LOVELIGHT FARMS

BOOKS BY B.K. BORISON

✳

Lovelight Farms
In the Weeds
Mixed Signals

LOVELIGHT FARMS

B.K. BORISON

Berkley Romance
New York

BERKLEY ROMANCE
Published by Berkley
An imprint of Penguin Random House LLC
penguinrandomhouse.com

Copyright © 2021 by B.K. Borison
"Bonus Chapter" copyright © 2022 by B.K. Borison
Excerpt from *In the Weeds* copyright © 2022 by B.K. Borison

Library of Congress Cataloging-in-Publication Data

Names: Borison, B.K., author.
Title: Lovelight farms / B.K. Borison.
Description: First Berkley Romance edition. |
New York : Berkley Romance, 2023. |
Series: Lovelight
Identifiers: LCCN 2023007762 (print) | LCCN 2023007763 (ebook) |
ISBN 9780593641118 (trade paperback) | ISBN 9780593641125 (ebook)
Subjects: LCGFT: Romance fiction. | Christmas fiction. | Novels.
Classification: LCC PS3602.O7545 L68 2023 (print) |
LCC PS3602.O7545 (ebook) | DDC 813.6—dc23/eng/20230307
LC record available at https://lccn.loc.gov/2023007762
LC ebook record available at https://lccn.loc.gov/2023007763

Lovelight Farms was originally self-published, in different form, in 2021.

Berkley Romance ebook edition / February 2023
Berkley Romance trade paperback edition / June 2023

Printed in the United States of America
1st Printing

Book design by Alison Cnockaert

For E, my favorite love story.
And for Ro, the best happily ever after.

Christmas Eve will find me
Where the love-light gleams.

—Kim Gannon and Walter Kent,
"I'll Be Home for Christmas"

1

"LUKA, LISTEN." I lean backward in my chair and fumble for the stack of papers on the file cabinet behind me, cursing under my breath when my fingertips barely glance the corner edge and it goes cascading to the floor in a flurry of white. "Listen, I need you to stop talking about pizza for a second."

There's a pause on the other end of the line. "I was just getting to the good part."

What he means is he was just getting to the part where he talks at length about homemade cheese, and I don't think I can handle him talking about mozzarella with that level of detail right now. As a data analyst, Luka is ridiculously thorough in all things. Especially cheese. I rub at the ache between my eyebrows. "I know you were, I'm sorry, but I've got something else to talk to you about."

"Everything okay?" There's a honk in the background, Luka's muffled curse, and the steady click of his turn signal as he merges into another lane.

"Everything is . . . fine." I peek down at the budget spreadsheets littering my floor and wince. "It's good. Okay, I mean. I just—" The fleeting confidence I entered this conversation with leaves me, and I slouch down in my chair. Every time I've called Luka this week or Luka has called me, I've chickened out. I don't think this time is going to be any different.

"I actually have to go. One of my vendors is calling." I frown at myself in the reflection of my computer screen. I have bags under my eyes, my full bottom lip is bright red from nervous chewing, and my mass of dark hair is twisted up into a bun that looks better suited to a haunted Victorian doll.

I look every bit as rough as the farm's budget sheets.

"One of your vendors is not calling you, but I'll play for now." Luka sounds amused. "Call me when you're done working, okay? We can talk about whatever you've been running circles around all week."

Reflection me frowns deeper. "Maybe."

He laughs. "Talk soon."

I hang up my phone and resist the urge to toss it clear across the room. Luka has a knack for cracking me right open, and I don't want that right now. I don't want it ever, to be honest, afraid of what he'll find when he starts connecting all of his data points.

My phone buzzes in my palm with an incoming text, and I flip it facedown on top of a stack of invoices. It buzzes again, and I pinch the bridge of my nose.

With the farm's finances the way they are, I'm quickly running out of options. I had thought—I guess I thought owning a Christmas tree farm would be romantic.

I had big dreams of a holiday season filled with magic. Kids weaving their way through the trees. Parents stealing kisses over hot chocolate. The stuff Christmas songs are written about. Young couples getting caught beneath the mistletoe. Low-hanging lights and oversized stockings. Wood railings painted red and white. Gingerbread cookies. Peppermint sticks.

And at first, it was great. Our opening season was as magical as it gets.

But since then, it's been one thing after another.

I'm eyeballs deep in debt with a fertilizer supplier who conveniently forgets my shipment every other month. I have an entire pasture of trees that look like something out of a Tim Burton movie, and there is a family of raccoons orchestrating a hostile takeover of my Santa barn. It is, in short, not a magical winter fairyland.

It is a frigid hellscape from which no one can escape, topped with a pretty red bow.

I feel lied to. Not only by every Hallmark movie I've ever seen but also by the previous owner of this land. Hank failed to mention he stopped paying his bills months ago, and as the new owner, I'd inherited his debt. At the time, I thought I had gotten a steal. The land was at a good price, and I had exciting ideas for expansion and marketing. With a little love, this little farm could make a big impact. Now though, I just feel stupid. I feel like I ignored several red flags in my desire to create something special.

I was blinded by the Douglas fir.

But I do have a solution. I'm just not sure the email sitting at the top of my inbox is something I'm willing to explore.

Honestly, at this point, harvesting my own organs sounds less scary.

"Stella."

I jump when Beckett elbows his way into my office, my arm knocking over my coffee, a halfway-dead fern, and a stack of pine tree–scented air fresheners. It all tumbles to the ground on top of my destroyed filing system. I frown at my lead farmer over the mess.

"Beckett." I sigh, and the headache pressing behind my eyes spreads, curls at the base of my skull. The man is physically incapable of entering a room in a normal, understated way. His knees are caked in mud and my frown deepens. He must have been in the south pasture. "What is it now?"

He steps over the pile of plant and cardboard and coffee and folds his large frame into the chair opposite my desk—a horrible, too-small leather thing I found on the side of the road. I had wanted to re-upholster it a rich velvet evergreen, but then the raccoons happened. And then the fencing by the road randomly collapsed twice.

And so there it sits. Horrible cracking brown leather with bits of stuffing spilling out onto the floor. It feels like a metaphor.

Beckett peers at the faded trees decorating the carpet, the cardboard curling up at the edges. One eyebrow shoots straight up his forehead. "Care to explain why you have seventy-five gas station air fresheners in your office?"

Leave it to Beckett to forget an apology and start digging into something personal instead. My phone buzzes again. Three staccato bursts in rapid fire. It's either Luka's dissertation on pizza crust consistency or another vendor looking for their late payment.

Beckett's eyebrow creeps higher. "Or perhaps door number two. Care to explain why you're ignoring Luka?"

I hate when Beckett is feeling clever. It almost always ends poorly for me. He's too astute for his own good, despite the dumb farmer act he plays a majority of the time. I bend down and pick up an air freshener, tossing it in the bottom drawer of my desk with all of the rest. A big ol' mess of tangled strings, stale pine, and unrequited feelings. A single pine tree for every time Luka has been home, starting back when we were twenty-one and stupid. I typically find them a week or two after he's left—tucked away in some hidden spot. Beneath my snow globe, under my keyboard.

Wedged in my coffee filter.

"I'm not and I don't," I mumble. Hard pass on both those options, thank you. "Care to explain what you found out there this morning?"

Beckett slips off his hat and runs his fingers through his dark blond hair, working a smudge or two of dirt in there. His skin is tanned by the sun and from spending his days in the fields, the flannel rolled up to his elbows displaying the color and ink on his forearms. All the women in town are crazy about him, which is probably why he doesn't go into town.

Also probably why he frowned at me when I suggested a Hot Farmer calendar to boost profits.

I swear, I'd have no financial concerns if he let me take that one to market.

"I don't understand," he mutters, thumb rubbing at his jaw. If Cindy Croswell were here right now, she'd drop dead on the spot. She works at the pharmacy and sometimes pretends she's hard of hearing when Beck comes in, just so he has to lean into her space and yell straight into her ear. I even saw that old bat pretend to stumble into a shelf so Beckett would help her back up. Hopeless.

"These trees are probably the lowest maintenance crop I've ever had to support." There's a joke in there somewhere, but I frankly don't have the energy. My lips tilt down until my frown mirrors his. Two sad clowns. "I can't think of a single reason why the trees in the south pasture look like—like—"

I think of the way the trees growing at the base of the hills curve and bend, the brittle texture of the bark. The limp, sad needles. "Like a darker version of the Charlie Brown Christmas tree?"

"That's it, yeah."

Strangely enough, there's a market for lonely looking Christmas trees. But these don't fall into that category. These are unsalvageable. I went out the other day, and I swear one of them crumbled when I looked at it. I can't imagine one of these things sitting in anyone's home—ironically or not. I pluck at my bottom lip with my thumb and do some quick calculations in my head. There are dozens of trees in that lot.

"Will we be all right without them?" Beckett looks worried and he has every reason to be. It's another hit we can't afford to take. He's the head of farming operations. I know I owe him the truth. That we're hanging on by the skin of our teeth. But I can't make the words come out. He took a leap of faith when he left his job at the produce farm to work here with me. I know he's counting on this being a success. For all of the promises I made him to hold true.

And so far they have, thanks to my savings. I've had to scrimp and save and eat ramen more nights than not, but no one who works here has seen a dip in their pay. I'm not willing to sacrifice that.

But that won't last forever. Something has to give soon.

I glance back at my computer screen, the email at the top of my inbox. "Well," I say, chewing on my bottom lip. In for a penny, in for a pound, and all that. If Beckett wants us to make it through this next season with the farm in one piece, there is something he can do. I breathe deep and summon the scraps of courage that didn't abandon me during my call with Luka. "Want to be my boyfriend?"

I'd laugh at the look on his face if I weren't so serious. He looks like I asked him to go out into the orchards and bury a dead body.

"Is that—" He shifts in his chair, the leather squeaking under his legs. "Stella, I'm not—I don't really see you—you're like my—"

When was the last time I heard this man stutter? I honestly can't think of it. Maybe when Betsy Johnson tried to cop a feel in front of a group of schoolkids during his Arbor Day presentation at the middle school.

"Relax." I press the toe of my boot into another air freshener and drag it toward me. "I don't mean a real boyfriend."

I'm struggling with dragging the piece of cardboard toward me, so I don't see the way Beckett's body goes ramrod straight in the chair. All I see is his leg jumping up and down a mile a minute. I snort. When I look up, his eyes are wide, and he looks like I've put a gun to his head. It's the same thinly veiled apprehension and mortification he wears on his face every time he steps foot in town.

"Stella," he swallows. "Is this—are you propositioning me?"

"What? Oh my god, Beck—" I can't help the full-body shudder. I love Beckett, but—*god*. "No! Jesus, is that what you think of me?"

"What do I think? What do *you* think?" His voice has hit a register I have never heard from him before. He gestures wildly with his hand, clearly not knowing what to do with himself. "This is all a little out of left field, Stella!"

"I meant like a fake boyfriend thing!" I shriek, like that was obvious. Like this is a normal thing people request from their very platonic friends. Like my overactive imagination and half a bottle of sauvignon blanc didn't get me into this mess to begin with. I click to open the email and stare at it mournfully, ignoring the animated confetti that explodes across my screen. I watch it three times in a row and pretend Beckett's eyes are not currently drilling a hole into the side of my head.

"I did a thing," I supply, and leave it at that.

"A thing," he parrots.

I hum in response.

"Do you want to share what that thing is?"

No.

"I—"

As if summoned by sheer force of will, Layla tiptoes her way into my office, a tray of something preceding her around the edge of my door. I smell cinnamon, dried cranberries, and a hint of vanilla.

Zucchini bread.

Like an angel descending from the heavens, she brought zucchini bread. The one thing that always, *always* distracts Beckett.

Beckett makes a noise that is borderline obscene, and I vaguely consider recording it and putting it on OnlyFans. That might bring in some dollars: *Hot Farmer Eats Zucchini.* I chuckle to myself. He reaches for the tray with grabby hands, but Layla smacks his knuckles with a wooden spoon she pulls out of her . . . back pocket, I think? She balances the tray neatly on the edge of my desk. I peer into it and almost weep. She added chocolate chips.

"Made you something, boss lady."

She nudges it forward with the edge of her spoon and rests her chin prettily in one hand.

While Beckett embodies rugged recluse with all the charm of a paper bag, Layla Dupree brightens any room she walks into with her sweet Southern hospitality and no-nonsense wit. She is striking with her crystal clear hazel eyes and cropped dark hair. She's kind to a fault and makes the best hot chocolate in the tristate area. I snatched her up to manage the dining options at my little tree farm as soon as I tasted one of her chocolate chip cookies at the firehouse bake sale. She's the third member of our humble little trio, and if she's bringing me sweets, she wants something.

Something I probably can't afford.

I shove a slice of bread into my mouth before she can ask, bound and determined to enjoy at least one thing before I have to tell her no.

My phone takes advantage too, buzzing merrily across my desk. Layla blinks at it, exchanges a glance with Beckett, and then looks at me.

"Why are you ignoring Luka?"

"I'm not—" A spray of golden, flaky, delicious crumbs accompany my denial. "I'm not ignoring Luka."

It sounds more like *M'snot snore ukeah*.

Layla hums and pivots. "So, I was thinking," she starts. Bingo. "If I add another stove in the back corner of the kitchen, we could almost double our output. Maybe even start some prepackaged things if people want to take a little basket out into the fields with them."

Beckett crosses his arms as I continue chewing my massive bite. I ignore Layla for now and stare him dead in the eye.

"It's still warm," I tell him.

He groans.

Layla relents and rolls her eyes, plucking a slice off the top and offering it to him.

"If people start leaving trash in the pastures, I'm going to have a problem with that," Beckett grouches. He shoves the whole slice of bread into his mouth and then collapses against the back of the chair in rapture, the leather once again releasing an ominous squeak of defeat. Just like I'm about to.

"I love the idea, but we might need to put a hold on any big purchases right now." I think about the sad little number in my savings account. How I was barely able to cover operational expenses this past quarter.

Layla's face falls, her hand reaching out to mine. She touches my knuckles once. It's a kindness I don't deserve, given that I haven't been completely honest about how bad things are right now. "Are we doing okay?"

"We're doing"—I search for a word to categorize *hanging on by my fingernails*—"all right."

Beckett finally swallows his ridiculous bite of food and kicks out a leg. "We were just talking about that, actually. Stella propositioned me."

"Oh? That's interesting. Don't understand how it plays into our operational status though."

"Yeah, me too. But that's what I got when I asked her the same question."

"Do I get to be propositioned too?"

I roll my eyes and choose not to dignify that with a response. Instead, I turn my computer screen around so they both can see the animated confetti in all its glory. Beckett doesn't so much as blink, but Layla throws both arms up in the air with a high-pitched screech that has me wincing.

"Is that for real?" She grabs the sides of my desktop and leans closer, nose practically pressed up against the screen. "You're a finalist for that Evelyn St. James thing?"

Beckett eyeballs the zucchini bread as it balances precariously on the edge of my desk, eyes glazed like he's been drugged. "Aspirin Saint what?"

Layla slaps his hand again without even looking at him. "She's an influencer."

Beckett makes a face. "Is that like a political thing?"

"How do you exist in this century? She's a big deal on social media. She does destination features. Sort of like a mini Travel Channel thing."

I feel a small burst of pride. She is *the* influencer for destination hospitality. Snagging a feature on her account is equivalent to thousands in ad spend—thousands we have never had the budget for. It would turn our farm into a place people want to visit, not just a stopping point for locals. And the $100,000 cash prize for the winner of her small business sweepstakes would keep us afloat for another year, if not more.

Too bad I lied on my application.

"Where does the propositioning come in?"

"I didn't—I didn't proposition Beckett." I swing my computer screen back around and minimize the email. I drum my fingers against my lips and remember the night that got me into this mess. I had been on the phone with Luka, a little bit dizzy off white wine and the way his eyes crinkled at the corners. He had been making some stupid joke about ham sandwiches and couldn't stop laughing long enough to get the full thing out. I still don't know the punch line.

"I said in the application that I own the farm with my boyfriend," I mumble. Color heats my cheeks. I bet I look as red as one of my barn doors. "I thought it would be more romantic than *Sad, lonely woman who hasn't been on a date in seventeen months.*"

"I hope to god you're having meaningless sex with someone."

"Why do you need a boyfriend to be successful?"

Layla and Beckett speak over each other, though to be fair, Layla makes a much more aggressive effort as she propels herself forward in the chair and yells her statement about my sex life. She collapses back, jaw hinged open, hand pressed dramatically against her chest.

"Holy cannoli, no wonder you are—" She gestures at me with her spoon-wielding hand, and I fight not to blush a deeper shade of red. We're probably hitting crimson territory by now. "The way you are."

I fidget in my chair and press on. I don't have to tell Layla that dating in a small town has its complications, let alone starting a no-strings-attached situation. "She's coming for five days for an in-person interview, and she'll feature us on her social accounts. The boyfriend thing, I don't know. I guess I thought having a boyfriend would make this place seem more romantic. She loves romance stuff."

Beckett sneaks another piece of zucchini bread. He's taking advantage of Layla's continued shock and awe at my celibacy. "Well, that's fucking stupid."

I give him a look. "Thank you, Beckett. Your input is helpful."

"Seriously though"—he breaks his zucchini bread slice in two—"you've made this place amazing. You. On your own. You should be proud of that. Adding a boyfriend doesn't make your story any more or less important."

I blink at him. "Sometimes I forget you have three sisters."

He shrugs. "Just my two cents."

"You sure you don't want to pretend you find me irresistible for a week?"

Layla shakes her head, finally emerging from her trancelike state. "Bad idea. Have you seen him try to lie to anyone? It's horrible. He turns into a monosyllabic fool every time he has to go into town for groceries."

It's true. I've had to pick up his order from the butcher more than once. I'm convinced he became a produce farmer purely so he'd have to make fewer stops at the Save More. Beckett doesn't enjoy people, and he especially doesn't enjoy the overt flirtations from half the town whenever he stops in. Sometimes I feel like Layla and I are the only ones immune to his good looks, probably due to his considerable lack of charm, but I suppose that's what happens when you've seen a man muttering obscenities to trees half the day every day.

And when your heart has been hopelessly occupied with pining over another person for close to a decade. It's hard to notice the charm of anyone who isn't Luka.

I grab another slice of zucchini bread and begin to nibble, considering my options. My non-Luka-shaped options. I could ask Jesse, the owner of our town's only bar. But he'd likely think it's more than it is, and I don't have the time or energy for a fake breakup for my fake relationship. I could look into escort services, maybe. That's a thing, right? Like, that's why escort services exist? For people to—I don't know, escort others?

I press my fingers under my eyes, forgetting that one hand is still clutching a piece of zucchini bread. There's an obvious answer here. It just—it scares me to death.

"There it is," Beckett mutters, and it takes every fiber of my being not to hurl this bread at his face. "It just hit her."

"I don't know why you're freaking out. It's a simple solution. He'd do it in a heartbeat," says Layla.

I peek through my fingers at Layla. She's smiling a smug little grin. She looks like she should be wearing a monocle and stroking a hairless cat Bond-style. Why I ever thought she was all sweetness is beyond me. She's a spicy little thing.

"Ask Luka."

2

THERE'S THIS BAR in the city that Luka and I like to go to. The beer is cheap, the floors are sticky, and when I kick the jukebox in the bottom right corner, it'll play Ella Fitzgerald thirteen times in a row exactly. It's perfect.

But sometimes on a Saturday night when the bar gets crowded and bodies press close, I have trouble holding my space. Emboldened by whiskey, it's always inevitable that a hand lands on my ass or some pretty, dumb thing who thinks he's a gift and a delight leers down my shirt. And always, Luka slips his hand over my shoulder, under my hair, and presses it to the nape of my neck. He pulls me close and tucks his chin on top of my head. I fit perfectly there, folded in close to his body. I find my space.

I've thought about that a time or two in the stillness of night. How his hand feels against my skin, his palm gently cupping the back of my head, the move both possessive and reverent. I've thought about what it might feel like for his fingers to tighten, to sift up into my hair, to pull and angle me until his mouth finds mine.

I've thought about a lot of things when it comes to Luka. Things you shouldn't think about your best friend.

We met when I was twenty-one years old. I ran smack into him as I was leaving the hardware store, lost in a shadow of grief I couldn't shake. It clung to me like an uncomfortable blanket, relentless since the passing of my mom just three months earlier. I remember standing in one of the aisles, holding a mismatched set of nuts and bolts, determined to do something with all my listless energy. Build a birdhouse. A new shelf for the hallway. I stumbled into Luka on the front steps when I was leaving, and he cupped his hands around my elbows to hold me steady. I remember staring at his caramel brown hair just starting to curl from beneath his baseball hat, the way his smile pulled at one side of his mouth before the other. It felt like the first time in a long time I noticed anything. Luka had cleared his throat, steadied my arms, and asked if I wanted grilled cheese. No "Hello." No "How are you?" Just "Wanna go get a grilled cheese?"

I don't know what made me say yes. I'd barely been talking to people I had known for years at that point. I was existing at best. Floundering at worst. But I went with Luka and ate grilled cheese at the little café in town. It turned out his mom had just moved to Inglewild, and he was helping her get settled. I offered him the array of hardware I picked up, and he had stuttered a surprised laugh. I can still remember the rasp of his fingers against my palm as he took the stupid wing knob I had aimlessly purchased.

Luka called it kismet. He had been on the way to the store for that exact piece of hardware.

From there, we fell into a routine. Whenever he was in town, he managed to find me, and we got grilled cheese. Grilled cheese turned into afternoon walks through the park and early morning farmers markets. Afternoon happy hours and trivia nights. His trips to Inglewild became more frequent, and he invited me to stop by if I ever found myself in New York. I got brave and tried, booking a bus ticket on a whim.

Luka filled the empty places in my life slowly, carefully, with his easy smile and stupid jokes. He brought me back to myself.

And it's been that way ever since.

Frustratingly, perfectly platonic.

This wouldn't be any different, I try to tell myself. Asking Luka to pretend for five days would just be . . . a friend helping a friend. I'd do the same for him or Beckett or Layla. It doesn't have to—it doesn't have to mean whatever my mind seems fixated on having it mean.

Layla's suggestion isn't the first I've thought of it. Of course I've thought of it. I've been trying to ask him all week. He's the reason I wrote it down in the first place. Call it wishful thinking or living a fantasy, but I know when I typed those words who I was thinking of.

But it does feel a little like crossing a line we've both been careful to hold. A line I have been absolutely meticulous in my desire to hold. Luka is the very first person in my life who hasn't disappeared. He's more than my best friend—he's tradition and familiarity. He is homemade Pop-Tarts on the first Saturday of the month. He is late-night viewings of *Die Hard* in the sticky summer heat, both of our phones propped up on our respective coffee tables. He is pizza with extra mushrooms and light sauce, a crust that has to be perfect.

The relationship I have with him is the closest thing I have to family. I can't—I wouldn't—risk that for a chance to see what we could be.

Even if I wonder. Even if the reason I haven't been with anyone in seventeen months is because I always inevitably compare every man against Luka, and I'm always left disappointed.

But maybe this idea—this pretending to be together—maybe this is the solution. After a week of pretending, I can get it out of my system. Get *him* out of my system. I can stop with the wondering and the comparing and just move on.

After all, if something were supposed to have happened with Luka, wouldn't it have happened already?

The thought aches like an old bruise, one I press my thumb in from time to time just to feel the dull hurt of it. Because the truth is, there have been times when I thought he might want something different too. Sometimes after a night of drinking, I'll catch his gaze lingering on the curve of my shoulder or the swell of my bottom lip. His touches become freer. A hand on my hip as he swings me around the tiny dance floor. His forehead pressed against mine. Moments frozen in time throughout the years, always just for a second or two.

But it has always been enough to make me feel like maybe he might want me the same way I've always wanted him. More than a friend.

More than anything.

But then I press that bruise and tell myself it's better this way.

Because this is the way I get to keep him.

"I'm not sure he's in town that week," I respond to Layla after a lengthy retreat down memory lane, very aware it's a thin excuse at best.

She gives me an unimpressed look. "He lives three hours away. Plus, haven't I seen him like twice this month already?"

Beckett decides this is a fine time to chime in. "And didn't you ask him to come home for the strawberry jam cook-off in April?"

I sink farther into my chair. "He loves strawberry jam."

Beckett heaves himself out of the tiny leather chair and wipes his palms on his thighs. He has officially removed himself from this conversation. Mentally, he's somewhere amongst the balsams humming a merry little tune, a fresh loaf of zucchini bread cradled gently in his hands.

"I'm leaving," he announces and turns on his heel.

Layla hops up to join him and curls her hand around his elbow before he can get too far. She points a threatening finger in my direction. "Ask Luka, or I'll ask for you."

I don't even want to know what that would involve. A PowerPoint deck, probably. My total and utter humiliation, likely.

As if on cue, my phone skitters across my desk. It gives one long violent buzz and then comes to a standstill. I turn it over carefully and stare at my notifications, a perfect storm of anxiety pulling in my gut and creeping over my shoulders.

7 MESSAGES
Luka

3 MESSAGES
Charlie

1 MESSAGE
Charlie, Brian, Elle

Ah, crap. Not many people have their dad in their address book with their first name, but that about sums up my relationship with my father. I decide to tackle that one first.

BRIAN: We'll be having our Thanksgiving dinner the first weekend in November. Estelle, you may bring a pumpkin pie.

I may bring a pumpkin pie. Awesome. I bet if I were the type of person to save text messages, I'd have this exact same message on this exact day at this exact time from last year. In fact, I'm not sure my father has ever sent me a text message beyond this little nugget. That explains the three text messages from Charlie, then. I delete the group chat with my dad, his wife, and my half brother and move straight to the next.

CHARLIE: He sure has a way with words, doesn't he?

CHARLIE: Don't let him get to you.

CHARLIE: Dare you to bring pecan.

I huff a laugh and send a stupid GIF—something with a dog and flames that sums up my overall feelings at being summoned like a petulant child. My dad and his family do not celebrate Thanksgiving on the first weekend of November, but it is the one I am invited to so my dad can check off his yearly holiday box. Maybe it assuages his guilt for the way he left me and my mom high and dry, or maybe Elle makes him do it. Whatever the reason, it is always a painfully awkward dinner broken up only by Charlie's well-meaning attempts at making conversation and my dad's sullen mumbling under his breath.

I'm definitely bringing pecan pie.

I pull up Luka's messages next, the stress of the day catching up to me. I think tonight will be a boxed-wine-*Sleepless-in-Seattle*-pizza-in-bed kind of night.

> LUKA: How was your vendor call?

> LUKA: You're cute when you're lying to me, by the way.

> LUKA: Also, why are there three episodes of Naked and Afraid downloaded on my TV? Do I even know you anymore?

I sometimes forget we share streaming services. Thank god I watched those porny Netflix movies at Layla's place.

> LUKA: Charlie is texting me about pecan pie.

> LUKA: Dear god.

> LUKA: Is Layla making pie now?

I shouldn't feel a stab of jealousy over pecan pie, but there it is, all the same. This is what Luka reduces me to.

> LUKA: Sleepless in Seattle is on HBO again.

I close my eyes and press my phone against my forehead. I tap it there twice and make a decision. I'm going to do it. I'm going to ask him. I'm going to ask him and it's going to be fine.

STELLA: Can we FaceTime tonight? I need a favor.

My phone rings almost immediately, a picture of Luka from five years ago stretched across the screen. It's from when I made him try seven different pizza places in one day because I couldn't find a sauce I liked. In the picture, he's wearing a stupid hat that looks like a giant slice of pizza. He looks ridiculous.

I love it.

I let it ring a few more times and try to channel a more resilient version of myself. A version of myself that maybe doesn't have maple syrup from this morning's stress waffles still on her shirt.

I can do this. I can ask Luka for this simple thing, and nothing has to change.

"Hey!"

It's overly perky and forced, and I'm immediately met with a ringing silence. There's muffled shuffling, a door closing, and then a huff.

"Can you please just tell me what's going on?"

I fiddle with one of the pine cone air fresheners I didn't throw in my bottom drawer, twisting the string forward and back over my thumb. "What do you mean?"

I'm officially a pathological liar.

"You've been weird all week."

"I have . . . not."

"You're being weird right now," he says. He sighs again, and I hear a flop like he's just thrown his body down on his bed. I imagine the way his long legs starfish out, ankles hooked over the edge. "Come on, Stella. What's going on with you? I can't remember the last time you asked me for a favor."

I frown and turn in my chair, peering out the large bay window that looks out over the trees. We're pretty isolated all the way out here. But if you travel down the narrow dirt road that leads to our farm, you'll find the tiny town of Inglewild. About twenty years ago, some-one tried to brand Inglewild as Little Florence, likening us to the stunningly beautiful city in Italy. It was an effort, I think, to pull in more tourists passing through to DC or Baltimore. Unfortunately for that marketing campaign, there are exactly no similarities between Inglewild and Florence. It didn't stick.

"About a month and a half ago," I tell him. "I made you bring me back three gallons of chocolate ice cream from that shop on the corner by your apartment. You had to buy a special cooler and everything."

His laugh rumbles over the line, and it tucks itself right between my ribs. "Okay, that's true. But you're being weird. What's up?"

My stomach grumbles and I shoot a glance at the clock. There's ramen waiting for me in my pantry. And I don't especially want to get into this here where anyone could walk in. I'd much rather have a glass of wine in hand.

"Could I call you back when I get home?" I stall for time, tossing the air freshener down on my desk. I have a bright red mark across my thumb from the string. Apparently, I want to draw this anxiety out some more. "I'm about to head out."

"Well, funny story," he drawls, "I'm actually in town visiting my mom. I can be at your place in twenty?"

Crap.

"Yeah, sure," I say faintly, panicking. Leave it to Luka. I remind myself that he is my best friend, and I have done far more embarrassing things in our long relationship than ask him to be my fake boyfriend. Like the time I threw up on his welcome mat after betting someone I could consume an entire jug of mystery wine. Or the time I cut my bangs and I wore a bucket hat everywhere we went together for eighteen weeks. I swallow the nerves.

"That sounds good."

3

EVEN THOUGH MY cottage is within walking distance of my office, it still takes me forty-five minutes to extricate myself from emails, gather my things, and begin my walk home. I make a note to follow up with Hank and see if he noticed any troubles with the trees in the south pasture. Or if he noticed the family of raccoons tearing the barn apart. Or if he had trouble with the fertilizer distributor.

And if he did, why didn't he say anything to me?

Because he knew this place was a money pit and he wanted to move to Costa Rica with his wife. My mind helpfully recalls the posters I had to peel off the office walls. Bright green jungles and lush waterfalls, practically bleached white from how long they had been hanging.

I wasn't exactly level-headed when I bought this place. Blinded by positivity, probably. Too focused on the cute little cottage that hugs the corner of the property, visions of curling up in front of the stone fireplace with a mug of tea dancing through my head. Imagining the first snow of the year, walking through rows and rows of trees. A place of my own. A place to belong—finally.

Growing up, my mom and I were always moving, chasing the next opportunity. I had trouble finding my footing when we popped up in a new town for a waitressing job or temporary seasonal help. It wasn't for lack of trying from my mom. She always did her best to make things special, connected. She kept us in one spot for as long as she could, painstakingly packing up our meager amount of possessions as we shuffled from place to place. Hanging the cross-stitch welcome sign in the same place every time, the same dish towels dotted with embroidered lemons and limes. But I was always afraid to plant roots, wondering if it would be for nothing. If the next month I'd have to start all over again.

A gust of wind whispers through the trees and lifts my hair, brushing at my cheeks as my boots crunch through the leaves of the mighty maples that line the edge of the property. There's a footpath that winds its way through a small meadow and the outer edge of the pumpkin patch that links the house to the office. It's a five-minute walk when the weather is good, but I find myself moving slower tonight, watching the way the sun dances lower in the sky, the light glancing off the leaves. Reds, oranges, and yellows dance in a kaleidoscope of color around me.

It's probably not a coincidence that I bought the place in October. There's a special kind of magic on nights like this, a certain sort of nostalgia when the past intermingles with the present and flirts with the future. I can smell the wood smoke from the fire Beckett has going in his place at the base of the foothills, see the plume of smoke as it lifts from his chimney. The branches rustle above me and a few owls call out, a solemn sound as the sun dips lower. For a single perfect moment, I feel like I'm in that picture my mom used to tape on the wall of whatever apartment we called home.

A farm. A single red tractor. A little girl with dirt on her knees. And a perfect collection of Christmas trees behind her.

It's been a dream since before I even had the courage to make dreams.

A light in the distance catches my eye, a warm glow cast out over the stone of my driveway. As I move around the last tree that marks the edge of my personal property, my front door swings open, and Luka steps out, resting his shoulder against the banister. He looks almost comically large on my tiny front porch in front of my tiny house with my tiny kitchen towel held between his hands. He swings it over his shoulder and crosses his socked feet at the ankles. I smile when I notice he's wearing the socks I got for him last Christmas, the ones with the tiny sriracha bottles. His mouth hitches up in a small grin, the one that pulls his bottom lip just a bit lower on the left, the October wind tousling his endlessly messy hair. His warm brown eyes reflect the setting sun, making them look almost amber in the fading light.

"Breaking and entering now?" I pick up my pace, getting a whiff of tomato and basil. If he's made his grandma's meatballs, I might never let him leave.

"It's not breaking and entering if you have a key," he calls back.

I laugh and his smile tips up into something beautiful. It's a moment I want to stamp into my soul for the nights when I feel a little bit lonely and a lot bit sad. I take in a deep breath and hold on to the moment. The pinks and purples that cast his face half in shadow, the pull of his sweatshirt across his chest, his socked feet creaking the aged wood of my front porch. The magic is in the details, my mom always used to say. And these details are perfect.

My feet find the bottom step, and he meets me halfway, two strong arms wrapping around my shoulders in a bear hug. He smells like marinara and the vanilla hand soap I keep next to my kitchen sink, and I suddenly, inexplicably, want to cry.

"Hey, La La." He rests his chin on top of my head, arms squeezing tight. "Long time no see."

I curl my arms around his back and press my hands into his shoulder blades. I breathe out slowly through my nose and rock us back and forth. "You saw me two weeks ago," I mutter somewhere into his chest. "We sat on the couch and watched *Independence Day* two times in a row because you have a Jeff Goldblum fixation."

"Something about that flight suit, am I right?" He pulls back but keeps his hands over my shoulders. His brown eyes search my face. This close, I can see the freckles that bridge over his nose and spread like constellations under his eyes. I bite back a sigh, and he frowns.

"What's going on, Stella?"

The panic is still there. And so I delay. I pat his sides and press up on my tiptoes, trying to see over his shoulder. "Feed me first?"

He frowns but nods, slipping his hands down my arms in a series of squeezes. He's done this since that first day when I steamrolled right into him, a one-two-three of his hands moving down my biceps, elbows, hands. Once we're inside, he retreats back to the kitchen, and I kick off my shoes by the door, noting his boots already neatly tucked beneath the entryway table. I toss my keys on top of his in the blue ceramic dish I made as an art class project in high school and loop my scarf on the hook next to his black denim jacket.

And isn't it silly to love the way someone's things look like next to yours? Little bits and pieces of lives lived in parallel.

I stare at his jacket for a minute too long before he shouts from the kitchen, asking after a bottle of red I keep in the hall closet. I'd be impressed at his memory if he wasn't the one to bring this red and hide it beneath my sweaters a few months ago.

I shuffle into the kitchen with the wine bottle in hand, another tucked under my arm. This conversation will probably go better if I have a bit of liquid courage. He glances over his shoulder when I place them both down, a lock of his hair dropping in front of his eye, that damn dish towel with the garden gnomes tucked in his back pocket. He looks absolutely ridiculous and deliciously perfect, worn jeans and faded sweatshirt, sleeves rolled to his elbows.

"One of those nights?"

"One of those years," I mutter in response, digging through my drawer for the bottle opener. Luka watches me struggle for approximately twenty-six seconds before he abandons whatever he's stirring at the stove and crowds my space, his chest pressing into my side as he reaches over our heads. Its sudden, his body against mine, and I tip my head back to watch his face. Like this, I could bite his bicep if I wanted to, the curve of it just an inch from my nose.

His eyes search my face, a grin curving his lips upward. "What in the world are you thinking about?"

"Devious things." A blush climbs my cheeks and I pinch his side. He winces but keeps patting around on top of the cabinets. "What are you doing up there?"

He holds up a wine opener in response, and I crane my neck to look above my cabinets with a frown. "What else are you hiding up there?"

"Whatever I don't want your little hands on."

I mentally remind myself to get the step stool out later and investigate. He takes the wine bottle out of my hand and, with a series of smooth movements that honestly shouldn't look as attractive as they do, uncorks it. He reaches over my shoulder and pours us both a glass, still with me plastered against his front. The top of my head barely reaches his shoulders, and I can see the jut of his collarbones peeking out from his sweatshirt. I stare at them with laser focus.

"Dinner will be ready in a few minutes," he mutters, his words a warm puff against my skin.

I blink and reach for my wine, clinging to it like a lifeline. I've noticed these things before, of course, but now it feels like everything about Luka is under a magnifying glass. Life in Technicolor, I guess.

"Thank you." I look around at my kitchen like I've never seen it before, dazed and confused. "Do you need help with anything?"

My voice sounds oddly formal, like I should add a *good sir* to the end of it. Luka gives me another narrow-eyed look and just points to the table in response. I follow his direction without comment and settle into the wobbly midcentury dining chair that absolutely does not match my farmhouse table. I stare and stare at the tabletop and do my best to not freak out, but it's hard not to when the thing I'm about to ask my best friend might make him laugh in my face, bolt out the door, or both.

By the time Luka slides a heaping plate of spaghetti and meatballs in front of me, I've drained my wineglass and worked myself into an emotional bottle rocket, ready to explode.

"Beck says the trees are looking good." Luka slides across from me, cozying himself in the chair. "Well, besides the pasture by the south gate."

I don't need the reminder. My eyes wander from my full plate of spaghetti to the cuff of his sweatshirt stretched tight around his forearm. I quickly redirect my gaze to the bottle of wine on the kitchen counter and the parmesan cheese sitting next to it. I hope that didn't come from my fridge.

I point at it with my fork, leg dancing under the table. "Where is that from?"

Luka stares at me. "The grocery store."

"Cool. Cool cool."

"Stella." Luka places his fork on the edge of his plate and leans forward, reaching halfway out to me like he wants to scoop my hands in his. I'm not sure that would help, honestly. He pulls back, sighs, and rubs his knuckles against his jaw. He picks up his fork. "What is going on with you?"

"Why do you ask?"

He arches an eyebrow. "I think you've moved this table halfway across the kitchen, for one."

"I just—I need to ask you something."

"Do you need a kidney?"

"What? No." Though an organ transplant sounds preferable right now.

"You're acting like you need a kidney."

"I need you to date me," I blurt out. My palms are sweating, my heart is somewhere in my throat, and my stomach has completely removed itself from the conversation.

Luka, for his part, doesn't so much as flinch. He just calmly twirls his fork around and around, collecting the world's longest spaghetti noodle. "Okay." He pops his fork into his mouth.

"It's fake," I practically yell at him. I don't know why I'm talking so loud. I make a conscious effort to turn it down. "It wouldn't—I meant to ask if you would pretend to date me. The pretend part is important."

He shrugs. "Sure."

Sure. *Sure.* I'm on the verge of a total mental break, but Luka says *sure*. I watch another elegantly cut meatball disappear behind his lips. I aggressively stab one of mine, and it flies halfway down the table. I ignore it, spear another, and shove the whole thing in my mouth.

"Cheeses or grandschmas?"

Luka calmly takes a sip of his wine, ignoring my deterioration into lunacy. "Pardon?"

I swallow and gently pat the corners of my mouth with the napkin resting in my lap. I am a lady. "Is this your grandma's recipe?"

"It is."

"Do you think she'd adopt me?"

"She'd kick me out and adopt you in a second." Luka huffs a laugh. "We both know it. Thanks, by the way, for bringing her dinner last week. She called me seventy-five times to brag about it and ask what you use in your snickerdoodles."

I did not make those snickerdoodles. But over my dead body am I telling that to Luka's grandmother, who makes her pasta from scratch. She once came over, saw a half-used jar of store-bought marinara in my fridge, and looked me dead in the eye as she threw it in the trash.

I wish he wouldn't thank me for spending time with his family. It's not a hardship. Going to visit his grandma and his mom and sometimes his aunt Gianna who lives two towns over is a nice distraction from the fact that my only family decides to celebrate Thanksgiving an entire three weeks early just so they don't have to explain my existence.

Also, his grandma is a badass, so . . .

"They were Layla's snickerdoodles, so you'd have to ask her."

"I'm more interested in why you need to fake date me, actually." He pauses with another dramatic sip of wine. I stare mournfully at my empty glass. "Aren't you dating Wyatt?"

I stare at him. Stare and stare and stare. How is it possible for someone to be so intricately woven into my life and yet not realize I haven't brought Wyatt around in a short eternity?

"Luka." I blink at him. "We broke up over a year ago."

Luka is a caricature of the comically shocked. Furrowed brows, fork frozen halfway to his mouth. It would be funny if it wasn't so shocking. "What?"

"Yeah, after last year's harvest festival. He texted me."

"He—wait, he broke up with you over text?"

Wyatt had been kind and sweet, if not a little immature. In a lot of ways, it felt like reverting back to my teenage self and dating the cute captain of the soccer team. A lot of heavy petting, a useless label, and zero emotional attachment. He texted me after last year's festival with a simple You're super cool, but I think we want different things. Friends? 😊

Super cool.

The smiley face sealed the deal for me. I had agreed and that was, well, that. I never heard from him again.

"I told you this."

He stares at me. "You did not tell me this."

I put my fork down and lean to the left, reaching for the bottle of wine. "Luka, how on earth would I have all this time to spend with you if I were dating someone?"

He blinks, his gaze far away like he's mentally reliving the last year of his life. His mouth moves soundlessly, and then he picks up his wineglass, draining it in one go.

"Okay, so not Wyatt."

"Not Wyatt. No."

"Am I your only option, then?"

I don't know why he sounds so upset about that. "If it makes you feel better, I asked Beckett first. He said no." His frown deepens, that tiny little divot between his eyebrows appearing. "I was going to ask Jesse, but—"

"You were going to ask Jesse before me? Christ, Stella." Now it's his turn to stab a meatball like it's personally offended him. "You should have asked me first. Now I feel like I'm your last resort."

I don't tell him that he is, in fact, my last resort. Well, besides the escort service.

"I'm sorry, Luka." I clasp my hands in front of me on the table, pleased when I sound only slightly sarcastic. "Did you want me to put more of an effort into asking you to be my fake boyfriend?"

"It wouldn't have killed you to," he mumbles. He runs both hands through his hair, back and forth and back again, a tuft on the left side sticking straight out. It's such a familiar gesture that it sends a pang of wistfulness straight through my chest.

"Luka, listen," I swallow twice, hesitant. This feels important, his reaction. If he's agonizing already, I don't want—

I don't want to ruin what Luka and I have.

I curl my hands around my cutlery. "This was a stupid idea. If you don't want to do this—"

"No, that's not it. Sorry, I'm just—" He cuts himself off by biting down on his words, brown eyes fixed on his plate. He picks his fork back up, twirls, twirls, twirls some pasta. "I keep getting off track. Why do you need a fake boyfriend?"

It's a redirect, but I allow it in the same way he allowed my procrastination earlier. I explain the social media contest to him, careful to leave out the parts about how much our farm desperately needs the cash prize. I focus instead on the national exposure, the influx of new customers, and hopefully an online presence we can capitalize on. By the end of it, I sound like I'm giving a presentation to the board, and given Luka's glazed look, he probably agrees.

He's a data guy. I should have just shown him a bunch of numbers.

He shakes his head slightly when I finish. "I think that's the first time I've ever heard the words *ingress* and *egress* come out of your mouth."

"Yeah, probably." I think for a second. "Though I feel like I probably mentioned it when I was complaining about the state fair."

He laughs at that. He is very familiar with my thoughts on the state fair.

We're quiet for a moment, the sound of tree branches scratching at my windows filling the space between us. Wind whistles through the cracks around the door, and I think about starting a fire. Wine in front of the fireplace sounds excellent.

Luka leans back in his chair and considers me. I'm content to leave him with his thoughts as I work to untangle my own.

"You think this will help? The pretending?"

"Yes," I respond without hesitation, the answer rising from deep inside of me. I don't know how I know that Luka is the key to all of this, but I do. This fake relationship, stupid and silly and cliche as it may be, it's the spark we need. It's the spark I need. I clear my throat. "I really do."

He knows me well enough to understand that there's something I'm not telling him, but he also knows me well enough not to press. It feels like we've run back-to-back verbal marathons since I walked in the door, and I think we're both okay with leaving the conversation where it is for the night.

Luka nods, a decision made. "Then that's what we'll do."

I mirror his position and kick back in my chair, grasping for something that will ground me. Something that will make me feel like I'm not stepping into a giant mistake.

Except nothing comes to mind.

4

I WAKE UP the next morning with a headache behind my eyes and a pull in my gut that's the result of one too many gummy worms, and probably a hasty decision to force my best friend into a fake relationship. Can you have a hangover from bad decisions?

It seems likely.

In the light of day, the decision feels like an unnecessary mistake. A boyfriend won't make or break my chances at this cash prize. I don't even know if Evelyn St. James read my full application, let alone the one place in the personal statement that I said I owned and operated the farm with my boyfriend.

Unless she did read it, my brain whispers. *And you're automatically disqualified for lying.*

I've done my research. As soon as I heard about the contest, I scoured Evelyn's feed. I looked for trends in her content, the type of businesses she liked to recommend. She always has a story to tell and she loves romance. Her last three features were all love stories in their own way. The couple in Maine with their bed-and-breakfast. The lifelong best friends that operate historical boat cruises from their little jetty in South Carolina. The newlyweds that met on a blind date and decided to open their own winery. Maybe this time, for once, I want my story to be something different than a sad one. I dig my palms into my eyes and kick my legs out from my tangled blankets. I'm tired of being the sad one.

I think about Beckett and Layla. The stack of bills that are getting harder and harder to pay. I think of the wrought iron gate that welcomes you to the farm, the two giant red bows I put on it last year. I remember the day I was given the keys, how the sound of the rusted chains slipping off the bars almost made me cry. I think about closing that gate and looping those chains back around the bars and almost want to cry for an entirely different reason.

I have to try. This is my best shot. Even if it sounds silly, it's the story I want to tell for this place.

I want Evelyn St. James to see all the things that made me fall in love with this farm that first winter I visited with my mom. When I was sixteen years old and programmed to hate most things but fell in love with the wide-open space that smelled like balsam and orange slices and just a hint of cinnamon. I want her to walk through the rows and rows of trees, just as the sun is setting, where it's quiet enough to hear the way your boots crunch along the frozen ground. Where pine needles tangle in your hair and you feel like you're the only person in the world. I want her to get a hot chocolate from Layla's bakehouse, go ice-skating in the rink Beckett organized last winter, and watch the kids chase one another by the barn.

I want her to see the magic.

"I was kind of hoping you weren't alone."

It's a testament to how deep in my thoughts I am that I don't even flinch when Layla appears in the doorway of my bedroom, a navy blue beanie pulled down low over her head. Also, an indication that I should reassess who has a key to my place.

I frown at her, my head halfway under my pillow, legs hopelessly tangled in the sheets. It looks like I went ten rounds in this bed. "Who would be in here with me?"

She rolls her eyes and kicks off her shoes, climbing up with zero hesitation. There's a rearrangement of limbs, an elbow in my solar plexus, and then Layla is curled next to me, her knees pressed into my hip. I love that she requires touch for most conversations, that she never hesitates to reaffirm with a quick cuddle. She pulls my fluffy duvet to right below her chin and gives me a look.

"You know who."

I blink at her. I have no idea. "Who?"

"I think it's obvious I am referring to Luka." She walks her fingertips up my arm and back down again. "I passed his mom's house on the way here and saw his car in the driveway."

"You saw his car at his mom's place but assumed he was here with me?"

"I figured he doubled back." She shrugs, burrowing down farther until I can only see her eyes. They're green today, reflecting the color of the trees outside my bedroom window. Her voice emerges muffled from beneath my blankets. "I don't know, he could have snuck out."

"He's a grown man. Why would he have to sneak out?"

She sighs. "I don't know, Stella, let me sink into this fantasy. I've been rooting for you guys for as long as I've known you."

That certainly explains all the slightly vulgar hand gestures she's been making behind Luka's back every time he joins us at the farm.

I frown. Layla notices and presses her pointer finger directly in the divot at the corner of my mouth. She pulls, attempting to force a smile on her own, and snorts when I make a grotesque face. Her lingering frustration melts.

"Did you ask him?"

I nod and pick at a loose thread on my duvet.

"And?"

"He said he'd do it," I mumble into cotton, having slowly pulled the pillow fully over my face. Last night when I asked Luka, I was so fixated on him saying no that I didn't consider the implications of him saying yes. Pretend dating. We'll have to pretend other things too. Pretend romance. Pretend affection.

Does Luka realize? We didn't really talk much last night after our dinner conversation. I was pretty aggressively against discussing any details, mortified with myself for even asking. I was too afraid to talk about it more. Have him change his mind. Or worse, have to explain the situation in detail.

We turned on *Sleepless in Seattle* and tangled ourselves on the couch. I fell asleep with my feet tucked under his thigh and my head on the armrest.

Layla tugs on a piece of my hair. "Then why are you so sad, honey?"

Embarrassment, probably. A little bit of loneliness. Fear of change, absolute terror at the idea of messing all this up. Luka finding out the truth about my feelings for him.

Take your pick, Layla. It could be anything.

Instead, I breathe out long and slow into the pillow and let that answer for me. Layla gently lifts the pillow from my face and tucks it under her cheek.

"I think it's time we have a talk about this."

"No, thank you."

"Stella."

I shake my head. "I don't want to. How about we talk about you and Jacob instead?"

Her eyes narrow into slits. Layla's track record with romance is interesting, to say the least. She has a tendency to pick the worst sort of guy. "We're not talking about me right now. We're talking about you."

"We could be talking about you."

"You have feelings for him, Stella."

I know that. Of course I know that. I'm just unwilling to act on those feelings.

"I'm—"

"You have big feelings for Luka, and he has big feelings for you, and I don't understand why neither of you has ever done anything about it."

It's easy for Layla. She's always been utterly confident in who she is and what she feels. Despite everything she's gone through, she's always managed to dust herself off and roll right along with sunny optimism. She is graceful in her disappointments. I am not.

And things with Luka are great—amazing even—just as they are.

"Honey"—her eyes trip back and forth between my own, a sad smile pulling at the corner of her lips—"just because you let yourself love someone doesn't mean they're going to leave."

But it sure as hell doesn't mean they'll stay.

"I think—" I swallow around the tightness in my throat and try to channel just a little bit of Layla's confidence. I curl up on my side and mirror her position, hands clasped under my chin. It feels like we're in a cloud, under my comforter like we are. Weightless. Here, like this, I confess my most secret thoughts. "I think if something were supposed to happen between Luka and me, it would have already happened."

Layla doesn't like that answer. I can see it in the twist of her lips. "Maybe he's waiting for you to say something."

I shake my head sadly. I once watched Luka walk up to a girl in a bar, prop his hand on the back of her chair, and tell her something that had her chin tipping back with a laugh. He was confident, charming. They left together not a half hour later. Luka has never been hesitant with vocalizing what he wants. If it were me he wanted, I think I would know by now.

"I think this is what we're supposed to be." I nuzzle down farther into my blankets, blinking against the prickling sensation in the corners of my eyes. "We're supposed to be friends. Just friends."

"Then why did you lie on your application?" It's a gentle accusation, but I feel the sting of it nonetheless. "Beckett was right. You didn't need to do that."

"I didn't plan all of this, if that's what you mean. I wouldn't trick him into pretending to be my boyfriend. I'm not—" I scrub both hands across my face. "I'm not that desperate."

I'm not. The lie in the application—I just wanted this place to seem romantic. Homey. When I turned in the personal statement portion, I didn't even think we had a chance. It seemed like a small, harmless detail. I wanted us to have the best possible chance.

Cool fingers thread between my own, the press of her rings against my skin leaving tiny indentations.

"Honey, no. That's not what I meant."

"Then what did you mean?"

Her eyes are kind as she tucks my hair behind my ear. "I'm just saying I think this might be the something you've both been waiting for."

❧ ❦

LAYLA'S WORDS PING-PONG around my head as I trudge my way over to the office. If last night was all the reasons I bought this place, this morning is all the reasons I probably shouldn't have. Walking in this direction, I can see the scraggly outline of dead and dying trees. There is decidedly not a supply truck in the driveway of the barn like I had scheduled, and one of the pumpkins that lined the stairway to the office is now smashed to bits on the ground.

It's the last thing, though, that has me cursing under my breath. If one of the McAllister twins thought it would be funny to trash the fields again, I'm pretty sure Beckett might commit murder.

Last fall, the high school population of Inglewild decided our farm was the place to be for illicit activities. I saw more pasty white skin belonging to sixteen-year-old boys than anyone ever ought to. Beckett and Luka had handled it in the way that any grown man would.

They dressed up in camo, hid in the cornfield, and scared the ever-living shit out of all the kids sucking face in their cars.

It's been quiet since then, and I've laughed to myself more than once walking through town, listening to the kids talk about the demented creatures that live in the fields at Ms. Stella's farm. I think about Luka and Beckett using my tiny bathroom to put on their camo paint. The absolutely ridiculous amount of green I had on all of my cute bathroom towels.

I've always wanted to be an urban legend.

I'm picking up the pieces of the pumpkin when a car door slams, two heavy boots appearing in my field of vision. Luka squats down and picks up the biggest piece of pumpkin carcass, an extra large take-out cup cradled in his other hand.

I catch a hint of hazelnut and immediately drop all of the pumpkin goop I'm holding. I reach out for it with both hands, a greedy little whimper caught in the back of my throat. He doesn't even fight me when I curl one hand around his wrist and the other around the cup. He just lets it happen.

Warm, creamy hazelnut welcomes me to nirvana as I take a deep pull. I make a slightly inhuman sound and then drink again. And again.

"What did you say to her?" I ask.

Ms. Beatrice makes the best hazelnut latte in probably the entire universe, but only when she wants to and only when you give her the oddly specific compliment she's waiting on. It's never the same compliment twice, there's never a clue, and god forbid you deliver it without the exact inflection of sincerity required.

She still only serves me decaf.

Luka huffs a laugh through his nose, a little puff of white in the cold October morning. He hands the cup over with a little nod of his head. "I told her that purple hair suited her mighty fine." He grins, bashful. "I think I made up a Southern accent? I'm not sure. I smelled hazelnut and it's all a blur from there."

I peek up at him, curling my hands around the cup and holding it close to my chest lest he gets any ideas about taking it back. God help me, he's wearing a black beanie with a forest green puffball on top. I'd bet the slim funds in my savings account that his mom made it for him. Ms. Beatrice probably took one look at him and blushed all the way down to her compression socks.

I take another drink of latte. "The things we do for good coffee."

"Yeah, sure, *we*." He laughs. He arches an eyebrow and extends his hand, gloved fingers not so politely requesting his drink back. "I got you a coffee too." For the first time, I notice an extra take-out cup resting on top of his car. "But I'm pretty sure it's still decaf."

I curse.

"Come on. Let's go inside and I'll split and mix."

Together we trudge into my office, the pumpkin pieces left scattered across the steps. I'll grab a broom later, or maybe I'll leave it for the raccoons. A peace offering of sorts. Luka collapses into the faded leather armchair, legs sprawled and elbows haphazard on the armrests. He always has trouble making his body fit, all long legs and toned arms. Maybe I'll make him and Beckett do that calendar together.

He shifts back and forth, a valiant attempt to get comfortable. I still haven't released his latte, and warm brown eyes jump from the cup to mine to the cup again. His gaze begins to get a little forlorn. Somewhere in that beautiful brain of his, he's realizing he's made a terrible mistake.

"I hope you had some of this in the car." I take a pointed sip.

He shifts, the chair squeaks, and he frowns. "It was too hot to drink in the car," he mumbles. "Are you going to give it back?"

"Probably not."

He grunts and shifts in the chair again. "Stella, listen."

"I'm listening."

"I've been a good friend to you, haven't I?"

I sit down primly in my chair. My perfectly sized, appropriately upholstered chair. "You have."

He leans forward, hands cupped loosely between his legs. "Do you remember the summer of 2016? I gave you my waffle at the First Friday block party."

I have no recollection of Luka ever once giving me a waffle. I slurp loudly.

"Stella. C'mon. I took you to the *Lord of the Rings* midnight show-ing when I didn't even know what a hobbit was. I got you a cape."

That's true. He did do that. And then proceeded to ask for seven consecutive weeks if he should grow his hair out like Aragorn. Like the universe needs Luka to be more attractive.

He continues. "I didn't tell my grandma your snickerdoodles were from Layla."

I raise my eyebrows and take another sip. I'm not afraid of her.

Not really.

Maybe a little.

He leans closer, tongue pressing at the inside of his cheek. His brown eyes flash a shade darker, and his voice drops. "I agreed to be your fake boyfriend for a week."

Suddenly it sounds like he's not teasing me at all. All my bravado and good humor slip away with that little comment, a rush of heat pressing at my cheeks. It's the tight curl in my stomach that I hate, and I avert my gaze to the top of my desk. Is this what it's going to be like now? Luka holding on to this as a bartering chip for the rest of our relationship? A funny little anecdote at cookouts and parties? *Oh, remember that time you were so desperate you asked me to pretend to date you?*

I get it. I'm the one who asked for this as a favor. But still, that felt . . . weird. Not good.

After an indeterminate amount of time staring at the nick in my desk from that time I got too aggressive with my stapler, I clear my throat and look back up at him, fixing my gaze somewhere over his left shoulder. I hand over the coffee and congratulate myself when my hand doesn't shake.

"Here you go."

His fingers overlap mine, but he doesn't let me release the cup. He has a deceptively strong grip, and that sends my thoughts tumbling down a separate, albeit more vulgar, path.

"Stella."

He manages to infuse a lot in those two staccato beats of my name. It's a gift. I blink my gaze away from the calendar on the wall and back to him, sighing when I see the way his lips are settled in a thin line. Concerned Luka. Damn it.

"Why are you upset right now?"

I try to pull my hand away, but he just tightens his grip. I'm worried for the paper cup. The hazelnut latte doesn't deserve to go this way. "I'm not upset."

He makes a sound in the back of his throat. "I have known you for almost a decade. Why are you upset?"

"I don't want—" His fingers flex on mine. I don't want him to do this because I forced him into it. I don't want him to hate every second of it. I don't want to be a bother, a nuisance, an obligation. "I don't want this to ruin anything."

"It won't. Stella, look at me please." When I manage to meet his gaze, those brown eyes of his are as serious as they've ever been. With the sun filtering through the window and that stupid hat on his head, I can see the flecks of gold in them. The light brown ring of color just at the edge of his iris that reminds me of coffee with too much milk. Hazelnut lattes. "This isn't going to ruin anything, okay? It's me and you."

I nod, and his hand squeezes mine again on the cup. My arm is starting to tingle from keeping it outstretched. He opens his mouth to say something else, his hand pulling, the front half of my body beginning to lean toward him, but the door to my office swings open, a very grumpy Beckett standing there with his hands full of smashed pumpkin.

"We have a problem."

Twenty minutes later, I'm standing in the pumpkin field staring at the carcasses of hundreds of smashed pumpkins. It looks like a battlefield but with more . . . orange. So much for my raccoon peace offering of a single pumpkin back at the office. They can have an all-you-can-eat buffet out here.

I make a mental note to google if raccoons can eat pumpkin.

"Well . . ." I stretch my neck back and forth. This is fine. This is—it's absolutely fine. Next to me, Luka hands over his hazelnut latte without a word. "Halloween is in two days. We were going to harvest these anyway for Layla. Maybe we could—I don't know. Turn this into a haunted field?"

Beckett makes some sort of grumbling noise under his breath. He's probably nervous I'll make him wear a zombie costume. "I'm going to kill those McAllister shits."

He sounds like an eighty-year-old man standing on his front lawn. It feels a bit like I manifested this.

I look around at the sheer range of damage. Every single pumpkin left on the vine has been caved in. It seems excessive for two teenage boys. It's too organized, too methodical. "We don't know it was them."

I guess I'll have to install cameras.

Luka and Beckett give me matching looks of disbelief, though Beck manages to infuse a layer of hostile frustration into his. It's difficult to take Luka seriously when he's wearing that poof-ball hat.

"All right, well"—I channel my inner optimist—"it's time we switch over to Christmas anyway. We'll leave the big decorations for next week, but we can start putting Halloween away. I'll ask Layla to make extra goodies for the bakehouse, and if anyone shows up for pumpkins, we can sell what we've already pulled off the vine at a discount."

"What are we going to do about whoever did this?" Beckett sounds like he has a few ideas.

I shrug. "I really don't know. What can we do?" I briefly consider using what I've learned in marathon viewings of *Law & Order SVU*, looking for shoe imprints in the dirt and clothing fibers on tree limbs. What I wouldn't do for Detective Stabler right about now. "I'll have some cameras installed at the major spots, but we can't cover the whole farm."

I can't afford to cover the whole farm.

The three of us lapse into silence. It's a good thing this happened at the tail end of the fall season. I can't shake the feeling that this—the fertilizer, the trees—it's all connected. No one is this unlucky, right?

"You think this has anything to do with your supply issues?"

I frown at Luka and press my fingers into the back of my neck. He's heard me complain about missing shipments and random incidents since I bought this place. My shoulders tense from yet another thing landing on top of them. "I don't know. Probably." I drop my hands by my sides and look around. "Maybe."

Whatever is happening, we need to figure it out. Preferably before the farm is featured before millions of people.

5

BECKETT TRAILS US on our way back to the office, the hazelnut coffee somehow ending up in his hands. I don't know why. It's not like he ever has any issues ordering from Ms. Beatrice.

"What are you doing down here?" he asks Luka. It's something I've wondered about too, but I haven't had a chance to ask him yet. Luka's sudden appearance is unusual. I usually know the weekends he's coming to hang out with his mom. New York is only a few hours from us, and he's been known to make spur-of-the-moment visits, but I usually get a text when he's decided to come home for the weekend. "I thought you weren't supposed to be home until Thanksgiving."

"Decided to come down early." Luka shoots me a look I have no idea how to interpret. "Hang out with Stella."

I frown at him, confused. Oh, does he want to . . . practice? Work on our story? It's probably a good idea. I clear my throat.

"Yes, we are dating now." My voice is overloud in the quiet of the farm, a nearby tree of birds taking flight. I bring it down a level. "We are—ah, people who date. He came to spend time with me, his—um, his girlfriend."

Beckett stops walking and looks at me, both eyebrows high on his forehead. I fidget under his gaze, belatedly reaching for Luka's hand. Luka laughs but tries to cover it with a cough. I squeeze his fingers hard enough to break.

"Yeah . . ." Beckett turns on his heel and heads over to the barn, the hazelnut latte going with him. "That's going to need some work-shopping."

I drop Luka's hand.

"We are people who date?" Luka's gaze is fixed on the tree line, a small smile making his eyes crinkle at the corners. He turns and peers down at me. "You know, I think that's how we should intro-duce ourselves when Ms. Instagram gets here."

I narrow my eyes and decide not to reply. I turn and continue walking to my office. He lets out a loud laugh and jogs to catch up, running a bit ahead of me just so he can walk backward and needle me some more. His coat opens in the breeze, a stupid sweatshirt with the Inglewild High mascot. He probably got it at the last fundraiser, eager to support his mom, who is a teacher and head of the PTA.

I never knew a man could look so good with a badger plastered across his chest.

"It does bring up a good point though."

"What's that?"

"If we are now people who date, does that assume we were once people who did not?"

I ignore him and pointedly don't remind him about the ancient maple tree he's about to smack into. But because the universe hates me, Luka smoothly sidesteps it without missing a beat. I tuck my hands deeper in my pockets and burrow my face into my scarf.

"I don't know. I was being stupid. Obviously."

"But it is something we should talk about. Stella, hold on a sec-ond." Strong hands cup my shoulders, bringing me to a stop. His face is still lined in amusement, but there's a seriousness there too. Like the time he said he wanted to learn all the words to Queen's *A Night at the Opera*, and he was kind of joking but also mostly serious.

"She thinks we're dating, right? This influencer?"

I nod.

"And she thinks we bought this place together?"

I nod again.

"Okay, well"—he shakes me slightly—"she's also presumably staying here in Inglewild. And that's going to be news to a town full of busybodies."

My stomach plummets somewhere down to my toes. I hadn't thought about that. In a town as small as ours, Luka and I suddenly proclaiming that we're dating and have been for years is borderline front-page news. The one time Beckett took off his shirt while plowing the backfields in the dry summer heat while Becky Gardener was driving by in her minivan, he had right column real estate in the *Inglewild Gazette* for three weeks running.

"I didn't think about that," I manage. I swallow awkwardly, a tiny almost comical *gulp* between us. "She's staying at the bed-and-breakfast."

Luka squeezes down my arms. The familiar one-two-three. "I've got a plan."

※ · ※

AN HOUR LATER, I'm standing at the stone fountain that marks the entrance of our downtown district. I'm not sure you can consider a small collection of buildings consisting of a bakery, a pizza shop, and a bookstore a district, but that's what it's been referred to as long as I've lived here. Luka likes to laugh about it when we're together in New York—talk about how he misses the bright lights of downtown Inglewild as we stroll along the bustling streets crowded with men and their briefcases, traveling food carts, and laughing couples spilling out of bars.

It's worth noting that the last time Luka Peters told me he had a plan, I ended up blindingly drunk off tequila, wearing a hula skirt, and singing nineties pop karaoke in a twenty-four-hour diner. Luka grins at the memory when I remind him of this, his hand finding mine and curling our fingers together.

"But you had fun, right?"

Sure. I also had a hangover for close to five days after. I had to lay down in a tree field the next day just to keep the horizon from tilting.

"Think of this as a practice run." He swings our hands back and forth, our footsteps in sync as we head toward Main Street. "We'll pop into a couple of stores, say hello, and go from there."

I fight the urge to wrestle my hand out of his grip and go running back to the farm. This feels sudden. And stupid.

"Shouldn't we have prepared for this?"

He mutters something I can't understand under his breath and releases my hand to throw his arm over my shoulder instead. I grumble but nestle easily into his side. We've always been affectionate with each other. This physical intimacy between us is nothing new. The result, I think, of two people who rely heavily on touch as a method of comfort and communication.

But with the story we're trying to sell, it feels different. A zip of awareness lights up my spine and settles where his arm rests heavily across my back. Tingles where his fingers play idly with the hair peeking out of my hat.

"What would you have done?" Luka asks.

I hum, distracted. I'm busy returning the steady stare of Mr. Hewett, the town librarian. He's stopped halfway down the steps of the library, broom in hand, as he sweeps up the leaves that crowd the stone walkway. But he's staring at us like we're doing something indecent. I wave and we keep walking.

"For preparation," Luka continues, not noticing the strange interaction. "How would you have prepared for this?"

"I don't know. Probably get our story straight, for one." I glance over my shoulder, my nose pressing into Luka's arm. Mr. Hewett is still watching us wander down the street, his tortoiseshell glasses practically fogging up.

"We have a story already."

"Oh yeah?" I stop worrying about the old librarian's googly eyes and look up at Luka instead. His jaw is set. Oh boy, I've seen this level of determination before.

> 2015: *The summer carnival. Over seventy-five dollars in game tickets to liberate as many goldfish as possible.*

> 2016: *Rio Summer Olympics. When he became convinced he could run a four-minute mile.*

> 2018: *The tiny studio apartment I had above the oil change garage. His sudden need to put locks on every single window and two on the door.*

"Yeah," he says. We turn left down Main. "Boy meets girl. It's a pretty simple story."

I'm suspicious. "All right."

"You see, Boy's mom decides she wants to move to a tiny town on the East Coast. She wants something different, something new, and keeps talking about Little Florence. Boy doesn't really get it, but he goes with her. Helps her get settled. When they're moving her in, Boy meets Girl. Runs right into her really. And she is—" He coughs, his arm tightening over my shoulder.

"She's incredible. Smart, funny, beautiful as all hell. But she's sad too. So he buys her a beer and a grilled cheese, and after that—well, after that, he keeps bumping into her. Buys her some more grilled cheese. And that's that."

That's that. I swallow hard. It's our story, but . . . different. He did buy me a grilled cheese and a beer. He told me it was an apology for practically mowing me down. It had felt like swimming underwater, all those months, and then Luka was there and my head bobbed above the surf.

I look up at him, stuck on one particular part of that story.

"You think I'm beautiful?"

He frowns down at me as we continue walking.

"Of course I do. I've told you that before."

I shake my head, a little bit dazed. I think back and try to remember that day and what came after. Falling into friendship with Luka had been effortless. Half the time I don't remember what it was like before him. It feels like he's always been a part of my life. And no wonder, after almost a decade.

And while we are comfortable with each other as all best friends are, I don't think he's ever called me beautiful. Luka has always seemed—*oblivious* isn't the right word. I guess I just thought he didn't think about me in that way. Friends don't think about friends like that.

You sure do notice his collarbones though, my brain helpfully supplies. *Never miss a glance at those biceps.*

"You have not."

"Oh." His frown deepens. "You're beautiful."

He says it almost like he's mad about it. And paired with that frown, well, it's probably the weirdest compliment I've ever received.

Though there was that one time a man told me I have nice teeth. And the lady at the supermarket two towns over who told me I have strong calves.

"But if you want some harrowing story of how I saved you from a rumbling trash can coming at you in the middle of the street while your boot was stuck in a storm drain, by all means."

"That sounds familiar," I mumble.

He grins, but I barely notice. My brain is still stuck on *beautiful*.

Beautiful, beautiful, beautiful. I'm ruminating as we continue walking, so I don't notice as he steers us into the greenhouse that sits prettily right on the corner of the street. It's huge, the curved walls covered in glass, an ornate dome painted in color at the top. The silhouettes of hanging baskets and wide leaves brush at the windows, the fog from the heaters obscuring the details of anything specific. When I was a kid, the high school boys used to sneak in here and draw penises on the windows.

I follow Luka blindly, ducking into one of the thick glass doors. Two things happen immediately. The thick humidity of the greenhouse welcomes me by instantly puffing up my hair, and Mabel Brewster screams at the top of her lungs.

Luka and I both jolt.

"Oh my god," I groan. "You thought starting here was a good idea?"

Mabel is weaving through the shelves of succulents at the back with an almost manic look in her eyes. Her long black hair is in braids, tied neatly back with a scarf around the crown of her head, the orange and red a striking contrast to her dark skin. While I can feel sweat starting to gather at the small of my back and the hollow of my throat, her skin is unfairly glowing in the humidity of the greenhouse, a light shine on her high cheekbones. She looks like a greenhouse Barbie, and I tell her so every time she visits the farm with fresh herbs.

But right now, she looks like a determined little stick of dynamite.

I groan again, just for good measure. Luka shifts on his feet, seemingly beginning to regret his decision when she knocks over two potted palms and doesn't slow down.

"Why does she look like that?" says Luka.

I know exactly what he means, I just want to hear him say it. "Like what?"

He curls me closer to his body like he can protect me from her frankly terrifying single-mindedness. I've known Mabel since high school. The last time I saw her look like this was when she caught Billy Walters drawing the penises on her dad's greenhouse windows. "Like she wants to chop our bodies into tiny pieces but also kind of make out with our faces."

I snort a laugh. Mabel is all of five feet, probably 125 pounds soaking wet. But what she lacks in stature, she more than makes up for in energy. She marches right up to us, staring pointedly at where Luka's hand is curled around my arm. He pulls me a touch closer and exhales a shaky breath against the back of my head. I want to cackle in delight, but I'm a little bit afraid of what Mabel might do.

"You two look cozy."

We remain silent.

She narrows her eyes. "Haven't seen you around in a bit, Luka."

"You saw me two weeks ago, Mabel. At the grocery store."

She hums but doesn't acknowledge his statement. "And you. Ms. Fancy Farmer. Have something you want to share with the class?" She practically burns a hole where my hand is clutching at Luka's jacket.

"Not much." I play dumb. "Oh, actually," I say and she perks up. "I'll have some fresh trimmings for you starting the third week of November. For wreath-making, if you'd like."

She looks like she wants to wring my neck.

"Wreath-making."

"Yes."

"All right."

There's a beat of silence as we all consider one another. I'm fighting a smile, and I can feel the rumble of a laugh trapped in Luka's chest. He tugs me around so I'm standing fully in front of him and folds both arms over my shoulders, pulling me flush against him. It's a perfect fit, the scratch of his stubble catching in the chaotic mess that is my hair in this heat. Mabel's eyes light up, and a smile starts to unfurl across her lips.

"We were hoping you'd make us a wreath for our front door," Luka offers, chin resting at the very top of my head.

Clever man. He could have come right out and told her. Instead, he's made it seem like it's something she should already know. A foregone conclusion. He's tapped right into the heart of this town's gossip mill.

Mabel threads her fingers together, clasping her hands over her heart. She grins as she rocks back on her heels.

"It's happening," she singsongs.

And just like that, our ruse begins.

꙳ ꙳

APPARENTLY, THERE IS an Inglewild phone tree.

We find that out as soon as we leave Mabel's and cross the driveway that spills out from the firehouse onto the main road. The truck bay doors are rolled up, and Clint and Monty are kicked back in the faded lawn chairs they use when the weather is nice. They both start applauding as soon as we're within earshot, a hearty whistle coming from somewhere deep inside. Gus, no doubt. He's probably stuck halfway beneath the paramedic van, tinkering away.

"Fuckin' finally!" calls Clint, lifting his energy drink in a toast.

Monty slaps him and gestures at the completely abandoned playground across the street like his curse words might linger and influence the currently nonexistent kids to start talking like sailors.

Clint waves him off. "Mabel called with the good news!"

"We were there like twelve seconds ago," I mutter.

"Busybodies. I told you." Luka tilts his chin up at Clint. "Cathy know you're drinking those?"

Clint glances down at the drink in his hand and then shoots Luka a cheeky grin. "Of course she knows I am drinking this fine, electrolyte-enhanced hydration beverage." He tilts his chin down and looks at us both over the rim of his glasses, a thin edge of warning in his smiling eyes. His wife, Cathy, would whup him up and down the block if she knew he was still drinking those after his last heart scare. "And it'll stay that way."

Alex at the bookstore gives us a tiny salute with his mug of chamomile as we pass by the large paneled windows of his store. Ms. Beatrice, contrarian that she is, only offers a frown when Luka pops his head in, my hand clasped in his, asking for a latte to go. And Bailey McGivens and her wife, Sandra, almost start to cry when Luka and I run into them on the sidewalk.

"We're so happy for you both," she manages, clutching onto Sandra's arm. "We've been hoping this might happen."

I don't know if she's talking to me or Luka, but I blush and stammer and do my best not to completely fold in on myself. I had no idea everyone was so invested. I sneak a look at Luka out of the corner of my eye to read for any awkwardness, but he's just smiling gently, taking all the congratulations in stride, not a hint of anxiety on his handsome face. Me? I'm a tightly wound ball of apprehension.

"You good?" He nuzzles the question into my ear, fingers finding a belt loop at my waist.

I almost jump out of my skin. "I'm fine!"

It's much the same as we wander through town. People I've known forever and people I don't know at all clapping us on shoulders, waving and cheering. It feels a bit like we're in a parade of two, and I'm infinitely glad Luka suggested we do this now and not when Evelyn is in town. Everyone is acting like we're the chosen ones and our union determines the fate of the world.

By the time we make it to the sheriff's station that bookends Main Street, I'm exhausted. I don't think I've talked to this many people since the last time Ms. Beatrice offered a buy-one-get-one-free special on her Nutella swirl mochaccinos, and the entire town showed up at open to wait in line.

Luka rubs my back before sifting his fingers through my hair, digging with his thumb at the base of my neck. I experience what can only be described as a full-body shiver, an absolutely obscene sound leaving my mouth. Luka makes an interested hum in response.

"Pizza when we get back?" he asks.

I nod, still focused on the one square inch of skin where his thumb is pressing little circles. Half of me wants to collapse face-first into the pavement, the other half wants to strip off all my clothes.

Luka arches a single eyebrow, brown eyes flashing a shade darker. His thumb presses again with intent, testing, and my shoulders roll back with a tiny shiver. I feel that press low in my belly, in the dip of my spine.

I've always been attracted to Luka. He's handsome in all the ways

I like best: tall, perpetually messy hair, strong jaw, and a smattering of freckles across the bridge of his nose. But it's always been easy enough to ignore it. Convince myself I don't see him like that.

I'm noticing it now.

A devious grin tugs at the corner of his mouth, interest clear in the lines of his face. "I didn't—" He clears the husk away from his voice, fingers inching across my skin until he has the nape of my neck cupped fully in his palm. His hand is big, warm. He squeezes once as his gaze searches my face. "I didn't realize—"

I don't know what he didn't realize, because we're interrupted by the very clear click and release of a shotgun being loaded.

6

LUKA USES THE hand on my neck to tug me backward, positioning his body half in front of me. I peek over his shoulder to see Sheriff Jones sitting on the front porch of the old police station, a shotgun resting casually over his knees.

"Those are good instincts, son." He tips his hat at Luka but keeps one hand firmly on his gun. "That'll be a point in your favor."

Luka laughs, his shoulders relaxing with a heavy exhale. His hand slips from my neck, relieved. "Oh, is this an evaluation?"

Sheriff Jones does not laugh. "It sure is."

Dane Jones, town sheriff, was the first person my mom and I met when we moved into Inglewild. He saw us unpacking our over-crowded hatchback and offered to help, shouldering one of my mom's mismatched duffle bags over his broad shoulder and balancing a box of my books in his other arm. He ordered us two pizzas, gave my mom his card, and told her to call if she ever needed anything.

I tuck a smile into the wool of Luka's coat and then press up on my tiptoes, waving at the good sheriff.

"What's going on, Dane?"

Dane blinks away from his stare down at Luka to smile at me. It's hardly a smile by the standard definition, but after nearly twenty years, I know what that tilt of his lips means. "Heard you two were dating."

"Oh?"

"Thought I'd congratulate you both." Luka makes a muffled sound of protest, no doubt curious as to how the shotgun translates into a *congratulations*. Dane's eyes slide back to him and hold. "And give the boy here a warning."

Ah, okay.

My smile widens, a warmth settling in my chest. Strangely enough, I feel Luka relax in front of me.

"That's all you've got?" He nods at the gun. "An unloaded gun and an ambiguous warning?"

"There's nothing ambiguous about me telling you I will break every bone in your finely structured body if I see even the hint of a tear on that girl's face. And I will take great pleasure in grinding you down physically, mentally, and emotionally." He rocks back on his chair and kicks his feet up onto the railing. He pats the gun. "And who's to say this gun isn't loaded?"

"Ah." Luka swallows. "Noted."

There's silence as the three of us consider one another. I look at Dane. Dane looks at Luka. Luka, for his credit, doesn't break his stare with Dane.

"You know," I offer, voice carefully even, "I dated Wyatt, and you never once showed up with a shotgun."

Dane's eyes trip lazily back to me and he gives me a look. "I think we both knew that was going nowhere, Cinnamon Stick."

I roll my eyes at the nickname he gave me when I was thirteen years old, tearfully confessing my great crime of forgetting to pay for a cinnamon stick sucker at the Save More on Third and Monroe. I sat myself down in front of his desk and cried myself silly, holding up my wrists for the cuffs I was so sure he would be forced to use.

Shockingly, he did not feel the need to put me into custody.

"Are you going to your dad's next weekend?"

I grimace. I had almost forgotten. "Yeah, the usual."

Luka turns and frowns down at me. "He's still doing that? The early Thanksgiving thing?"

Yes, my father is still making me come to an early Thanksgiving at his house to avoid the horror of entertaining his illegitimate child on an actual holiday. And yes, my father is still the worst combination of self-centered and egotistical, his false humility a sour cherry on top.

But he's the only parent I have left. And that should count for something.

Even if *he* doesn't want it to.

"Yes," I say simply. "I'm bringing the pie."

I can feel the dead-eyed stares of both men on me. Luka looks like he has some thoughts on the matter. I think I've seen him frown more in the last two days than I have in the entire duration of our relationship. Dane has gone back to running his fingers over his shotgun, looking contemplative.

"Let him know I say hello," Dane offers. "And that I still think he's not fit to lick the tar off Satan's ass."

I bust out laughing. I'd love to see the look on Brian Milford's face if I delivered that message. I'll have to text it to Charlie later.

"All right." I hook my arm through Luka's and begin towing us back toward town. If we're lucky, Matty might still have some deep-dish pepperoni left, and we can get a pie to go. "Always a pleasure, Sheriff."

"Right back at you, Cinnamon Stick. I'm watching you, Peters."

I half expect him to point at his eyes and then point at Luka before dragging his finger across his throat. But apparently, that is a step too far for the man currently sitting in front of the police station with a gun in his lap.

Luka is quiet as we walk back. I glance up at him, noticing his frown hasn't budged an inch. I clear my throat. What I wouldn't give to go back to the levity of his fingers twisted through my belt loop.

"Did it bother you?" I say.

"Hm?"

"The sheriff? I think he was mainly joking. You know he's protective."

Luka goes to run his fingers through his hair but remembers at the last second he's still wearing his hat with the poof ball. He coasts his hand over it instead, nudging the cap up until a thick riot of hair pokes free in the front. With his rosy cheeks and dark messy hair, he looks like something that should be in a snow globe. I sigh.

"No, that was fine," he says. A grin cracks through, some of his melancholy fading. "Actually, that was fantastic. I like that you have people looking out for you."

"He checks in on the farm every couple of weeks. I think he even has some of the deputies do roadside cleanup on the stretch of road that leads down to us."

And he always buys three trees. Every year. He grabs enough pumpkins to place on every banister of his front porch. He makes sure to grab a hot chocolate from Layla and fresh produce from Beckett. He's a good man.

"Why are you still going to your dad's house though? You're always so—" He considers his words carefully, assessing me from the corner of his eye. "You're not yourself. Seeing your dad makes you sad."

I shrug and focus on the way our feet march out the same beat on the pavement. Luka's legs are so much longer, but he slows to meet my pace, two sets of boots in perfect harmony.

"I'm not sad, I'm just . . . tired, I think. It's always exhausting."

"Then why do you still go?"

"I like to see Charlie. And Elle is nice."

"So? You can see either of them whenever you want. You don't have to entertain this weird nonholiday your dad insists on doing year after year."

I'm not so sure it's my dad's idea. I think he plays along with it, of course. And it is certainly more convenient for him if I attend this version of Thanksgiving and not the large bash he throws on the actual holiday for the board of directors that oversees his financial management firm. But in the beginning, the invitation had come directly from Elle.

I sigh and decide to opt for honesty. "It's nice to have somewhere to be," I say quietly. "It's nice to have a family to visit."

Even if the entire dinner is an awkward ninety minutes of small talk, it's a tradition in its own right.

"What's that supposed to mean? Are you telling me—" I'm surprised to hear that Luka sounds angry. Furious even. "Stella, I have invited you to every single Thanksgiving."

I know that. And I've declined every time. Instead, I spend my day at a shelter on the outskirts of Baltimore serving mashed potatoes and turkey sandwiches until it feels like my arms might fall off. And on the way home, I stop at Sheetz and eat my body weight in tater tots and fried mac and cheese.

And that's okay. Perfect even. It's exactly how I want to spend my holiday. My mom used to piece together a similar feast for us every Thanksgiving. We could never afford the turkey and sweet potatoes and green bean casseroles, so she improvised. We got TV dinners and set the table with our fanciest plasticware and laughed ourselves silly toasting each other with Dr Pepper.

It's my own little tradition.

"I see you the day after," I hedge. "You know I don't like to miss the bookstore Black Friday sale."

He stops walking and curls both of his hands over my shoulders. I look up at him and catch sight of that poof ball again. It really is infuriating. I frown back at him.

"Why haven't you been spending Thanksgiving with me and my mom?"

Because Luka's mom still pinches his cheeks when he walks in the door. Because his grandma and all his aunts make dinner while yelling over one another in Italian, slapping wrists with wooden spoons when you get too close to the pot. Because it's warm and loud and chaotic and perfect. Because it feels too much like all the things I'm missing out on.

I shrug.

He mutters under his breath. "Well if I can't stop you from willingly spending your day with that asshole, I'm not going to let you do it alone." He stares down at me, and I can see that he means business. He looks like he should be delivering this proclamation from atop a hill before a wide green field. A sword or something in hand. Maybe a kilt. "I'm coming with you."

I struggle to shake the mental image of Luka in a kilt out of my mind. "What?"

"I'm coming with you to forced fake Thanksgiving."

"Uh, no you're not."

"Why?"

"Well, you're not invited, for one."

"All right, well. Charlie loves me. I'll just text Charlie."

It's true. Charlie does love him. Charlie would invite him in a nanosecond.

"What's for two?"

"What?" I startle and stare longingly at the neon pizza sign two blocks away. If they've run out of deep-dish pizza in the time we've been having this discussion, I might never forgive Luka.

"You said 'for one.' What's for two?"

"For two . . ." I search for an appropriate response.

"See." He's smug. I roll my eyes and begin speed-walking down to the pizza place. I'll get a deep dish for myself, and Luka will be left with only the gluten-free thin-crust vegetable special. "There is no two."

"There is a two," I snap. I don't want him to hear the way my dad talks to me. How sometimes he doesn't even acknowledge my existence at all. Like I'm an inconvenient shadow at the table. I don't want Luka to see what my Thanksgiving looks like when his is so wonderful. "I don't want you to come."

That gives Luka pause, and I feel his steps falter next to mine. I fight the immediate instinct to take it back.

"That's not true," he says quietly, and my chest pulls tight when I hear the hurt in his voice. "You don't mean that, Stella."

Shit. I stop on the sidewalk with one last longing glance at Matty's Pizza and then turn to face Luka, gripping my hands just above his elbows like he often does to me. I shake him once.

"Luka." His face is almost comically sad. I have no idea how his mother ever managed to discipline him as a child. "Luka, you are already doing so much for me. I do not want you to come to . . ." I search for what he called it. "I don't want you to come to forced fake Thanksgiving."

He perks up a bit. "Is that why? Because you think I'm already doing so much?"

I nod, hesitant. He blows out a puff of air and rocks back on his heels. "Okay, well, that's easy."

"That's easy?"

"Yeah, I'm coming with you. We've been friends for almost ten years, Stella. Stop keeping score."

Luckily for Luka, there is still deep-dish pepperoni pizza when we finally arrive at Matty's. As per usual, Luka waits at the curb while I run in and grab our food. Matty gives me a wink and a smile from the back kitchen and lets me know it's on the house for the lovebirds. He even arranges the pepperonis in a heart. It goes a long way to soothe my Luka-related frustrations.

He says not to keep score, but I can't help it. I've always had trouble accepting help, and that seems like all I've been asking for lately. I don't know how I'll ever repay him for all of this.

∗⢌·⢀∗

WE'RE QUIET ON the way back to the farm, the murmur of the radio filling the silence between us. Every so often, there's the creak of the cardboard box as I sneak my hand in for a pepperoni or two. I try to be stealthy about it, but by my third one, Luka reaches over and curls his hand around my wrist, guiding one perfect, greasy pepperoni to his mouth.

The edges of his teeth bite against my fingers, his bottom lip catching and dragging on the pad of my thumb. There's a hint of tongue, and my stomach drops down to my toes.

He makes an exaggerated groaning sound as he chews, and I have to roll down the window half an inch.

I keep the pizza box shut after that.

As we turn onto the narrow road that leads down to the farm, I see Beckett waving us down, elbows resting on the fence post that circles the land we use for produce. Luka slows the car to a stop, and I roll down the window. I snap a quick picture with my phone to upload to the farm Instagram, and Beckett grimaces. It's his own stupid fault for standing like that. Luka snickers somewhere behind me.

"Why have I gotten four calls about you two?"

"Four calls?"

"My sisters and then the phone tree."

My eyebrows shoot up my forehead. "You're on the phone tree?"

Beckett frowns. "Everyone is on the phone tree."

"I'm not," Luka supplies from over my shoulder. "Neither is Stella."

"Oh well." Beckett shrugs, wholly unconcerned. Honestly, I didn't even know the man owns a cell phone. When I need him, I just step outside my office and bellow his name into the fields. "You got the word out, if that's what you were looking to do."

I frown, something about that twisting in the back of my mind. In all the excitement, I feel like we've forgotten something important. Beckett waves us off and goes back to doing whatever it is he does when alone with the potatoes, and Luka guides us down the back roads.

I remember my earlier hesitation in the day, how we're jumping into this without a plan. It had worked out this time, but what comes next? I'm stuck on that as I climb out of Luka's car and dig around in my bag for my keys, shouldering open the door and letting us into the cluttered hallway. I kick off my boots and ignore the way Luka almost immediately straightens them, discarding my scarf on a table. I mindlessly wander into the kitchen and find the gnome-shaped plates that match the dish towel left by the previous owner and are frankly too hilariously weird to get rid of. I grab a slice of pepperoni and stare out the little window above the sink.

I'm two bites in when I realize the problem.

"Luka."

He's ignored my introspective mood and set up camp on my couch, a college football game on the television and an IPA in hand. He turns to look at me, long arm stretched out over the back of my love seat.

"You figure it out?"

I nod and shuffle a step closer. I take an extra bite of pizza for strength and fortitude.

"Everyone thinks we're dating," I start. He gives me a look that quite plainly says, *Was that not the point of today?* I eyeball him back and remind myself that he can't read my mind. "It's just—if they think we're dating, what are they going to think when we're—not dating?"

Everyone we ran into today had been so happy for us. Invested. Bailey McGivens had teared up. Mabel almost took Luka to the ground when he insinuated we were living together. I know I should have thought about this before, but this whole thing is starting to feel messy. And Evelyn hasn't even arrived yet.

He takes a long draw from his beer, a little line forming between his eyebrows. "I don't follow."

I circle the couch and perch on the edge. "We don't have an exit strategy."

"Do we need an exit strategy?"

As in, fake date forever? Walk around town on Saturdays arm in arm, only to go home to two separate houses? That seems like . . . an odd choice. My face must betray my confusion, because Luka chuckles, holding up both his hands.

"Hold on, hear me out." He shifts his body until he's fully facing me, resting his beer bottle on my knee. I narrow my eyes at him and reach for it, taking a quick swig. Deliciously bitter hops explode in my mouth, and I calm fractionally. "I get that today was a little bit of a spectacle, but when this is all over, after we charm Evelyn Stackhouse—"

"St. James," I correct.

"—or whatever, and you win this contest, what really has to change? We didn't act any different today than we normally do. I just laid out some innuendos for Mabel to pick up on."

I think of the way he curled his hand around my neck, how I could feel the thrum of his heart against my back when he pulled me against his chest. I think of how he nosed below my ear when we walked past the bookstore, pointing out the new nonfiction serial killer anthology. True, we act like that sometimes. But I'd hardly call it normal.

Luka continues, oblivious to my dubious look.

"I mean, what were you thinking? Did you want to send out a memo or something? How about we just . . . continue."

I blink at him. He takes a behemoth bite of pizza, pleased with himself. I have no idea what he's talking about. *Continue what, Luka?* I want to grab him by the shoulders and shake. *Continue what?*

"We will—" I almost don't even want to say it. I reach for his beer and down it in four gulps and then wince. IPAs are not for chugging. I hand him the empty bottle and then thread my fingers together on my lap. I employ my patient voice, the one I use when the kindergarteners visit the farm on their annual field trip and I show them how to plant their seeds. "Luka, what do you mean when you use the word *continue*?"

He looks at me like he knows exactly what kind of voice I'm using.

"Say we were dating for real." His gaze softens, hazy in the light of the TV, brown eyes warm and reassuring. A half smile tips up the corner of his mouth, like the thought pleases him. Like he can't possibly imagine anything better. "It wouldn't change this part, right?"

"Pizza on the couch? Absolutely not." Though it would probably be pants optional. The idea of it sends a prickle of awareness through me.

"No, I mean . . ." He searches for the right words, tilting his chin to look at the ceiling like he might find the answer somewhere up there with the support beams. His face is all clean lines in the setting sun. The sharp angle of his jaw. The dark brush of his brows. His straight nose and the freckles that dance over it. He took off his hat as soon as we came in, and his hair hasn't quite figured out what to do, wild and unkempt and sticking out in every direction. "I mean like if we were dating for real, I'd like to think that no matter what happened, we would still act exactly as we do now. That even in the event of a breakup, like you're worried about, we would still be friends and still do this. We would continue."

"So you think—" I try to follow his logic. "Oh, you think because we have a friendship, it wouldn't matter if we break up or not."

He nods. "Yeah, exactly. We don't need to say anything to anyone. We'll just keep doing what we've always done, and if someone asks, we can tell them, I guess. But it's not likely."

"Won't that—I don't know—won't it impact your activities when you're back in town? After this?"

He looks confused as he runs his hand back and forth over his hair, somehow managing to mess it up further. "Activities?"

"You know." I make a vague gesture with my hands. "Like if you go out and want to pick up a lady friend or something." I sound like I am one hundred and seven years old.

He blinks at me. "Who am I going to pick up? Ms. Beatrice?"

"Luka."

"I have never once done that here."

I grimace, remembering a night out at the bar when he visited on his college spring break, his hand on a tourist's thigh beneath the bar, his nose brushing her shoulder as he leaned in close.

I clear my throat. "You have once or twice done that here."

He frowns like he has no idea what I'm talking about. Like the idea of it is preposterous. "I have not."

I am not willing to continue this conversation, nor explain why every, ah, encounter of his is seared into my brain. "The point remains," I say with an iron-willed determination to be relaxed about this, "that if we *continue* and people think we're dating, you might have some—um—trouble. Doing that."

"Which is not a point that matters," he counters, looking confused and a little hurt. "Because that's not something I've done in, like, five years, Stella. And especially not here."

"All right." He's wrong, but all right.

"Okay."

"Fine."

A frustrated huff of a laugh leaves him, and he kicks his legs out, sprawled across the couch. I still have my reservations, but it's a little late to walk back this afternoon. Worst-case scenario, we can tell everyone that we decided we work better as friends.

Or I could fake my death and move to Mexico. I bet a holiday tree farm would do great there. I could sell tiny little palm trees in coconut shells on a beach somewhere.

After a few minutes of the both of us staring unseeingly at a college wide receiver rocketing down the field, his socked foot nudges mine.

"Everything is going to be fine, La La. No matter what happens, I'm not going to disappear on you. Okay?"

Leave it to Luka to touch on my deepest fear while I have pepperoni grease clinging to my chin. My dad left before I was born and it destroyed my mother. She died when I was in my twenties. We moved around too much for me to make lifelong friends. I've never gotten to keep anyone.

"Do you promise?"

I'm not ashamed of how my voice shakes around the edges, the tightness in my throat. He needs to know how important this is. I'm not willing to do any of it if it means losing him in the process.

He laces our fingers together and squeezes. His eyes are earnest, and it's easy to believe him.

"I promise."

7

THE WEEK BEFORE my dad's version of Thanksgiving passes quickly. Luka spends it in New York handling some mysterious work project that he explains using only vague adjectives, and I fill my time by getting things organized for the farm's holiday switchover.

After he's gone back to the city, I find a pine tree air freshener hung neatly in the middle of the doorway of my house like a sprig of mistletoe. I pull it down with a smile and put it with the others, wondering if he stops at the little gas station on the edge of town every time.

Beckett, Layla, and I clean up the damaged pumpkin patch, and I install a couple of cameras along the property line. I had to drive nearly twenty minutes to find an electronics store with any sort of stock. Barry of Barry's Electronics informed me that while the cameras aren't as high-tech as some of the other things on the market, they will let me know if anyone is coming onto the farm without my knowledge.

Or if the raccoons have developed a thirst for pumpkin destruction.

In a stroke of absolute genius, Beckett turns the twisted trees in the south pasture into a haunted forest on Halloween night. The best part is he needs to do absolutely nothing to make it look like something from *Pan's Labyrinth*. Susie Brighthouse takes one look at it while picking up catering from Layla with her mom, declares it *totally twisted*, and the next thing I know, the entire sophomore class is running through the grounds like a horde of drunken zombies.

It's the most guests we've had since last holiday season, and despite it being a group of hormone-addled teenagers, it's enough to give me a buoy of hope. Beckett, Layla, and I celebrate accordingly and sit at the edge of the fields with a thermos of spiked cider, listening as they shriek back and forth at one another.

"What did you put in there to scare them?" I ask Beckett.

"Nothing."

"Nothing?"

Beckett takes another swig from the cider. "Maybe they're afraid of their own stupidity."

All in all, it's a good week. I wake up the morning of forced fake Thanksgiving and expect the worst, but I'm pleasantly surprised. Nothing on the farm is destroyed, all shipments arrive on time, and no one appears in my office to tell me something is on fire. Half of me expects a sinkhole to open up and swallow me to the depths of hell as I wander across the fields to the big red barn. But I see nothing but the well-tended garden boxes by the road and trees in the distance, a couple of empty baskets by the trail that some produce collectors must have forgotten.

I gather the empty baskets and loop them over my arm, piling them by the door as I duck inside the barn and begin to pull down the boxes with holiday decorations. It's my favorite part of the year, the transition between fall and winter. When I unbox all of the things that make this place magical.

Hank did his best to make this place festive, but he was more focused on the trees than the experience. He had left behind a few sad-looking wooden reindeer, a sled made out of old shipping crates, and a moth-eaten Santa suit. All of the lights strung along the buildings had burnt out years ago, and the signpost for the North Pole was faded and weathered. Layla called it *Nuclear Wasteland Christmas* our first week on the farm.

Most of my budget last year had gone into rehab. I wanted people to drive down the narrow dirt road and be greeted with a tunnel of big bulb lights, just like the ones their grandparents had. I wanted them to pull through the front gates marked with two extra-large cherry red bows, guideposts painted with spirals of red and white. I wanted families to climb out of their cars and look up at rows and rows of trees on the foothills, kids running ahead to snag a spot in line for the ice-skating rink.

I wanted it to feel like stepping inside a Dolly Parton Christmas special.

I grab the ladder and start to haul boxes down, pulling back lids and poking through carefully wrapped packing paper. I run my hands over the North Pole sign I spent hours stenciling, red paint on my fingertips for weeks. Some of the tension in my shoulders releases by the fifth box. It looks like everything is here and accounted for. Even the tiny tin reindeer made out of beer cans by Beckett, his white elephant gift to me last year.

I hold up one of the giant red bows and run my finger along the bottom edge. It's silly to get emotional about a ribbon of all things, but here I am. With everything that's happened, I had figured the ribbons would be in tatters or stolen or stained or something else ridiculous. But they're here, perfect and pristine and ready to sit pretty on our wrought iron gates. I'm grateful. I send up a wish to the ghosts of Christmas past, present, and future. I just need this little bit of magic to continue through the end of the month.

"Please," I whisper, wishing I had a sprig of mistletoe to wave around. Maybe some peppermint incense.

"Is that what you're wearing tonight?" When I turn, Luka is propped up against the open barn door, donut in hand. He is loose angles and relaxed shoulders, eyes traveling in the same one-two-three pattern his hands always press into my skin. I have an excuse ready on the tip of my tongue, anxious to backtrack, to explain, but he doesn't make any indication that he heard my begging to the barn rafters. He takes a bite and nods at the very large bow in my hands, obscuring half my body from view. "Bold yet festive. It should leave an impression."

Feeling silly, I hold it close to my chest and drape it over me, sticking my leg out from underneath and arching my neck back. I am Jessica Rabbit in a pretty red bow. There's a choking sound, and I straighten to find Luka bent in half, struggling to swallow his donut.

Concerned, I toss the bow on top of the boxes of decorations and rush over, smacking the heel of my hand in between his shoulder blades repeatedly. I try to remember what they taught us in our high school CPR class. Strike to the beat of a song? I hum under my breath before Luka swats me away, his chuckle a little bit raspy.

"Why are you humming Earth, Wind and Fire as I almost choke to death?"

Ah, that was . . . not the correct song.

Luka coughs once more and straightens, a devastating smile pulling his mouth wide. It's easy like this to think of him as mine. This Luka, with this smile, in this place. Brown laced boots and a sweater over plaid. The surge of possessiveness is so fierce it takes my breath away, and I rub at my sternum in an effort to rid myself of the feeling. I feel like our display in town has cracked open the tiny steel box I keep all my Luka feelings buried in.

I need to remember that Luka isn't mine. Not even when playing pretend.

He cocks his head at me and considers, something tightening in the lines by his eyes. What I wouldn't give to know what's going through his mind. The moment passes, and I struggle to find my footing.

"You ready to go?"

No, I'm not. I want to stay here in this barn with him and my pretty red bows for the rest of time. I want to forget everything else exists. I want Layla to drop off apple cider donuts at the door for sustenance. Maybe a pizza or two.

Instead, I sigh and glance behind him to where his car is parked on the gravel lot just outside the barn. I indulge in a passing fantasy of slashing all the tires so we have to stay here instead.

"I guess I have to be."

❧ ❦

"IS IT DIFFICULT for you? This weird Thanksgiving thing?"

I rest my forehead on the window and watch as the farmlands and pastures outside my window slowly change into strip malls. A bustling suburbia with drive-through Starbucks and Burlington Coat Factories. Houses that look like they've been stamped by a cookie cutter with their pristine white fences and a single towering oak tree in the front yard. Perfect for a tire swing. I dreamed of houses like that when I was a kid.

It is difficult for me to go to my father's house, but not for the reasons Luka thinks. He probably thinks it's hard for me to see the house and the yard and the wine cellar and the four-car garage when, more often than not, my mom and I shared a one-bedroom apartment. He probably thinks it's difficult for me to see the home he made with Elle and Charlie that he chose not to make with me and my mom. That's true, sort of, but it's harder for me to sit at that table on a day meant for family and realize just how much my dad and I look alike.

We have the same round face, the same wide blue eyes. We both have dark curly hair. The first time I met Charlie, it was jarring. It was like looking in a mirror. My mom used to joke and say the only thing I inherited from her was her whimsical inclinations and killer right hook. She liked to pretend that she was okay, that being alone was a choice she wanted. But as I grew older, I saw how lonely she was. She never dated, as far as I can remember. My dad ruined her when he left.

That's why it's hard for me. I sit at that table, and the whole time I wonder if every time she looked at me, she saw him. I wonder if it made her sad.

I draw a smiley face with my pinky in the condensation on the window. "Yes," I reply simply, and leave it at that. I can see Luka shooting me concerned glances out of the corner of his eye, but I ignore it. Tonight will be . . . fine. It will be fine. It always is.

Any hesitancy I had about Luka coming with me has faded in the face of a deep appreciation that in the worst-case scenario, I can get blindingly drunk on my dad's absurdly expensive wine, and Luka can cart me home and pour me into bed.

I wipe the smiley face away with my thumb and lean back in the seat, tilting my head against the headrest to look over at Luka. There are two mediocre pies on my lap. I didn't ask Layla to bake anything. My dad doesn't deserve a Layla pie.

"We've passed at least three Wendy's drive-throughs. Want to skip dinner and I'll get you a frosty?"

"No," I sigh. Though the offer is tempting. Maybe on the way back. "It will be good to see Charlie."

Luka hums. "It will be good to see Charlie. I haven't seen him since"—he considers, his mouth moving soundlessly as he thinks back—"Fourth of July? I think?"

Of all the strange, isolating things that happened after my mother died, Charlie is the one bright spot. I had looked up my father and reached out in a misguided attempt at offering closure. I had figured he might want to know—well, I thought he might want to know that the woman he had a child with had passed away. I still remember the dress I was wearing when I pulled up in his driveway on that warm spring day. How angry I was at all the flowers blooming in the garden. How could flowers still bloom when my mom was dead? How could the sun still shine so bright? Why were people laughing on their porches, drinking lemonade like nothing was wrong?

A pale blue dress and bright red flats. I wanted to look nice. I knocked on the door and waited, my heart in my throat, a stack of letters my mom had written him clutched in my hand. Charlie had answered the door, his greeting hastily aborted the second his gaze landed on me. His wide blue eyes—my eyes—blinking in shock.

Charlie was born exactly eight months after me. A lot of things became clear after that.

And despite the inherent awkwardness of your father's love child showing up on your front porch on a random spring day, Charlie and I had become fast friends. I guess both of us wanted a sibling.

"Was it the Fourth of July when he insisted on doing a keg stand and projectile vomited on the side of Beckett's house?"

Luka snickers under his breath. "It was, yeah. I told him not to."

"You did not. In fact, I think you encouraged him. You were chanting."

"Ah, hell. Yeah, I was. Layla's Jell-O shots had me feeling some type of way. She makes them sneaky tasty. You don't even know you're half a bottle down until you're wearing an Uncle Sam hat, demanding that a grown man do a keg stand."

"We're too old for Jell-O shots and keg stands."

"Clearly," he laughs. "I think it's a fine time to transition to boxed wine and an early bedtime."

"I would agree."

I'm grateful for the distraction. I don't even realize we've arrived until Luka parks the car on the street at the edge of the driveway. He tells me it's for a quick getaway with a cheeky little wink that has me laughing all the way to the front door. It's a nice change from the slow, defeated march I usually do.

I knock and stare at the perfect navy blue paint on the door. Not a single nick. I straighten my shoulders inch by inch until I am fortified, unmovable. I almost jump when I feel fingers thread through my own. Luka squeezes my hand.

"Frosty," he mouths and shoots me a wink.

8

STANDING IN THIS house is always a strange experience. A tradition in its own right, I suppose. Elle welcomes us into her home, effusive and lovely as usual, not a single blond hair out of place. Her white blouse is tucked neatly into a beautiful royal blue skirt, pin straight without a wrinkle. I wonder how she manages to sit in it for it to look like that. I picture her propped up against the wall. Lying flat across the couch.

We step into the foyer, the sun reflecting off the marble floors to the ornate chandelier that hangs in the middle of the . . . *reception room* as Elle calls it. It's impossible not to endlessly compare the life here with what my mom and I had. The kind of woman my mom was and the kind of woman Elle is. My mom would have answered the door with jam on her face and a pen stuck in her hair, bare feet and chipped toenail polish. No reception room for us.

"Did you get here okay? No traffic, I hope?"

Bless her for acting like this is actually Thanksgiving and not a random Saturday in November. I follow her to the kitchen and dutifully place the pies on the countertop.

"Everything was smooth sailing."

"I'm glad to hear it," she says. She glances at Luka and clasps her hands underneath her chin. She looks like she should be posing in a J.Crew catalog, the holiday edition. "And I am so glad you brought a friend."

"I'm glad to be here. Thank you for having me on such short notice." Luka hands her a bouquet of flowers handpicked from the farm.

She buries her nose in the blooms, cheeks flushing pink. I smile into the palm of my hand. It's nice to know I'm not the only one affected by Luka.

"I've heard so much about you from Charlie and Stella. It's nice to finally meet you in person."

Her eyes dance back and forth between us with what I assume is weighted significance. I forget, sometimes, that despite all the ways Charlie and I have welcomed each other into our lives, my interactions with Elle are still very limited.

"I can only imagine the horror stories you've heard, then."

"Nonsense." Elle places the flowers in a vase she pulls from above the fridge and then click-clacks her way over to the oven and checks inside. I don't think I've ever walked around my house in stilettos. I don't think my shoes have ever made it past the threshold of my door. "My children have nothing but good things to say about you."

It's a quick slip of the tongue. Two words really, a possessive pronoun. The entire kitchen instantly feels as if all the air has been sucked out of it. Maybe I make a sound, or maybe my body is talking loud enough for that not to be necessary, but I feel electrocuted with it. Stiff and creaky, like a scarecrow in a cornfield.

Elle stands quickly, face pinched. For the first time since I met her, she looks flustered.

"I just meant"—she tucks her hair compulsively behind her ears—"I just meant . . ."

"It's all right." I give her a small smile and clear my throat. "I know I'm not—I know what you meant."

"Stella." She looks stricken. "I—"

Whatever she was going to say thankfully gets lost in a commotion from the front door. This dinner is enough without the added reminder that I am the child her husband had with another woman.

I hear several bags hit the ground, a muffled curse, and then the very clear sound of glass shattering against marble. Elle drops her head back and looks at the ceiling with a rueful little smile.

"That would be Charlie," she says.

I snort a laugh, and the tension slips from the room right along with Elle, off to collect Charlie from the foyer. He is a grown man masquerading as a bull in a china shop. I sigh and shake off the strangeness of the conversation, the confusing cocktail of surprise and regret. Surprise makes sense. Regret I don't know what to do with. Luka shuffles closer, those brown eyes of his warm as he squeezes gently at my arm. His knuckles brush gently under my chin.

"Okay?" he asks quietly.

"I'm fine," I say, and I'm surprised to find that I am. Or at least fine enough that I don't want to reach for a wine bottle and start guzzling. That's a positive change from how I usually feel at this point of the evening. I give him a smile and tip my head toward the fancy crystal wineglasses set out on the counter. We're debating which wildly expensive bottle to open first when the door to the kitchen swings open, hard enough that it smacks right into the wall and comes back again.

"You brought a date?" Charlie booms in place of a greeting, arms full of the scattered remains of what he's brought to dinner. Large torn pieces of a paper bag, the twine that I assume was once a handle. The crust of a pecan pie and what looks like the lip of the ornate ceramic vase that was sitting in the entryway. Charlie's eyes dart from Luka's shoulders to me and back again, narrowed in confusion. I don't know what's more amusing—that Charlie doesn't immediately recognize Luka or that he's managed to channel a lifetime of protective brother aggression into a single question.

Luka glances over his shoulder at Charlie, away from where he hasn't stopped twisting open a cabernet sauvignon. His forearms flex and release, flex and release as he twists the corkscrew around. I am transfixed. "Hey, man. Long time no see."

Charlie bobbles the collection of items in his hands again, a majority of them returning to the floor. "Oh my god, it's happening."

I flush scarlet, Charlie should be on the Inglewild phone tree. I snatch the bottle of wine from Luka and pour myself a hearty glass. So much for not wanting to drink the discomfort away. "Nothing is happening, Charlie. Luka just came to dinner."

"With you," Luka adds with a sly grin and a wink. I huff. "Together."

There is some silent exchange between Luka and Charlie—a raised eyebrow, two in return—that has Charlie practically wiggling in delight. *Honestly.* Luka takes the wineglass from my hand and sips—a pointed, silent exclamation point on whatever that conversation just was.

"I mean, sure, technically we arrived in the same car," I babble. I don't slap him away, but it's a near thing. I let him have my glass and fetch a new one. "So yes, we are here together. Together as friends in harmony."

"Sure seems harmonious," Charlie quips, rolling his lips between his teeth.

I roll my eyes at him and he returns the gesture. It's a strange thing to see my expressions mirrored on his face. The same big blue eyes, dark cobalt when the light hits them right. We could be twins if not for the sheer width and breadth of his shoulders. He towers over my small form, and I feel every inch of our height difference as he takes three steps across the kitchen and scoops me into his arms. My feet dangle uselessly as I curl my arms around his shoulders, the toes of my shoes tapping against his shins.

"Good to see you, short stack."

I pinch between his shoulder blades, and he chuckles warmly somewhere above my head. "Good to see you too."

He releases me and wanders over to Luka, giving him the same treatment short of picking him up off the floor. I smile into my wineglass as I watch them hug, a bit of pie crust still stuck to Charlie's arm.

Luka mutters something in a low voice, and Charlie barks out a laugh, his eyes shining bright when they find mine again.

"Are we eating or what?"

By the time all the dinner platters are situated on the table, my dad still hasn't arrived, his absence hanging ominously over all of our heads. It's like the thick black clouds that roll in before the storm, lightning flashing in the distance. You know something bad is coming, but you can't outrun nature. Elle ushers us into the formal dining room, not to be confused with the cozy family dining room or the breakfast nook just off the kitchen.

The table looks like a Norman Rockwell painting. A pristine white tablecloth and shining silver dishes. It's a far cry from the dixie cups and paper plates I grew up with. The only touch that indicates actual humans intend to eat this meal is the tiny cardboard turkeys marking out the places where people should sit. They are well loved and faded, the names written with an unpracticed hand. It makes me smile to think of a much smaller Charlie painstakingly putting pom-poms on toilet paper rolls to make them look like little turkeys. I can imagine him putting them together as a kid, the same wild curls I have chaotic on top of his head, tongue sticking out in concentration.

My name is marked with a much newer, much more professional name card. A simple *Stella* printed on a tiny piece of cardstock held with a heavy paperweight that looks like a leaf. The edges just barely brush the bottom curve of the *a*. This isn't one that is carried from year to year. It was probably printed this morning. Ordered from a fancy supplier, stamped on heavy cardstock with grooved edges.

I find my seat and see a new card keeping mine company. *Luka* with a burnt orange leaf. I stare at that for a long time until everyone else is settled and seated.

"Will Dad be joining us?" Charlie stares hard at the empty chair at the head of the table. I know they have their struggles, my dad and Charlie. Charlie often bears the weight of unfair expectations. He works at the same firm as my father, primed to one day fill his shoes.

It sits heavy on his shoulders, a dull meekness settling over him every time they're in the same room. I hate it. I hate watching him cave in on himself, tucking away all the parts of himself that make him so wonderful.

"If we're lucky, no." Elle calmly fills her wineglass to the very top. A heavy pour if I've ever seen one. Charlie and I stare at her. Luka makes a sound like he's trying not to laugh. I've never heard Elle say anything negative about anyone—let alone Brian. Not even when I showed up on her front doorstep, the worst kind of surprise, I'm sure. She took one look at me, made a humming noise under her breath, and offered me a lemonade.

Charlie recovers first. "Feeling okay, Mom?"

"Delightful, sweetie. Did you want some wine?"

"Is there any left?"

She tilts the bottle back and forth. "Just a touch."

Charlie puts his hand out for it and drinks directly from the bottle. Sitting next to Elle, I see the subtle similarities between them. The same turn to their lips. A dimple that winks in the flickering light of the candles. Mischief that hides in the corner of Elle's eyes but sits boldly in Charlie's. The kind that grows now as he finishes off the bottle. "This might be my favorite Thanksgiving yet."

I'm about to agree when I hear the front door open, clumsy, lumbering footsteps moving in the direction of the dining room.

Charlie curses under his breath. "I spoke too soon."

We all listen in silence as my father meanders his way around the first floor of the house, nonsensical in his direction. He takes two steps forward and then circles back. Stumbles, trips, and then hurries his steps toward the kitchen. It sounds like he slips at one point, and catches himself with his shoulder against the wall.

Luka leans closer to me. "Is he—"

"Drunk?" Elle takes a very long sip from her too-full wineglass. "Probably."

That's a new development. I don't think I've ever seen my dad drunk. He usually shows up late, booming an excuse about the office, a client, a new deal, something about how important and needed he is at the firm. But I don't think I've ever seen him with so much as a hair out of place. He's always buttoned up, pristine. Cold and untouchable.

He finally elbows his way into the dining room, his movements uncoordinated, messy. His arm catches one of the silver candlesticks as he slowly makes his way around the table, knocking it over and almost setting the tablecloth on fire. Charlie snatches it up before anything can catch, the butter dish moved neatly on top of the small black ring of burn. His series of movements are effortless, anticipatory. Like he has practice cleaning up messes exactly like this.

I always thought I was the one with the short end of the stick. Brian Milford left my mom high and dry as soon as the pregnancy test turned positive. But here, seeing this, watching Charlie warily observe his dad as he slumps in his seat at the head of the table—I can't help but feel like I lucked out.

"Happy Thanksgiving," he mutters, staring directly at his dinner plate, not bothering to look anyone in the eye. He reaches forward and scoops some mashed potatoes out of the serving bowl . . . with his hand.

And I can't help it. I don't know if it's the tension of coming here, the continued disappointment of my father and all his shortcomings, or the stress of the upcoming visit from Evelyn, but as I watch the self-declared corporate god nibble mashed potatoes out of the palm of his hand like a toddler, I—I lose it. My shoulders shake as I try to keep the hysteria at bay. I swallow compulsively, over and over. But it's a losing battle, and as soon as Luka's hand finds my thigh under the table, checking on my mental state, I'm sure, a loud bark of laughter leaves my mouth.

Oh, how badly I wish that Norman Rockwell painting looked like this. I might commission something.

My dad frowns at me. It's the first time he's looked directly at me in close to a year, I think, and he has some gravy stuck to the corner of his mouth. "Estelle," my name is slurred around the edges. "Control yourself."

My giggles continue, albeit more subdued. "All right," I acquiesce with a little head nod, agreeable as ever, but with a healthy dose of sarcasm I've never been brave enough to use with my father. I can't help it. Not when he's reprimanding me with a handful of potatoes. "Sure, I'll do my best."

Charlie's laughter slips loose at that—a boom of a chuckle that has my dad jolting in his chair. I peek over at Luka, and I see him smiling into a bite of green bean casserole. With his hand still on my thigh, fingers just barely grazing the inside of my knee, I am suddenly, absurdly glad he's here with me. That I won't have to tell him about this later over FaceTime, curled up alone on the couch. Having him here, it's a shot of comfort and confidence. I find his hand under the table and squeeze, his warm eyes darting up from his food and holding mine.

Charlie was right.

Best Thanksgiving ever.

⇛· ⇚

ELLE DOES NOT agree with that overall sentiment. That much is clear as soon as my dad passes out face-first with his forehead narrowly missing the cranberry sauce. It's the fancy stuff too. No wiggling mass of cranberry that still looks like the can here. There are actual berries and slices of orange, and I'm strangely disappointed that I won't get the visual of my dad's face stained pink to reference the next time he's an asshole.

Though I think the mashed potato thing will do just as well.

We decide to treat him like a fixture at the table, no more life to him than the cardboard turkeys. I wonder if Elle is going to gently coax him to bed, but she stands and disappears to the kitchen, returning with my two pies and a fresh bottle of wine. Charlie snaps several pictures on his phone with a wistful sigh.

"I know we were all worried about the type of shit this guy was going to pull tonight," he says. Elle makes a face at Charlie's string of profanity. She has a rule about language at the dinner table. "Sorry, Mom. But all in all, I think everything turned out nice."

My dad snorts, his entire body jostling once. He resettles, and one of his hands lands in the gravy bowl.

"I mean, look at this tablescape." Charlie snaps another picture. "Perfection."

Luka's hand is still on my thigh beneath the table, his palm curved slightly, fingers almost tucked in the crease between my knee and leg. That hand feels like it weighs ten thousand pounds, every place his skin touches mine lighting up like a circuit board. He squeezes every now and again, and when his pinky lightly caresses the inside of my leg, I jump so hard I knock over a basket of dinner rolls. He hides his smile in his napkin and leaves his hand where it is.

"Are these Layla's pies?" Charlie's hands are already reaching for the pumpkin pie closest to him, fork caught between his teeth. I shake my head.

"No, they're a sugar-free recipe I made at home." At Charlie's horrified stare, I chance a glance at Elle. While this evening has been different from all the others in her obvious dismissal of my dad, I'm still not sure what I can say in front of her. I don't want her to think I'm ungrateful. I don't want her to withhold an invitation in the future. I am hungry for family, connection, and roots however they come.

But when I slide my gaze over to her, she's smiling serenely into her wineglass, a secret look in her eyes that tells me she already knows what I'm going to say.

I shrug, sheepish. "I wanted the pie to taste bad."

Charlie collapses back in his chair. "God, Stel. You could have bought pecan like I said! That would have been contrary enough."

I could have. "Just save this pie for Brian in the morning."

Elle raises her glass with a hiccup. "Cheers to that."

❧ ❦

"THAT IS NOT what I expected."

We're halfway back to the farm, an extra large chocolate frosty clasped between my hands. Luka has a carton of spicy nuggets held securely between his thighs, half of one caught between his teeth as he maneuvers us onto the highway. I breathe a little bit easier the farther we get, the stars beginning to peek out as we head away from the suburbs.

"It's not usually like that."

"You mean your dad doesn't typically eat out of dishes with his hands before passing out?" Luka offers me a nugget, and I shake my head.

"Yeah, that was a first." I let my head rock against the back of the seat and watch as the streetlights dance across his skin. Yellow, orange, deep muted red. A soothing pattern that lands heavy on his cheekbones and the tip of his nose. He flexes his hands on the wheel. "I know I gave you a hard time, but I'm glad you came."

Luka looks pleased, his entire body straightening half an inch. He shoots a quick glance over to me before his eyes find the road again. "Yeah?"

"Yeah, if only so you believe that it happened."

He laughs. "Yeah, I'm not sure I would have if I hadn't seen it for myself."

"And for moral support," I add a bit more seriously, feeling brave. I remember what Layla said in my bedroom the other morning, how just because you tell someone how you really feel, it doesn't mean they'll leave. I don't think this is what she had in mind, but it's a step in that direction. As big a step as I can manage right now, anyway.

"You don't have to thank me for that."

"I know. I'm not. I'm just—" I think of his hand on my knee, the way he hugged Charlie in the kitchen. How Elle pressed a kiss to his cheek when she saw us out the door. His hands on my shoulders as he helped me into my coat, his fingers slipping under my collar to untuck my hair. "I'm just glad is all."

My Luka box is rattling in my chest, all sorts of things threatening to spill out.

I check the farm's social accounts as we rumble along, a pleased little wiggle in Luka's heated seat when I see that Evelyn has commented on the picture of Beckett I posted the other day. You can't make out his face in the shot, just the silhouette of a tall man in the golden light of the setting sun, miles and miles of fields rolling out behind him. Evelyn has commented, Can't wait to be here in two weeks, with a complicated series of emojis, and it lights a thrill of excitement and opens a pit of dread at exactly the same moment. Excitement because our follower numbers are already climbing with just that one comment and dread because, well, now I have to lie in the bed I've made for myself.

I darken my phone and rest it against my chest, chewing on my bottom lip.

"We should probably practice." It's something I've been thinking about since our walk through town. Given my reaction to his hand on my neck and his palm on my thigh, I think I need a little bit more exposure before Evelyn is here. I don't trust myself not to squeak every time Luka kisses my cheek.

"Practice what?" Luka is unconcerned, his hands relaxed on the steering wheel, thumb curled along the bottom curve.

"Being a couple."

A couple that touches each other. Kisses each other.

"Oh?" He hits the turn signal even though there isn't another soul for miles, headlights glancing across cornfields as he makes the turn down the long winding road that leads back to the farm. "Was tonight not a solid go at it?"

It takes a moment for his meaning to sink in, but when it does, I have to hold my body still. I don't want to give anything away with the curl of my shoulders, the set of my jaw. Not that he could see it anyway. We're far away from streetlights now—on the backcountry roads that light up only with the full moon.

I breathe out slowly through my nose. I didn't think tonight was part of our plan. I thought tonight was us. The real us.

"Is that why you came? To pretend?"

9

I FIGHT NOT to sound winded when I ask the question, though I feel a bit like I've been sucker punched. Of course. Of course that's what it was. The touches, the glances, the easy smiles. It was all an opportunity to practice in front of an unknowing audience. Just like our walk through town. I shake my head. I need to remember. I can't keep getting confused with Luka.

Embarrassment settles in my stomach like a lead rock the longer the silence lingers between us. This is why I should have gone with the escort service. I bet I wouldn't be getting this flustered with a rent-a-date.

I try to change the subject.

"I think I'll start with the holiday prep tomorrow," I mutter, hunching down in my seat. I bring my knees to my chest, mindful of the way my skirt flares out around my thighs. The bows. I'll put the bows up tomorrow and pretend this conversation never happened. It was a stupid thing to suggest anyway. What are we going to do—practice kissing? We aren't in high school. We are capable of kissing each other without working on it. "I'd like to get everything settled before Evelyn arrives."

Like my sanity.

"All right," Luka drawls out the words, the car beginning to rumble beneath us as dirt changes to gravel. "But let's go back a step. You think I came with you tonight to—what—squeeze in some more practice? Figure out how to hold your hand?" I watch as he shifts in his seat, elbow landing on the ledge by his window. He rubs above his eyebrow, frustrated. "I don't need to practice holding your hand," he mutters.

I sink farther, my knees knocking into the dash, and bundle my arms around myself. "It was just a thought."

"Well, it was a dumb one."

A laugh sputters out of me. "Thank you."

My laughter must soothe whatever's agitated him, because his shoulders creep down from his ears. He glances at me once from the driver's side, starlight haloed around his head. "But I do think you have a point with the rest of it."

"Rest of what?"

"The practice thing."

I blink at him. "You just told me that you don't need to practice."

"I said I didn't come tonight to practice. There's a difference." His thumb traces the bottom curve of the steering wheel. "I think it would be good."

That surprises me. "You do?"

"Yeah, I think—" It's his turn to shift in his seat. "Well, with us being a couple, Addison—"

"Evelyn," I correct. I don't understand why he can't remember her name.

"She'll probably be confused if we're a couple that doesn't touch each other at all."

I know it was my suggestion, but my mind goes instantly to the gutter. I think of his hand on the inside of my knee. How warm it felt, how much space he could cover with his palm, his fingers wrapped slightly along the inside of my thigh. I think of him sliding that hand higher, under the skirt of my dress. Higher still, his nose against my throat, my legs spread wide over his hips.

He's still talking on his side of the car, explaining about something or another, but I've heard none of it.

I clear my throat. "What was that?"

He swallows hard, a dip in the road making the car rock beneath us. "I'm just saying. Wouldn't it be weird if we didn't kiss?"

"It would be weird if we didn't kiss," I agree. I sound winded, like I've just been shot in the foot.

"No need to sound so thrilled about it, La La."

When I don't say anything in response, still stuck thinking about his hands on my legs, he sighs, knuckles straining on the steering wheel with the flex of his hands. "I'm sure we can work around it."

"Wait," I turn in my seat, the strap getting caught at my shoulder. "Why are you upset right now?"

"Because you're acting like I just handed you a death sentence," he grumbles.

"What are you talking about?"

I can only make out the corner of his jaw in the dim light from the console, the bridge of his nose. But it's enough to see that he's deliberately holding himself in check. There's a rigidness to his body that means he's upset. I reach for his forearm and squeeze. We're almost back to the cottage now, darkness curling around us like a blanket. The stars are hidden by a thick layer of clouds, and everything feels closer, quiet, and still. He pulls us to a stop in my driveway but leaves the car on, a heavy sigh gusting out from somewhere deep in his chest.

"I don't know. This conversation got out of control." He runs his hand down his face. "I think you have a point about practicing," he says, an attempt to start over. The tension that twisted him tight starts to slip from the stiff line of his body. "So that the first time we try in front of an audience you don't suck at it."

"Suck at it?" I'm offended. "I don't suck at it. You probably suck at it."

"I can assure you I do not suck at it."

"What, do you have a survey you send out? Rate your level of satisfaction from one to ten?"

He barks a laugh. "That's not a bad idea actually. I'll add it in with my postcoital gift basket. A little QR code they can scan."

I roll my eyes and climb out of the car. Good to know we can quickly bounce back to our normal selves. "I never want to hear the term *postcoital* come out of your mouth again."

Two doors slam, boots echoing up the stone walkway.

"Why?" Luka's trailing me, his stroll leisurely, his hands in his pockets.

Because I don't want to think about Luka with anyone. Because his hand on my thigh at dinner is going to haunt me for decades. I clear my throat as I try to find my keys in my bag, Luka crowding my space.

"I think *coitus* is a weird word," I tell the inside of my bag. One day, maybe I'll be a more organized person and won't have to hunt for my house keys every time I need to get inside. But it won't be this day.

His laugh whispers across the nape of my neck. I shiver and hope he doesn't notice.

"What word do you prefer, then?"

"Hm?" I finally manage to get my key in the lock and practically fall through the door. My cheeks feel hot despite the chill in the air, my breathing too fast. I unwind my scarf and drop it on the table.

"If you don't like *coitus*"—Luka does his best to bite back his grin, but it fights its way through—"what do you prefer?"

I prefer to not have this conversation.

"I don't know if I've thought about it," I manage. I kick off my shoes and wander to the kitchen, Luka following after his requisite reorganization of my space. I'm glad I had the forethought to set out the good whiskey this morning, knowing I'd want a hot toddy immediately upon my return. Whiskey, lemon, tea, honey—it's all set out neatly on the countertop. Also the remnants of a pumpkin loaf, courtesy of Layla.

I hold up the whiskey bottle in silent question and Luka nods. He finds a seat at the old rocking chair that sits at the head of the table, mismatched and hideous but surprisingly comfortable. I snag the lemon and the cutting board.

"Pound Town? Bumping uglies?" I narrowly miss slicing my finger off as Luka lists options. "The no-pants dance?"

"I can't say anyone has ever asked me to Pound Town."

"Something more direct, then." He rests his chin in his hand and levels a stare at me that I feel low in my belly, in the backs of my knees. "*Fucking*, yeah?"

I swallow at that, a whole slew of imaginings falling through my mind like dirty dominoes. I can honestly say I have no idea what we're discussing anymore. I hear that word, out of his mouth, and lose the thread of conversation. All I know is the pulse of heat that pulls sharp between us, his brown eyes dark in the stillness of my kitchen. This is new territory and . . . not unwelcome. Mouth suddenly dry, I wet my bottom lip with my tongue. "I, um—" I shake my head and reach for the whiskey. "What?"

"Fucking."

Luka and I have discussed sex exactly two times, and only in vague terms and suggestive hand gestures. Once, when I alluded to the complete lack of commitment to foreplay by the entire male population, and another time after watching a period piece with a very confusing love scene, when we argued about blow jobs for seven minutes.

So I am . . . confused. Confused and flushed from my head to my toes. "I don't—" I shake my head and slice the lemons, turn on the burner for the teakettle. The fact that I can even manage these basic tasks when it feels like I'm having an out-of-body experience is astounding to me. I'm going to hear Luka saying *fucking* for the rest of eternity. "What is happening here?"

Luka balances his ankle on his knee and rocks back once. "I don't know. I got carried away, I guess." A faint blush brushes at his cheeks, his gaze lingering on my shoulders, skimming down the curve of my back. I've never seen him look at me like this before. I feel it like a caress. "It's easy to get carried away," he adds as an afterthought, voice a whisper in the stillness of the kitchen.

I study him, unsure if he's messing with me or serious. I can't tell. It almost feels like he's—like he's flirting with me. I don't know what to do with it. I shake my head slightly and fight to get this conversation back on track. "This is not what I had in mind."

"No?"

"I don't think anyone is going to ask how I refer to sex."

"That's a fair point."

"Thank you."

We stare at each other in silence, the air heavy. My eyes don't know where to land. His fingertips, tracing back and forth along the arm of the chair. His long legs spread just slightly. The flush of pink on the tips of his ears. My perusal is interrupted when the kettle begins to whistle on the stove. I turn my back to him and fish for two mugs in the upper cabinet, pressing up on my toes.

Usually, I have mugs scattered throughout the kitchen. It's not that I'm messy; I just prefer convenience. I drink a lot of coffee. And tea. And whiskey. And tea with whiskey. Sometimes mulled wine. And the occasional cake in a cup. Mugs are my cup of choice and, as such, are typically left at various places around my home.

But I've been trying to be neater, more organized, and Luka's arrival has heralded the usual two-week trend of cleanliness. Which unfortunately means I'm putting my mugs back in the most unreachable place in the kitchen. I hear the creak of the rocking chair, easy footsteps across the hardwood, and then I feel Luka behind me, close enough for his knees to brush the backs of my thighs. My breath rushes out of me when one of his hands finds my hip, the other reaching above our heads for the mugs.

"Here we are again," I mutter. I never did get out the step stool to check what he's got stashed up there. Feeling a little indulgent, I press my head back slightly so I can feel the catch of his stubble in my hair.

His laugh rumbles against my back, one mug and then two set neatly in front of me.

"What does Charlie call you? Short stack?" Luka doesn't step back as I reach for the kettle and pour, handing me the whiskey over my shoulder with one hand, his other still on my hip. He squeezes once.

"Yeah, he's been trying out nicknames. Trying to find one that sticks."

"Maybe he should try Cinnamon Stick. Isn't that what Sheriff Jones calls you?"

I hum, my entire existence focused on where his thumb drags against my hip bone. He presses into me farther, just for a second, his body weight a delicious, heavy pressure against me. His nose drags through my hair, nuzzles once beneath my ear.

"You do smell like cinnamon," he says, voice quiet, serious, unbearably sweet. I turn my head slightly, my temple against his jaw.

"A hazard of the job."

"Do all tree farm owners smell like cinnamon, then?"

"And sugarplum fairies."

Luka laughs at that, the strange tension between us splintering. He steps back, but his hand holds against my hip, fingers slipping away with reluctance. I look up at him in the dim light of my kitchen, and for a single breath, I see a wild, ferocious hunger. But he blinks and it's gone. He's my Luka again, the change so quick I think I've imagined it. Brown eyes soft, smile crooked, hair a wild mess.

He drops a slice of lemon in my drink. *"Saluti."*

"Thanks." I hand him his mug, an old chipped thing that has a fox on it and says, OH, FOR FOX SAKE. He takes a sip and I tilt my head at him. "And thanks for coming with me earlier. It means a lot."

"You don't have to keep thanking me," he mumbles, the thinnest edge of frustration in his voice. He looks like he wants to say more but swallows it, eyes searching my face. I feel it like a fingertip at my jaw, the hollow of my throat, the corner of my lips. "I'm not doing this for your thanks, okay?"

He reaches over my shoulder and plucks a piece of pumpkin

bread off the counter, holding it between his teeth as he tugs me once toward the couch. "We're going to watch *Die Hard*, and you're going to do your Hans Gruber impersonation."

As we settle onto the couch, a flannel blanket thrown over our laps, I don't even think to ask. If he's not doing this for my gratitude, then why is he doing it?

❧ · ❧

I START MY morning in the big red barn by the road, armed with a giant plastic candy cane and a wooden cutout of a nutcracker soldier. I look like some vengeful holiday knight. The only thing missing is a bow and arrow made out of gingerbread. But I heard rustling in the corner by the door when I came in, and I have no intention of getting rabies before Evelyn arrives. Foaming at the mouth doesn't really fit in with the aesthetic I'm trying to achieve.

I hear it again, a little louder this time, one of the giant metal arches that we use over the road for the lights swaying back and forth.

"Shit," I curse, and search the ground. Maybe I should have one of the firehouse guys down here to take a look. They'd know what to do with a family of raccoons, right? The arch gives another shake, and I abandon my candy cane and head for the door.

I'm not willing to tempt fate today. Tomorrow is a new day.

The barn door is heavy beneath my hands when I try to slide it open. It doesn't budge the first two pulls, and I huff a laugh under my breath. Of course I'd get stuck in here with endless piles of decorations and whatever critter has decided to move in. It feels like a sign from the universe to not lie on contest applications.

I pull again and press the toe of my boot into the bottom edge to help the weathered wood stay on its tracks, all of my concentration focused on sliding it open without breaking the damn thing. It finally gives, a foreboding shriek accompanying its incremental movement, enough space for me to slide my way through. Only as soon as I start to step out of the barn, someone else decides to step in.

I knock my knees against Luka, my hand losing its grip on the door. It begins to slide closed, and Luka mutters a string of obscenities under his breath, curling my body close to his and moving us both out of the way. I'm still pressed up against him when the door falls shut.

"Hey," I manage, staring wistfully at the door. I have no idea how I'm going to open that thing again. Luka might have to give me a boost to the narrow windows on the south-facing side. I'll have to wiggle my way out. Hopefully, Beckett and Layla are somewhere else on the farm, and no one has a camera. I've been that dumb before, and I have a Christmas card courtesy of Layla's camera phone to prove it. I blink back to Luka. "I wasn't expecting you."

"Yeah, I wasn't expecting me either." He rubs one gloved hand over his face, brown eyes peering at me through the fan of his fingers. He lets his hand drop with a heavy sigh, frustration tightening his features.

"Everything okay?"

"Stella, I have to head back to the city." He says it with the same gravitas as one would announce, *I have cancer*, or *I've discovered a Civil War ghost in the attic*.

"Okay." I try to move past him, but he shakes his head and walks us farther into the barn, his hands curled around my upper arms. It's disorienting walking backward, and I shoot a glance over to the arches. No movement now. Hopefully whatever critter was over there is long gone.

"I didn't think I'd have to go back before Evelyn gets here."

I give his chest a little pat through the down of his jacket. I definitely didn't expect him to spend the entire month of November in Inglewild. He works remotely from time to time, but even so, I had assumed he would be back and forth between here and his office. I know they rely on him for presentations to clients, and he can't do that from behind his computer. "That's all right. You won't be missing anything here. We'll just be setting up for Christmas. And potentially getting a new barn door." I nod over his shoulder and take another look at the door. It seems to still be on its track, at least. "When will you be back?"

"A week, I think. And then I'll be here through—" He swallows, not finishing his thought. "I'll be here."

"Okay?" I still don't understand why he's so worked up. He's holding himself still despite his hands curled around my arms, a perfect two inches of space between our bodies. He flexes his fingers once, twice, and then levels me with a determined look, his tongue poking the inside of his cheek.

"I think we should practice now, before I go."

"Um, okay?" I swear I know another word, but my mind is like a record skipping on the memory of him in my kitchen. Holding that stupid mug, smelling like lemon and whiskey. The way his voice rasped and the things he said. How his body pressed to mine against the kitchen counter, his chest against my back, the countertop digging into my hips.

After he left last night, I tossed and turned in bed, the sheets twisted around my bare legs, my hand low on my stomach beneath the soft cotton of my T-shirt. I lingered there, fingertips dragging back and forth just below my belly button, an ache I hadn't felt in ages.

"Because here's the thing, Stella," he says. I breathe in deep through my nose and hope what I was just thinking about isn't written all over my face. "If we don't practice today, you're going to think about it all week."

He's right. I will absolutely think about it all week. I will fixate, freak myself out, and probably start stress eating Layla's peppermint mocha brownies until there are none left for customers. She just started making those too.

"Okay?" I clear my throat and look for other words. "Okay."

Great.

Luka is not bothered. "I'm going to kiss you, and we're going to deal with it like two mature, consenting adults. And when I come back, and when Evelyn is here, you won't be worked up about it. And it will be fine."

Except I am not a mature adult, and I decide I'm going to kiss him first. Like ripping off a Band-Aid. I grip the collar of his coat with both hands and use the momentum to press myself up and into him. The force of it has our mouths meeting awkwardly, my bottom lip slightly on his chin, our noses pressed at an awkward angle. I don't try to correct it, don't linger, and drop back to the flats of my feet, hands still curled around him.

"There," I say, pleased with myself. I feel like I've finally gained the upper hand. I kissed him first. I kissed him and it was fine. "Done."

He blinks at me, his hand coming up to press against his mouth. "What was that?" he whispers.

I shrug. "You wanted a kiss. I gave you a kiss."

"What you gave me is a concussion. Is that how you kiss?" He looks genuinely concerned.

I roll my eyes. "Stop."

"I'll probably need some dental work." He pulls his hand away like he's checking for blood.

"What happened to dealing with this like mature, consenting adults?"

He hides his smile behind the palm of his hand. "Okay, you're right. Let's try that again."

"Again? I think that was fine."

"It was not fine," he fires back, gaze lingering on my mouth. He's a healthy dose of stubborn, the amber that usually lights up his eyes dimmed to a warm chocolate brown. "If anyone sees us kiss like that, they'll know in half a second we are full of shit."

It's a fair point.

"Okay, then you try."

"I am trying to try," he mutters, exasperated. He heaves a deep breath through his nose and considers me, eyes dark. There's a single beam of light that filters in from the windows at the top of the barn, early morning sunshine beginning to wander its way across the floor. The light just barely catches an old box of garland, a shower of gold exploding like a kaleidoscope as the sun shimmers through the strands.

Luka doesn't say anything. I watch as he searches my face in the dancing light, the gold reflected in his gaze. He's looking for something in my expression, and when he finds it, the right side of his mouth hitches up in a smile, a smooth pull of his lips. It's my smile—this one. I hoard it like all the others, bundle them up and put them in the same drawer as my cardboard pine trees.

In an achingly slow movement, he leans forward and brushes his nose against mine. I keep my eyes open even though it makes everything a little bit blurry, gold sparkles twinkling at the edges. Close like this, with his bottom lip just barely brushing mine, I can count every individual freckle on his nose. A burst of them on the bridge, less as they fan out below his eyes. Once when we were younger, we got drunk off tequila and I drew constellations on his skin, hovering over him with my hair curtained around us. I remember the weight of his eyes on me, sprawled across my living room floor, how he curled his fingers around my ankle like he had to hold himself steady.

He catches my mouth in a kiss the same moment his gloved hands find mine, fingers gently skimming until our palms press together. I'm frustrated by the thick material covering his skin, unable to feel the heat of him, the calluses on his palms. He squeezes once as I shuffle farther into him, a reward for good behavior. When I sigh, his lips smile into mine, a curve of his mouth that I want him to imprint everywhere. Into my cheek, my neck, the soft skin of my thighs. It feels like the beginning of every argument we've ever had. Me impatient. Luka teasing. It's a reassurance that despite tipping the scale of our relationship, we're still us.

Luka holds me there, our hands twined together, his lips soft and searching. *Like this*, he says with his mouth against mine. *Slowly*. It's the deliciousness of a kiss that isn't intended for more. Patient. Chaste.

It drives me insane.

He hums under his breath when I slip my hand from his to find the nape of his neck, a tiny sound of surprise that has me catching his bottom lip between mine. I want to pull at it with my teeth, see if that sound deepens, sharpens. I want to shift my hand up and tangle my fingers in his hair, use it to angle his mouth against mine. I want to untangle all his gentle calm until he's as impatient as I am.

He pulls back instead. Eyes closed, he hovers with his nose against my cheek, forehead tucked to my temple. I can't tell if my hands are shaking or his.

"Um," I clear my throat. I wet my bottom lip with my tongue and taste hazelnut coffee. It is, quite frankly, a lot to handle. I clear my throat for a second time. "I think that will work."

He pulls away completely, and I keep my eyes on the box of garland in the corner. The sun has moved past it now, cast it half in shadow. He lets go of my hand and I curl my fingers into fists.

"Yeah, that was good." I gather my courage and look up at him, watching as he runs his hands over his hair, front to back and back again. He looks like he just got home from the grocery store. Like he had to stop on the way to fill up the gas tank. Calm. Unaffected.

Business as usual.

I tell myself to get it together.

"I'll see you in a week?" I say.

Luka nods and wanders over to the door, bending at the waist and tinkering with something near the ground. "I'll call you when I'm leaving the city."

"Great."

He unfolds his body from his crouch and pulls on the handle. The door slides back smoothly. A burst of sunshine floods the room, and I curl my arms around myself.

"Want me to walk you back?"

"Nah." I gesture toward the pile of decorations, the fifty thousand lights that are tangled together. "I'm going to work in here for a little bit."

I don't care if there is an entire family of raptors hidden in this barn. I need some time to myself to unpack that kiss and then pack it right back up again.

He hesitates in the doorway. "I'll see you soon."

I wave him off and busy myself with unpacking. It's the exact type of mindless movement I need, too focused on lights and candy canes and signposts to think through that kiss in any sort of detail. It was a good kiss, yes, but only because we were both determined to make this work. Because we're both committed to making this fake relationship seem as real as possible. Just because I felt it all the way to my toes, it doesn't have to mean anything.

By the time all the boxes are stacked and sorted, I have successfully convinced myself that I am as unaffected as Luka.

I call it a morning when my stomach begins to rumble. On my walk back to the office, I tuck my hands into my coat pockets. It's starting to get colder, the winds coming down off the foothills and whipping across the fields. If we're lucky, we'll get some snow when Evelyn is here. I picture what it's like out on the fields when that first layer of white kisses the branches of the trees. The cold stillness, the heavy expectation in the sky. The soft flutter of snowflakes as they land on my cheeks, my lashes, the tips of my ears. If I could live out in the fields during the snowfall, I would.

I flex my fingers in my pockets and feel the sharp edge of firm paper, a piece of string catching on my pinky. I pull it out and smile.

A pine-scented air freshener in the shape of a tree from the gas station just down the road.

10

"YOU KISSED?"

I studiously keep my attention on the tray of peppermint bark and not Layla. I hadn't meant to start our conversation with that little bombshell, but I've been holding it in for days, and I needed to tell someone. So much for not fixating.

Luka has texted me multiple times since he left. A selfie of him with a pumpkin cannoli from the Italian deli on his street, a look of horror pulling at the corners of those golden eyes, the straight, sharp cut of his jaw. A diatribe about how *nothing is sacred* and cannoli deserve to be consumed how God intended, with fried dough, ricotta, and chocolate chips.

Another selfie twenty minutes later of his eyes closed in absolute bliss, cannoli wrapper empty, a touch of pumpkin clinging to the corner of his mouth. I change his contact photo immediately.

A text asking if I've changed the password to HBO Max, and oops, no, he just used the incorrect amount of exclamation points. Did I see that they just added the full collection of Harry Potter movies? A quick note that he left popcorn jammed in the cabinet by the stove when he brought dinner over the other night. Movie theater butter, none of that kettle corn crap.

A picture of him and Charlie out to lunch, both of their faces twisted in exaggerated comical frowns. Wish you were with us, it said.

And a voice memo reminding himself to pick up fresh tomatoes and chicken stock, voice out of breath, the heavy sound of weights in the background. That one had me picturing Luka sweaty and flushed, hair damp just behind his ears. Arms flexing and releasing. I listened to that voice memo twice before I deleted it completely from my phone, concerned with myself.

A text message seventeen minutes later with an apology, he had meant to send it to himself, and I just happened to be at the top of his messages. But while he's thinking about it, do I need him to pick up anything from the grocery store on his way back into town?

All of them completely normal. Not a single indication that he was thinking about our kiss.

"Yes." I pick up a mallet and smack the peppermint bark once in the middle. It cracks and I hit it twice more. Now I know why Layla is always making seasonal chocolate bark. It's very cathartic. "But it was a pretend kiss."

"Ah, okay. A pretend kiss." Layla shuffles across the kitchen as I continue to pound the bark.

We converted an old tractor shed into a cooking space and bakery for Layla, the ceilings low in the back, where she does all her cooking, the front replaced almost entirely with glass. Full evergreen and balsam trees press in on every side, brushing up against the windows. When it's especially cold, the windows frost at the bottoms, and you can just barely make out Layla bustling behind the counter, trays of cookies and brownies and tarts in neat little rows in each display case. Mugs stuffed with candy canes and a chalkboard with the daily special. The dining space is filled with small red-top tables with walnut chairs, cozy green booths along the walls. There are picnic tables with space heaters just out front, and they spill out into the fields. I love that this place is tucked away like a little gingerbread house for our visitors to discover.

I came over this morning with a box of replacement bulbs for the string lights Beckett hung over the weekend and quickly got roped into peppermint bark labor.

She curls her fingers around my hand on the hammer. "We need this to be peppermint bark, honey. Not peppermint dust."

I release the mallet and frown at the countertop, collecting a little pile of peppermint and chocolate with my fingers. Layla picks up one of the bigger pieces I left behind and offers it to me.

"Explain to me what a pretend kiss entails."

"I don't know. Exactly what it sounds like, I guess." I shrug and think of the sound he made when I put my hands in his hair. That low little hum. I nibble at my peppermint bark. "We thought it would be a good idea to practice kissing before we have an audience."

Layla gives me a look. "All right. And so you, what? You just kissed each other?"

"Yep."

Layla sighs and reaches around me. She gives the peppermint bark another hard whack. "You're not giving me anything to work with here."

"I don't know what to tell you."

"I need details, obviously."

"Like what?"

Layla gives me a look like she wants to use the mallet on my fingers. "Like what," she mutters. She puts the mallet down and props her hand on her hip, sifting through the peppermint bark shards until she finds one to her liking. "Did you talk about it first? How long did it last? Was there tongue? Come on, now. Don't be shy."

It's not that I'm shy. I'm just a little . . . protective, I guess. Right now it feels like mine—well, mine and Luka's—and holding it close feels right.

"It was . . . fine."

At Layla's slightly murderous look, I feel a bit of the tension release from my shoulders. I huff a laugh through my nose and reach for the bags we're supposed to be putting this bark into. Not stuffing our faces with.

"It was a nice kiss," I offer quietly, thinking of the way gold danced across his skin, how his palm pressed to mine as he tugged me closer, into the curve of his body. I sigh. "It was a really nice kiss."

"A nice kiss."

"Yeah."

Layla hums under her breath, her inquisition fading, a thoughtful gleam entering her gaze as she cocks her head to the side. She reaches for a pair of scissors and drags the blade along a strand of cherry red, the ribbon curling beneath her fingers.

"You know, you're allowed to enjoy spending time with Luka."

"I know. I always enjoy time with Luka."

"I meant"—she ties the ribbon into a bow and repeats the action, forest green nails moving flawlessly through the maneuver—"I meant more like you are allowed to enjoy kissing him. Enjoy pretending."

And that's just it, isn't it? I do like the pretending. Too much, probably. It's the end of the pretending that'll be the problem. The part that comes after. I can't stop thinking about it, despite Luka's plan to just *continue*.

We lapse into silence, the crinkle of the bags and the curl of the ribbon the only sounds between us. I am once again grateful for work that keeps my hands and brain busy.

"It's been a while since I've had a nice kiss," she says, a little bit wistful. I think of her and Jacob, her current boyfriend. The way his eyes stay stuck on his phone rather than anywhere near her when they're together. I frown and reach for her hand, squeezing it once. She gives me a tight smile and squeezes back.

A timer beeps in the background. Another tray of goodies ready to come out of the oven. Layla is still looking at me thoughtfully after the interruption, rubbing her thumb back and forth over her bottom lip.

"What?"

She blinks, a sly smile curling her lips. "I would have paid so much money to watch."

I sputter a laugh, cheeks flushing red. Sometimes shy, sweet Layla surprises me. I pinch the skin just above her elbow. "Don't make this weird."

"Too late," she singsongs, heading toward the ovens.

❧ · ❦

I'M IN THE pharmacy browsing nail polish I absolutely don't need when Gus pops up in front of me, a bag of peanut butter cups clutched in his hand and a goofy smile stretched across his face. He's a handsome guy, especially when he smiles, two twin dimples appearing in his scruff-covered cheeks. There's a rumor going around town that he has something going on with Mabel, and I think the pair of them are adorable together. He reaches into the front pocket of his EMS uniform and pulls out a stack of haphazardly folded bills, holding them out to me with two fingers.

I take the stack of greasy bills after a moment's hesitation. He must have gone to Matty's for lunch. "What's this?"

Gus leans back against the concealer display, an elbow propped up against various shades of foundation. He unwraps a single peanut butter cup carefully and then offers me the bag. I shake my head, my hand still occupied with the stack of bills held between thumb and forefinger.

"Gus, why did you hand me a wad of cash?"

He smiles at me around a mouth of chocolate. "It's your cut."

I groan. "Please don't tell me you're growing something on the farm without my knowledge."

He laughs, knocking over an entire row of tiny glass bottles. "It's not that. Jeez, Stella."

"Then what is it?"

"The betting board."

"Okay," I wait for him to continue, but he just keeps smiling at me, another peanut butter cup in his giant paw of a hand.

"You see, I had a foolproof equation." He holds up one hand between us like he's presenting in front of a lecture hall, fingers spread wide as he lays out his words. "Distance, timing, and good old-fashioned tension. That picture you posted on Instagram of you out in the fields helped too. But that was more a stroke of luck. Can't take any credit for that."

I struggle to keep up with the conversation, my mind grabbing onto that last part. I had posted a picture on the farm account of me in the fields, yes, but that was over a month ago. I don't typically feature myself, but it had been a perfect day working quietly out amongst the trees, and I had dirt all over my hands and cheeks. It was silly, impulsive. Two bright blue eyes laughing through a mask of dirt. Cheaper than a Sephora mud mask, I had written.

"Gus." I suddenly understand why Layla wanted to murder me with a spatula yesterday. "What are you talking about?"

He opens his mouth to respond, but we're interrupted by Dane strolling down the aisle in full sheriff regalia, hat tucked under his arm. He takes one look at me and frowns, eyebrows slanted low.

"A word, Stella. If you don't mind."

His voice grits along the edges, a sure sign that I'm about to get yelled at.

"Uh-oh. Someone is in trouble," says Gus.

I shoot a look at him. He shrugs and turns on his heel, heading toward the checkout counters and leaving behind his mess of makeup. Coward. I hope he pays for those peanut butter cups he's destroying. I almost tell Dane Gus is about to shoplift so we can postpone whatever this conversation is.

I shove the wad of cash in my back pocket and give the sheriff my full attention, watching as his fingers drum on the bill of his hat.

"I don't know anything about the betting pool, if that's what you're worried about." I cross my arms over my chest and watch as Dane's mustache twitches. "So if you're here to question me about an underground—"

"Why am I finding out about property damage on the farm from Luka?"

I blink.

"He stopped by the station a few days ago, says you've been having trouble. A fence collapsed, and now pumpkins are being smashed?"

Damn, he must have stopped by on his way back to New York. I scratch at my eyebrow and fight not to fidget under Dane's steady stare. "I was gonna come down to the farm, but I spotted you in here. What's going on, Stella? Why didn't you come to me?"

"I didn't—I didn't think it was a big deal." And it's not. Or it wasn't. Separately, it's all tiny things. The fence, the pumpkins, the stolen signpost from the main road. The missed deliveries and the barn door left wide open back in August, half our supplies getting soaked by a summer thunderstorm.

My brow creases in thought and I rub my palms against my thighs.

"Don't you have your magazine highlight coming up?" I don't correct him and explain it's a social media feature, not a magazine. I don't have the energy to explain TikTok to him right now. I tried to show him Instagram once, and he frowned so fiercely I thought his face might freeze that way. He was grumbling under his breath about cat filters for close to a month. "Even more reason to make sure everything is buttoned up."

"You think it's connected?"

Luka had implied something similar, and I can't say I haven't been thinking about it. It does seem like an awful amount of bad luck, but what could possibly be the explanation? I can't imagine a pack of high schoolers would be so methodical. And I'm not sure who else would. I don't have any enemies in this town.

He rubs his palm across his jaw and peers over my head, gray eyes scanning the pharmacy. It's empty as far as I can tell, Cindy somewhere in the back working on restock. "I don't know," he says quietly. "But I think it's worth lookin' into."

He settles his hat back on his head, tipping the brim up with his pointer finger so I can still see his face. "I'll stop by the farm this afternoon and take a look around." He pauses and shuffles his feet. "Will Layla be there, you think?"

I narrow my eyes. "Why?"

A light blush climbs his cheeks. "I wouldn't say no to one of her bear claws, if that's what you're asking."

I huff a laugh. "Yeah, she'll be there. I'll let her know you're stopping by, and she'll fix you up with something nice."

"No need to go through any trouble," he mumbles.

"No trouble." I smile and curl my hand through his elbow, towing him to the front of the store and ensuring he can't get away. I have something I've been meaning to discuss with him, and now is the perfect time. "Now, while we are on the subject of things we've kept from each other, I've noticed you've been spending an awful lot of time over at the pizza shop."

Dane's blush goes from a light pink to a fierce burning red in a matter of seconds. I cackle and tug on his arm, just short of hopping up and down in glee. I *knew* it.

"I knew it," I poke him in the chest, right above his badge. "I knew it, I knew it, I knew it."

"You know nothing, Cinnamon Stick." He swats me away, but I can see that he's fighting back a smile. His hand finds the brim of his hat again, and he pulls it down low before pushing it up, unsure what to do with himself. He clears his throat and peers at me out of the corner of his eye. "I like the pizza."

"Sure," I hum. "And it has nothing to do with a certain handsome pizza shop owner, huh?"

I've caught Dane loitering outside of Matty's a couple of times. I didn't think anything of it until I spotted him standing just outside the window, gazing longingly at the handsome pizza man behind the counter. I followed him in and listened to him stutter over his order for a pepperoni pizza and some garlic knots, and I *knew*.

"They have a good special on Tuesdays."

"That certainly explains why you're there Saturday, Monday, and Thursday as well, then."

"Easy. Or I'm going to be the one smashing your pumpkins."

I bite back on my laugh and guide us down the street, back to the sheriff's station, and coincidentally, the pizza shop. I have a few errands left to run while I'm in town, but giving Dane a gentle nudge in the right direction is a detour I'm happy to make. He grumbles under his breath as he realizes where we're walking but keeps my hand tucked in the crook of his arm, patting it absently.

"When does your contest lady arrive? The one who is doing the story for the farm." He's officially switched off sheriff mode and is asking as a friend.

"About a week and a half. The Monday after Thanksgiving. She'll stay through the weekend and leave that Sunday."

"Feeling ready?"

I am, surprisingly. Most of the decorations and lights are up. The only thing I still need to do is replace the burnt-out bulbs from the strings that lace through the fields and place the bows on the gates. We made the decision last year to start the lights on the road and weave them back to the very edge of our property line. At night, every inch of our farm glows. Beckett, Layla, and I did a dry run last night as soon as the sun dipped low enough to cast everything in a faint purple glow. The second the lights twinkled alive, I felt my breath catch in my throat. Layla smiled ear to ear, and even Beckett gave a nod of approval. Everything was falling into place.

"I feel ready. The farm looks great. It has me in the holiday mood."

Dane snorts at that. "I think you're in the holiday mood twenty-four seven. Three-sixty-five."

It's true. I've always loved Christmas and everything that comes with it. It's the one time of year where everything feels like magic. Hopeful, earnest, and kind. The whole world slows down and . . . believes for once.

Mom and I would do the same thing every Christmas, no matter where we were. The large, colorful bulbs on the tree by the fireplace. Thick red stockings in the hallway. Pie for breakfast on Christmas morning and ice-skating in the afternoon. I still keep those traditions, even though she's not here. It's like holding a piece of her close, the sweet ache of it always sharpest in the center of my chest.

"I think you have to be if you own a Christmas tree farm." I shake my head to clear the cobwebs of the past and steady myself with a deep breath. It's been almost . . . god, it's almost been ten years since my mom passed away. I like to think everything happens for a reason, but I still don't understand why she had to go so soon. I'm still angry about it.

We're outside of the pizza shop now, the light from its hazy humid windows glowing warm and bright. I look at Dane out of the corner of my eye. I doubt he realizes that he's the one who stopped us here, focused on the man working at the ovens behind the counter. The air around us smells like oregano and tomato sauce, a siren's song spilling out onto the pavement.

I nudge Dane once with my shoulder. "You gonna go in?"

He shrugs, a little helpless, and I squeeze his arm. I only want the very best things for Dane. This man who chose to be a father to me when my own refused. He scratches his chin and then fusses with the collar of his shirt.

"How did you—" He clears his throat. "How did you, you know, with Luka?"

For one mortifying second, I think Dane is asking about our kiss in the barn. "What?"

He clears his throat again, a little bit louder this time. "How did you tell him how you feel? How did you ask him to—to take a chance on you?"

Something in my chest shifts at that, a little pluck that I feel reverberate down to the soles of my feet. I squeeze his arm harder until he looks at me.

"You're not a chance, Dane." I want to shake his shoulders, get the megaphone he keeps in the passenger seat of his cruiser, and scream it in his face. Instead, I settle for a whisper that wobbles around the edges and the best smile I can manage when my throat feels so tight. "You're a sure thing."

I tuck myself behind a light pole across the street and watch as Dane wanders his way into the pizza shop, pretending to look at cannoli in the glass case at the front before he shuffles his way over to the ovens. Shoulders by his ears, he fidgets, his hat tucked back under his arm. Matty half turns, about to ask after his order, I'm sure, and their eyes catch. Matty's smile splits into something wide and beautiful, and Dane's shoulders roll back, his forearms finding the counter. Finally relaxed.

A sure thing.

I hide my smile behind my fingertips and wander my way back up Main Street, shooting Layla a text to let her know that Dane will be stopping by later to take a look around. The wind kicks up at my ankles and twists around my calves until it lifts the ends of my jacket, curling under my sweater and brushing a hello at the small of my back. It's my favorite time of year, this in-between of fall and winter. It feels like the whole world is holding its breath. Stillness and sweetness all rolled into one.

I'm not watching where I'm going, too caught up in tracking my boots against the pavement, the black sharp against the browns and creams of fallen leaves. They're almost all gone now, the only branches bursting with life are the ones on the farm. Sturdy little swipes of green dotted all along the fields and hillside. A splash of red here and there from the holly trees that Beckett planted purely because they looked pretty.

My phone buzzes with a text. I check it and see a string of messages from Charlie.

> CHARLIE: Don't think I'm going to forget about you bringing Luka to dinner.

> **CHARLIE:** We discussed you at length during lunch the other day.

That's interesting. I wonder what they talked about. I'm just tapping out a reply when another message pops up.

> **CHARLIE:** Won't kiss and tell though.

I roll my eyes.

> **CHARLIE:** Also, isn't this amazing?

A picture pops up of my dad facedown on the Thanksgiving table, except Charlie has added dancing turkeys all over him. I immediately save it to my phone.

I'm just typing out my response when I slam into a body, the momentum almost taking me to the ground. I stumble and catch myself on a light pole. Unfortunately, the person I've run into is not so lucky.

I reach out a hand to help Mr. Hewett up, cheeks blazing in embarrassment. It's not like me to be so careless, though I suppose I have a lot on my mind.

"Mr. Hewett, I'm so sorry." He's busy rearranging his glasses on his face, brushing off brown leaves from the edge of his coat. "I didn't see you. I wasn't watching where I was going."

He scowls up at me from behind the slightly magnified lenses of his tortoiseshell glasses, gray eyes narrowed in disdain. His jacket is faded at the elbows, well loved and worn often, the collar sticking up unevenly on one side. His patchy gray hair is a bit of a mess, tousled by the wind now whipping in earnest. He's a small man, but he holds himself tall, chin tilted up in defiance.

It's the look on his face that has me taking half a step back, the aggressiveness out of place on this tiny side street. It feels angrier than any sidewalk bump-in deserves. I suddenly remember the stroll Luka and I took through downtown last week, with Mr. Hewett watching us from the steps of the library, that same furious look on his face. I had thought it had something to do with Luka and me together, but it seems like I might be the common denominator.

"I'm really sorry," I say again. I haven't been to the library in ages, and it seems like I've missed some things. Like whatever I might have done to piss off Will Hewett. "Can I—"

"'It is better to have your head in the clouds and know where you are,'" he recites, voice oddly formal, a bit nasally, "'than to breathe the clearer atmosphere below them, and think you are in paradise.'"

I blink at him, confused. "Um."

Is that an insult? A warning?

"That's Henry David Thoreau."

Apparently, it's Henry David Thoreau.

I was going to offer to buy Mr. Hewett a hot chocolate to apologize for bulldozing him, but now I just want to quickly remove myself from this odd conversation. I do my best to be kind to everyone in this town, grateful for their role in helping me put myself back together after the death of my mom. But I'm not sure I can tolerate a stilted conversation about New England transcendentalism. Not even for a peppermint hot chocolate with extra whipped cream.

"That is . . . nice, I think?" When Mr. Hewett only offers silent contempt as a response, I shove my hands deep in my jacket pockets and look for an escape route. The pine air freshener from the other day is still there, and I grip it like a lifeline, edges digging into my palm. "All right, well, I have a few things left to do in town. I'll stop by—" I am not going to lie to this man. "I'll see you around town, I'm sure."

I hurry down the street, careful this time to note where I'm going and if there is anyone else on the sidewalk. What a strange little man. I search for my phone in my oversized pockets, intending to finally text Charlie back when it suddenly comes to life, buzzing in my hand.

I smile when I see the picture of Luka and the pumpkin cannoli on my screen and swipe to answer.

"Hey, I was just about to text you."

"Oh god, is she there already?"

I frown at the way his voice sounds slightly out of breath. Like he's running or—I hear the clink of a coffee cup in the background, the faded tones of some sports show—pacing his apartment.

I look around me at the almost completely abandoned side street. Just me and a couple of sparrows, collecting crumbs from an old half-eaten bagel. "What? No, Evelyn isn't here for another week or so. The Monday after Thanksgiving."

"Not Evelyn," he breathes out, and I imagine him scratching at the back of his head, just where his hair starts to curl. "My mother."

I swallow back a laugh at his deeply foreboding tone. Mainly because I know how much Luka loves his mom. His relationship with her is like a Hallmark card. He doesn't go a day without calling her at five thirty on the dot so she doesn't have to eat her dinner alone. Once he got caught up in a meeting but still managed to call her from the hallway just outside the boardroom, adding me into the group call so she'd have someone to talk to. He brings her flowers when he visits and dresses up in the school mascot costume when they can't find anyone else. Because she asked him once and he doesn't want her to have to ask again. He is the picture-perfect son and dotes on her constantly with genuine affection.

"What's going on with your mom?"

"I don't want you to panic, Stella."

Unease scratches at the back of my throat, and I swallow around it until I can manage my voice. If anything's happened to Luka's *mom*—memories rise like a swelling tide. Hospital visits, prescription bottles, how small and brittle my mom looked at the end, still trying so hard to smile for me.

"Luka—" I can't seem to catch my breath. I press shaking fingertips to my chest. "Is your mom okay?"

"Ah, shit. Yeah, Stella. She's okay." All the air whooshes out of me. I feel like I need to bend at the waist and rest my hands on my knees. "She's okay. I'm sorry. That was . . . not a great lead-in."

"I think you've known me long enough to understand that telling me not to panic will only cause me to panic."

I swear I can hear his smile over the phone. I close my eyes to imagine it. A little bit rueful, tugging sharply on the left side of his bottom lip.

"You're right. I'm sorry."

"All right, so . . ." I head toward the bookstore—my last stop before heading home. Alex called yesterday to let me know he just received a shipment of *A Christmas Carol* bound in fabric with gold foil etching. I want to get some for the office and one for Evelyn's room at the bed-and-breakfast. I'll add some cookies from Layla and a fresh bag of coffee from Ms. Beatrice. Maybe one of the mini trees that Beckett grows in the greenhouse behind his house. But Luka is distracting me with . . . whatever this is. "What's going on?"

"My mom knows," he offers in explanation. I hear the TV in the background click off, and the heavy gust of a sigh as he collapses into his couch. "I underestimated the power of the phone tree. Also, Betsy Johnson."

My boots crunch over leaves along the pathway, birds scattering as I walk. "That's not a problem though, right? She knows it's—" I glance around me at the empty sidewalk. I drop my voice. "She knows it's not real."

Luka is silent on the other end of the phone, and I feel that uneasy feeling again.

"Luka."

Lying to Evelyn is one thing. The town another. But lying to his mom, of all people. That feels like a step too far. I never anticipated lying to his family. I never thought we'd have to. My oversight, I guess, but I can't believe he's considering it. The man who buys a sweatshirt with an angry badger on it every year and wears it unironically on the weekends because it makes his mom happy.

"Luka," I say again, this time with a hint of pleading, "tell me you didn't."

"If by *didn't* you mean I didn't say anything when she called me in rapid-fire Italian to tell me that she was bringing you manicotti and lasagna, then yes, you would be correct." I hear the clink of a coffee cup again, and I fight not to change direction and head to the bar instead. "She was—she was really excited, Stella. I couldn't tell her we're just faking it."

"That's exactly why you should have done it! If she finds out we're lying to her, she'll be furious." Worse, she'll be hurt. I can't bear to disappoint his mom. I can't have her look at me differently after all of this. "Luka, this is a mess."

"Look at it this way. If we tell her this is fake, she'll tell her sisters, yeah?" That's true. Luka's aunts are always around, and they keep exactly nothing from one another. I once heard his aunt Gianna tell his mom about her hemorrhoid cream. "And my aunt Sofia will absolutely tell Cindy Croswell. They play bridge together every other Sunday."

I scratch at my eyebrow and fight not to scream into the sky. Never in my life have I had more childish impulses in the span of a single month. "I don't know, this is—"

"It'll be fine, La La."

I try to assure myself with the calm confidence in his voice, but it's difficult. It actually only pisses me off more. *It'll be fine. We'll just continue. It's not a big deal.* His nonchalance over every single detail is frustrating. He's not the one with everything to lose here.

I try to explain. "I just don't want her to think of me differently, is all. At the end of all of this."

"What do you mean?"

"When we—" I glance around the street again to make sure I'm alone. "At the end of all this, when we are no longer fake dating. I don't want her to be hurt."

He sighs, frustration around the edges, his deep voice rumbling a bit. I imagine him in his apartment with his feet kicked up on the coffee table, his cup of coffee resting on his knee. "We talked about this already, Stella. We don't have to say anything to anyone."

He's unbelievable. "We will absolutely need to say something to your mother when she's inviting her son's girlfriend to family dinners."

"Or maybe I'll take advantage of the fact that you're being guilted into consistently attending family dinners. Finally."

This isn't the conversation I want to be having. I have enough on my plate right now without Luka's laissez-faire attitude toward the most important relationship in my life. It's like he doesn't even care what happens after all of this, doesn't care what people think of us— think of me. Angry and a little bit hurt, I pick up my pace on the sidewalk and blink at the frustrated tears burning at the corners of my eyes. I've always been an angry crier, no matter how hard I try to stop myself. And it only makes me more upset as I trudge along the sidewalk. I know this whole thing was my idea and a consequence of my actions, but Luka isn't—he's not taking the fallout seriously.

"All right, well, I'm at the bookstore, so I have to go," I fib. The bookstore is at least three more blocks down the street. "You know Alex doesn't like people talking on the phone in the shelves."

"Stella, wait."

"I'll call you later."

I don't wait for him to respond, ending the call and tossing my phone in my pocket so I'm not tempted to read whatever string of text messages he decides to send through. Luka has never been the type of person to let things lie. Unfortunately for us both probably, I absolutely am.

Right on cue, my phone buzzes. I ignore it and keep walking.

11

THERE'S A CAR waiting in my driveway when I finally make it home, a stack of brand-new books and a self-indulgent pepperoni pizza on my passenger seat. Matty had been walking on air when I stopped in before heading home, humming under his breath as he pulled pizza from the oven. It had been enough to temporarily lift the little storm cloud that settled over my shoulders following Luka's call.

Now though, I feel rumbles in the distance as I watch Luka's mom climb out of her bright red Kia, a stack of Tupperware in her arms and a grin on her face. It's a strange thing—to feel both crippling guilt and heartwarming flattery in the same breath. But I manage all the same, raising my hand in a wave as I sigh.

Luka's mom is stunningly beautiful, with rich chocolate brown hair that tumbles down her back. She has streaks of gray just behind her ears, with light gray eyes to match. I've heard the kids in town talking about her "spooky eyes" and how she misses absolutely nothing. The rumor is that the little Italian doll that sits on the edge of her desk in her eighth-grade classroom is a spirit object. It lets her watch her class when her back is turned to the board. It's hysterical, and Luka bought his mom three more after he found out.

She's intimidating in the way all good teachers are—quiet, knowing, and sure. She'll let you know when you're not reaching your full potential and then hug you through it. Everything is a lesson; every moment is an opportunity to learn. Luka likes to complain about how she made him write reports on holiday TV specials during Christmas break. Practice fractions with his asparagus at family dinner.

I climb out of my car, my arms loaded with books and pizza. She takes one look at the cardboard box stained with grease in my hand and narrows her eyes to slits, the change in her demeanor so comically swift I have to swallow around my laughter.

"Hi, Mrs. Peters."

"Stella, you make me feel old when you call me that." She hoists her tower of Tupperware in one arm so she can point at my pizza. "What is that?"

I glance down at the box. We only have one pizza shop in town, and Matty's boxes have a fairly obvious blue-and-white logo printed across the top. It says MATTY in a large bold font along the sides. "It's a pizza."

"From Matty."

I check the box again, just to be sure. I can just catch the edge of the blocky blue letters. Still, I hesitate, because Carina Peters looks like she's one step away from using her Tupperware as a weapon against the dinner in my hands, and I'm really craving pepperoni. I clutch it a little tighter and nod toward the house.

"Want to come inside? It looks like your hands are full."

She tightens her grip on the containers stacked neatly in her arms. White with blue lids, a triangle pattern printed at the very top edge. Luka has the same stack of Tupperware in his fridge in the city, left-over risotto and manicotti and tiramisu that I always sneak bites of when I stay over. She has two trays and another three smaller canisters, all with labels taped cleanly on the side. It looks like enough food to feed me for weeks.

"Come inside," I say again. "I think I have some biscotti leftover from Luka. You can even have some pizza if you want."

She follows me up the stairs to my porch, back to glaring at the box in my hands. "I wouldn't eat that pizza if it were the last thing on this planet."

I'm pretty sure she wouldn't eat Matty's pizza if someone was holding a gun to her head. I've heard her refer to it as an insult to the people of Italy, a bastardization of culture.

Eating there with Luka is always a master class on evasion. He has never once actually dined in the building, and he makes me go in alone when we get takeout. His mother almost caught him once, waiting at the curb for me to come back with our dinner. He had driven away so fast, the street cleaner had to buff out his tire marks. I came out with our food to an empty street and had to walk four blocks down to the alleyway behind the café to finally get a ride home. His hands were shaking when I slid into the passenger seat, wide-eyed terror on his handsome face. He slept on my couch that night, too afraid to go home and face his mother if she happened to have seen him.

"No Italian in their right mind would put cheese in the crust of a pizza," she shakes her head like she's never heard of a more ridiculous thing in her life. "And the stromboli. Did you know stromboli doesn't exist in Italy? It is a crime to create such a thing."

I do know this. She's told me before. And Luka tells me every time he orders a stromboli.

"It's very delicious though."

She slashes her hand through the air with a sharp gesture, cutting right through my words. "I have been asking that the school stop using his food for fundraisers, but the kids love it. I gave my eighth graders a lesson on Italian dining"—I have no idea how she managed this as a math teacher—"*real* Italian dining, mind you, and they had the audacity to ask if mozzarella sticks were considered antipasti." She places a hand against her chest, her fingers covered in rose gold rings. One from her late husband, another from her sister Cecilia, and another from Luka. They glint in the sunlight as I reach for the tin of cookies Luka hid in my cabinet. "The damage this man is doing to our young people."

She shakes her head sadly and turns on her heel, heading straight for the fridge. She manages to open it without a single dish toppling from her arms and begins to rummage inside. I watch as she takes a bag of wilted mixed greens and throws it in the general direction of the garbage, arranging and rearranging to fit her collection of Tupperware.

"Do you know he's from Boston?" She tosses an expired bottle of mustard after the bag of greens. "I bet he doesn't even have a drop of Italian blood in his body. I once asked him what part of Italy his family is from, and he said the northern coast. The northern coast, Stella! I do not believe this to be true."

"Why wouldn't it be true?"

She turns to glance at me over her shoulder, a lock of thick dark hair cascading over her right eye. A single eyebrow arches, and I now know what it feels like to be one of her students caught on their cell phone in the back of class.

"Because the northern coast is known for their risotto al nero di seppia." The words trip off her tongue in the faint accent she hasn't quite managed to get rid of despite thirty years living in the States. "And I have never seen the man so much as look at squid ink."

I make a face and her lips quirk up at the corners, a little sharper on the left side, the look so reminiscent of Luka that I feel an answering tug in my chest. "It is better than you think."

"I'll take your word for it," I tell her. I hand her a plate loaded with biscotti. "All right, here you go. I'm sorry I don't have any Illy on hand. Luka complains too."

"My son is giving you a hard time?"

I think of Luka standing at the stove just two feet from where she stands now, my hand towel in his back pocket. How he made me dinner and packed up leftovers, hid groceries around my kitchen. I think about his shoulder pressed to mine on the couch, my hair catching in the scruff along his jaw as I faded in and out of sleep. How I woke up in my bed with a thick blanket tucked around me, a glass of water on the nightstand.

I think about him in the barn, gloved hands holding mine tight. The taste of peppermint and hazelnut coffee.

"No." I smile at her, heat brushing at my cheeks despite my best efforts. "He's not. You raised a really wonderful man."

Even when I don't want him to be. Even when I'm upset with him.

She preens at that, a proud look on her face. "I did, didn't I?" She takes a bite of her cookie and settles into one of the kitchen chairs, patting the space diagonal from her in invitation. "Though I suppose some of that goes to his father as well."

"He doesn't—" I hesitate, unsure if I should say that Luka rarely talks about his dad. Is it wrong for me to share these things with her? Is it dishonest to Luka and the relationship we have if I talk to his mom about it? I don't know where I stand with this fake relationship and how it blurs the lines of my real ones.

She gives me a knowing look as I slide into the seat across from her. "He doesn't talk about his father?"

"Not really, no."

He'll let things slip sometimes. An unconscious mention of something his dad once did or said. But as soon as he realizes, he bottles it back up. Tucks away the memories piece by piece until they don't hurt as badly. I do the same thing with my mom, in a way. Sometimes it sneaks up on you when that constant ache turns into pain so sharp it steals your breath.

She nods. "He doesn't speak of him with me either." One finger traces the edge of her plate, back and forth, her gaze drifting out the window. "It makes me sad. We should remember those who have left us with fondness. Speaking of them keeps their memory alive."

"My mom said something similar to me right before she, um, right before she passed." I still remember the smell of antiseptic, so strong and so chemical, burning at my nose. How my shoes squeaked across the floor as I bent at the waist and tried to find a free electrical outlet for the scent diffusers I brought. Lavender, her favorite. "She said she only wanted me to have happy memories."

I try my best. I try to remember her when she was healthy and happy and spinning around our kitchen to the beat-up old radio she kept on top of the fridge. But some days are easier than others, and while it's mostly fondness now like Luka's mom says, it's also a healthy dose of longing too.

Carina's hand reaches for mine. "I sometimes forget that you lost your mother. She passed away right before I moved here, yes?"

On a Tuesday at 3:13 p.m. It had just rained, and there was a rainbow arching over a tree in the parking lot where I sat on the curb, both my legs splayed in front of me, hair plastered to my forehead. I was smoking a cigarette I got from one of the security guards, and I had never touched one before in my life. I nod. "She was sick for a while. Cancer."

"Cancer is a terrible thing," Carina says. She makes a short sound under her breath, a quick *tsk*. "I do not know if there is an easy way to lose someone, but with Leo, it was so quick. He left for work as he always did. He kissed me twice, Luka twice, and the last time I saw him, he was walking out the front door yelling over his shoulder that he wanted zucchini flowers for dinner." She swipes under her eyes quickly with her fingertips. "He was a bossy man."

I recognize the sadness in her words, the loneliness of remembering someone all by yourself.

"You should try to talk with Luka about him," I offer gently. "I think it would be good for both of you."

She nods and wipes at her face again before waving her hand between us, a finger pointed at me in mock accusation. "This is not why I came here, to cry at your table." She pulls her hand from my grip and presses both palms flat to the tabletop, situating her body in the chair until she has me pinned with her stare. "I came for an interrogation."

"Oh?" Now her questions feel like a welcome break from the heaviness of our conversation. This is what I was expecting when I saw her car in my driveway. I lean back in my chair and reach for a cookie from the tin. "I hope you put some tiramisu in the fridge, then."

She laughs, a bright burst of it that lights up my small kitchen. "Oh, there you are. I was worried for a second that you'd play coy with me now that you're dating my son." She settles in her chair. "Now, tell me. How did you and Luka go from best friends to something more?"

⤜• ⤛

I KEEP IT as close to reality as I can. I tell her that after so many years of friendship, we just sort of fell into dating each other. That in the end, dating wasn't so different from . . . being best friends. She arched an eyebrow at that, an interested hum beneath her breath.

We talk about the kids in her classroom, her sister Eva's foray into ballroom dance, and the ridiculousness of Ms. Beatrice and her merit-based ordering system. It seems the only way Mrs. Peters can get a hazelnut latte is by enlisting Luka's help as well.

It's nice having her in my kitchen. It's cozy and warm, and she fills the space with her loud laughter, her rings clinking along the edge of the table. She devours the rest of her cookies and declares that she has to go bother Giana with Thanksgiving preparations, abruptly pushing back from the table and handing me a folded-up piece of notebook paper out of her back pocket with reheating instructions. She leaves with a kiss to both of my cheeks and a slightly threatening invitation to family Thanksgiving called over her shoulder.

Disappearing in a cloud of kicked-up dirt, her little Kia rumbles away down the road back to town. I watch her go with my shoulder against the banister of my front porch, the lights in the fields beginning to twinkle alive as the sun dips below the horizon. I hear my phone in the kitchen but choose to ignore it for now, watching Mother

Nature paint the sky in shades of purple. Corn stalks blow gently in the breeze, the only remnant of the fall season. We'll cut those back soon enough and fill the space with precut trees, ready for families who don't want to make the trek all the way out into the foothills. Layla handles that portion of our business, sawing down trees and loading them up in the little tractor Beckett uses to make trips back and forth. She says it's good for her suppressed rage. Beckett says it's good for his back.

When the sky finally fades to a deep indigo, I head back inside, eyeballing the phone on my counter. I don't like arguing with Luka. I never have. Our disagreements never last long, but they always leave me feeling like I've put on an itchy sweater, uncomfortable in my own skin. I tap his number.

"Stella, listen." He sounds a little bit breathless, uneven. "I'm sorry."

I collapse onto my couch and kick my feet up on the coffee table. I drag the cable-knit throw he was using the other night over my lap. It still smells like him. "I'm sorry too."

He exhales slowly, and I imagine him falling back into his plush couch, his arm spread wide against the back of it. "Was she—did my mom stop by?"

"She did." I glance over my shoulder at the fridge. I wish I had grabbed that tiramisu on the way over. "She brought me food."

Luka groans long and loud, and it pulls my belly tight. Hearing those sounds from him has never been easy, but now that I know what he tastes like, it's borderline unbearable. I shift under my blanket. "That means she also brought the inquisition."

"She called it an interrogation."

"Stella, I'm so sorry." His voice drops lower, a little bit muffled, like he's speaking through a pillow or his face is pressed to the nearest flat surface. "I should have been there."

"And what would you have done? You can't lie to your mom."

"I absolutely can. I do it all the time. How do you think I've survived my mother and all her sisters? You have to be agreeable. You have to tell them their pasta sauce is the best thing you've ever tasted. You have to say you like smelts."

I frown and cozy down farther in the couch, pulling the blanket up to my nose. "Do I want to know what a smelt is?"

"No. You do not."

"She invited me to Thanksgiving," I mumble. "So I'll probably find out then anyway."

"You'll actually come?" He sounds surprised.

"Of course I will. Your mother invited me."

He scoffs. "I have invited you. For years. And you always make excuses."

"It's not an excuse if I already have plans."

"And those plans, you suddenly don't have them this year?"

I'll still go to the shelter in the morning and help serve meals, but I can be back in time to go to the Peters' for Thanksgiving. It's easy to tell myself it's for our secret so no one suspects that we aren't being truthful. But honestly, it would be nice to not be so alone on the holiday. I think about what Mrs. Peters and I talked about—about remembering and happy memories. I don't think my mom would want me wallowing alone on my couch on Thanksgiving, eating gas station food.

"I think—" I start slowly, careful with my words. Layla told me I'm allowed to enjoy this time, and I think she's right. There's no harm in spending a holiday with my best friend and his family. "I think I'd like to try something different."

Luka makes a happy little sound. I hear the shuffle of fabric against leather, the clink of a glass against his coffee table. "I'm really glad to hear it."

"Me too." I wiggle my toes in my thick socks and pick at a loose thread in the blanket resting over my chest, hesitant to bring up what else his mom and I discussed. I want to talk with him about it, but I'm not sure how he'll react.

"What is it?"

I chew at my bottom lip. "What is what?"

"Whatever you're not saying."

"Your mom and I talked about a few other things too," I say. When he says nothing in return, I continue. "We talked about your dad a little bit. I think—I think it makes her sad that you don't talk about him with her."

Luka had been twelve when his father passed away. There's never a good time to lose a parent, but Luka had to grow into a man without his dad. His mom has a picture of him in the hallway of her house, hanging just as you begin to walk up the stairs to the second floor. It's a high school spirit night or something similar, Luka's body gangly in the way most teenage boys' are, his hair shaggy and unkempt. It's a picture of all the young boys and their dads, with Luka standing proudly with his arm around his mom. Every time I'm at their house and every time I see it, I feel an overpowering rush of sadness. Because I can see it in the strain of his arms, in the weak edges of his smile. He missed his dad.

He misses his dad.

Luka clears his throat. "Did she say what she wanted to talk about?"

"No, just that she wants to talk about him. She said talking helps keep a memory alive."

He's quiet for a long time at that. So quiet I check the phone several times to make sure he hasn't hung up on me.

"Luka."

"He made me grilled cheese," he says softly, a heavy pause following his declaration. I can hear the click in his throat when he swallows. He takes a deep shuddering breath in, holds it, and then releases it. I grip my phone tighter, the edges pressing indents into my palm. I wish I were with him, my knee pressed to his hip on my couch.

"He was—he was a shit cook, actually. Always blamed my mom and called her bossy in the kitchen." I huff a laugh, thinking of Carina saying the same thing just an hour ago. "But he would make me a grilled cheese. Whenever I was sad."

That day at the hardware store, when Luka caught me from face-planting into the cement, he took one look at me and asked me if I wanted to get grilled cheese. Did he know I was sad? Could he tell?

I rub at my nose, the rush of fondness for this silly, stupid man overwhelming. I firm up my voice, make it as steady as possible. "You can—whenever you want to talk about him, Luka. You can."

He's still quiet, a stillness that I feel even through the phone. "I wish you were here right now," he confesses.

Something squeezes in my chest. I nod and pluck at the blanket in my lap. "Yeah. Yeah, me too."

Another lengthy pause. His voice, quieter this time. "Thanks, La La."

12

"ALL RIGHT, GUYS. This has been fun and all—" I rest my hands on my hips, facing the depths of the barn. Something has managed to unwind half the garland that I twisted around the support posts, and two ribbons are missing from the wreaths on the door. "But it's time to clear out."

I'm well aware that raccoons are nocturnal creatures, but my courage is fleeting. I had tried to come out here last night with a flashlight and a tennis racket, but that seemed like a bad idea as soon as I took two steps into the fields and heard an unexplainable noise in the dark. The flashlight went tumbling, and I went jogging back to my house. What I planned to do with a tennis racket, I'll never know. Now, by the light of day, it's certainly less scary. And I should be able to at least find out where these critters are nesting.

Again, I have no idea what I'll do with that information. But we need this barn for Santa, and unless we can convince these raccoons to put on antlers, they need to find a new home.

Something rustles in the far corner and I steel myself. I can do this. I have done scarier things than this. I found that whole little family of cockroaches when we were gutting the tractor shed. I had nightmares of tiny legs crawling in my hair for weeks. This is nothing compared to that.

I take a step closer. There's another shuffle of movement and then a . . . meow? A little braver, I make my way across the barn and poke my head over the top of our old-fashioned metal mailbox. Nestled just behind it, with some of the garland that went missing and a velvet red ribbon bundled together in a little nest, is a mama cat and her three kittens. All white with black spots around their eyes.

"Well"—Mama cat peers up at me with no shortage of distrust, curling her body closer to the three balls of fur tucked against her—"this is not what I expected."

A half hour and a couple of phone calls later, Beckett, Layla, and I are staring down at the little family in my office, nestled in a laundry basket with the bit of the garland Mama refused to let go of. She hadn't left her home without complaint, but as soon as she saw me place her babies gently in the basket and coax her to follow, she was agreeable enough. Now all four are dozing, sweet little snores from their tiny pink noses.

"This is fucking adorable," Beckett mutters, almost angrily. He twists his baseball hat around backward and folds his arms over his chest. "What are we supposed to do with them?"

"Take them to the shelter?"

Beckett unfolds his arms and brackets his hips with his hands, shooting me a glare. I hold both hands up.

"Okay, maybe not. I just—I don't know what to do with four cats."

"I think we should take them to Dr. Colson and go from there." Layla lowers herself down to a squat, pressing her face up against the slats of the laundry basket. One tiny paw boops her nose, and she practically melts to the floor in a puddle. She sighs dreamily. "They really do sort of look like raccoons."

With their coloring and the spots around their eyes, it's no wonder I mistook them for raccoons all this time. Frankly, I had slid open the barn door once, saw a flash of black and white, and called it a day. I just always thought a very emotional raccoon was leaving those scratch marks on all the posts.

"Maybe we should name the mom Raccoon," I wonder aloud, and both Beckett and Layla give me a look. "What?"

"If we're naming the cats, it's likely we are keeping the cats." Layla stands back up, brushing her hands on the back of her jeans. I look back down at the tiny balls of fur and feel a sharp pang of longing. I always wanted a pet growing up, but we never had the time or the space. And with our busy season coming up and Evelyn arriving in a week, we certainly don't have the time now. But maybe, with the three of us, we could—

"We are not naming her Raccoon." Beckett huffs. "It's insulting. I think it's obvious what we should name them."

Layla and I exchange a look, her smile hidden behind the tips of her fingers. Beckett hasn't looked away from the cats once.

"Yeah?"

He points at the smallest bundle of fur, tucked in tight with her face hidden in her mom's chest. "Comet." He points at the other two curled together. "Cupid, Vixen." He points at Mom, who has turned her face up to look at him with what, I swear to god, is the cat version of heart eyes. Beckett cups her tiny face with his large hand and she purrs, nuzzling into his palm. "She's Prancer."

"Well," Layla sighs. "I guess we have cats now."

☙ ❧

AFTER A THOROUGH bath and examination, the town vet, Dr. Colson, declares Prancer and her babies ready to head home. He prescribes a medicated shampoo, just in case, and some food laden with supplements to help Prancer bulk up a bit. When he asks if I have all the necessary items to house a family of cats, I stare at him dumbly. I barely have the necessary items to house myself. I don't even know where the closest pet store is.

But Beckett swoops in with a frown and pulls the laundry basket tight to his chest, muttering something about Amazon shopping lists and an old dog bed at his place. Some leftover feeding dishes from when his sister tried to foster two Frenchies. Sensing she's back in the arms of her one true love, Prancer rises gracefully from the basket, hops onto Beckett's shoulder, and curls herself into his neck with a purr. Dr. Colson and I watch with amusement as Beckett swings open the exam room door and wanders his way through the waiting room, a cat on his shoulder and a basket of kittens in his arms. He's likely to obliterate the entire female population of Inglewild if he goes too far like that.

Apparently, I wasn't the only one who wanted pets as a kid.

By the time we get back to the farm, the sun is hanging low in the sky, and there's still plenty I need to do. But for once, I don't feel the weight of the incredible amount of pressure I put on myself. Instead, I feel nothing but a bubble of joy as we turn down the lane. Giant arches lined with lights. Red-and-white striped posts. A massive sign with crisp white paint welcoming you to the North Pole. It really does look perfect.

"I haven't had a chance to talk to you this week with how busy we've been, but it looks amazing. Even better than last year," Beckett says from the passenger seat, Prancer still draped across his shoulder, little Comet snoozing away in the front pocket of his jacket. "This place is what it is because of you."

I turn left and head toward his cabin at the base of the foothills. Hank said the people who owned the land before him tried to use this place as a hunting lodge or something similar. But hunting has never been very good on the Eastern Shore, and they closed up shop quickly. I have one cottage, Beckett has another, and the third we turned into our administrative office and welcome cottage. I offered him the place as a part of his work here. It's easier for him to live on the property with his early mornings, and before this, he'd been sharing a home with his parents and youngest sister, with his other two sisters stopping by frequently. He's always been the first to take care of others, almost to a fault.

"It's because of you and Layla too."

I feel terrible every time I get a compliment from either of them. I still haven't been completely honest about our finances. I'm too afraid of their reaction, of their disappointment. I swear I'd chop off my arm before I let them down.

"Listen, Beck. This thing with Evelyn. It's not just a good opportunity."

"What do you mean?" He's busy trying to move a comfortable Prancer from her perch across him to the laundry basket. She meows softly and he hushes her with a whisper, knuckles brushing under her chin. It's unbearable.

"The exposure is great, and I'm hoping it can bring in more customers. But I'm more interested in the prize money. It would—it would help us out a lot."

He blinks at me, face unreadable in the setting sun. "Are we in trouble?"

I shrug my shoulders, my heart in my throat and tension in my belly. "We could use a holiday miracle."

He considers me, weighing my words. It's the closest I've ever come to telling him the truth. It's still less than he deserves, but the rest of the explanation sticks in my throat. After a moment, he hefts the laundry basket in his arms and slips from my car. He ducks his head back down with an arm braced on the door, face serious.

"Then let's make some fucking magic."

❧ ❦

I WAKE UP in the morning buried beneath a heap of blankets, the smell of coffee tickling my nose, the sound of clinking glasses in the kitchen pulling me from the cusp of sleep. I blink blearily at the weak sunlight pouring in from the window over the dresser and stretch out my legs, bare toes peeking out from the bottom of my blanket as I try to remember if there's supposed to be someone in my kitchen. If it's a burglar, they're being awfully polite by putting on the coffee.

I hear movement in the hallway, socked feet against the hardwood.

I don't know how I know it's him, just that I do, a comfort in listening to his movements around my house. When I was a kid, I hated how quiet our apartment was when my mom was working late. I always felt better when I heard her come home and start the tea kettle, reheat her leftovers in the microwave.

Luka appears in my doorway in the middle of a fierce yawn, eyes screwed shut, sweatshirt on inside out. His hair is flat on one side like he was wearing a hat when he came in and just now remembered to take it off. I dart a quick look at his toes. He's wearing his *Nugs and Kisses* socks—the ones with dancing chicken nuggets holding hands.

"What time is it?" I mutter, snaking my hand through my nest of blankets to reach for the mug of coffee in his. It's the only part of my body I'm currently willing to move. He sits at the edge of my bed and pats my foot, handing me the mug and making sure I have a good grip before he pulls away.

"Seven. Sorry it's so early."

I squint at him. "Did you leave at three in the morning?"

He shrugs, noncommittal, avoiding my eyes to look at something on my headboard. I'm not sure the stitching on my discount upholstery is that interesting. There's something he's not telling me, but it's too early in the morning to try and figure it out. I'll let him have his secrets for now.

I take a sip from his mug. Whatever this is, it's certainly not the coffee I keep in my cabinet. It's rich and delicious, and I take another long pull, moaning when I get a hint of mocha. Luka's gaze trips a shade darker, and I slip down a little farther in my bed. It's different now, knowing that his eyes turn the exact same color when his mouth is on mine.

I clear my throat. "I thought you were supposed to call me from the road."

"I meant to," he says and leaves it at that. His voice is scratchy around the edges with sleepiness, an adorably flustered softness to him in his exhaustion.

"I'm kind of glad you didn't if you left at three in the morning." I look at the circles under his eyes, at the way he's listing slightly to one side like he can't commit to holding himself upright. I curl myself to one side of the bed.

"Luka."

He hums, eyes closed, mug raised to his mouth but not actively drinking from it. It's like he forgot what to do with it halfway to his mouth. I bite my lip against a smile and flick back my blankets. "Luka, lay down. Come back to sleep for a little bit."

He looks down at me, eyelids drooping with heavy, slow blinks. "I can sleep on the couch."

I take the mug out of his hands and put it on the nightstand. "Don't be ridiculous. We've shared a bed before."

"I was going to sleep on the couch," he mutters again, letting me pull him down and collapsing into my bed with a borderline pornographic moan. "Is this memory foam?"

All I can see of him through the mound of pillows and blankets is a tuft of brown hair and the curve of his ear. The mattress bounces slightly as he shimmies beneath the blankets, his feet slipping under my calf, his hand at my hip a second later. He squeezes once as I burrow myself back into my pillow.

"Get some rest, Luka."

All I get in response is a light snore, his foot twitching against my leg.

❧·❧

I WAKE IN increments, sunlight warming my cheek and the jut of my ankle where my foot is twisted out of the bedsheets. It still smells like coffee, but it's muted now, the birds fully awake in the trees that sit at the very edge of my yard. I can hear them calling to one another, jumping from branch to branch. I squint one eye open, and golden, sparkling sunlight fills the room, dancing off the snow globe I have sitting on my dresser and the old vintage floor mirror I found at a flea market in the city and made Luka strap to the top of his car.

I've almost forgotten there's someone in bed with me until fingers flex on my belly beneath my sleep shirt, a heavy palm sliding lower against my bare skin. Still caught in the haze of sleep, it feels like the edges of a delicious dream. I tuck my body closer to the man curled behind me, his knees nudging against the backs of mine. Two spoons in a drawer.

"Skin's soft," he mutters somewhere into my hair, voice rough, nosing until he finds my shoulder. His hand flexes again, thumb dragging up once and then back down, memorizing. Goose bumps light up my arms, a heavy tug low in my belly. Warmth settles and spreads, and I push back into him, wiggling, trying to get closer. He grunts, and his hand shifts from my belly to my hip, holding me there. For a second, I think he might angle me away, roll onto his back and fall asleep with his forearm over his eyes, but he doesn't.

He tightens his hand at my hip just as his left knee pushes forward, nudging mine until I'm off-balance, surrounded by his heat. Our bodies touch everywhere—his chest flush with my shoulders, his belly to the small of my back. I can feel every inhale he takes, the cotton of his sweatpants soft against my bare thighs. I arch my back and shift again, restless, and feel a hardness press into the curve of my ass. Luka shies away from me with the motion, tilting his hips just slightly until we're no longer touching. And maybe it's the sticky slowness of a lazy morning, or maybe I'm just tired of pretending all the time, but I chase his touch and rock back into him once, his sharp inhale answering against the shell of my ear.

It's still between us, nothing but birdsong and the pounding of my heart. He doesn't move at all except for fingers gripping and releasing at my hip, his pinky slipping half an inch down beneath the hem of my sleep shorts. It's an innocent touch, all things considered, just his finger brushing the bare skin at my hip bone, but it feels like another step forward in this strange dance we're choreographing together. I feel that touch in the hollow of my throat, in the tips of my breasts. A silent conversation, his body asking, *Is this all right?* I lean my head back into his shoulder. He tightens his grip and uses the leverage to pull my hips back into the cradle of his, more insistent this time. *What about this?*

It's a slow rhythm, his body rocking forward, mine curling back. It's a bit like being out on the bay in one of those little dinghy boats we sometimes rent in the summer, a rise and fall with every whispered exhale. It's gentle, searching, and the heat in my belly grows and spreads until my breathing shallows out, a single bead of sweat rolling down between my breasts. He nudges harder, hips rolling, and I hold on to his wrist, urge his palm up until his hand is pressed flat just beneath the swell of my breast. I want him to move that last bit himself, cup me in his hands until it's nothing but bare skin. It's a delicious tease, all movement and no friction, and it's creating an aching wetness between my thighs. His thumb smooths up, tracing once along the bottom curve of my breast. We both groan.

"Luka," I stutter. I want to ask what we're doing. I want to ask for more. He makes a noise deep in his throat at the sound of his name, half groan and half growl. He pushes into me harder for a perfect moment, body heavy against mine. "Luka, could you—"

My words break the spell between us, a shiver of awareness rolling from his body to mine as our rhythm falters and slows. I swear I can feel the blood rushing under my skin, pulsing hot in the places I want him the most.

"I'll do whatever you want, Stella," he says, voice caught on the rasp of his breath, forehead against the back of my neck. His skin is flushed hot, slightly sticky with sweat. Suddenly my bedroom is an inferno. I hear him swallow. "We don't—we don't have to talk about it if you don't want to."

Something about the way his voice splinters around the edges, the tremble in his hand that he tries to hide—it doesn't feel right. I twist in his arms and get distracted by the sight of him. Pink cheeks, dark eyes, a single lock of hair plastered to his forehead, bottom lip red from where his teeth were holding it. He looks like he was dropped into the washing machine and set to heavy cycle.

I brush my toes to the top of his foot beneath the blankets. "What do you mean?"

Does he think I want to stop?

Oh god.

Does he want to stop?

His hands fight to hold me close as I try to pull myself to the opposite side of the bed, his hand gripping at my hip, still tucked beneath my shirt. "Stop, no." He pulls my wrist to his mouth and drops a quick kiss on my pulse point. It sends another lick of heat curling up my spine, and I shiver. If he notices, he has the decency not to say anything about it. "No, I just meant— if you wanted to stop. We could stop and—" He swallows. "We don't have to talk about it."

I absolutely do not want to stop. He's watching me so carefully that it's like I've spoken the words aloud. His entire frame softens, the fingers around my wrist spreading out, thumb stroking the center of my palm. One dark eyebrow arches high on his forehead. He looks like sugar and spice and everything not so nice, sleep rumpled and flushed in my bed.

I've had dreams that started and ended exactly like this.

"Or . . ." he says, and leaves it at that.

I shuffle closer. "Or what?"

The hand that's been tracing patterns on the bare skin of my hip slips from beneath my shirt and finds my chin instead. His thumb drags lightly over my bottom lip, back and forth. "Or we could try something."

"What something?"

I wish my voice didn't sound so breathy, that it wasn't so obvious I want his touch everywhere.

He licks at his bottom lip, eyes mapping the curve of my jaw, the tangle of my hair twisted like a crooked halo against my pillow.

Whatever hesitation he had is gone now, a thoughtful intention in the way he curls a lock of my hair around his finger.

"I could see how much it takes. The sounds you make," he says, voice low and intimate, a grit to it I've never heard before. His bedroom voice, I think faintly. Half of his mouth curls up in a wicked grin. His brown eyes are burnished with gold—molten and warm. "If you're quiet or loud."

I swallow hard and squeeze my legs together. I want that. I want that very much.

"Why?" I ask. His answer is important.

"Because I really fucking want to," he releases on a breath.

His words settle like snowflakes against warm skin. A single shock of cold and then warm melting heat. A confession. I blink twice but don't give myself a second to think it through, to agonize over the consequences. I keep myself in the moment.

"Okay."

Luka twists his hand until our palms are pressed together, same as that day in the barn. I close my eyes in anticipation and listen to his body move beneath my sheets. He whispers a quiet "Okay" in response and drags his nose along my cheek, bumps it lightly against mine. I tip my chin up into him, the barest brush of lips, when a horn blares from my driveway.

Luka collapses against me with a groan, forehead at my collarbone. I card my fingers through his hair once, tugging lightly until he makes that sound again, a bit more strangled. Whatever awkwardness I should feel in the face of dry humping my best friend is strangely nonexistent. I feel nothing but a happy lightness fizzing in my chest, popping like champagne every time I feel the flutter of his eyelashes against my skin.

Maybe I'll settle into an anxiety tailspin later, but right now I'm reveling. I am floating on a cloud of flushed endorphins. I bet I could run seventeen miles in two minutes.

Another round of honking sounds from the front yard, this time to the general tune of "Jingle Bells." Luka angles himself up on one arm above me, lifting the corner edge of my curtain to look outside. One of his sweatshirt strings drags along my collarbone and pools in the hollow of my throat. I can feel him hard against my thigh. I swallow.

"Why is Beckett on his tractor with a family of cats draped over him?"

I grind the palms of my hands into my eyes and try to ignore the way Luka's hips are pinning me to the bed. My hazy morning happy bubble has officially been popped. "I'm supposed to watch them today." I had forgotten we agreed to that when we left the vet last night.

Luka peers down at me from his balanced position above me, his arms bracketing my head. If I turn my head slightly to the left, I could catch the delicate skin at his wrist with my teeth. His eyes slip from golden amber to rich melted chocolate like he knows what I'm thinking. We stare at each other, considering.

Another round of honking, this time something from the Trans-Siberian Orchestra. I didn't realize someone could be so musical with a compact utility machine.

Luka shakes his head with a rueful grin and looks back out the window. I can see it in his eyes. He wants to rip that horn off Beckett's tractor and do something creative with it. "Since when do you have cats?"

I don't. Beckett does. Or maybe it's a shared custody thing, I don't know. The details aren't very clear.

"They're raccoons," I mutter as Luka leverages himself off me, slipping from my bed and trudging down the hallway. He adjusts himself as he moves toward the door, and I flush hot, staring at the back of his sleep-mussed hair. I wait for the inevitable rise of regret. I hold myself still and close my eyes, breathe deep through my nose like I learned in those yoga videos Layla is always sending me links to.

But it never comes. There's simmering arousal, a liquid heat that plucks at my skin. A drumbeat of desire. And a giddy awareness, a tiny flame of hope.

That didn't feel like faking.

13

I CRAWL OUT of the bed with a groan and grab the oversized sweater hanging off the edge of my doorway. It's a miracle that Luka managed to ignore it and not fold it into submission and tuck it into the proper bureau drawer as soon as he entered the room. He'd have a heart attack if he checked my closet and saw the sheer amount of things stuffed in there.

I slip the cardigan over my shoulders on my way to the front porch, elbowing my way out the front door, the floorboards freezing cold under my bare feet. I hop up and down in place until Luka nudges an old pair of rain boots in my direction, the inside lined with thick flannel. I slip into them gratefully. Luka's boots are unlaced, a ferocious yawn opening his mouth wide as we both stare blearily into the late morning sun. I glance briefly down at the front of his sweatpants. He notices and gives me a rueful look.

"Like I'd walk onto your front porch with a boner," he grumbles.

"Morning."

I jump at Beckett's overly cheerful voice at the edge of the porch. I don't know how he infuses so much innuendo into a single word, but he manages, standing in front of his tractor with the cats perched atop him like he's their king. Prancer has claimed her usual spot in the curve between his neck and shoulder, the three kittens fighting over the front pocket of his flannel.

I squint and wrap my sweater tighter around me, crossing my arms over my chest. I wish I had grabbed a pair of pants too. The wind is cold against the backs of my knees. "Why are you serenading me with your tractor horn this morning?"

Beckett smirks at me, stomps up my steps, and hands Luka a kitten. "Didn't want to interrupt anything."

Comet gives Luka a curious look, tiny head tilted to the side, likely trying to figure out if he can be trusted or not. They stare at each other, brown eyes on gold, blinking in consideration. Luka's hair is wild from sleep, sticking in every direction. I wish I had the opportunity to sift my fingers through it, thread and pull and tug. Comet seems to be of the same mindset, because after a moment's consideration, she lets out a plaintive meow and scampers up his arm to curl atop his head.

I understand the impulse.

"You didn't want to interrupt anything, but you proceeded to work your way through an early nineties Christmas hits catalog via your horn."

Beckett shrugs and looks pointedly at my bare legs. "I didn't want to see anything."

I grumble. "Nothing to see." There would have been, maybe, if he had been twenty minutes later.

I shiver as I scoop a sleeping Cupid out of Beckett's shirt into the palm of my hand.

Only Luka's eyes move as he tries to get my attention, the rest of his body held unnaturally still due to the kitten using his hair as a nest. "I still don't understand where these cats came from."

I hold out my arms to Beckett for the rest of the little family. Prancer gives me the same distrustful look as yesterday, pulling her mouth back in a hiss. I actively resist doing the same. Instead, I shush her gently and attempt to extricate her from Beckett's grip, her claws holding on to his shirt for dear life.

"It's all right."

One of the babies, at least, has decided I'm worth trusting. Vixen walks herself up my arm from Beckett's pocket and sits primly on my shoulder, tail tickling at my ear. Cupid purrs into my hand, still asleep and unbothered by all of the commotion. Prancer, meanwhile, is shredding the front of Beckett's shirt in her anxiety. I curl my hand around her and try to pull. "Easy, you'll be back with your true love soon enough."

"They're the raccoons from the barn," Beckett explains to Luka, gentling my grip on Prancer and curling his large hands around her. He pulls her up and nuzzles her nose once with his, her grip releasing on his shirt with a tiny meow of farewell. It is sickeningly sweet, and I'm absurdly disappointed my phone is still sitting on my nightstand.

I just watched Beckett give a cat a goodbye kiss. I feel like we should put a plaque on this front porch. He watches me as I tuck Prancer into the crook of my elbow, the longing clear on his face. It's both comical and endearing. He shuffles his feet, rocking back on his heels once with his hands deep in his pockets. "I can pick them up tonight if you want?"

I tell myself to look solemn, to not make fun of the man for cat separation anxiety. "Do you want to?"

"It's nice to have the company."

I soften at that. It's hard to think of Beckett as anything other than stoic, but I recognize the shades of loneliness in him the same as me and Luka. It's another reason I'm grateful for this farm and the weird little family we've pieced together. We're all a bit less alone.

"Pick them up whenever you want. I'll be in the office."

He nods and heads back to his tractor, still rumbling in my driveway behind Luka's crossover. We watch him go, Prancer declaring her disgruntlement with her claws in my hair.

"Okay, but they're not raccoons, right? They're cats."

"Correct."

"Still so confused."

Luka reaches above his head for the dozing kitten and cradles her in his arms, following me into the house. I drift into my thoughts as I work to set the kittens up on a pile of old blankets in the corner, and Luka reheats the coffee, pulling down two mugs with winking Santa faces. Comet saunters her way over after she leaps out of Luka's arms, settling into her new blanket home with her family. They tuck themselves together in a happy pile of content meows, dozing in the sunlight painting patterns across my hardwood.

I suppose I should be more tangled up about what happened this morning, but the truth is simple enough. I want Luka. I've always wanted Luka. And this morning felt like just the type of indulgence everyone is always telling me I need.

Didn't Layla say I should enjoy my time with him? Didn't I do exactly that?

I glance over at him standing at the sink with his hand curled around a mug of coffee. He's been stirring with the same spoon for close to a minute now, the metal clinking against the ceramic every rotation around the cup. I watch as his lips turn down at the corners, and he shakes his head slightly, just once, like he's having an argument only he can hear.

"Should we—" I swallow around my hesitation and watch as Luka blinks back to himself. A jolt in his shoulders as he straightens. "Do you want to talk about this morning?"

He pauses and then sets the spoon in the sink, the split second of indecision lodging my heart firmly in my throat. I don't want him to hesitate with me. I never want to lose the ease between us.

He meets me in the living room, extending a hand to help me from my crouched position on the floor. There's no jolt of electricity when our skin touches, just the sweet, settling warmth I always feel. Like the first bite of pie after waiting for it to cool on the racks next to the oven, tart and delicious. Or clothes fresh out of the dryer in the middle of winter. Steady and sure. A familiar comfort.

He pulls his hand away and tucks it into the front of his sweatshirt, flipped back to the proper direction at some point this morning.

His knee shakes up and down, and he takes his hand out and runs it through his hair instead. He looks up at me from under his lashes, reluctant, and settles his hand on the back of his neck. "Uh, do you want to?"

"I think we should," I say quietly, dropping onto the cushion next to him. Another hesitation, and I tuck my feet under his thigh. His entire body collapses at the movement, shoulders curling in with relief, a sigh escaping from somewhere deep in his chest. His hand finds my ankle and wraps around it lightly, thumb over ring finger. It's the same way we've always fallen together on this couch, and there's a reassurance in that. He gives me a sheepish smile.

"I didn't—" He squeezes my leg once. "I didn't make you uncomfortable, did I?" When I don't answer right away, his hand squeezes harder at the back of his neck, knuckles turning white. "I didn't expect for that to—"

"No, I wasn't uncomfortable." The opposite, actually. "I just—" I think of how he moved against me, the way his bottom lip dragged against the skin at the back of my neck. I clear my throat and wrap my sweater tighter around my torso. "We haven't done that before."

We've hugged. We've cuddled. We've twisted ourselves around each other on the couch watching movies. But we've never panted into each other's skin. Moved together to chase friction and heat and wanting.

"No, we have not," he says, a little bit shy. He finally releases his neck and smiles into his coffee. I like this version of him, almost as much as I like the version of him that sits with his legs spread wide in my rocking chair, saying the word *fucking*. "Was it weird?"

I've been waiting all morning to feel the awkwardness, the panic. To feel weird about my best friend whispering into my ear about the noises I make. But I've felt only the same bubbly feeling of contentment I've felt since he kissed me in the barn. I don't know, maybe I'll have a breakdown about it later, but right now, I feel—I feel okay. Good.

"It's weird that it wasn't weird, I think. Does that make sense?"

He straightens a bit at that. "That makes sense," he offers. "We've been friends forever, and that was—" A knowing smile hovers on his lips, and I practically feel the drag of his gaze over the hollow of my throat. "I was dreaming of you, and when I woke up, you were warm and soft, and . . . I guess I couldn't resist." One finger strokes against my ankle bone. "That's been a temptation for a while."

I blink at him. "What has?"

"Well, I mean, not specifically grinding against you in bed," he says quickly, and then pauses, tilting his head back and forth in consideration. "Actually, I guess, yeah. Specifically grinding against you in bed." He gives me a cheeky smile, color rising in his cheeks. I pinch at his ribs.

"Be serious, please."

"I am being serious." He laughs, pulling himself out of pinching distance. He comes right back to me, though, when I settle into the couch and reach for the kittens, stroking their tiny heads with my knuckles.

"I think—" He shifts in his seat, places his coffee on the table, and grips my ankles, maneuvering my legs so they're tucked at his side. "This social media person arrives Monday, right? And she's here for a week?" He rests his chin on my knees.

I nod.

"A recap, then. We don't feel weird about this morning. And it's weird not to feel weird. But it's a good weird?"

I nod again and he smiles, a dip of sunlight catching in his hair. I glare at it, half expecting a family of bluebirds to fly in through the crack in the window and settle on his shoulders.

"Okay, so how about this. We're supposed to be pretending anyway. What if we use this week as a trial period? For me and you. See how it goes."

"A trial period?"

"Yes."

"See how it goes?"

"Are you just going to repeat back what I say to you?"

I rub my thumb into my temple. "I think I need you to explain it."

"Okay, so"—he narrows his eyes and tilts his head—"like how we're acting in public. What if we tried that when we were alone, too? Take this morning as an example. We wanted to try it, so we did. And we're still okay. I think— I think if it feels right, we should follow it."

"Meaning?"

"Meaning if we're here, and I want to press you into the counter-top and see what you taste like, then I can try that." My stomach swoops low. He nuzzles my knee. "If you want."

"Is that what you want?"

"Obviously."

It is not obvious to me.

"Like a friends-with-benefits situation?" I don't like the idea of that.

He shakes his head, making a sour face. It reassures me. "No. I think—I think we both feel the tension between us, yeah?"

I nod. I can't believe I'm admitting that I've thought about him like that, about us like that.

"Then this will just be, I don't know, a week of actual dating and all that entails. We don't have to turn it off when we're alone."

I consider it. I'm not sure how I feel about a seven-day-guarantee approach to the most important relationship in my life. "And we'll still be friends? No matter what?"

He nods firmly. "No matter what."

"Do you promise me?"

I need a promise. In fact, I'd prefer a legally binding document with our names signed in blood at the bottom. I know Alex at the bookstore notarizes documents from time to time. I wonder if he'd be willing to press a seal to something written on the back of a take-out menu. This feels like an oversimplification of a complicated addition to an irreplaceable relationship. I've watched enough romantic comedies to know this is probably going to end badly for one of us, and my money is on me.

Luka tugs at my bottom lip with his thumb until I release it, tracing the indents left from my teeth. He is earnest, open, and I'm grateful that he seems to be taking this as seriously as I am.

"I promise you, Stella. Cross my heart." He makes a little *x* over his chest. "This is as low pressure as it gets. No expectations. We don't have to do anything we don't want to do."

That's the problem. I can't think of many things I don't want to do with Luka, and I'm not so sure indulging in a week before cutting myself off forever sounds like a good plan. I once tried to give up caffeine cold turkey. Layla found me shivering in my office in the middle of summer, chewing frantically on sticks of gum. I don't know if they make gum strong enough for Luka withdrawal.

"Right at this moment though, you know what feels right?" He leans forward until the tip of his nose drags against my cheek, and my heart leaps to my throat, that same delicious tension from earlier this morning pooling low in my belly when his hands drag up my shins, over the outside of my thighs. He lingers there with his palms cupping my bare skin, fingertips just barely brushing under the hem of my shorts. I can think of plenty of things that would feel good right now, starting with me pressed out flat against this couch.

Luka smiles at me, one side of his mouth hitching up, then the other. I stare at the pattern of freckles just under his left eye. "Omelets with bacon," he whispers.

❧ · ☙

WE EAT OUR omelets at the table like civilized human beings, a respectable 2.5 feet of solid barn wood table between us. Despite our decision on this new aspect of our relationship, there is no more lingering in each other's space. There is no kissing or touching or even heated glances. There's just me and Luka, a half-empty carton of almost expired orange juice, a stack of crispy bacon, breakfast potatoes, and his fork on my plate every other bite, trying to steal my cheese.

"I don't understand why you don't just put cheese in your omelet." I pull my plate out of his reach again and grab a slice of his bacon for good measure. He's driving me nuts.

"I don't like cheese in my omelet."

His wandering fork says differently. He reaches for the orange juice and gives it a good shake before topping off my glass and his. He looks more rested now, the faint circles under his eyes gone. The restorative properties of dry humping, I guess. He catches me staring at him.

"What?"

"Why did you leave the city so early?" I fork another bite of egg into my mouth. I don't know how he manages to get the bacon so crispy once it's inside the omelet. Witchcraft, probably.

He shrugs but looks away from me, frowning at his egg whites and spinach. Eyes full of longing slide over to my plate. Eggs with cheddar and bacon and Old Bay. I tug it closer to my side of the table. If he wanted a delicious omelet, he should have made one for himself instead of the health prescription he has loaded in front of him.

"Wanted to," he mumbles. Pink touches the tips of his ears. "I missed—I missed home, and I couldn't sleep, so I just drove back."

I don't like the idea of Luka not being able to sleep. I frown. "Does your mom know you're back?"

He nods toward the coffee machine. "Where do you think I got that from?"

"You stole your mom's coffee?"

"No, she had it sitting out with a bright blue sticky note that said, 'For Stella,' along with some creative threats in Italian if I took any liberties with your coffee." He leans back in the chair and hooks his arm around the back of it, feet kicked wide. It shouldn't look so indecent. All he's doing is sitting in my kitchen chair. But the sheer amount of space he takes up with his body and remembering how much space he took up in my bed—it has me shifting in my chair. "I saw it and figured I'd just come over. Crash on your couch."

"I'm glad you didn't."

One dark eyebrow jumps on his forehead. "Crash on your couch?"

I nod and he smiles. He looks down at the tabletop and then back up to me, bashful with a touch of heat. "Yeah, me too."

We settle back into silence as I think through my list of what needs to be done today. One of the kittens is investigating the orange juice, another weaving through the salt and pepper shakers. Prancer and Vixen haven't moved from their cozy spot by the window, bathed in a halo of sunshine. I'll return them to Beck tonight, and it's likely he won't volunteer to ever bring them back. I guess our shared custody agreement is officially over.

Tomorrow is Thanksgiving, and the following day our official holiday season is open. We've had some customers here and there, mainly people from town visiting Layla for their sugar fix. But we've had a couple of people come for trees too. One family in particular, with a beleaguered-looking dad and two overexcited preteens hopping up and down in their matching winter coats. They had declared it Christmas at the start of November, apparently, and were tired of waiting for their tree.

"I don't think I'm going to stay in New York much longer," Luka says. He partners that bombshell statement with a sip of his orange juice and a crunch of bacon. Comet skitters away from the condiments and hurries back to her pallet of blankets and sunshine. He shrugs a little bit. "I'm not really happy there."

I blink at him and think through some of our recent conversations. Didn't he spend forty-five minutes the other day explaining the superiority of good public transit? I'm pretty sure he composed a poem about that halal chicken cart in front of his apartment.

Stupidly, that's what I fixate on. "I thought you liked your street chicken."

He ignores me. "There's a start-up in Delaware that's been trying to recruit me. They're small, and it's really different from what I'm doing now. Less client-facing stuff, but I'd be closer. And I could—I could work remotely more."

Luka in Delaware. That's only—I can drive to the Delaware border in twenty minutes. There's even a fish taco stand on the way if I head toward the coast and take the scenic route. We could meet at the beach on summer mornings and have coffee with our toes in the sand. I tamp down the rush of excitement and try to channel the part of me that's supposed to be an impartial best friend, a sounding board for big decisions like this.

"Is that what you want to do?"

As far as I know, New York has always been his plan. Working at a big marketing agency, leading the data team—it's always seemed like something he's happy doing. He scratches at the back of his head and meticulously extricates a piece of spinach from his omelet with the tip of his fork. He gives it a look like it's insulted his mother. "I'd be happy being closer. I don't know. I don't think the city is for me anymore. It feels too big. And my mom says she's tired of taking the bus up for visits."

She has never once taken the bus. Luka always books her a ticket on the fancy Acela train that runs up and down the coast, and she's delivered to New York in less than two hours, tipsy off mini bottles of cheap wine. She says the train reminds her of Italy, but instead of the rolling golden hills of Tuscany vineyards outside her window, she's forced to look at a wasteland of capitalism.

"But would you be happy? In Delaware?"

The tension slips from his shoulders, and his hand loosens its grip on his hair. He gives me a look, a half smile curled across his lips. There's a secret there, hidden in the lines of his face. "I think I would, yeah."

I can't help my grin. It spills out of me like the sunshine making my kitchen glow. I let myself indulge in the fantasy of it for a moment, the possibility of Luka close by. "You know there's a—"

"Fish taco stand, yeah." His fork finds my omelet again, but this time I let him. I'm feeling magnanimous. "It's not street chicken, but I think I'll manage."

I push my plate in front of him and let him have at it. All I wanted was the bacon anyway. I pluck the rest of his from his abandoned plate. "While we're on the topic of living arrangements, we should probably figure out this week."

He doesn't look up from where he's shoveling food in his face. "I'm supposed to bring you to Thanksgiving tomorrow by any means necessary," he says around a mouthful of potato. "My mother specifically said that she doesn't care if you're unconscious at the table, just that you wake up in time for pie."

"That's . . . violent, but not what I was talking about."

"Oh." He sits up and drags his thumb across his bottom lip, catching a bit of ketchup before popping it in his mouth and licking it off. I am sufficiently distracted. "What are we talking about, then?"

"Evelyn thinks we own this place together. If you're staying at your mom's while you're here, she'll probably think that's weird."

Luka nods and spears a leftover breakfast potato. "Then I'm glad I brought the good coffee, roomie."

14

THANKSGIVING AT LUKA'S house is a perfect type of chaos. We let ourselves in the front door to a chorus of shrieking and laughter from the kitchen, armed with enough bottles of red wine to take down a small militia. I have one in each of my hands and another tucked under my arm, a fourth in my bag next to the flask of whiskey Luka snuck in just before we left. Luka is laden with bouquets for his mom, grandmother, and each of his aunts, a veritable walking greenhouse. He pauses in the hallway, Italian and English and David Bowie drifting in from the kitchen. I hear his aunt Gianna yell something about stuffing without oysters, and Luka winces.

"I'm having some second thoughts," he mutters just as all the women begin to cackle, his mom yelling something in Italian. Luka's ears turn bright red. "Quick, I think we can turn around before anyone notices us."

I go to rub his shoulder with my hand, but I'm still holding the bottle of wine. I tap it against him in what I hope is a comforting gesture. He frowns down at me. "It'll be fine. This isn't the first time I've been around your family."

But it is the first time I've been around them when they think I'm dating Luka. Whatever goodwill I've built up over the years disappears as soon as I step foot in the kitchen, five sets of startling gray eyes narrowed in on me. This must be what it feels like to be trapped behind enemy lines. I wave with a wine bottle and Aunt Eva shuffles over.

"Are you late because you were having sex?" She grabs the bottle of wine out of my hand and nods at the label. I hear Luka mutter a creative string of curse words behind me. "Just because you two are humping like bunnies now doesn't mean you can just show up late to things."

A bouquet of mums is thrust between us, Luka's eyebrows slanted low. "We're twenty minutes early, Aunt Eva."

She reaches up and pinches both of his cheeks, following with kisses. "I'll be the judge of that, *Cucciolo*. You"—she points to me and then points to an empty place at the counter where there looks to be about seventy-six pounds of potatoes—"peel."

"She's a guest, Aunt Eva."

"She is not a guest. She is family and she peels potatoes."

I go to peel the potatoes. After Luka makes his round of greetings, cheeks a bright red from being pinched incessantly, he's put to work as well, arranging and rearranging the table settings under the careful direction of his mother. Luka's grandmother comes to me at the sink, peeler in hand. She grabs a potato and makes quick work of it, nodding in the direction of the dining room as Luka moves the gravy boat half an inch to the left, jaw clenched.

"It is tradition to make him flustered." She winks at me. Poor Luka, the only son for all these women to torment. His aunts are intentionally and somewhat notoriously single. He says growing up, the little Italian town they lived in called them *lupi che ululano*. The women wolves who howl. "We like to guess how long it will take for him to start begging mercy from *San Pietro*."

It takes another twenty minutes and an argument half in English and half in Italian about what should go on top of the sweet potatoes. He throws the bag of marshmallows clutched in his hand at the pantry in exasperation and stomps into the basement, hissing something about folding chairs. I notice he makes a stop at my purse first, a flash of silver in his hand. As soon as he's gone, all the women start to laugh. There's an exchange of money, and then Carina is sweeping over to me with mischief in her eyes, a kiss pressed to both of my cheeks.

"We are so happy to have you here, Stella."

"I'm happy to be here." I smile.

In fact, as the evening goes on and Luka emerges from the depths of the basement with two folding chairs under his arm and whiskey on his breath, I'm pretty upset with myself for saying no to this for years. Aunt Sofia pulls out an album of Luka baby pictures during appetizers, her face positively alight with glee. I take it from her with greedy hands and get a glimpse of a sailor suit before Luka slams it shut again, taking it and tossing it on top of the fridge. It's funny that he thinks I'm not above climbing up there.

He doesn't bother hiding his flask after that.

It's cozy and silly and sweet and a perfect holiday with family. Luka grabs my hand halfway through dinner and twines our fingers together, thumb brushing over my knuckles. I don't know if it's for the benefit of his aunts, or if this is one of those things that feels right, but I lean into it, resting my shoulder against his and scooping a bite of pie off his plate. By the time we're leaving, I am stuffed to the brim with good food and even better company, my chest light for the first time in months. Apparently, a dinner with the full Peters-Russo family is a suitable distraction from a predominant fear of failure and abandonment.

I stand by the door, once again eyeballing a tower of leftovers that seems to stretch from floor to ceiling. This Tupperware is different, more modern, and I wonder if Luka's mom picked it up after seeing the state of my fridge last week. I still haven't managed to work my way through the dishes she brought over. I am out of tiramisu though. That went quickly once Luka found its hiding place wedged behind the spinach.

She adds another small dish on top as Luka pulls on his coat by the door. I have no idea what I'm going to do with all this food. "He likes cranberry with croissants in the morning," she tells me with a wink.

Luka flushes pink for probably the hundredth time this evening. I'm delighted. "*Grazie*, Mama." He kisses both her cheeks and then pulls her tight against his chest. He whispers something in her ear, something I can't hear, and she closes her eyes tight, rocking into him. When her eyes blink open again, they're shining with tears but smiling, and I avert my gaze to the baseboards.

"When are you visiting again?" she demands as he pulls open the door, a rush of cold air sweeping into the hallway.

"Can I leave before you ask?"

She pinches her mouth shut and watches pointedly as he takes a step onto the porch. He holds a hand out for me, taking half the Tupperware out of my arms. As soon as we're over the threshold, she asks again. "And when will that be, Luka?"

I laugh. "How about you come to the farm this week? We're having a guest, and I'm sure she'd love to meet you."

Luka stares at me with a comically distraught face. *Mistake*, his eyes say, even as his mom claps her hands together and jumps in place. He just rolls his eyes and holds back a smile.

That's all right. I'm smiling enough for the both of us.

"Oh, that's right! You're in that contest. The kids have been talking about it all week. There was some sort of sign-up sheet going around. They've been assigning shifts. Mr. Holloway confiscated it, thinking it was for the drugs"—Luka mouths *the drugs* behind her—"but handed it off to the PTA when he realized what it was. The adults decided to sign up too."

I'm confused. "Sign up for what?"

"For visiting," she says. She leans on the open doorway with her arms crossed over her chest. "We can't have an empty farm for you while your fancy TokTok lady is in town. I think you'll have a steady stream of visitors through the holiday season, the last I saw of it. Mabel is even hanging the Christmas decorations so we all look our best for you."

I rapidly blink against the warm press of tears, Luka's hand gentle at the small of my back. "Everyone—" I clear my throat. "They're doing all of that for me?"

"I have my suspicions at Cindy Croswell signing up for a visit every day, of course, but yes." She curls her fingers around the edge of the door, light and warmth and laughter spilling out onto the porch. "Don't you know yet, Stella? This is your home. What is it—I know it in Italian, but—*chi si volta, e chi si gira, sempre a casa va finire.*"

Luka's hand slips up my spine and curls over my shoulder. "No matter where you go, you will always end up at home."

"Yes." She snaps her fingers at her son. "And with home comes family."

⊰ ⊱

"HOW CAN YOU eat right now?"

Luka is stretched out across my couch, thick sweater bunched slightly around his middle, the bottom half of his button-down exposed. I got a glimpse earlier at his collar, but now I can see the pattern better. He has little turkey drumsticks dancing all over his shirt, tucked underneath a snug green knit. He forks another mouthful of pie out of the tin.

"I don't know." He groans. "I have no self-control."

I feel like I'm the one with no self-control as I watch the way firelight dances over his skin. His mouth curls around the fork, a bit of whipped cream clinging to his top lip. I want to crawl on top of him, tuck my thighs against his hips, and lick it off.

He points at me with his fork. "Your thoughts are written all over your face."

I sink farther in the cozy armchair by the window. "Are not."

"You're lusting after pie."

I huff a laugh. I feel heavy with wine and want. "Am not."

Luka levels me with a look and then carefully sets the pie tin on the coffee table, relaxing back against the couch, body loose angles. "Stella"—he swallows once, my name just as sweet on his tongue as that pumpkin pie—"you can't say things like that."

"Why not?"

"Because." His gaze is dark in the flickering light from the fireplace. "Because it makes me want to kiss you, and you're all the way over there."

He rolls his head against the couch cushion to look at me, his hand resting on his belly. I wish I were resting right there. Awareness snaps between us, a thin string of desire pulling tight.

"I know we said we'd follow what's right," he says in a low voice. His eyes linger on my lips, captivated. Mine drift over the straight line of his jaw, the length of his throat, the jut of his collarbones through the crooked collar of his ridiculous shirt. I don't think I've ever felt such anticipation before, the curl of it heavy in my chest. "But you've gotta go first. I don't want to feel like I'm pressuring you into anything."

"That's not fair." I slip my legs out from where they're tucked under me and place my mug of tea on the end table. Luka watches me, hands shifting to spread his arms wide against the back of the couch. I rise and take a step closer, and his knees tip open in invitation. "I don't want to pressure you either."

"How about this." He grits his teeth, impatient, hands reaching out to me as soon as my feet step between his open thighs, fingers wrapping low around my hips. He tugs once, my left knee falling to the worn leather at his side. He tugs again, not satisfied until I'm balanced above him. He hums under his breath, contentment in the lazy slouch of his body, my thighs neatly bracketing his hips. Just how I wanted. "How about we pressure each other?"

I smile and rest my hands on his shoulders. "That sounds like a line."

His nose scrunches, an adorable furrow between his brow. "If it is, it's a bad one."

"I don't know, it seems to have worked out for you."

I ignore the brief flash of warning in the back of my mind, the bright neon sign that's blinking *Wait, slow down*. It's hard to think about the consequences when his palm is warm on the small of my back, dragging up my spine. He tangles his hand lightly in my hair and tugs gently, just once, a flash of something decadent in amber eyes when I make a small noise in the back of my throat. He likes that noise, I can tell. He wants to hear it again.

I fix the collar of his shirt until it's straight, my thumb brushing the bare skin at the hollow of his throat. He has freckles here too, lighter than the ones on his face. I drift my fingertips across a cluster of them at his collarbone, tracing a line to the center of his chest. He shivers against me.

"Still weird that it's not weird," I say, and he hums low in his chest, his body relaxing farther into the couch as I settle more fully on top of him.

It's a delight to touch him like this. I watch him watching me, the hand in my hair uncurling from a fist to a gentle stroke, strands slipping through his fingers. He cups the back of my head and then lifts again, this time my curls cascading around my shoulders and surrounding us both in a thick curtain of black. A smile lights up his face.

"Your hair is soft too," he whispers.

I feel soft. Soft and relaxed and languid in his hold, our chests brushing together with every inhale. I changed into an oversized sweater and an old pair of his sweatpants as soon as we got home, and I want him to take advantage. Dip his hand under the hem and find out if I'm soft everywhere.

But he doesn't. One hand stays in my hair and the other stays at my hip as he tips his chin up, nudging my nose with his until I slip my hand to the back of his neck and brush our lips together.

"I've been thinking about kissing you all week," I feel him say against my lips.

That's nice. I've been thinking about kissing him since I was twenty-three.

The first time we kissed, it was gentle. Careful. He held my hand in his and curled around my body and kissed me like I was made of glass.

I do not extend the same courtesy.

I lean forward and catch his mouth with mine, my teeth grazing his bottom lip. I move my hand from the back of his neck to his jaw, guiding his mouth open with mine. He grunts like he's taken a blow, the wind knocked out of his lungs. I can feel the question in the tense line of his body, the *Should I* that I lick off the tip of his tongue. He makes another pained noise, and then his body melts, his hands grab, and Luka shows me just how much he was holding back when he kissed me in the barn.

He's insistent, impatient—a little bit greedy. It's like he wants everything I have to give all at once. He chases my kiss, his thumb at my chin tipping my mouth open until everything slows into a wet slide of heat. He tastes like cinnamon and the whiskey he kept stealing sips of all night, and I let myself sink into the languid pull of it. Because now it feels like I'm the one that's been punched in the chest, my heartbeat loud in my ears. I can feel my pulse everywhere. In the small of my wrists, the base of my spine, the place between my thighs where I'm spread over him. The hand at my hip traces down to curve over my ass, pressing me forward, tucking me close. It's like that morning in my bedroom, except better, because I can feel him now, hard and ready. The button of his jeans digs into my belly as I move closer and grind down a little, and he groans around my tongue—my favorite taste yet.

He breaks away from my mouth and drags biting kisses over my jaw to the hollow just behind my ear. I shiver and thread my fingers through his hair, rocking over his lap. He huffs a laugh, and I tug until I can see his face, the dancing flames from the fireplace casting him half in shadow, half in light. He smiles up at me and drops a kiss where my sweater has slouched down over one shoulder. He considers the stretch of bare skin and then tugs the sweater down a little more, kissing the soft skin just above my bra. He sighs and leans his forehead there, his muttered curse a benediction.

"I think I should sleep on the couch tonight."

I hum and scratch my nails at his scalp. His whole body practically vibrates, and he nips at my chest where his mouth rests. I hope it leaves a mark.

"It'll be a tight fit, but I think we can make it work."

He groans and shakes his head, hips thrusting the slightest bit beneath me. I want to chase the friction until the winding pressure within me builds and builds and snaps. I want panting breaths and tension stretched like taffy until I break. I want it on this couch. I want it in the hallway. I want it spread out on my dining room table.

"I wanna take my time," he says, face somewhere in my sweater. "I wanna do this right."

He tilts his head back to rest his chin against me, dark brown eyes hot on mine. "When did you get so tempting?"

His arms wrap fully around me, holding me close but also keeping me from moving against him. I recognize the moment has passed. Slow is probably a good thing when it comes to us, but right now it feels like my heart is ready to beat right out of my chest.

"I used to have control over myself," he mutters, arms flexing around me.

I know the feeling.

15

I WAKE UP in the middle of the night with a body pinning me to the bed, Luka's breathing steady and even against my neck. He's always been a cuddler, shifting and rolling and moving in his sleep until he's wrapped around me. The first time we ever shared a sleeping space, we were camping together at the beach, the edges of the tent shaking in the heavy winds off the water, our sleeping bags in parallel, a lantern hanging in the corner. He had sheepishly tried to make a little wall between us with sweatshirts and a bag of tortilla chips, mumbling something about chronic cuddling. I had thought he was joking until I woke up with Luka's thigh across my hips, his arms twisted around my torso, and the bag of tortilla chips wedged under my back.

I scratch my nails lightly down his forearm and smile when he nuzzles closer. It's nice to have him here. It's nice to wake up with him next to me.

Or on top of me.

I shift and yawn and peer at the clock on the corner of my dresser, Luka's left arm wrapping tighter around my middle with the motion. It takes me a second to understand why I'm awake, and then I hear it again, a metallic *ping* from my phone. I reach for it, and Luka grunts, turning onto his side and burrowing under one of the seven thousand pillows against my headboard.

Every man I have ever dated has complained about the number of pillows I keep on my bed. But not Luka. Tonight before he collapsed into an exhausted heap, he muttered a quiet "Fuck yeah" before smothering himself with a cozy chenille. He was asleep in less than thirty seconds.

I wince at the bright screen of my phone in my dark room, navigating to the camera app. The alarm system has gone off a couple of times in the middle of the night since I installed it. Once it was a family of deer grazing at the dried-out corn stalks stacked by the tractors. Another time it was Beckett, doing whatever it is he does out in the fields before the sun rises. The last time it was an inquisitive robin, nothing but a flash of her feathers as she pecked at the top of the camera, the whole thing shaking.

So I don't know what I'm anticipating when I swipe to open the notification about movement on camera three, but it's certainly not a hooded figure throwing rocks.

Awareness has me jolting up in bed, watching as the person abandons the rocks and looks at the ground by their feet for something else instead. I watch with my heart hammering as they find something long and thin—a rake, it looks like, left out of the barn—and reach up. The picture jolts, swims, and then goes dark.

"Luka." I toss my phone and practically fall out of bed, looking for my sweatpants. They're folded neatly over my desk chair. I try to hop into them, my hands shaking too badly for me to get a good grip on the waistband. "Luka, wake up."

He groans and shimmies farther down into my mountain of pillows. "I can't take you to get tacos right now, La. M' sleeping."

I find my left boot half hidden under my bed and jump on one foot as I attempt to pull it on. "There's someone outside."

That has Luka sitting up, blinking blearily at me, hair sticking up in wild disarray. "What?"

"The cameras," I explain. "Someone just knocked one out with a rake."

He throws back my comforter, feet finding the hardwood. "Just now?"

"Yeah." I reach for my phone, dark on my bedspread. I don't know why; there's no use in showing him a disconnected camera. "The notification from the camera woke me up and I saw someone."

He pulls his sweatshirt over his head and then looks pointedly at where I'm still trying to jam my foot into a boot. "And you were going to, what, go outside and strike up a friendly conversation?"

I frown. "Obviously I have to go out there and see what's going on."

He scratches at the back of his head roughly, making his hair stick up even worse. It would be cute if I could focus for half a second. "No. Not *obviously*. Stay here and call Beckett," he tells me. He takes a step toward the hallway and then turns back to me. "Call Beckett, and then call Dane."

I trail after him out of my bedroom. "I'm going with you."

"You are not."

I follow him to the entryway and grab my coat before he can shove it out of my reach in the closet. I stuff my arms into the sleeves, defiant, and grab a hat, pulling it down over my tangled curls. It feels like I'm arming myself for battle. Luka frowns at me with a heavy sigh, quickly pulling on his jacket.

"Do you still have that softball bat?"

I nod. "What are you going to do with it?"

"Hopefully nothing."

I call Beckett when Luka is half buried in my hall closet, emerging with the softball bat I used for maybe three years when I decided I was going to make it to the Junior League Softball World Series. It's bright pink with a tie-dye hand grip, and I refuse to get rid of it because my mom worked overtime for a month to buy me that thing. I love it. I hit exactly zero home runs with that bad boy.

Needless to say, I did not make it to the Junior League Softball World Series.

Luka hefts it over his shoulder and peeks out my front door like the boogeyman himself is about to jump from behind a fence post.

He tries to close me in, but I hustle after him, keeping my steps light down the front stairs. Beckett answers on the third ring.

"Why are you calling me at—"

"There's someone on the farm," I rush out, keeping my voice low just in case. Just in case what, I have no idea.

Luka gestures at me, a wordless question. *Where?* I point toward the Santa barn, sitting large and ominous on the other side of the ice-skating rink we had installed three days ago. The farm looks different in the middle of the night, the moon blocked out by a heavy cover of clouds, a breeze whispering through the trees. Everything sounds like footsteps, and I feel like our hooded intruder is going to come tearing out at us at any second.

I grip Luka's arm. "Someone knocked out the barn camera."

"Are you alone?" Beckett asks. There's rummaging in the background, a string of creative curse words, and a crash.

"Luka is here. We're heading that way."

"I'll be right there."

Luka stays close to me as we round the rink, fists clenched tight around the colorful handle of the bat. He nods at my phone as I hang up. "Dane."

"You really think I need to call the police?"

The look he gives me is one part incredulous, another part unadulterated exasperation. "Dane," he says, through clenched teeth.

I doubt whoever knocked out the camera is a real threat. It's probably just one of the kids from the high school messing around. They were wearing a hoodie with a badger, for goodness sake.

I call Dane and he answers on the first ring.

"What's wrong?"

"Someone is on the farm," I repeat for what feels like the hundredth time. "My alarm went off, and it was someone knocking out the camera. It's disconnected now."

I stare hard into the dark, looking for any sort of movement. My eyes are playing tricks on me. Every twitching tree branch is someone's leg. The big banners that circle the rink a flash of a sweatshirt.

"Why are you whisperin'? Stella, I swear to god—" Another round of creative curse words, and these phone conversations are starting to get repetitive. "Are you outside right now?"

I run my bottom lip between my teeth. "Maybe."

"Go back inside."

"I'm with Luka."

"Then the both of you go back inside. Do not engage the trespasser on your property, Stella Bloom, or I will lock you up myself. The same goes for Luka." He exhales a breath like he's just run fifteen miles with a barrel strapped to his back. "Now go sit in your house, lock all the doors, and wait for me to get there. Do you understand?"

I glance over at Luka. We're almost at the barn now, the tall red siding within arm's reach. We hug close to the side, keeping to the shadows. Luka nods toward the disabled camera. "We'll check the locks on the barn real quick," he whispers. "Then go back."

"Do you understand, Stella?" I hear a car door slam and then the rumble of an engine.

"I understand," I say quickly, eager to get him off the phone. I understand why he wants me to do that, but I don't necessarily agree. "See you soon."

He starts to say something else, but I end the call, tucking my phone in my back pocket. Together, Luka and I creep toward the large sliding doors, both of my hands wrapped firmly around his arm. He's going to have ten tiny bruises on his bicep from my fingers. My heartbeat pounds through me, adrenaline making me shake. Luka stops abruptly next to me, and I almost stumble forward, preoccupied with looking at the bits of camera scattered on the ground. Luka steadies me and then points at the barn door.

It's open.

We stare at each other. Suddenly, Dane's instructions make a lot more sense. I shake my head and gesture back toward my house.

Luka frowns and points once at the ground and then nods his head forward, clear instructions for *Stay here while I go look*. Absolutely not. He is not going into the dark barn by himself with nothing but a baseball bat. I shake my head furiously. He rolls his eyes.

Fortunately, our standoff is interrupted by a figure strolling out of the barn.

I almost bite my tongue clean in two, a squeak of surprise as Luka forcefully drags me behind him. I wish we had never come out here and just waited for Dane like any other sane human being would have. Luka was right. What's my plan here? Ask him nicely to stop destroying my things?

The shadowed figure stills, clearly having spotted us. Luka raises the bat in front of us. I wish I had one of those plastic candy canes. If Luka is right and this is the same person who has been causing all my problems since we opened, I'd like to get in a whack or two.

"What're you guys doing?"

Luka drops the bat with a heaving sigh and bends at the waist, bracing himself on his knees. Tension releases me in a rush, leaving me lightheaded and pissed off. I pick up a piece of camera off the ground and lob it at Beckett. He smacks it away.

"What the hell are you doing sneaking around out here?"

"I was checking to see if the barn is locked. What are you two doing?" He squints at Luka, who is still recovering from a heart attack, bent in half. "Is that a pink bat?"

"It's rose gold," I snap. "Were the doors locked?"

Beckett nods. "No damage inside. Just the camera here."

"Someone jammed the door a week ago," Luka offers. "It wasn't closing all the way."

"Is that what that was?" I knew something was wrong with the damn thing, and I didn't think twice about it. "Do you think they're still here?" I look around us as Luka picks up the bat and straightens. I've just now noticed one of the kittens is in Beckett's front pocket. Vixen, by the looks of it. Maybe Comet.

"Do you still have everything on the switch?" Last year we connected all of the decorations to a single, digital switch. It makes it easier than Beckett and me walking all over the farm, unplugging more than a hundred extension cords. Beckett hilariously still refers to it as "the switch," like flicking on the light when you step into the garage.

"Good idea," whispers Luka.

I hand Beckett my phone. "What idea?"

The farm suddenly blazes to life around us, every single light blinking on at once. It's like that scene in *Christmas Vacation* when Chevy Chase pulls the extension cords over his head. I'm pretty sure you can see us from space right now. I blink against the sudden brightness and then see it, a flash of white and a knocked-over rake, the trees rustling in the entrance to the west pasture.

"There," I point, and Beckett hands me the kitten before tearing in that direction, Luka quick on his heels with that ridiculous bat held loosely in his left hand. I briefly consider going after them, but there's no way. Luka and Beckett both ran track in high school, and no one knows these fields better than Beckett. Good luck to whoever thinks they can outrun them.

I hold Comet/Vixen up to my face and give her nose a tiny kiss. She meows at me. "I know, sweetheart. Let's go back to the house and wait for Dane."

It's less intimidating to walk home with all of the lights on. Still, I'm careful to pay attention to my surroundings. I have no idea if this person was alone or not, and Luka took my bat with him. If Beckett is right and it's the twins wreaking havoc, it's likely one of them is still hiding close to the barn.

But my trip back to the cottage is uneventful. I sit down on the front steps of my little cottage and strain my ears, listening for any sound of Luka or Beckett or our trespassers. I chew on my lip and watch the lights sway back and forth, the pinprick of two headlights appearing at the entrance to the farm. Dane races down the dirt road like a bat out of hell, the crunch of gravel loud beneath his tires. He's out of his car door before the vehicle has even come to a complete stop, wearing his full uniform and with a fierce frown on his face. I wonder if he sleeps in his sheriff's badge.

"I told you to stay in the house."

I hold up the kitten in an effort to distract him and respectfully don't point out that I am sitting on the steps of my house.

Dane frowns and glances around the yard. "Where is Luka?"

I wince. "You're not going to like the answer."

He sighs and rolls his shoulders back. I've just aged him five years with one late-night call. "Where is he?"

"With Beckett."

"Are you being deliberately vague right now?" He tips the brim of his hat up with his knuckles and gives me the same look he gave me when I was nineteen and telling him I had no idea how that PBR can ended up in my hand. "Where is Beckett?"

I debate my options. Dane pinches the bridge of his nose, and I decide to be honest.

"They took off into the fields when we saw someone."

Dane sighs, a few choice words on the tip of his tongue before he swallows them down with obvious effort. "Was it when you lit it up?"

I nod. "Beckett's idea."

"It was a good idea. Woulda been a better idea had you waited for appropriate backup." He turns and looks over his shoulder as another set of headlights appears down the road. He jerks his thumb over his shoulder. "I called in Caleb. Because I understand the importance of protocol and support." Whew, shots fired. I'm pretty sure if Dane could get away with slapping me in handcuffs and stowing me in the back seat of his car for an indeterminate period of time, he would. He sets his fists to his hips as Caleb's cruiser rumbles to a stop next to his car. "Which direction did they run?"

"West pasture," I offer.

Dane turns on his heel.

"Wait a sec." I hop off the steps and stride over to him, wrapping both arms around his chest. I squeeze tight, Vixen/Comet meowing happily from her place smooshed between us. "Thank you for coming," I mutter into his sheriff's badge. "I'm sorry I didn't listen."

One hand briefly presses between my shoulder blades, his chin tapping at the top of my head. He sighs and I squeeze tighter. "Just glad you're safe," he rumbles. He pulls away from me and rounds the front of his car. Caleb is just climbing out of his, a little bit sleep-rumpled, his uniform shirt untucked and his deputy badge clipped upside down. "Stay here with Caleb. I'll go get the boys."

Caleb and Dane confer at his bumper. Dane points to me and then points at the house three times in rapid succession. It seems like he's just saying, *Keep her in the house, keep her in the house, keep her in the house*, over and over again, but Caleb nods like it's day one at the police academy, eager to take instruction.

Caleb is a good guy. We went to high school together here in Inglewild. I remember him as shy and a little bit awkward, tall and lanky with glasses too big for his face. He's certainly shed that image with age. He's downright handsome now, with dark brown eyes and a wide smile. A dimple that winks to life in his left cheek every time he laughs. Beautiful olive skin. His thin frame has filled out with muscle, and he keeps his dark hair cropped close to the sides and a little bit longer on top. It's sticking up a bit in the back right now, and I wonder if he's annoyed he had to come all the way out here in the middle of the night.

I heard Becky Gardener talking at the grocery store once about how it's a crying shame he hasn't dated seriously in all the time he's been deputy.

Dane climbs into his car and backs down the driveway and Caleb gives me a little wave.

"Hiya, Ms. Bloom." He nods to the kitten curled in the crook of my elbow while doing his best to hide a yawn. He shakes it off and tucks his hands into his pockets. "Evening, Ms. Kitten."

The kitten stretches in my arms and kneads her paws into my shoulder twice before resettling. Must be Comet, then. "You've known me for years, Caleb. I think *Stella* is fine." I smile at him, shivering a bit in my wool coat. He must be freezing in just his button-down. I jerk a nod back toward my house. "Come on inside. I'll put some coffee on while we wait."

It's hard not to worry. Even though I'm convinced it's a bored rotation of teenagers terrorizing the farm, I'm still nervous that Luka and Beckett are out there alone. I try to reassure myself that they're together, that Dane is on his way, but my heart is having trouble settling in my chest. Its unlikely caffeine will help, but I need to do something with my hands. Caleb follows me into the house and I gesture toward the table. My gaze drifts to the couch and I blush furiously, remembering how I straddled Luka on it just hours ago, his body warm and solid beneath me. How his hands traced under the hem of my sweater to the bare skin of my back, fingertips dragging until I shivered and rolled my hips against his hardness.

I clear my throat and deposit Comet on the little pillow fort of blankets I still have set up in the corner.

"Thanks for coming all the way out, Caleb. I appreciate the help."

He nods and lingers in the doorway of the kitchen, studying the collection of artwork, greeting cards, and photos I have pinned to the wall. He smiles at a picture of me and Layla, the two of us at a barbecue with our arms wrapped around each other, half collapsed in laughter. He straightens it with his pinky. "It's no trouble. Part of the job."

"Still"—I collect mugs out of the dishwasher while the coffeepot gets to work—"I imagine you don't get many late-night calls."

He finds a seat at the table and stretches out his long legs, palms pressed flat against the tabletop. His gaze keeps darting to the plate of baked goods in the middle of the kitchen island, a collection of different things Layla has been working on for the holiday season. "Not many," he agrees. "Though I feel like the high schoolers have been finding all sorts of mischief this year. Dane says Mercury must be in permanent retrograde at this point."

"Oh yeah? Anything interesting?"

He's looking at the peppermint bear claw with such naked longing I have to hide my smile in the collar of my sweater. "Just, ah—" He shakes himself out of his sugar-related fantasies. "Without naming names, we found a couple of kids skinny dipping in the fountain in the middle of town. Another pair of kids parked behind the café and were missing their shirts. Ms. Beatrice had something to say about that when she saw them on her security camera."

I laugh. "I'm sure she did."

He gives me a shy smile, cupping his hands together and sitting up straighter in the chair. "She was trying to put up WANTED posters in her shop, right behind the counter. I think she had them printed special. You know, those sandwich board posters? It took me almost two hours to convince her not to."

Now that he's mentioned it, I have seen Eliza Bowers and that Stillman kid working there on the weekends. I reach for the pot of coffee. "Is that how Ms. Beatrice is staffing the café now?"

"With blackmail and threats?" Caleb grins. "Yes, ma'am."

I snort and we lapse into silence. I peek out the window that looks out over the fields. Nothing but the usual: string lights over the expanse of dark trees winding to Beckett's house and over the foothills. I wish I had been able to put cameras all over the property. I'd be able to see what's going on out there.

"You've been having some trouble?"

I shrug. "Not much really. Nothing serious at least. This is the first time I've felt—" Afraid? Maybe. Concerned, I think, is more likely. Worried that someone is actively trying to hurt my business. "Well, I suppose this is the first time I've thought it's intentional."

"Dane said something about smashed pumpkins. Some broken fence posts?"

I pour two mugs of coffee and snag the plate of baked goods, meeting him at the table. His pretty eyes light up like I've just handed him a winning lottery ticket. He helps himself to the bear claw, and I choose a muffin for myself, picking at the top.

"That and some missing shipments, a couple of other odd things that don't make sense. It felt like a string of very bad luck, but now I don't know." I think of the trees in the south pasture that have gone rotten for no good reason. The flat tires on all the tractors three months ago. The broken barn door. "Luka and Beckett think it's all connected."

"You're not so sure?"

"I guess I don't know," I say, playing with the edge of the plastic wrap. It has little Christmas trees dotted all over it, a special order from a catering company in California. I bought about a hundred rolls for Layla last season. "Who would want to bring down a Christmas tree farm?"

"I suppose that's true," he muses. "Though if I've learned anything doing this job, it's that people always have a reason. Even if it's a strange one."

"You think there's a reason someone knocked out my camera?"

"I think it's likely that person didn't want you to see what they were planning on doing tonight. You didn't see anything odd or out of place?"

I shake my head. Just the broken camera. "Luka says the door to the barn was wedged open last week."

"Dane will figure out what's going on. Nothing gets past him," Caleb says and takes a monstrous bite out of his pastry, his face the picture of bliss. When he blinks open his eyes, he blushes a bit, color rising high on his cheeks.

"Layla makes the best stuff," he says bashfully around a mouthful of crumbs. He swallows and chases it with a sip of coffee. "I was pretty jealous when Dane came back to the station with a basket of goodies the other day."

"He didn't share?"

Caleb looks at me like I've got four heads and one of them just asked for a tissue. "You don't share Layla's bear claws."

I look pointedly at the half of a bear claw that's still clutched in his hand. He curls it closer to his chest. "I'll let her know you send your compliments."

At that, the blush on his cheeks intensifies to a bright fiery red. Interesting. He fidgets in his chair, crossing and uncrossing his legs beneath the table. "She's—ah—no problems over at the bakehouse?"

I smile down into my coffee cup, amused. "She found a window open when she came in about a month ago, but nothing was stolen or damaged. I think a bird flew in, but he found his way right out again when she unlocked the doors."

"Just like Snow White." He sighs and, oh boy, I think Caleb has a crush. It's pretty obvious as I watch him bounce his knee under the table, a question on the tip of his tongue. I let him sweat it out.

He manages to last about thirty seconds.

"Um, is she—" He forcibly stills his leg under the table. "Is she still seeing that Jacob guy?"

I raise an eyebrow. "Is that part of the investigation, Deputy?"

At his flustered and slightly embarrassed look, a bright laugh bursts out of me. He peels a bit of peppermint off his bear claw and lobs it at me, that blush still burning over his cheeks and down lower to his neck. It's a delight to see someone so buttoned-up get a little ruffled. I hear the stomp of boots on the porch stairs and push my chair back, a smile still tugging at the corners of my mouth.

"She is. But between you and me, I think she deserves better."

16

LUKA WON'T STOP glaring at me.

Well, more specifically, Luka won't stop glaring at Caleb. He's saving his special brand of annoyed looks for me, a narrow-eyed glance every minute or so. He thinks he's being sneaky about it, but Beckett has rolled his eyes no less than fourteen times since they came back into the house inexplicably caked with mud, my pink bat as pristine as when they left. No one has even started to explain what happened out in the fields, distracted by baked goods and warm coffee.

I prop my hands on my hips. "So? Anyone want to step away from breakfast for a second and tell me what's going on?"

Caleb beams at me from where he's lording over a brioche bun stuffed with maple walnut cream. "I told you"—he chews, oblivious to the man glaring at him from next to the refrigerator—"they're the best."

Okay, clearly Caleb needs a moment alone with his pastries. And Luka isn't feeling very talkative at the moment. I turn to Dane and raise both eyebrows. He takes his time working through a mouthful of cinnamon apple Danish.

"Didn't find the trespasser," he offers, succinct as ever. "Did find these two mud wrestling though."

Beckett sighs, weary. The early morning antics have been too much for him. He scoops up Comet from where she's dozing and drops her lightly back into his front pocket. "I'm going home," he announces, swiping a cinnamon roll off the quickly diminishing pile of baked goods. "I'll catch up with you later, Stella."

He disappears out the front, the quiet *snick* of the door behind him. My gaze trips over to Luka.

"Mud wrestling?"

Luka huffs, a bit of his frustration easing with the smile that winks to life in his eyes. It's a relief. I'm not used to grumpy Luka. "Beckett fell while we were running. And then I fell over Beckett."

I imagine it, the pair of them tangled up in a muddy heap. I roll my lips to contain my smile.

"That's when Dane found us."

"Did you get a look at who you were chasing?"

Luka shakes his head, disappointment clear in the harsh slant of his brows. He slouches back against the kitchen counter, legs crossed at the ankles. He leaves a smudge of mud at the baseboard of my cabinets that he'll probably scrub out by this time tomorrow. "Just a glimpse. They had too much of a lead on us, and we were both wearing boots."

"But they had to get out here somehow, right?" I turn to look at Caleb and Dane. "Was there a car parked along the road when you guys came in?"

They both shake their heads. "We'll do some poking around on our way back into town. But Stella, I'd like it if you filled out a formal report. List all the things we talked through the other day."

I twist my hands together in my lap with a frown. "You think that's necessary?"

Dane nods. "I do. This person was obviously planning on doing something more, on account of breaking the camera. You probably interrupted them before they could get started."

"Best to be overly cautious," Caleb agrees, and Luka is back to scowling over his coffee. I shoot him a questioning glance that he ignores. "We'll make a note of it as well, but it's best if the complaint comes from you directly."

"All right," I say. It's all a bit overwhelming. Evelyn arrives in a couple of days, and it feels like all my carefully laid plans are spinning out of control. It's hard enough maintaining the charade of a fake relationship, now I have some mystery trespasser wreaking havoc. Sensing my unease, Luka catches my hand in his and brushes a kiss on my knuckles. I squeeze his hand gratefully. I look to Dane. "I'll stop by later today."

I walk Dane and Caleb out to the driveway, waving from the front porch as they rumble back down the road. The sun is just starting to rise over the horizon, a dull glow from behind the clouds. I sigh and scratch between my eyebrows, pull my phone from my pocket and flick the switch off. All of the lights blink out at once.

Is this what instant Karma feels like? Is this what I get for lying about Luka?

Luka is rummaging through the cabinets when I step back into the kitchen, his shoulders tense. I'd ask what's bothering him, but frankly, I'm too tired. I sit and wait, picking at the remnants of my blueberry muffin, the silence strained and awkward between us. I want to go back to when we were curled together on the couch, Luka's arms tight around me.

"Why didn't you ask Caleb to be your fake boyfriend?"

"Um, what?"

"Caleb." Luka slams a cabinet door shut and opens another. "You two looked cozy. Why didn't you ask him?"

If by *cozy* he means we were sitting at the table talking cordially like normal adults, then yes, we were cozy, I guess. I stare at him across the kitchen. The grumpy glares, the tense line of his body, the way he's practically ripping my cabinet doors off the hinges. Luka's jealous. He walked in, saw us at the table laughing, and got jealous.

It's amazing. I rest my chin in my hand, amused.

"I hadn't thought about it," I reply slowly. It's not the answer Luka is looking for, his frown deepening until little lines are bracketing the sides of his mouth. I want to press my thumb into them, smooth them out. "Isn't there a rule about police officers lying or something?"

He doesn't laugh at my joke.

I sigh and reach for honesty instead. "Luka," I say. He mutters something about missing biscotti and ignores me. "I didn't ask Caleb because there was only one person I wanted."

Luka glances at me from over his shoulder, and I feel it again, the heavy thump of my heart banging around in my chest. It's both wonderful and terrible to feel like this every time he looks at me. I don't know how I've managed to survive it this long.

"It was Clint, wasn't it?"

I bark a laugh and lift myself from my chair. "You know I love a man who appreciates a hoagie."

"Jesse?"

"I'd probably get a discount at the bar."

Luka sighs and tilts his head back to the ceiling, eyes closed in agony. "It was Billy, I know it."

Billy works part time at the funeral home two towns over. It's honorable work, sure, but I think he's a little too enthusiastic about his job. He started sleeping during the day. He calls himself a night-walker. I saw him in a black leather trench coat in August.

I step between Luka's legs and wrap my arms around his waist. He tilts his head back down until we're nose to nose. His smile is devastating, honest in its own way.

"It was not Billy," I tell him. "It was you, you great big moron."

He sobers, his smile settling into something gentle and warm. He traces the curve of my cheek, the sharp angle of my chin, my chapped bottom lip. He brushes over it once, twice, and then curls his hand around the nape of my neck. His thumb rubs at the top of my spine, and I shiver, forehead against his chin. I tighten my arms around him.

"I'm glad you wanted me to be your fake boyfriend."

"Me too," I agree. "Were you jealous, fake boyfriend?"

He scoffs, hand spreading wide to trace between my shoulder blades. He works out a particularly stubborn knot on my left side, and I melt into him. I expect him to deny it, to change the subject, but he surprises me again.

"Of course I was. You were holding a plate of donuts. And you're wearing your sleep shorts that have dancing nutcrackers on them." We both snicker and look down at my shorts. "And you looked happy, Stella. You were laughing when we came in." He tips my chin up with his hand, eyes searching. "That was—" He swallows roughly. "That was my smile."

It's a heady feeling, to know that I'm not the only one who wants to possess every moment of happiness. Collect every laugh and pocket it, hoard them like tiny treasures. I beam at him. His greed has me bursting at the seams.

"Okay," I say. I take a half step back and reach around him to the flour jar, move it to the left and hand him the box of leftover biscotti behind it.

He blinks down at the box and then back to me. "Okay?"

"Okay, you can have them." I nod at the cookies in his hands. "My cookies and my smiles."

He swallows again, a heavy bob of his throat that has me wanting to press myself back against him, drag my teeth up the length of his neck. Instead, I take another step back. And then another.

"Careful." He's looking at me like I'm a peppermint mocha bear claw with extra walnut cream cheese frosting. "You can't take that back."

"There's nothing to take back," I promise him, but I don't tell him the other things. That my smiles have always belonged to him. A big chunk of my heart too. All my best memories.

And the toaster oven I stole from his apartment six years ago and have hidden in the pantry beneath two leather jackets and a tennis racket.

I rub my fingers over my lips. My best kiss now too. Luka has pretty much everything cupped in his hands, and he doesn't even know it. The thought makes me sad.

"I don't think I can go back to sleep," I say. The hope of that disappeared as soon as I woke up and saw someone slinging rocks at my camera. I glance out the window, up the foothills. "I think I'm going to go out and get a tree for the living room. I want it to be festive here too."

I could use the fresh air and distance from flat surfaces. I see Luka nod out of the corner of my eye, cookie tin tucked under his arm.

"I'll join you."

❧ ❧

"YOU NEED TO relax," says Luka.

Let it be known that telling a woman to relax has never once resulted in said relaxation. I suck in a lungful of air and press it out again through clenched teeth. Like a dragon. Luka laughs from his relaxed position in the corner of the couch. I pull the tinsel down from around the tree and start again. I can't get the damn thing to hang right.

"I am relaxed," I mutter. "You relax."

"As you can see, I am very relaxed."

I look over at Luka. His hands are tucked behind his head and his eyes are half-lidded, a smirk at the corners of his lips. He's got his little duckling socks on tonight, one foot propped on the arm of the couch, the other flat on the floor with his knee bent. There's a book folded open across his chest, some ancient science fiction novel he found in my TV stand.

He looks obscene.

I roll my eyes and go back to the tree, attempting to thread the gold tinsel through the bottom branches at exactly the right angle. How is Evelyn going to take me seriously as a Christmas expert if my tinsel is a mess? She won't. She'll see the crooked tinsel, she'll know

I'm a fraud, and we'll lose the contest. I'll have to shut this place down and work late nights at the funeral home with Billy.

Luka sighs from the couch. "You're spiraling."

"I am not spiraling," I reply, absolutely spiraling.

"Come here, please."

I throw the tinsel into a heap and shuffle over to him. He shifts his head to look at me and pats his leg once. I arch an eyebrow.

"What?"

"What do you mean, what? Come here."

I look down at him dubiously. He's taking up all the space on the couch. The only place to go would be on top of him. He pats his leg again.

"I'm not a dog," I grumble. I press one knee on the couch and swing the other over his hips. My hands find his shoulders. I sit there, awkwardly perched, my body hovering over his. I frown. "You were right, this is great. I am so relaxed," I monotone.

"Sit," Luka says with a laugh. His hands find my hips and he pulls once, a sharp tug that sends me off-balance and has me tumbling into him. "Stay." My chest smashes into his, my legs fan out until our hips are flush and my nose digs into his collarbone. He sighs, happy, and wiggles down farther into the couch, both of his arms wrapping around me like a boa constrictor. "That's better."

I huff and rearrange my legs so they still receive circulation. I tuck my elbows under me and rest my palms flat on his chest. I tell myself to relax, but my brain can't let go of the thousand things I still have to do before Evelyn arrives.

Typically during the holiday season, I'm either in my office or out on the farm from dawn to dusk. But Luka had appeared in my office doorway two hours ago with a candy cane hanging out of his mouth and a promise of homemade Bolognese, and I trailed after him without a backward glance. We spent way too long in the fields debating the proper tree, then hauling it back.

Now I feel all my responsibilities piling up. My shoulders pull tight with it, my breathing shallow. Now isn't the time for me to get distracted with whatever it is Luka and I are doing. I have to be focused. I have to be flawless.

After I went to the police station to file my report about the weekend's excitement, I stopped by the bed-and-breakfast to make sure everything was in order for Evelyn's arrival. Cozy flannel sheets, a wreath from Mabel on the door, daily coffee delivered—even a box of Layla's sugar cookies to go with her key upon check-in. I felt some of my anxiety settle after that. At the very least, she'd be comfortable.

And fully in the holiday spirit, judging by the decorations covering every square inch of our little downtown. Thick rows of garland wrapped in twinkling lights twisting around the streetlights. Heavy wreaths anchored with cherry red bows on every door. Over the fountain, a handwritten sign wishing everyone a happy holiday season, a shimmering snowflake hanging like magic from the center. A giant Christmas tree decorated with handmade ornaments from the school, a small wooden plaque declaring it homegrown at Inglewild's own Lovelight Farms.

A heavy palm sweeps up my back to that magic spot on my neck, Luka's fingertips grazing instead of pressing. I still shiver into it, burrowing myself farther into his chest. "What do you need?"

I sigh into the warm skin of his neck. He smells delicious here. Like peppermint and basil and the fancy grapefruit body scrub he keeps stealing from my shower. "For everything to go perfect," I whisper. I curl my hands into his T-shirt and then relax them again. "For my brain to slow down."

"The first is a given," he says, and now his thumb presses deep. My legs go completely limp on either side of him, and he makes a pleased sound deep in his chest. I feel it rumble beneath me. "The second I can help with."

I make a vaguely inquisitive sound, still focused on that perfect bit of pressure at the nape of my neck. He slides his hand down between my shoulder blades and then back up.

"What do you know about causal analysis?"

It's safe to say I know absolutely nothing about causal analysis. I grumble something into his collarbone and focus on his hand on my neck instead, his palm cupping gently under all my hair. He combs it to one side and wraps it around his fist. Releases and lets it slip through his fingers.

"It's used to determine cause and effect." He brushes a kiss under my ear and my whole body shivers. "There are four elements you need to establish, but the most important ones are correlation and sequence in time. Does that make sense?"

"Sure." It makes no sense. I'm more interested in his gentle touch guiding my head farther to the side, his teeth grazing my neck. I curl my fingers into his hair and grip tight.

He laughs into my skin. "Hold on, this is important. I'm teaching you something. Sit up for a sec."

I groan but do as he asks, sitting up on his lap. He laughs when he sees my pout, shuffling up on his elbows and fanning his hands out on top of my thighs, fingers drumming. "To determine the effect of a specific cause," his hands glide up and then back down again, thumbs against the inseam of my comfy pants. "You need to correlate two actions with sequencing. The cause has to come before the effect."

"Okay." I'm frankly too focused on his hands on my thighs to further contribute to this conversation.

No wonder he's always the one to present to clients. I have no idea what he's talking about, but he's hot when he talks about data. I want to ask him to pull up an Excel sheet, maybe sort by ascending value. He leans up farther against me until his hands are gripping my hips, our chests pressed together. With one quick move, he flips me backward, flat against the couch.

"Good distraction so far," I say, eyes wide. He loosens his grip at my waist and slips his hands up over my ribs, palms teasing at the sides of my breasts. He urges my arms up and gathers my wrists in his hands, holding them lightly against the arm of the couch.

"For instance," his eyes are dark, his tongue at the corner of his mouth, "if I kiss you here—" He ducks his head down and presses his lips gently to the line of my collarbone. My legs shift beneath him, my ankle curling over the back of his knee. He pulls back and holds my arm out, pulling my sleeve up to my elbow. "You get goose bumps here."

There's a sharp stillness between us, the both of us watching to see what the other will do. He studies me with my arms above my head, the way my sweater has tugged down low on one side. He trails his fingers back up my arms in a sweet caress, thumb hooking in the collar of my shirt. He pulls it down low until he can see the cut of my plain white cotton bra, his eyes darkening further, his teeth holding his bottom lip. My breath catches and then releases, Luka's thumb grazing my ribs

"If I do this," his voice is smoke and spice as he leans forward, teeth gripping the edge of my bra, pulling back and snapping it against my skin. He whispers a laugh into me when my fingers curl into the couch. "That happens."

He pushes up on both hands and smiles down at me, bright and boyish. I'm panting, an ache low in my belly and between my thighs. He pats the top of my legs and I almost growl.

"These are good data points, Stella."

Frustrated, I arch up beneath him and reach my hand behind my back. With a twist of my fingers, my bra unhooks, the snap of it wiping the smug look right off his face. The material slips a bit under his thumb until I'm barely covered by soft cotton and a cozy knit. Judging by the way his jaw has gone a little slack, I think Luka likes that more than bare skin. The hint of something more. The tease of what's beneath.

"We should probably find some more," I breathe. "You know. For science."

He kisses me then, his hand threading through my hair and angling my mouth to his until our lips meet. Our little game has officially turned from a tease to an ultimatum. It's possession in a kiss, Luka braced on his elbows above me, his mouth aggressive, hungry. It feels like all of our almost moments are balanced on the tip of my tongue, and he's coaxing them free, his teeth lightly nipping. When I almost reached for his hand at the bar, because I liked the way his fingers felt between mine. When I almost kissed him at the jam festival, because I wanted to see if he tasted like strawberries. When I almost told him I loved him every single time he answered his door and his amber eyes lit up at the sight of me.

A million little almost moments spilling free.

"When I do this—" He pulls his mouth from mine with a gasp and starts to press deep, sucking kisses to my neck. I shift my legs wider around him and wrap my hands around his shoulders. "When I do this, do you get wet here?"

He presses his hand between my legs over my leggings, and black spots appear at the edges of my vision. I grab his forearm and hold his hand there, rolling my hips, seeking friction. It's a delicious frustration to keep finding ourselves here. We keep working ourselves up with no relief, and I feel the pull of it everywhere. My skin is too tight, the place between my legs aching. I strain up into Luka, and he drops his forehead to my shoulder, hand moving with me between my legs.

"Can I—" He swallows around the rest of his question, voice rough, distracted with the length of my collarbone and his teeth against it. "Can I touch you?"

I'm nodding before the last word leaves his lips. I don't care that it makes me seem eager. This is Luka. He's already seen all the messy parts of me.

Except for this one. This piece of myself that is flushed and panting as his big hands find the waistband of my leggings. He noses between my breasts as he slips his hands down inside the stretchy soft fabric, cupping the curve of my ass. He squeezes once with a pained moan, like this is hurting him, like this is torture. I laugh into his hair and tilt my head, brushing a kiss to his temple, the shell of his ear. I pull it between my teeth and bite, and the length of his body pushes me deeper into the couch, his hips against my thigh. I feel him there, hard beneath his jeans.

"Fuck," he whispers. One hand moves, slipping around my hip and dipping down, the movement clumsy with his wrist trapped by the fabric of my pants. But where I expected hesitation, there is none. His fingers fan out over my skin like a brand, his thumb brushing once at the soft skin below my belly button. I exhale into his neck. It's barely a touch, a glance of his fingertips, and I'm shivering beneath him, body strung tight.

"When I touch you here—" He moves his hand lower and hooks his thumb just right, a single firm touch where I need him the most. I make a gasping sound, a whimper caught in the back of my throat. He nods into me and makes a rough circle that has me holding on to him for dear life. "Yeah, you make that sound."

I don't know what sounds I'm making. I don't know where I am. All I know is Luka's hand grinding into me, my hips chasing his touch, his bottom lip caught between his teeth as he watches me with heavy eyes. I don't think I've ever been touched so carefully. I don't think I've ever been so close to the edge with all my clothes still on.

The thought has me huffing a disbelieving laugh into Luka's warm skin, my forehead tucked against his shoulder so I can look between us. He starts a smooth rhythm, a rolling motion with his palm and fingers that spins the tension in my belly tighter. I chase it with my hips and watch as we move together, his hand beneath my leggings, his hips pressing into my thigh. Every time I thrust up, he pushes into me, his forehead against my chest. I want his touch there too. His mouth warm and teeth biting.

Luka nudges at my chin with his nose, his fingers playing me higher. He slips two inside me, and my hands close into fists against his shirt, trying to rip the soft material from his body. It's a wonder I don't strangle him.

"What's so funny?" he breathes, and it sounds like he's in the middle of a marathon. Mile marker twenty-three. He's started to move his hips against me, tiny stilted movements that are almost unconscious, his body chasing friction. It's a comfort to know he feels it too. This pull. This need.

"Nothing, just—" I flex my hips down into his touch, and he answers with a sharp thrust that has my head falling back against the couch, eyes closed. Everything within me sharpens until I'm balanced on the very precipice. "Oh, god."

He stops the motion of his hand, and I make a desperate noise, embarrassing if this were anyone but him. I have half a mind to slip my hand next to his and finish the job myself, but I want to see where he takes me. I peek open one eye to glare down at him. He's grinning at me, cheeks flushed, hair a mess from my hands. "What's so funny?" he repeats.

I roll my hips, forcing his touch, and he gets a glazed look in his pretty amber eyes.

"It's never felt like this," I whisper, feeling those sparks start up again. "It's just—it's never felt this good."

That does it for him. My confession has him frantic, the hand that's been squeezing my ass and guiding me against him suddenly up and out of my leggings. He pulls at the collar of my sweater, dragging it down over my shoulder until the cotton of my bra is the only thing keeping him from my skin. He groans at the sight of it, muttering something under his breath, the hand between my legs pressing, shifting, rolling with me. It's overwhelming, the sudden change in pace and pressure, especially when he licks the soft skin just above my bra, catches it in his teeth and drags it down.

His mouth finds the tip of my breast at the same moment his fingers speed up against me, thumb rubbing hard perfect circles, and that's it. It's a fracture low in my belly that rolls hot through the rest of me, spreading slow and sweet like honey. He holds me tight and guides me through it as I shake and unspool beneath him, one hand clenched tight in his shirt, the other frantically pulling it up until I find bare skin. He's sticky with sweat—but then, so am I. Delicious heat unfurls from between my legs and sings through my blood until I'm limp below him, panting against his neck.

If he's at mile marker twenty-three, I'm collapsed at the finish line, begging for electrolytes. He shifts against me and grins, slipping his hand from between us.

"That was nice." His voice scratches against the edges of the words, a huskiness to match the heat in his eyes. His hips press into me once. "You look pretty when you come."

My stomach swoops like I've just walked off the side of a building. I blink twice. He's said it like *That's a nice sweater* or *You make a great cup of coffee*. I don't know what to say.

Instead, I reach between us, my thumb tracing the button of his jeans. He makes a pained grunt and catches my wrist in his hand. His fingers are still wet and I blush. His mouth hitches up in a grin, a secret dirty smile that has that blush spreading lower. He watches its progress with fascination, nose chasing it down over the breast that's still exposed by my twisted bra.

"I'm okay," he rasps somewhere into my skin. He nudges at my breast with his nose and exhales a shaky sigh when I arch into him.

The tent in his pants would disagree. I twist my hand in his grip and stroke my palm over the length of him beneath denim, and he drops his head against the arm of the couch with a groan. "Doesn't feel like it," I reply.

"I don't want to—"

I pause my motion at that. I don't ever want to make him do something he doesn't want to do. Our agreement is a week where we chase what feels right. And if this doesn't feel right to him, then I don't want it either. I pull my hand back and wait, patient.

He picks his head up, the smile tugging at his mouth sheepish. "It won't take much," he explains, twin spots of pink blooming on his cheeks.

Like the idea that he got close from doing that to me, watching me, is something he needs to be embarrassed about. Like the thought of him getting pleasure from giving me pleasure isn't—isn't enough to have heat tugging low in my belly again.

"Hold on, I want to see if I understood the lesson." I bite at my bottom lip and slip open the button of his jeans. "If I do this—" I drag down his fly and curl my palm around him. He's heavy and hot in my hand, a wiggle in his hips when I try to pull his jeans lower. Impatient, I stroke him once, and he braces his hands on the armrest above me. I stroke again and he groans out my name, a broken "Stella" that I want to record and set as my ringtone. I've never seen him so disheveled, so perfectly undone. "Then you say my name like that," I smile with my hand around him. "Am I getting it right?"

He doesn't answer. He tips his head back, the long line of his throat and the sharp line of his jaw laid out like a buffet. I start at his collarbone and kiss there once, the motion of my wrist smooth and easy over him.

"You're gonna kill me," he whispers with a breathless little laugh, and I think I like that best, even more than the way he moves above me, greedy for my touch. I like how easy it is to laugh with him, even as we do this. I don't think I've ever smiled during sex, ever done anything more than close my eyes and try to get myself there. But with Luka, it's easy. The way we touch each other, the way we breathe and move together. It's so easy.

I lick and bite my way up his neck until my teeth catch the lobe of his ear. He groans then, long and loud, and I smile into his skin.

"You're pretty, too," I whisper. I grin and twist my wrist, earning a catch in his breath. I hum with approval and bite at the place where his shoulder meets his neck, his skin warm.

He lets loose a steady stream of curses, his hand curling around my wrist and holding me tight against him as he rocks his hips, fast and messy. His orgasm is quiet—body shaking, brow furrowed, warmth across my stomach as he chases his high. I wait until his hips stop moving before I pull my hand back and rest it on his stomach, scratching once with my nails at the trail of dark hair below his belly button. His hips jump and I grin.

He blinks at me, gaze heavy, shirt half pulled up on his torso from my frantic hands, and jeans low on his hips. He has a dark line of hair down the center of his abdomen, a stack of surprising muscle that I trace with my fingers, walking my fingers up until I can press my palms to his chest. There are freckles here too, dotted across his skin in clusters and bursts. I'm never going to be able to sit on this couch again without thinking of exactly this moment. His smile says he knows it.

"And that"—he whistles a breath through his teeth and collapses at my side, wedged between me and the back of the couch—"is everything you need to know about causal analysis."

17

I AM SUFFICIENTLY calm and happily distracted through the rest of the weekend. Luka is adorably affectionate and a little smug after our shared moment on the couch, burying his nose in my hair every time I stand at the sink to wash dishes, threading his fingers through my belt loop as I bend to hang ornaments on the tree.

I thought maybe it would be like scratching an itch, that maybe the tension between us would pop like a balloon. Instead it just feels like I've turned the heat from simmer to full blast. I can't stop looking at him. His permanently ruffled hair, the spread of his fingers around my knee, the lines by the corners of his eyes when he laughs. And for all my looking, he can't stop touching. His thumb at the base of my neck, his lips against my temple.

It's like instead of easing something, we unleashed it instead. Amplified it. I just want more.

I have a feeling I'm only ever going to want more where Luka is concerned.

The afternoon of Evelyn's arrival sneaks up on me, the sky a perfect crisp blue as I wait in my office. Luka is out in the fields with Layla, helping trim the trees in the far field for the preselected tree lot. Beckett is in the barn with the group we bring on for seasonal help, walking them through their training. And I am here, ready to welcome Evelyn with a mug of hot chocolate topped with whipped cream and a peppermint stick. But what I'm really doing is staring blankly at various spots around the office as I remember what Luka's hands felt like on my bare skin, his stubble brushing between my breasts, his hair tickling my neck as he panted above me.

I shake myself out of it, careful to keep the hot chocolate from spilling over onto my hand. All of our work is resting on this. Evelyn loving us enough to award us one hundred thousand dollars in prize money, and her millions of followers loving us enough to visit.

I watch a little car rumble its way down the entrance path, a cloud of dirt kicked up behind it. I know it's her as soon as she turns into the lot, her wide smile visible even through the tinted windows. I exhale a deep breath and shake my hair out behind my shoulders. I can do this.

Evelyn is just as beautiful in person as she is online.

Impossibly long legs, flawless honey-colored skin, dark shiny hair that hangs down to the middle of her back. She climbs out of her car in front of the office and tips her head back, smiling as she looks at the wooden licorice I painted at midnight two nights ago to make this place look like a gingerbread house. Luka had begrudgingly helped me hammer the wooden gumdrops approximately seven inches apart across the porch hangover, even scaling the roof to drape fake white icing around the chimney.

I meet her on the front porch, and her smile tips into a grin as she bounces on the balls of her feet. She really is stunning, taller than I imagined her to be.

"Hi," I say, and smile through my nerves. "Welcome to Lovelight Farms."

"Holy shit," she says back, and just like that, my anxiety fades. My brittle smile melts into a laugh, and I step down to where she's gazing out at the fields with her hand shielding her eyes against the setting sun. I asked her to meet me at this time for a reason. There's nothing like the farm just as the sun begins to dip in the sky, bright blue fading to deep cobalt, pink just starting to bloom from behind the clouds. I stand next to her and try to see it the way she does as a first-time visitor: The endless rows of full green trees. The lights that string throughout, just starting to blink awake in the early evening. The big red barn by the road with hand-painted arches. The climbing towers for the kids and the open hayloft lined with lights and filled with old broken-down tractors painted like reindeer. The ice-skating rink in the middle of it all, Bing Crosby crooning over the speakers.

I hand her the hot chocolate, and she curls her hands around it with a happy sigh. "This place is amazing."

I grin. "Wait until you see the rest."

❧ · ❧

FOUR BROWNIES LATER, and Evelyn looks like she's ready to sink into the booth and sleep through the rest of this trip. We're set up in my favorite spot in the bakehouse, a cozy little nook in the corner next to the stone fireplace. It's a high-back booth with green velvet seats and a mountain of plaid pillows, a dark-stained wood table in the middle. Evelyn grabs a pillow and nuzzles into the corner, an indulgent sound as she looks out the windows to the trees beyond.

She's easy to like, easy to talk to, and I suppose that's why she's such a captivating personality online. I'm a little surprised I haven't seen her phone in her hand yet, and I say as much during a lull in our conversation.

She waves her hand between us, eyeballing the still half-full plate of brownies at the edge of the table. "I like to experience the places I visit first," she says, rubbing at her bottom lip, "which sounds super pretentious, I know, and I realize I'm a person who makes their living on social media, but I hate how it robs us of that sometimes, you know? People get too caught up in how things look instead of how things feel." She shrugs. "I'll start content tomorrow. We'll do live coverage, of course, and then a full highlight that will be published in a couple of weeks. You'll have a mention on the blog, all of the stuff my team talked to you about."

A mention on the blog, an official listing as a contest participant on her website, and a highlight on each of her social channels. Even without the cash prize that will be announced at the end of her trips, it's enough to make a serious difference in our future.

She drags the brownie plate closer and then pushes it away again with a groan. "Though I might be in a chocolate coma by then."

"Layla has a gift."

Evelyn's dark eyes light up. "That's right. Your business partners, Layla and Beckett."

I nod. "Layla does all the baking here on-site with her team. We serve during farm hours, and she does some catering for the town too."

"Which is the cutest, by the way."

I'm so glad she thinks so. Our little town isn't everyone's cup of tea. The postal system has trouble delivering here, and we don't have the big department stores where you can get everything from decor to mascara to a box of wine in one trip. You would have to make at least three separate stops for those things in Inglewild. Everyone is in everyone else's business, and you can't leave your house without running into at least four people you know. But there's always someone to ask me how I'm doing. And a helping hand when I need it.

We're a family. A strange one that you sometimes want an extended vacation from, but a family nonetheless. I glance at the table in the corner, where Gus, Clint, and Monty are destroying a box of French crullers. Apparently, this is their time slot on the farm visitation schedule. Bailey and Sandra were here yesterday running around the hayloft like a couple of teenagers.

"Beckett handles all of our farm operations and oversees his own staff. Mostly crops and maintenance, but he dabbles in other things too." Like fostering a family of cats, apparently.

She nods, her eyes still darting between me and the brownies. I shift the plate closer to her, and she takes another with a laugh. "Thank you. And Luka, your boyfriend." My stomach drops and my smile falters at the lie spoken aloud. I tell myself it's for the farm, that it's harmless in the scheme of things, but I still feel that wiggle of doubt in the back of my mind. "What's it like working with your partner? I'm not sure many people could do it."

I think of Luka flat on his stomach on the office roof, a nail between his teeth as he hammered fake licorice across the shingles. How later that night he rested his chin on my shoulder as I looked at expense reports, a quart of ice cream in his hand as he adjusted my Excel equations to make data input easier.

"It's perfect," I say, because it is. Too perfect. I want it forever, not just this week. The fake relationship hangover is going to kick me right in the teeth. How do you go back to boundaries when your best friend has had his hand down your pants? I have no idea. I clear my throat. "We're a good team."

I glance at the clock above the counter and banish all thoughts of Luka and that couch from my mind. "They should be here soon, actually. I told them to meet us around now."

Excitement lights up her dark eyes. "Good. I want to kiss Layla on the face for these brownies."

"Who're we kissing?" Beckett appears at the edge of the booth with a Santa mug, a frown on his face and a kitten on his shoulder. I recognize Cupid, the little black heart-shaped spot on her front paw giving her away. I reach my hands out for her and cuddle her close when she happily leaps into my arms.

"Layla, on account of the brownies," I explain. He grunts in what I assume is agreement. "Beckett, let me introduce you to—"

I turn to the booth to look at Evelyn, and I'm surprised to see the look of shock on her face, her mouth hinged open. She snaps it closed quickly when I raise both eyebrows and immediately looks down at the table. I look back to Beckett in question, and he's frozen with his mug halfway to his mouth, gaze glued on the pretty woman sitting opposite me.

"Um," I say, eloquent as ever. I feel my face pinch in confusion. Beckett hasn't looked away from Evelyn, and Evelyn hasn't looked away from the tabletop. Cupid meows from the cradle of my arms. "Uh, Beckett, this is Evelyn. Evelyn, this is Beckett."

Silence.

"Uh," I start again and desperately try to get Beckett's attention. I kick him once in the shin and he flinches. I raise both eyebrows at him meaningfully.

"Nice to—" He clears his throat and puts his mug on the table, rubbing at his jaw. "It's nice to meet you."

Evelyn nods quickly and darts her eyes up once only to shoot them back down to the table. Her knuckles are white where she's gripping the edge of it. I frown and urge the brownie plate closer.

Beckett slides into the booth next to me after another lengthy hesitation, and the three of us sit in silence. I peer down at Cupid.

"Uh, we rescued these cats," I offer, hoping to dispel the weird tension that's settled over us. I have no idea what's going on, no idea what happened when Beckett arrived. Could it be that she finds him attractive? I mean, sure, Beckett is nice to look at. Objectively speaking. I've seen him fluster the women who come to the farm more than once. But I can't imagine that he would render someone like Evelyn mute. I stroke Cupid's soft little head. "They were living in the Santa barn. I thought they were raccoons."

"She's a cutie," Evelyn mutters without a single ounce of enthusiasm. I frown. She looks up at me, a little fission of anxiety in the place between her perfect brows. "Listen, Stella, I have to run back to the hotel real quick, okay?"

I frown. "I was going to—"

But she's already moving, scooting out of the booth and sending pillows tumbling in every direction. "I'll be back in the morning, and we'll get a fresh start."

She strides out of the bakehouse without another word. I stare at the door, the wreath hanging on the front swinging back and forth with the force of her retreat. Beckett takes a brownie next to me with a long-suffering sigh.

"Stella."

I narrow my eyes. Beckett only uses that tone when we have a problem. Cupid slips out of my grip and rubs herself against Beckett's forearm. I'm going to have to talk to him about having the cats in the bakehouse. He looks at me and takes a giant bite of brownie.

"Please explain to me what just happened."

He swallows and looks up at the ceiling then down at his hands. "Well—" He shifts in the booth and puts his elbow on the table and then picks it up again. I don't think I've ever seen Beckett at such a loss for words. "Ah, well. I slept with that woman."

"Beckett"—I do the math—"she's been in town for six hours."

He rolls his eyes. "Not today." He messes with the cuff of his sleeve. "Do you remember when I went to that conference in Maine? The one about organic farming?"

"You didn't stop talking about how synthetic fertilizers are the worst for close to a month. You're telling me you slept with Evelyn on that trip, and synthetic fertilizers is what I heard about?"

He scratches roughly at the back of his head and sends Cupid skittering across the table. He scoops her back up and places her in his lap. "I don't—we don't talk about stuff like that. And it was a one-time thing." His eyes go hazy, a small smile kicking up on the right side of his mouth. I want to punch him in the face. "More like a three-time thing, I guess. She was staying at the same bed-and-breakfast I was. We met at a bar."

I remember seeing her pictures from a tiny bed-and-breakfast in Maine. Her photos of the wildflower bedspread and the fresh-cut herbs on the windowsill. It's mind-boggling to me that Beckett was there. He was under that bedspread.

"Did it end badly? Why did she have that reaction?"

He shrugs and takes another bite of brownie.

"Beckett." He chews and keeps his eyes firmly on the tabletop. This little booth has never been inspected so thoroughly. "Explain this to me."

He shrugs again. "I don't know, Stella. I can't even explain this one to myself." He finishes his brownie and reclines back in the booth. I have no idea what this means for the contest, for her trip here. Will she leave early? Are we disqualified? "She was probably just surprised. We didn't—we didn't exactly talk much." A furious blush lights up the back of his neck, and despite everything, I feel a bubbling burst of laughter catch in my chest. This whole situation is unreal.

I invented a fake boyfriend so Evelyn would find this place romantic. Beckett unknowingly slept with her on a weekend trip to Maine. We have a mysterious trespasser dead set on disrupting the farm.

It would be comical if it wasn't such a mess.

"She was the one who left first. We were, um, we spent the night together, and when I woke up in the morning, she was gone. All of her stuff was gone too."

"You never tried to find her? Never saw her on social media?"

He scowls at me. "You know I don't do anything on social media. I figured she had a reason for leaving the way she did. I don't chase after people who don't want to be chased."

"That's fair," I say.

We fall into silence. I survey Beckett and catalog the tension in his shoulders, the way he hasn't stopped moving since Evelyn left. His fingers against the tabletop. His knee bouncing beneath it. A shift of his hips every few seconds in the booth seat. In my surprise, I forgot the most important thing.

"Hey," I curl my hand just above his elbow and tug once. "You okay?"

He nods, ducking his head just a bit. "M'fine. Embarrassed mostly. I don't want to mess anything up for us. I know how important this is."

I flinch. He has no idea how important this is because I haven't been honest with him. A flash of red in the window catches my attention, Layla's bright jacket as she and Luka trudge toward the entrance of the bakehouse. She laughs at something he says, both of their cheeks flushed pink with the cold. I make a decision.

"About that, I need to talk to you and Layla. Luka too."

I wait until everyone is situated in the booth, warm drinks for Layla and Luka after their morning in the fields. Layla's been talking about proper sawing techniques since they came in, a bemused Luka trailing after her from the door to the back kitchen to our cozy booth in the corner. But she cuts off abruptly when she notices how tense Beckett is at the edge of the wooden bench, the frown on my face.

"Weird vibes," she says, and I feel Luka's booted foot nudge mine under the table, a silent *Are you okay?* with the arch of his eyebrow. He's wearing his tree hunting boots, the ones with the flannel.

"We have some—" I shoot a glance at Beckett, who looks like he wants to melt into the floor. I pat his back once in solidarity. "We have some updates."

"I slept with Evelyn," Beckett offers without an ounce of lead-up or context. Layla bobbles her hot chocolate and spills half of it on the table between us. Luka just stares at him, brows furrowed. I toss Layla a stack of napkins.

"I'm confused." Luka looks at me, then Beckett, then me again. "Didn't she just get here?"

Beckett shares the same limited details with them as he did with me. Bed-and-breakfast. Maine. Farmer conference. He sounds like he's recounting a trip to the dentist, not a wild, sexy weekend adventure. Layla's eyes grow bigger at every staccato sentence until she's practically draped across the table, enraptured. Beckett concludes his story and slumps back into his seat. Cupid nudges once at his chin with her tiny paw.

"Beckett"—Layla breathes—"I didn't think you had sex."

He shifts and grumpily crosses his arms. "Of course I have sex."

"Clearly."

"I'm just private about it."

"Obviously."

"Okay." I rub at my forehead. "That's enough of . . . that." Beckett looks like he wants the floor to open beneath him. "I have something I need to tell you guys." Three pairs of eyes focus their attention on me, Luka's narrowed in concern. I muster my courage and straighten my spine. I owe them an explanation. I've owed them an explanation for a long time now. "I've been pretty vague with how the farm is doing financially. The truth is, it's not great."

Beckett narrows his eyes. "That is an equally vague statement."

"Even though we had an amazing year last year, we still aren't turning a huge profit." Maybe if I say it faster, it will be easier. Luka's boot is still between mine, and he taps my foot once. "Which I expected and accounted for. What I didn't budget for was all the extra repairs we had this last year, the loss of the south pasture, the missing shipments, and the debts we owe to a couple of different suppliers—"

"Excuse me, what?" says Beckett.

I ignore him and continue. "All that is to say, we are sort of hemorrhaging money right now. I'm hoping this season will help our numbers, especially with the added attention of having Evelyn here. But I'm really banking on that grand-prize money."

"I don't understand," Layla starts slowly. "How are we having money problems? I still get my paycheck every other week. So does my team. They haven't been late or short once."

Beckett breathes out sharply through his nose. "Same." Given the thunderous expression on his face, he knows exactly why that is.

"Stella." Luka's voice is quiet, pained. I guess he figured it out too. I keep my eyes on the wet napkins clumped together in the center of the table.

"I'm not ever going to cut back the paychecks of anyone who works here. I made you both a promise when you decided to join the farm, and I'm going to keep it."

I was afraid, I want to say. *I didn't want you to think I was a failure. I didn't want to let you down. I didn't want you to leave.*

"And what about your paychecks?"

My pantry is chock-full of ramen noodles. Luka stuffs protein bars in my glove box every time he comes home. The cottage came with the farm and my car has been fully paid off for years. I don't need a consistent paycheck, not like Beckett and Layla do.

When I'm silent, Beckett stands with a huff from the table. "I'm leaving," he announces, succinct as ever. I expected this, but I still wince at the heavy thud of his boots against the tile of the bakery. He strides to the door, changes his mind halfway, and comes walking back. The firefighters in the corner do their best to look like they're occupied, studying the last French cruller on their plate like it's invented electricity.

Beckett returns to the edge of the booth and stares at me. His disappointment is the worst of it, the sadness and hurt that lingers in the firm press of his mouth. He swallows once.

"This isn't what partners do," he says quietly. I watched Beckett argue with two of his sisters once. He had been quiet while they yelled, arms crossed over his chest, letting them carry on while he just stood there. At the time, I thought it was amusing. Look at them wasting all their energy just to face a brick wall. Now though, I can sympathize. Quiet, disappointed Beckett is a thousand times worse than any show of anger.

I nod once.

This day hasn't gone at all how I planned.

He leaves to the merry jingle of silver bells above the door. I wish he would have slammed it instead.

Layla reaches across the table and grabs my hand. "While I am just as angry as Beckett at you hiding this from us, I want to add that I love you." She stands from the table and pulls her jacket back on, flipping the hood up and over her head. She looks like a grumpy Arctic explorer. "We'll talk about this later. I've got an order to deliver in town."

"You'll be back?"

She gives me a sad smile. "Yeah, honey. I'll be back."

I watch her leave with a thousand apologies on my tongue, but I bite them back. Shouting after her isn't going to change anything. I slump in the booth and avoid Luka's eyes, collecting the mess from the spilled hot chocolate. I know there's a lesson here in telling the truth, but I can't bring myself to apply it to our situation. Maybe when I see Evelyn tomorrow—if I see Evelyn tomorrow, my brain helpfully reminds me—I can be honest with her. That Luka isn't my boyfriend, that this has all been a misunderstanding.

"Wanna walk home?" Luka asks.

I nod at the tabletop and take a deep breath that wobbles around the edges. Luka hears it and sighs, his hand cupping my elbow and pulling me into him as soon as I'm out of the bench seat. I hold the wad of wet paper napkins from the spilled hot chocolate over his shoulders and try not to get his jacket wet.

"It'll be fine," he says somewhere above my head. His arms squeeze tight, but he doesn't do his one-two-three. I tell myself not to read into it. "We'll figure it out."

$$\rightsquigarrow \cdot \leftsquigarrow$$

FIGURING IT OUT apparently means going over all my invoices and budget spreadsheets in excruciating detail while Luka hums under his breath and makes various other sounds that do nothing to soothe my frayed nerves. A cough into his hand when I show him the spreadsheet with our missing shipments. A low grumble under his breath when I pull up the invoices with amounts due in red. A sigh when we look over the estimate for the trees in the south pasture and how it impacts our bottom line.

He rubs his fingertips along his jaw and clicks around on my computer while I resist the urge to rip the laptop out of his hands. Going from sharing this with no one to sharing it with everyone has me agitated and off-kilter.

Luka doesn't spare me a glance as I stomp my way into the kitchen.

"You could charge admission," he offers as I wrestle with my wine bottle. I am about three seconds away from breaking the neck off on the edge of the counter. "That would help you out moving forward."

"If you look at spreadsheet three at the bottom"—the cork finally gives with a satisfying *pop*—"I projected out those numbers. I don't want to charge admission if I can help it. It makes it more cost-prohibitive to families. We're the only farm in the state that doesn't charge at the gates, and I'd like it to stay that way for as long as possible."

Luka clicks over to the spreadsheet in question with a humming noise. I drink directly from the bottle.

"You could charge anyone over the age of twenty. That way there's still an appeal for families with kids and teens. You could even lump tickets into a full package. Include hot chocolate, the ice-skating rink, and twenty percent off a fresh-cut tree."

That is . . . a good idea. I'm annoyed I didn't think of it myself. I take another pull from the bottle as Luka stands from the couch, placing my laptop on the kitchen table on his way to me. I offer him the bottle, but he shakes his head, collecting that too and putting it with my laptop.

He holds out his arms. "C'mere."

His cheeks are still flushed pink from his time outside today, twin spots of color against his golden skin. I stare at him, his open arms, the soft faded material of his thermal shirt. It clings tight around his biceps, and I get distracted there for a second, teeth sawing over my bottom lip.

"Why?" I ask, suspicious.

He huffs a laugh through his nose and steps closer, his hands over my shoulders. He tugs once and slips his grip to my wrists, adjusting my hands until they're looped around his neck. He spins us to the refrigerator in two smooth steps, my knees knocking against his the whole way.

"What's happening here?" I ask again, doing my best to follow his movements.

He ignores me, reaching above the fridge for the old radio I keep up there. There's a burst of static when he turns it on, twisting the knob to find a clear station. It was my mom's. Every place we lived, she put it up on top of the fridge. She liked to dance to Bruce Springsteen during dinner. AC/DC during cleanup. We'd wash dishes, and she'd swing her hips and shake her hair. She used to say she could have been one of those girls climbing on top of the cars in the music videos. Teenage me had been horrified.

"I want to talk to you," he says.

I stare pointedly at my hands curled around his neck, my chest pressed to his. "And this is talking?"

He finds what he's looking for, the smooth sound of Louis Armstrong crooning through the old speakers about a silent night. It's a little tinny and crackling with static, the old radio not the best in audio quality. But I love it.

Luka tugs me close and spins me into the center of the kitchen, one hand at my hip, the other between my shoulder blades. "Why didn't you tell me you were having trouble?"

"Um." It's hard for me to think when he's holding me like this. Slowly swaying around my kitchen with his nose at my temple. "Why are we slow-dancing?"

Luka rests his chin on top of my head. "This is how my parents argued," he confesses quietly, a grin in his voice. "Or I guess, this is how they had big conversations. My dad said he liked to keep my mom close, but I really think he wanted a way to politely restrain her."

I huff a laugh and relax into his hold, letting him spin me slowly. It's nice to hear him talk about his dad, to have a good memory. I try to picture a younger Luka, rolling his eyes at his parents dancing in the kitchen. It makes me smile. His grip tightens when he feels me soften in his hold, palm slipping down from between my shoulders to the center of my back. "So, why didn't you tell me?"

There's a thin thread of hurt in the quiet question, a lingering sadness around the edges that has me tucking closer, resting my forehead against his collarbone. He smells like pine here, another remnant of his time in the fields. The reason I didn't tell Luka is the same reason I didn't tell anyone. "Because I thought I was handling it," I tell him, a lick of frustration slipping through. "I am handling it."

My plan is a good one. Get through this trip with Evelyn. Charm her senseless. Win the contest and settle our debts with the suppliers. From there, we should be solid enough to make it through to spring. At this point, even if we don't win the prize money, I think we'll be okay. The added influx of customers from the feature on Evelyn's channels should be enough to pull us out. I'll just—have to eat ramen for a little bit longer.

"You still could have told me," he says, tipping his chin back until he's looking down at me. He looks younger like this, tired from a day in the fields, a yawn creaking at his jaw.

"I didn't want—" I think about those early days when I realized how deep in it we were, the numbers on my computer screen not making sense no matter how many times I sorted and rearranged the columns. I had wanted to call Luka so badly, ask him to take a look, reassure me. But I also wanted to do this myself. This farm, this business, it's the first thing that's ever been mine and mine alone. "I didn't want you to rescue me."

His eyebrows jump in surprise. "Helping friends is off-limits now?"

"It's not like that. It's just—do you remember that year I decided I wanted to learn how to ride a skateboard? And you said you'd help?"

He smiles at the memory. "Yeah, you bought that red helmet with the flames on the side. Knee pads to match. You were so cute."

I roll my eyes. I wasn't trying to be cute. I was trying to be safe and a little badass. I did like that helmet though. "Well, as you remember, those knee pads paid off. I was horrible."

The tug of a grin spreads until he's laughing, no doubt recalling my tumble into the fountain in the middle of town. "You were tragically horrible," he agrees.

"Right, and what did you do? How did you help me achieve my dream of coasting down the street on a skateboard?"

His laughter settles into a warm rumble of a chuckle. "I gave you a piggyback." He smiles. "I hopped on the skateboard with you on my back, and we flew down Main Street."

It's a good memory. I can still remember the way I clutched tight at his shoulders, every bump in the sidewalk as we rocketed past the bookstore, the greenhouse, the little park with daffodils at the entrance. I nod. "Yeah, you helped me do the thing I wanted to do by literally putting me on your back." I smile and run my fingers through his hair, helpless not to touch him. Not while he looks so happy and so sad at the same time. "You have done that countless times in our friendship, and I'm so grateful. But this time I wanted—I wanted to be my own hero. I wanted to do it myself."

He pushes his head into my hand, closing his eyes. "Leaning on other people doesn't make your achievements any less yours." He opens his eyes, dark like melted chocolate. "Do you remember when I convinced myself I wanted to run a half marathon? What did you do?"

I hated that idea. I woke up every morning before the sun and grumbled all the way through putting on my tennis shoes and pulling on my sports bra, Luka grunting on the other end of the line. We had entire conversations through sounds alone those mornings.

"You woke up every morning with me for my run and did an equal distance here at the same time. So I'd feel less alone."

"About that," I mumble. "I may have just ran to Ms. B's and got a plate of cinnamon rolls."

He blinks at me. "What? But your GPS—"

"I paid one of the high school kids to run my route. He'd meet me out front of the bakery, and we'd do the exchange. He was trying to make the cross country team, so it worked out."

Luka laughs, eyes crinkling at the corners. He nuzzles once at my temple and spins us back across the kitchen, over to the fridge. "Regardless," he hums. "You woke up with me. You sent me healthy snacks. You believed in me and encouraged me. You even made a sign for the race."

A bright pink sign with gold glitter that said YOU THINK YOU'RE TIRED? I'VE BEEN HOLDING THIS SIGN SINCE 9:00.

On the other side: I'M SO PROUD OF YOU, LUKA.

"What I'm trying to say is that you can trust me. You can trust me to help you carry the load. You don't have to do all of this alone." He catches an errant curl, rubbing it gently between thumb and forefinger. He twists it lightly and tugs once. "I know you can take care of yourself. You've been doing that as long as I've known you. But let me hold your hand while you do it, okay?"

I nod, a hot pressure behind my eyes. The music switches to Nat King Cole, and I practically melt into Luka's arms, another turn around my kitchen.

"All right," I say.

He brushes a kiss against my temple and whispers back. "All right."

18

EVELYN FINDS ME in my office the next morning. She's bundled up in a beautiful white jacket with a thick sash at the middle, her dark hair braided over one shoulder. I get a whiff of hazelnut and stare longingly at the take-out cup in her hand, my lukewarm coffee balanced at the edge of my desk. It's nice to know Ms. Beatrice can be kind when she wants to.

I try to surreptitiously stack the chaos of paperwork on my desk into a neater pile, brush away the crumbs from a leftover muffin. I wasn't exactly expecting company. I've been waiting for a call from the bed-and-breakfast all morning. The owner, Jenny, letting me know that Evelyn has decided to check out early.

Evelyn smiles and takes the seat across from my desk, perched on the very edge. I'm glad at least I decided to sew up the tears on the upholstery in a fit of procrastination. Her posture is immaculate, her legs crossed gracefully. I don't think I've ever looked that put together in my life.

"You seem surprised," she says and takes a long drink from her latte. "I told you we'd get a fresh start today."

"I thought you might have left." I fiddle with one of the pine trees sitting on the edge of my desk, wrapping the string around my thumb. "I was worried you'd be uncomfortable here."

"I owe you an apology," she says, and my elbow knocks a stack of paperwork to the floor. So much for looking organized.

A quiet "um" is about all I can manage in response.

"Beckett came to talk to me last night," she offers. My face must do something strange at that, because she flushes pink and ducks her head. "Oh jeez, not like that. He just—he explained how much the farm means to you, to him, to your town. He asked if I'd consider staying. He said he'd make himself scarce if I—if I wanted him to."

A balloon of affection for Beckett rises in my chest. "And do you?" It's not the question I should be asking, but I'm curious. "Want him to?"

Evelyn shrugs. "I don't think that's necessary. We're both grown-ups, and what happened between us is—" That flush on her cheeks burns darker, and she waves her hand between us, shooing the thoughts away. I hide my smile in the lip of my coffee mug. "Well, it doesn't matter. That was then, this is now. I'm resolved to be professional and see this trip through. You deserve it."

I probably don't. The truth sticks in the back of my throat, the confession that my relationship with Luka isn't the romantic tale I've led her to believe. I press my palms flat to my desk and trace my thumb over the wood grain. "Listen, I should tell you—"

My sentence is abruptly cut off by my office door swinging open, Luka on the other side with that damn poof-ball hat and two take-out cups. He's wearing a scarf today too, a thick evergreen I'm pretty sure his grandmother made him.

"I think this is still decaf, but Ms. Beatrice did give you hazelnut, so that's— Oh, shoot." He tucks one of the cups into the cradle of his elbow and extends one gloved hand to Evelyn, a smile already lighting up his eyes, golden in the morning light. It really is unfair how pretty he is. "Hey. You must be Evelyn."

Evelyn smiles and stands from her chair, taking his hand in a shake and then tipping her cup to his in a mini cheers. I feel my resolve wither away. "Luka, I'm so excited to meet you."

"I was just swinging by to drop off a coffee before I head out to the ice-skating rink." His amber eyes find mine, a smile lifting the corners of his mouth. I left him this morning before the sun was up, buried beneath the pillows on my bed. He had curled his hand around my elbow with a sleepy grumble, a muffled request to "come back and cuddle." It was a tempting offer.

"Beck texted about some of the panels on the far end being loose." I notice a hammer hanging out of his jeans pocket, a folded-up piece of canvas tucked under his arm. He sees my questioning glance and grins. "Mom gave it to me," he explains. "Some of the kids made a sign. I think it'll look nice over the panels. Sort of like those ads you see at hockey games."

"As long as no one is checking one another into the boards, that's fine. What's the sign say?"

"Wouldn't you like to know?" He rumbles with a laugh. He drops my coffee on the edge of my desk and presses his palm flat to the wooden top, leaning forward to brush a kiss across my lips. As far as distractions go, it's a good one. I sigh into it and he smiles, another quick kiss before he leans back. I see Evelyn grinning at us from the corner of my eye.

"Can I join you?" she asks. "I didn't get to see much yesterday. I'd like to see the rink."

"Yeah, no problem. I'll give you the unofficial tour, and Stella will give you the more professional version later."

She claps her hands together once, back to the energetic, excited woman she was when she first arrived. "That's perfect."

I tell myself that it's fine, that we're not really lying to her. We're more . . . bending the truth, I guess. I'm not exactly sure what Luka and I are to each other right now. Sure, we're friends, but after that night on my couch, we're also something more. I've convinced myself it's not so much a lie anymore as it is an embellishment.

I swallow around the unease. "I'll meet you out there in a little bit."

≫· ≪

I BARELY MANAGE to make a dent in my email before I have another set of visitors.

Beckett strides into my office with a determined look on his face, a stack of papers wedged under his arm. He slaps the booklet down on my desk and then collapses into the same chair Evelyn was sitting in an hour ago, arms crossed over his chest.

Layla hustles in behind him, out of breath, a giant piece of poster board in her hands. "You would not believe how this thing catches the wind," she says, placing the huge board in the unoccupied chair, corner down. She tears off her jacket and gestures toward the stack on my desk. "Beckett brought you the appendix. Good."

"Didn't have time to laminate," he says, still glaring at me.

"Don't you have your own machine?"

"Broken." He grunts.

I tried calling both of them last night after Luka and I had slow-danced around my kitchen enough for my heart to settle. All of my calls had gone straight to voicemail. I flip the stack of papers around on my desk so I can read the top page: LOVELIGHT FARMS BUSINESS PLAN in boldface.

Now I see why no one was answering their phones.

"Should I sit?"

Beckett and Layla nod in unison and then proceed to walk me through a forty-five-minute presentation. There are color-coded sections in the booklet on new suppliers, references to local ordinances about tax breaks and credits, and even a budget spreadsheet that looks suspiciously like the one I showed Luka last night, a column highlighted in yellow with our baseline numbers if we started charging admission rates.

I flip the page and look at salary projections, my eyebrows knitting in confusion when I see the numbers. "These are wrong," I say, interrupting Layla midsentence and wincing in apology. "Sorry, just, I'm looking at the paycheck section, and your numbers are wrong."

Beckett rubs at his chin with the heel of his hand, legs kicked out. Layla has led most of this presentation, but he did get pretty passionate when talking about fertilizers, as per usual. He flips to the corresponding page in his booklet and arches an eyebrow. "They're not wrong."

"They are off by about thirty percent." I squint my eyes. "Mmm, actually. About—"

"It's a forty percent pay cut for Beckett and me," Layla says without a lick of hesitation. "With backpay built in for what you've cut for yourself."

"It's a fifty percent cut for me," Beckett grumbles. "I don't pay any rent on my house. That should be included in my compensation package."

I swallow and keep my eyes on the numbers. "And everyone else?" I clear my throat until my voice doesn't wobble. "The seasonal help and your staff? Their numbers don't change?"

"Everyone else stays where they are. The pay cut for just the three of us should be able to get us through another couple of months, even without the prize money."

I press under my eyes and keep my gaze firmly on the spreadsheet. I'm afraid if I look up, I might burst into tears. "I can't let you do that."

"Well, we're doing it, so . . ." Layla props her hands on her hips. She gestures to the posterboard, where she's drawn a chart in red and white, outlined with glitter. A candy-cane financial projection through the next three years. "And there's another thing. Beckett and I discussed it. We want to be full-on partners. We'd like to split ownership and all financial obligations three ways."

Beckett jumps in. "We'll need to see your start-up costs, a full breakdown of what the land cost you and all the renovations. We'll evaluate it and split it. There's some legal paperwork to be done too. On the account of ownership. But if you're willing to let us be a part of this, we're in."

Layla nods in agreement. "We're super in. All the way in. It should have been this way from the start, Stella. This feels right."

I suck in a lungful of air and look up at Layla. Her face is open, none of the hurt resignation from yesterday. Now she just looks determined. She gives me a tiny nod, barely a tilt of her chin.

Beckett is different. He's all harsh lines and furrowed brows, arms still crossed over his chest, the sleeves of his flannel rolled to his elbows. The colorful ink painted across his skin is a fine distraction from the way my heart is pounding in my chest. I stare at the ivy vine that loops around his wrist. The crescent moon on the inside of his elbow.

"Beck? You're sure?" I blink back up to his face and something there shifts. A recognition. A realignment.

"This," he says quietly. "This is what partners do."

❧ ❦

BY THE TIME I make it out to the ice-skating rink to catch up with Luka and Evelyn, I'm jittery from too much caffeine and the relief of renewed hope. I made Beckett and Layla go over the numbers with me another three times, line by line. I eventually talked them down to a thirty percent pay cut, with only half the back pay they projected. With those adjustments, we should be able to run smoothly for a while yet.

I'm still hesitant about starting admission prices. Not having to pay to get into the farm was a big reason why my mom and I came here so often when I was a kid. It was free for us to wander around the trees, sipping on hot chocolate we smuggled in with our bags. If there was an entrance fee, I'm not sure my mom would have ever brought me here. The thought makes me sad. I bought this place so everyone could experience the same magic. No one should feel left out.

I turn the corner on the stone walkway that leads from the office to the main entrance area, Mariah Carey over the speakers. There's a chill in the air today, a brisk wind that's tripping through the trees. I watch them sway and dance on the foothills, their branches waving in the sun. By the end of the season, these hills will be golden brown instead of rich green, all of the trees sitting happily in their new homes. I like to think of that sometimes—where my trees end up. Strung with lights and tinsel and ornaments. Presents stacked neatly beneath, just begging to be opened. A piece of Lovelight Farms in someone's home, helping make their holiday special.

The ice-skating rink is full when I arrive, a group of high schoolers whipping around in figure eights, laughing and holding hands and chasing one another. I see Cindy Croswell off to the side using one of the skater helpers shaped like a penguin that we specifically bought for children. Bailey and Sandra McGivens skate slowly along, hand in hand, whispering to each other, pausing for a kiss beneath the mistletoe every time they pass under the entrance arch. I grin and let my gaze move along the siding, the reinforced pieces of wood, and the banner strung neatly overtop.

Red and green paint, a little bit sloppy at the edges, like whoever was painting it was in a rush. MERRY CHRISTMAS, LOVELIGHT FARMS. FROM ~~INGLEWILD HIGH~~ THE JOLLIEST BUNCH OF A-HOLES. They've drawn a tiny cityscape beneath, lights strung over Inglewild's rooftops. I lean my elbows up against the arm rail with a laugh and snap a picture with my phone.

"Do you like it, Ms. Bloom?" One of the high schoolers—Jeremy, I think—comes to a sudden, forceful stop against the wooden boards right next to me, his skates slamming in first as a shower of ice shepherds his arrival. He shakes his hair out of his face and leans right next to me.

"It's very creative," I say diplomatically. We'll probably have to cover up that last part if we leave it up, but it makes me laugh. "*Christmas Vacation* is one of my favorite holiday movies."

"Me too," he agrees, and he does that hair flip thing again. I don't know how he manages to stay conscious with such an aggressive head jerk every thirty seconds. "We have so much in common."

"Um, sure."

"You know, you're pretty hot for an older woman," Jeremy tells me, flipping his hair twice in the space of fifteen seconds. Does this work on the girls at Inglewild High? I sure hope not. I let that comment sit for a moment. He's staring at me with a cocky grin kicking up his mouth. Oh, to have the confidence of a young white man.

"Want a tip?"

"From you, baby? I want more than the tip."

Ugh, gross. When did high schoolers become so terrible? I make a mental note to let Mrs. Peters know that Jeremy sucks, though I'm sure given his less-than-subtle approach to life, she has an idea. "Don't call women old," I tell him. "In fact, don't call women anything. I think you'd benefit from probably not talking to women in general for five to seven years."

He looks down at his skates, shoulders curling in. "Sorry," he mumbles.

"It's all right, just—you can't say vulgar things like that. Use this as a learning moment."

He blinks up at me. "What sort of things should I say?"

I consider that. "Maybe if you like someone, tell them what you like about them." He opens his mouth and I give him a look. "Something that isn't physical."

He looks confused.

"Their personality," I offer. "Like they're funny or smart or especially kind. You could say something not"—I consider my words—"not gross about their appearance. Maybe their eyes, their hair, the way they smile."

He nods, still confused. He looks dubious. "And that will work?"

"It will only work if you truly mean what you're saying and you're respectful of what they say in return. Got it?"

"I think so." He shifts on his skates.

I feel an arm slip around my waist, a broad chest at my back. Luka rests his chin on top of my head. "Jeremy, you better not be creeping on my woman."

Jeremy grins and takes off to the other end of the ice-skating rink without a word, another spray of ice behind him. I'll have to get a Zamboni if the high schoolers keep coming.

I turn in Luka's arms, my hands clasped at the small of his back. I liked the way that sounded, *his woman*. A little bit too much. He glances down at me with a grin, brown eyes searching my face. "Everything okay?"

I nod. "Beckett and Layla came to see me."

He hums, his smile twitching at the corner of his mouth. "Oh?"

"Yeah," I squeeze him harder, fingers digging into the thick material of his jacket. I rest my forehead against his chest, and his palm drifts from the small of my back up between my shoulder blades. He rocks us back and forth once. "Thank you," I whisper.

"Nothing to thank me for. It's all you," he says. He hums again, a low rumble against my ear. "I just wanna hold your hand, Stella."

I rest my chin on his chest and look up. "I think I'll let you."

"Glad to hear it." His smile tips into something softer, thumb tracing the apple of my cheek. "Listen, we haven't really had a chance to talk. About—about the other night."

"Oh. Okay."

"Was it—" I feel his hands twitch at my sides. "Was it weird?"

"Weird that it wasn't weird," I tell him, a laugh at the tip of my tongue. No part of me regrets what happened between us the other night, even though it feels like I should. We're well beyond blurring the lines of our relationship. "What about you?"

His shoulders relax. "I can't stop thinking about you," he whispers, thumb tracing down from my cheek to my bottom lip. His eyes go hazy, unfocused. A shiver curls over my shoulders and slips down my spine. "The sounds you made, La La, I—"

The group of high schoolers whips by us again, screaming and laughing. Luka blinks and clears his throat, squeezes my hips tight.

"Weird that it wasn't weird," he agrees faintly, his gaze meeting mine. His eyes are dark, sharp with intent, and I look over his shoulder to the barn. We could probably make it there without anyone noticing. Find a nice and dark cozy corner to hide in.

"I left Evelyn at the bakehouse with Peter," Luka says, reminding me of what I should be focusing on. I shake my head. "She seemed intent on getting her hands on more brownies."

"Is she having a good time?"

"She seems to be. I took her out to the fields and showed her around. She really liked the sleigh. She was snapping all sorts of pictures on her phone."

The sleigh is an old beat-up 1954 Chevy 3100 truck left in the fields by Hank—or maybe even the owner before Hank. When Beckett found it, it was rusted out and home to an entire colony of birds. It still is home to the birds when they migrate back in the spring, but now it's painted cherry red, multicolor Christmas lights strung over the cab. We keep a big canvas sack in the bed of the truck stuffed with boxes—Santa's magic bag left behind. The kids get a kick out of it.

"That was a good idea to take her there."

"To be honest, I forgot about it." He rubs the back of his neck. "I might have got turned around with all the trees. I spotted it and just sort of made it seem like that was the goal."

I laugh. Leave it to Luka. "Either way, thanks for that."

My phone begins to ring in my front pocket, and I step out of the cradle of his arms to search for it among the crumpled candy wrappers and old receipts currently occupying my jacket. I find a foil-covered peppermint chocolate bar and hand it over to Luka. His attention is quickly diverted by the group of high schoolers as they make another raucous lap of the ice-skating rink, his eyes narrowed on Jeremy.

I answer the phone with a smile, not bothering to check who it is first. "Hello?"

"Hey, Stella."

"Dane."

Luka turns back to me and arches an eyebrow in a silent question.

I shrug. I haven't heard from Dane since the early morning chase through the fields over the weekend. "What can I do for you?"

He sighs. "I've got some news. Can you come down to the station?"

19

WHEN DANE SAYS *some news,* he means he caught the person throwing rocks at my security camera. He tells me this in place of polite small talk, and I launch myself out of the chair across from his desk, knocking over a cup filled with pens and a miniature model airplane.

"You what?" I glance around me like the suspect is about to pop out from behind his curtains. "Who is it? Why did they do it?" I squint through the glass wall of his office to the small kitchenette, the holding cell, and the receiving area for walk-ins. I point toward a door in the back corner. "Do you have them in interrogation?"

Dane rubs his fingertips between his eyebrows and gestures to the chair, a quiet command to sit. "That's a utility closet, Cinnamon Stick."

I sit back down, balanced on the very edge. "Did they confess?"

He nods. I want to punch the air in victory.

"Do you need an interrogation partner?" All my binge-watching of *Law & Order* is about to pay off. I feel like I should go home, change into a smart pantsuit, and grab a briefcase. "Want to do good cop, bad cop?"

"That is not a thing that happens."

"Says you."

"Says literally every law enforcement professional in the country. Listen"—he levels me with a look, a frown tugging at his lips—"there's no need for an interrogation. He's already told us everything he's done. I'm having trouble with this one because I'm a little miffed on your behalf, and I'm not embracing my usual"—he rubs at his jaw as he searches for the word—"impartiality, I suppose you could say."

"Did you punch him in the face?"

Dane shakes his head with a faint smile. "I did not punch him in the face." It looks like he wanted to punch him in the face.

"Then I don't see the problem. You don't have to be impartial if he's already confessed." My mind races with the possibilities of who it could be, their motive. Luka had wanted to come with me, but I forced him to stay at the farm in case Evelyn needed anything. I caught a glimpse of her just before I left, hot chocolate in hand. Interestingly enough, Beckett wasn't too far behind.

"They're here now"—I open my mouth to ask—"not in the interrogation room that does not exist."

"They're here now. And no, they are not in interrogration. We are a small town. There is no interrogation room."

He is exhausted by me. He grabs a stress ball out of his top drawer and starts to squeeze it. "How would you like to handle this?"

"I guess I want to know my options." I'd like to throw some rocks at this person, for starters. An eye for an eye and all that. But I don't think that's going to fly with Dane.

"They're facing several counts of malicious destruction of private property. That's a misdemeanor in the state of Maryland. Because it was done willfully and resulted in thousands of dollars' worth of damage, he could face jail time."

"Jail time?" I'm upset about the camera and the missing shipments and the broken fence posts, but I'm not sure I want someone to go to jail over it. I frown and settle back in the chair. "Is that the only option?"

"It's up to you if you want to press charges or not." He starts to squeeze the ball again, harder this time. "He asked if he could—he asked if he could talk to you. Apologize."

I blink. "I suppose that's probably a good start, yeah?" It would be nice if we could handle this civilly.

Dane's mustache twitches. "Sure."

"All right, then lead the way to interrogation."

"It's not—" Dane sighs and gives up. "This way."

I don't know who I am expecting it to be. Some grungy gargoyle of a human, maybe. I think part of me hopes it was someone doing all of this in a plea for help. Maybe they were throwing rocks at my camera because they needed to feed their family . . . or something. Maybe they just ran because they were scared, and this has all been one big misunderstanding.

I certainly don't expect Will Hewett sitting at the conference table in his tweed jacket and tortoiseshell glasses, nursing a cup of tea in a paper cup.

"Where'd you get the tea?" Dane grunts in greeting as I stand motionless and confused in the doorway.

"Deputy Alvarez," Mr. Hewett responds, looking up at me briefly and then back down at his cup. I feel like I'm part of an elaborate practical joke. Caleb slips quietly into the room behind us, notebook wedged under his arm. Dane gives him a look.

"We're serving tea to criminals now?"

Caleb blinks and looks at the tiny paper cup of tea. "Want me to take it away from him?"

"Obviously."

Caleb reaches for the cup and I wave him off, taking the empty chair across from Mr. Hewett. He doesn't look up at me again, and I fight the urge to whisper, *What the fuck?*

"I'm confused," I manage. I look up at Dane, standing over my shoulder with a thunderous expression, arms crossed over his chest. I turn and frown at Caleb, reclining against the door. I settle and glance back at Mr. Hewett. No one in this room is being particularly effusive. "Is this a joke?"

All three men shake their heads with varying degrees of enthusiasm.

"Okay, well—" I'd like some tea too. With a healthy dose of whiskey. "Can someone explain to me what's going on? I'm having trouble understanding. Mr. Hewett, you destroyed my camera?"

"Why don't you start from the top, William."

It begins with the sale of the farm, long before I drove past and saw the FOR SALE sign. Mr. Hewett explains that he had a gentleman's agreement with Hank to buy the land, but he needed more time to get the money together. While he was trying to liquidate some of his assets and free up the cash, I swooped in and bought the farm from under his nose.

I vaguely remember Hank mentioning there was another interested buyer when I put in my offer, but nothing ever came of it. I had been tucking money away for years in the hopes of opening my own place, the payout from my mom's insurance policy sitting untouched in my bank account. I had been saving it for something special, something meaningful. I saw the sign, made the offer, and the next week, Hank was in Costa Rica and I had the keys to the place.

"You wanted a . . . what?"

Mr. Hewett picks a piece of paper off the edge of his cup, disdain in the curl of his lip. Whatever altruism that led him to confess hasn't impacted his overall perception of me. "An alpaca farm," he mutters.

"An alpaca farm."

"It's my dream," he replies with thinly veiled impatience.

Dane snorts behind me. Clearly, there have been some thoughts shared between the men in this room on the concept of an alpaca farm.

I hold up my hands. "And you were upset with me because you thought I took the land from you," I reason. I duck my head and try to meet his eyes. "But you have to know, I had no idea you were interested. Hank never said anything to me about your agreement."

He nods. "I realize that now."

"Okay, well"—I shrug—"I still have some questions."

He gives me a jerk of a nod and shifts in his chair, clearly uncomfortable. His eyes glance over my shoulder to the room beyond with a wistful little sigh.

"Why did you tell Dane the truth about everything?"

"That night, when I broke your camera and Beckett chased me through the fields, he almost caught me, I ended up lying in a ditch for three hours covered in pine needles in an attempt to hide. I realized then it was time to take a hard look at my choices."

Okay, fair. I'd imagine anyone might reconsider their actions after lying in a freezing cold dirt ditch in an attempt to evade a pissed-off farmer.

"And what were you doing?"

He sighs. "I started with small, inconvenient things. I just wanted you to feel like the farm was a burden and maybe think about selling. To me. But nothing gave you pause. I broke some fence posts, called your vendors and canceled some orders. I took some of your decorations from last year—they're in the basement of the library if you'd like them back."

I nearly snort. "I would, thank you."

"And nothing seemed to frustrate you. It was maddening. Your lack of frustration was . . . frustrating. I knew I had to do something bigger, so"—he swallows and glances at Dane before looking back down at the table—"I tinkered with the drainage system in the south pasture. I, well, there's quite a bit of literature on Fraser firs in the library, you know."

Dane clears his throat, not interested in whatever educational resources the library offers on Fraser firs. Even sweet Caleb looks disappointed. The south pasture. The twisted and dead-looking trees. My stomach sinks.

"What did you do to my trees?"

"If you oversaturate the soil, the roots become overwhelmed and can't pull oxygen from the ground. I disabled your soil moisture sensor and gave your trees root rot."

Poor Beckett spent hours out in those fields on his hands and knees checking each individual tree for clues. He ran the equipment through countless tests and audits, drove himself into the ground trying to figure it out.

"But those trees don't look like they have root rot, they look—"

"Like something from an alternate realm, yes. I'm not—I'm not entirely sure how that happened. I repaired your drainage system after a couple of weeks, just after the rot took hold, so you wouldn't notice the cause. And things just sort of deteriorated from there. I bet the local university horticulture department would be interested in taking a look—" Dane coughs again, sounding more like a grumbling bear than anything, and Mr. Hewett shrinks in his chair. "But I suppose that's up to you."

I collapse back in my chair, winded. Mr. Hewett has caused thousands of dollars in damage to my farm over the course of a year in an effort to get me to sell so he could establish his very own alpaca farm. The truth can certainly be wild.

I rub my fingers over my lips. "I don't know what to think," I say faintly. It's a relief to know that all of our troubles can be explained away. That the challenges we've had will likely disappear now that he's confessed. But the saddest thing to me, the absolute heartbreak of it all is—

"Mr. Hewett, I would have happily given you space for your alpacas," I tell him, "if only you'd asked me."

We could have given them reindeer headbands in the winter. Sold Christmas sweaters made of alpaca wool in the gift shop. It would have been adorable.

Something in his face shutters and breaks at that, his eyebrows slanting low as he looks down at the table in front of him. He places his mangled cup off to the side and takes off his glasses, rubbing furiously at his eyes with his knuckles.

"I'll do whatever you want to make it up to you." He looks up at me, meeting my gaze steadily for the first time since I've stepped into this cramped noninterrogation room. "I'll do the time."

I don't know what I want to do yet, but I do know that this man going to jail for wanting to have an alpaca farm seems a little ridiculous. I push back from the table and stand. "Could I have some time to think about it?" I look to Dane. "The charges?"

He nods. "I think so, but not too long, yeah?" He shifts his glance to Mr. Hewett. "And if you even step a foot down the road that leads to Lovelight Farms, I will personally keep you locked up in our drunk tank for the foreseeable future. Do you understand?"

Mr. Hewett nods frantically. At least I can rest easy that no one will be smashing security cameras while Evelyn is here.

If only I was as confident with the rest of it.

⊰ ⊱

I MANAGE TO corral Luka, Layla, and Beckett into my office as soon as I'm back on the farm, Beckett pacing furiously in front of my desk. He hasn't stopped moving since I told him his drainage system and moisture sensors were disabled. Mr. Hewett is lucky Beckett wasn't with me at the station. As it is, I kind of fear for my flooring.

He stomps one way, pivots, and stomps back to the other side of the office. I need to expand this room by about three football fields. Layla watches him with a thoughtful frown on her face.

"Was he the one who unplugged my refrigerator overnight?" Layla asks. "I lost two weeks' worth of ingredients from that."

I nod. Dane had given me a written list of all of Will Hewett's actions against the farm before I left the station. It's two pages long, single-spaced. I hadn't even realized one of the tractors was missing a tire.

"The crooked mailbox at the edge of the road?"

I roll my eyes at Luka and his too-innocent expression. "Nice try. I know that was you. You always take that turn too sharply."

"Filthy soil-tampering motherfucker," Beckett fumes. He turns to face my desk with his eyes blazing, grunts, and continues his ritual hate stomp around my office. My head is starting to pound to the same beat.

"We need to figure out what we're going to do about it. I thought since we're partners now"—I glance at Layla and Beckett—"we ought to make the decision together."

"Is exile a thing? Can we ship him to Peru? His alpaca-loving heart would finally be satisfied."

"Beckett, be serious please."

"You're right. He'd be too happy there. Let's ship him someplace miserable. Like Florida."

"All right, so we'll come back to you when you feel like contributing something useful." I look over to Layla. "What do you think?"

"I mean, I'm upset, obviously." Her eyes flicker over to Beckett trying to strangle one of my chairs with his bare hands. They widen in an expression that clearly says, *Not quite that upset*. "But also relieved. It's kind of nice to know that all of this insanity will stop now. I was getting tired of constantly waiting for the other shoe to drop. Or I guess, a refrigerator to randomly unplug."

I nod my head. I am familiar with the feeling. "Dane says we can press charges if we want to, potentially file a civil suit for damages incurred. But he said that charges would probably include jail time, especially since losing the south pasture is worth thousands of dollars."

"Lock him up," Beckett mutters from the corner. He's backed himself into the space next to my office tree, cloaked half in shadow. He looks like the Grinch, sounds like him too. "Throw away the key."

"Don't you think it's ridiculous to put a man in jail for an alpaca farm?"

"I don't know, Stella." I'm surprised to hear this from Luka, silent up until now. He shrugs at me when my attention whips over to him, his long legs stretched out in front of him. "This is your dream, and he tried to take it away from you. Shouldn't he pay for that?"

Now, there's an idea. I would very much like for him to pay for it. All of it, down to the penny. Luka arches an eyebrow at me and reaches for the old-school calculator I have sitting on the edge of my desk, the packet of papers Dane gave me detailing the damages. He starts to tip-tap away as I look at Layla and Beckett.

"We'll take a vote."

❧ ⋅ ☙

IN A SHOCK to no one, Beckett votes for jail time. Layla and I agree to hold Mr. Hewett financially responsible for all of our losses with no additional charges pressed against him. All three of us agree on a restraining order to keep him off the farm indefinitely.

I glance at the clock above my door and wince, standing and brushing my hands over my jeans. "I'm supposed to meet Evelyn for a tour." I look over to Luka, one of my pens held between his teeth as he continues to poke away at the calculator. It shouldn't be as hot as it is. Something about the way he's pushed his hat back on his head so just a tuft of his chestnut hair pokes through the front, wild as usual, nose scrunched in thought as he drags his thumb down the page, checking his numbers. I clear my throat. "I'm going to invite Evelyn over to have dinner with us if that's all right with you."

"Yeah, of course." He blinks up at me from the paperwork, trying to clear his eyes after staring at numbers for so long. I've told him a million times he should wear reading glasses, something to help him so he doesn't have to squint when looking at small print. I'm almost glad he didn't agree. I don't know what I'd do with Luka in glasses. "I'll make ravioli."

The simple domesticity of the moment hits me right in the chest. This is what I'll miss the most, I think, when our week is up. Not the touches and the kisses and the way he makes me forget my name with his hands in my hair and his mouth on my neck, but this. Wandering down the little pathway to my cottage and rounding the bend by the big oak tree and seeing Luka through the window standing at the stove in the kitchen, one of my silly towels over his shoulder. Stepping in the front door and having him brush his lips to mine, the radio turned low in the kitchen. The smell of basil and tomato and garlic. Something sizzling on the stovetop.

I don't know how I'm going to give that up.

"What kind of ravioli?" Layla asks from her corner of the room.

Beckett must have slipped out at some point after our vote, off to take out his frustration on a tractor engine or maybe check the drainage systems in the south pasture. I wouldn't be surprised if I find him at the ice-skating rink. He's actually pretty good. Some mornings I come out to check on things early before the sun is fully up, and Beckett is quietly doing laps, wearing the old beat-up hockey skates he used as a teenager.

"Butternut squash, probably. I think my grandma put some in Stella's freezer," Luka says.

That's another thing I'll miss. The amount of homemade Italian food stockpiled in my refrigerator. Will his family still feed me when we fake break up?

Layla's eyes light up. "Bring me leftovers tomorrow?"

"You're welcome to join us, you know," I offer.

"Got a thing with Jacob," she explains. Luka makes a face at the mention of her apathetic and chronically boring boyfriend. "Plus, this will be good one-on-one time with Evelyn. You two"—she points at me and then Luka—"are charming together."

Heat rushes to my cheeks. Layla does not possess a subtle bone in her body. By the time I've managed my emotions over any mention of Luka and me together, this week will be over.

"Almost a decade of practice," Luka quips. He stands and deposits the calculator and stack of papers neatly on the side of my desk, making sure the edges are parallel to one another. I appreciate the effort to try to keep my desk clean. I want to nudge it out of place with my pinky, just to see what he does.

He grips the arms of my chair and ducks down, brushing a quick kiss to my lips. "See you at home," he murmurs, casual as can be. "I'll get dinner started."

He nods to Layla as he leaves, but she's too busy staring at me with a smug little grin to notice. I fidget in my chair, putting random papers in random folders in an effort to look busy. I wait for her to leave, but she just settles down farther in her seat.

"What?" I ask, not bothering to look up. There's a receipt in the top drawer of my desk for six hash browns from the drive-through. That must have been a bad day.

Layla snickers. "You know what?"

"I'm sure I don't."

Her snicker turns into a full-blown laugh, bright and loud in my tiny office. She stands to follow Luka out the door. "Oh, Stella honey. You're in deep."

Don't I know it.

☙ ❧

I FIND EVELYN in the Santa barn leaning up against one of the posts as she watches little Evan Barnes tell Clint what he wants from Santa Claus this year. We've kept the barn fairly simple on the inside. A wide-open space for the queue on our busiest days marked with a deep red velvet rope. Cozy armchairs and love seats in lush greens and midnight blues for people to sit while they wait. A wide hearth on the wall and an oversized rocking chair right next to it. A stack of board games close by. Mismatched, faded rugs crisscrossed over one another on the floor for kids to run and jump and tumble. It's one of my favorite places on the farm. Sometimes I come out here at night when the farm is closed and just lie in the center of the room and stare up at the white lights and barn wood, a sliver of the night sky visible through the slats of the roof. The same way I did beneath the Christmas tree when I was a kid.

Clint, for his part, is taking his job very seriously. He's sitting in the big rocking chair with a notepad in hand, tongue between his teeth in concentration.

"That's the LEGO City Mars spaceship?" Clint asks. He's wearing his full firefighter uniform with a big cherry red badge over the left breast that says OFFICIAL NORTH POLE REPRESENTATIVE. Layla made them for all of our volunteers last year and got a little overzealous with the glitter glue.

Evan nods, pushing his glasses back up his nose. "Yes, the research shuttle with the rover. That's important."

"Research shuttle with rover," Clint notes, writing slowly and carefully. He looks up when he's done and claps Evan on the shoulder. "Noted, kiddo. This will go directly to the big man in red." He peeks over at Evan's mom, and she gives him a subtle thumbs-up. "I have a feeling you're going to get everything you're asking for, buddy."

Evan's face lights up. "Even the pony?"

Evan's mom winces and she shakes her head. Clint laughs. "You didn't mention a pony on this list, big guy. Maybe next year, okay?"

"This is a cute idea," Evelyn whispers to me, nudging me with her shoulder. "It's a nice twist on an old tradition. And no children have to sit on a stranger's lap."

I laugh. "We tried to get a Santa here last year, but they're surprisingly hard to book. Inglewild stepped up and IGLOO was born: Inglewild Gift List Operation Operation. They really wanted to make it an acronym, so they listed *Operation* twice." That had been Dane's idea, and I didn't have the heart to tell him Inglewild Gift List Ornamental Operation would have done in a pinch . . . or hundreds of other options. "We have a rotating fleet of volunteers that sit with the kids and listen to their lists. They write them up and put them in the official North Pole post over there." I nod toward the corner with the big metal mailbox, which is painted red with NORTH POLE stenciled in gold. "We deliver the lists back to the parents or caregivers just in case they haven't got their shopping done yet."

"That's brilliant." Evelyn breathes.

I feel a flush of pride for myself and what I've managed to create here, and for the town, coming together to do something nice for the kids. Evan runs off to drop his list in the post, making sure to stamp it three times with the special reindeer stamp we have on the side.

"Also, Beckett refused to wear the costume."

"I'm sure the kids would have had questions about all the tattoos."

"And there probably would have been a whole lot of women in line with the children." I wince, remembering too late Evelyn's history with Beckett. "Shoot, I'm sorry."

She waves me off, and we watch as a little girl with pigtails skips her way over to Clint. "Don't worry about it. He gets a lot of attention, whether he likes to admit it or not."

I guess she saw Cindy Croswell with her cell phone out while he was flat on his back under a tractor earlier. And the gaggle of middle school moms pretending to be interested in the specifics of the coarse mulch that covers the herb garden in the winter, just to have something to talk to him about.

"I don't—" Evelyn eyes me warily. "To address the elephant in the room, I just want to make it clear that I'm not—I don't—" She puffs out a frustrated breath, mouth in a firm line. "I don't typically do things . . . like that. And I certainly didn't expect to see him again."

That was made abundantly clear, on account of her sprinting from the bakehouse.

"Oh, you don't have to—"

"It was just—" She shrugs, gaze far away like she's remembering something. "It just happened. He didn't know who I was and . . . that was nice. A nice change."

I sometimes forget the extent of Evelyn's influence. She has over 1.7 million followers on Instagram alone. I wonder what it's like for someone to recognize you everywhere you go. For people to think that they know you.

Exhausting, I'd imagine.

"He's a good guy." I begin slowly because, above all things, I want Beckett to be okay. I don't want anyone coming here and making things more difficult for him. Hurting him. "The best guy."

Evelyn nods and gives me a smaller smile, more timid. She tucks a lock of dark hair behind her ear, bright red nails glinting in the twinkling lights that line the heavy beams at the ceiling. "I'm not in the business of hurting people, Stella. I can promise you that."

I relax, not realizing how tense I'd become during that conversation. We watch the little girl lean over the arm of the rocking chair, pointing to something on Clint's list. He laughs and scratches with his pencil, then writes again.

"I bet she wants a pony too," says Evelyn.

I glance at the little girl with pigtails. "Not likely with Roma." I saw her at the summer outdoor games in the middle of town. She eviscerated the competition in the sack race and almost knocked a little boy unconscious during tug of war. "She's probably asking for a rocket launcher."

20

WE DON'T TALK about Beckett again. But we do walk what feels like every square inch of the farm. We stroll through the fields with hot chocolate from the bakehouse, past the "sleigh" and through the Hidden Gumdrop Forest. Evelyn laughs when she sees the cluster of trees decked out in bright, colorful lights. It's another surprise for families to stumble over, with a tunnel in the middle constructed out of old barrels for the kids to climb through. Layla calls it our tiny Lincoln Tunnel. Evelyn twirls around the trees, fingertips glancing over red, blue, and yellow lights.

"This place makes me feel like a kid again," she says.

"Everyone should get to feel like a kid this time of year."

It's nice spending so much time in the fields. Once winter hits, I'm usually chained to my desk answering emails and handling the paperwork. I like the quiet, the stillness, the cold brush of winter air on my cheeks. I make a promise to myself to do this more often. Lose myself in the trees.

As we walk, we talk. An informal interview, I guess. Evelyn asks me about the farm, about why I bought it. All the changes I made last year and how I brought on Beckett and Layla. Luka is mentioned often, not in any sort of way to convince her of our romantic story but because he's been with me through it all. I tell her how he brought me a bottle of champagne the first night I owned the place and we wandered out to the farthest pastures, laid flat on our backs beneath the stars, and drank ourselves silly. He told me that night he was proud of me, that he couldn't imagine anything better than me here, doing this.

"He was right," she tells me. "You've thought of everything. I know I've said it already, but this place is incredible. I can't believe what you've managed to accomplish in a year. I didn't see what it looked like before, obviously, but you've got something special here."

Pride warms me to the core. All I've ever wanted to do is make a little magic.

Talking to Evelyn is like talking to an old friend. It's comfortable and easy, quick to dissolve into laughter. We wander through the pastures until our feet are numb with cold, bellies grumbling with the promise of a warm dinner. I can see smoke rising from the chimney as Evelyn loops her arm through mine, and we trudge down the last hill before the cottage.

"I never want to leave this place," she says on a sigh, burrowing her face into the collar of her jacket.

"You're welcome to stay as long as you'd like," I say, chin tilted up to the sky. The sun's long since set, shorter days well and truly upon us. Tonight's sky looks heavy with clouds, a different kind of stillness settling over the trees. "Open invitation."

"I think the finalists I'm supposed to visit next week might have a problem with that," she laughs.

"Do you like what you do? The traveling?"

"You know, I think you're the first person in a while to ask me that." She smiles at me, her eyes crinkling at the corners where they peek out from behind her scarf. The thought makes me sad, and I wonder how many people around her are close to her just for a taste of her influence. "I do like it. I like telling stories. That's why I started all this."

I've been following Evelyn for a while. She started on Instagram, posting photos of ordinary people with no filters, no editing. Sharing their stories and thoughts and dreams, even when it was uncomfortable. That slowly morphed into highlighting small businesses and then transitioned into what she has today. She showcases the hidden beauty up and down the coast, revealing places that people might not know exist. Small-town coffee shops, independent bookstores, nonprofits that help families put food on the table. Those are the stories I love the most, the ones where a community comes together to support their own.

"But lately, I don't know. It feels like some of my stories are written before I even take a look." I know what she means. Most of her stuff these days is sponsored by companies trying to tap into the social influencer market. "I try to be discriminatory in who I work with, but social media is—I don't enjoy it most days."

"You mean you didn't dream of being a social media influencer?"

She laughs and shakes her head. "I wanted to be a journalist. For a while, I thought social media was the best way to do that. But now I don't know. I feel like I haven't told a real story in a while. I just want to help people." She knocks her shoulder into mine. "People like you, just trying to get their dream off the ground."

"You're helping me," I tell her. Already our followers have tripled, more booking inquiries for reserved time slots than we've ever seen before. And Evelyn hasn't posted the bulk of her content. "I can't tell you how grateful I am."

"Everyone deserves to experience this place," she says. A gust of wind lifts her hair, and she smiles, bright and disbelieving. "Oh, you've got to be kidding me."

I look up to where she's looking, head tilted up. A light snow has begun to fall, fat snowflakes drifting silently from the heavy clouds above. The first snow of the year.

"A real-life North Pole," she mutters faintly, a hint of awe in her voice.

I smile and look up at the sky. A perfect moment of holiday magic.

❧ ❦

WE WALK IN the door of the cottage to a blast of Christmas jazz from the kitchen, the smell of warm butter and garlic and something sticky sweet. Luka appears in the hallway with an apron on, a wooden spoon tucked in the front pocket. I have no idea where he found that thing, a dark midnight blue canvas material with SANTA'S LITTLE HELPER printed over the chest. He looks ridiculous.

"Hey, good timing."

He doesn't budge from the entrance to the kitchen as I wander over, rubbing my hands to chase some of the chill away. When I arch an eyebrow at his blockade, he points silently above our heads, a sprig of mistletoe that definitely wasn't there this morning. I snort a laugh and lift up on my toes, pecking a kiss on his cheek.

"Cheater." He chuckles and catches my hips with his hands before I can slip away, ducking down and pressing his mouth to mine in a short, sweet, scorching kiss. He sucks briefly on my bottom lip and then deposits me back on my feet, brown eyes amused when I wobble on unsteady legs.

The line defining fiction and reality is obliterated. I have no idea if that was because Evelyn is behind me or because it's something he wanted to do.

He gives me a wink, and I find I don't really care.

Enjoy it, a voice that sounds suspiciously like Layla whispers in the back of my mind. *Don't overthink it.*

"Is that butternut squash?" Evelyn exclaims from her spot hovering over the stove. She's kicked off her shoes and her jacket, an oversized sweater with a wide neck artfully draped over one shoulder. "Oh my god, is this pumpkin pie?"

She sounds suspiciously close to tears.

"Garlic bread is in the oven," Luka adds. "Should be out in a few. Go. Sit. Have wine." He nods toward the table, where two bottles of red are waiting. He's turned on all the decorations in the cottage, the small, cozy space filled to the brim with fresh pine and lights and handspun garland made from old tartan. Candles in every window and a full balsam fir in the living room bursting with lights and orna ments and tinsel that hangs just right. I watch as Evelyn takes it all in, wide eyes lingering on the row of miniature houses above the cabinets, lit up in an almost perfect replica of Inglewild.

She grabs the bottle of wine and pours herself a hefty glass. "Fuck, this place is perfect."

Dinner is a dream, my tiny house filled with laughter for the first time in a long time. Luka is charming and kind, telling silly stories about the kids in his mom's class, that time he and Beckett crouched in the fields for close to four hours when they were trying to catch the teenagers having illegal ragers. How I had dark green face paint on my hand towels for months after.

None of this feels like faking or pretend. I don't have to act at all when Luka winks at me over his wineglass, foot nudging mine beneath the table. I don't feel dishonest at all when I clear the plates from the table and drop a kiss on Luka's head as I pass by, his fingers catching mine with a gentle squeeze.

"How did you guys start dating?"

It's the first question she's asked about our relationship, and I fumble one of the serving dishes, the spoon clattering to the floor. Luka takes the lead while I collect myself.

"My mom moved here about ten years ago. I think Inglewild had a tourism campaign at one point, something like Little Florence, I don't know. I think she saw an ad in the paper and decided to move here. She misses Italy."

I laugh at the sink. It must have been a shock when they arrived and not a single thing resembled the picturesque Italian city. "Stella had lived here a while. We ran into each other when she was leaving the hardware store."

I know this story well. But Luka surprises me with a detour.

"I thought she was so beautiful. She was—she was wearing a

bright yellow dress with little daisies at the bottom edge. I couldn't stop looking at those daisies. I thought about that yellow dress for days after I left. Every woman I saw in a yellow dress in New York . . ." He trails off and clears his throat. "And when I came back to visit my mom again, I went—" His eyes glance over to me at the sink, standing with my back to the faucet, dirty dishes forgotten. "I took so many long walks around town, just trying to run into her again." He laughs. "My mom thought I was suddenly into power walking. But I eventually ran into her, coming out of the bookstore this time. I don't remember what she was wearing, but I do remember she smiled at me. A big, full Stella smile."

That was my smile, he had said when Caleb was in my kitchen. Evelyn and Luka share a laugh, but I'm busy having a medical event at the sink. I turn off the water and dry my hands on a towel.

Evelyn scoots around in her chair, looping her arm around the back of it and eyeing me with a grin. "And what did you think of Luka? When you first met?"

I still remember with startling clarity the moment I slammed into his chest, even though I was buried in a fog of grief so dense I could hardly manage to put one foot in front of the other.

"Luka isn't just using a figure of speech when he says I ran into him outside the hardware store. I practically tackled him to the ground." I fold up the kitchen towel and look over at Luka, his long legs kicked out under the table, a glass of red wine in his hand. "My mom had just died, and I was . . . sort of floating along. I stumbled off that step, and he caught me, made sure I had my footing. He's sort of been holding me steady ever since."

I wonder if they can hear all the things I'm not saying. That I don't remember what he was wearing, but I do remember he smelled like fresh orange slices and basil. That I could hardly catch my breath the whole time we were sitting in the tiny bakery eating our grilled cheese. That I've liked him forever and loved him just as long.

"I've never told you this," I say to Luka directly now. "But I had no reason to be in that hardware store. I was just—I was just sort of wandering around. Trying to convince myself to be productive. And when I ran into you—" I suck in a sharp breath and blink up at the ceiling. It's no surprise that the lady who owns a Christmas tree farm is sentimental. Luka puts his wineglass down on the table and sits up straight, concerned. "I don't know, I've always sort of thought my mom delivered you to me. I don't think I had ever stepped into a hardware store before in my life and—I don't know. I guess I just like to think that." I shrug. "It's silly."

I don't believe in fate or kismet or any rule or reason to the universe and all its random, wonderful, terrible happenings. But I do believe I found Luka when I needed him the most, and I like to think my mom played a part in that. It's a comfort. Like she's still looking out for me. Still holding my hand. Luka stands from his chair and takes three long strides across the kitchen. He wraps me in his arms, my hands clinging tight to his sides.

"La La," he says, rocking me back and forth. He presses a kiss to the side of my head, and I clench my fists into the back of his button-down. This might not last beyond this week, and I might never tell him how I really feel, but he deserves to know this.

Everything he's given back to me.

❧ ❦

THERE'S A HEIGHTENED awareness between us after that. Luka's eyes linger on me as I finish washing the dishes, his gaze discovering new inches of me. The skin just above my wrist, the hollow between my collarbones, the small of my back when I reach to put a plate away on one of the top shelves. He smiles when I roll my eyes at him over my shoulder, tongue peeking between his teeth, hands clenching and unclenching on the arms of his chair.

Evelyn leaves shortly after another round of wine and pumpkin pie, calling our town's single Lyft driver. Luka snoops over her shoulder at her phone, laughing when he sees where Gus is coming from.

"I guess Gus and Mabel are still a thing."

I join him, and we watch the little car animation leave from the direction of the greenhouse. Luka settles his palm at the small of my back, his thumb slipping low to slide under the hem of my sweater. I shiver.

"So he drives the ambulance and does Lyft?" Evelyn pockets her phone with an amused grin. "Small towns are so funny." She tilts her head to the side and the grin slips from her face. "Wait, he's not picking me up in the ambulance, right?"

Gus does not pick her up in the ambulance. He picks her up in his very sensible Toyota Camry, honking twice at Luka and me as they disappear back down the road. We stay on the porch together as they rumble down the driveway, watching as the snow continues to fall in big fat flakes. It melts as soon as it touches the ground, everything too warm for it to properly stick. But there's a fine layer on the trees, a little dusting of white. Like someone's shaken up a snow globe and left everything to settle.

I turn to head back into the house, but Luka stills me with his hand. He tugs once until I turn to face him and then again to get me down on the top step of the porch. I laugh and curl my hands around his, head tilted toward the sky. Like this, with the glow of the light from inside burning warm through the windows, the snow almost looks like tiny pieces of glitter. I smile as a flake lands on my nose.

"What're you doing?" I laugh, another snowflake tangling in my lashes. I brush it away with the back of my hand, and the laughter catches in my throat when I look at Luka.

His eyes glow amber in the light spilling from the house, a smile tilting his lips. It's a secret smile, this one. One I haven't seen before. I want to trace it with my fingers and feel the weight of it against my skin. I want to lean up and catch it on my tongue like a snowflake, see what it tastes like. His smile grows into something bigger, snowflakes landing in his hair. He looks divine like this. Utterly mine.

"I want to kiss you," he says, nice and easy, like the look on his face isn't one step away from absolute hunger. He ducks his head closer until his nose brushes mine. "Isn't it magic to kiss someone in the first snow of the year?"

If it isn't, it should be. Because it feels like magic when I lean up and catch Luka's bottom lip between mine. He whispers out a sigh, a breath, and wraps his arm around my back, pulling me closer, tugging me up and into him until our hips knock together. His knuckles brush at my collarbone while he kisses me slowly, his hand skimming up, his thumb pressing a melting snowflake into my skin. I feel every single fingertip as he trails his touch up my neck to the soft skin under my ear. I've never thought that to be a particularly sensitive part of my body, but Luka's made it one. Of course he has. He lingers there with soft circles until I gasp into his mouth, his tongue tangling against mine just as his fingers curl into my hair, cupping the back of my head and tilting me back so he can lick deeper, hotter. I've never been kissed like this before, with the night sky pressing down on me and Luka everywhere else. Snowflakes touching my skin in tiny pinpricks of cold.

"Did you mean it?" he whispers into the same space below my ear he was discovering with his thumb, my head collapsing to my shoulder to give him more space. His palm maps the bare skin of my back under my sweater, the material bunched at his wrist. "What you said?"

I don't even know my name right now. Luka tastes like red wine and cinnamon, and I don't want him to ever stop kissing me. "What did I say?"

He peels himself away from me and rests his forehead against mine with heavy, panting breaths. Each one is a small cloud of white between us, twisting up into the night sky with the snow and the stars. "That I've been holding you steady," he says. He dips his head back down and nips at my bottom lip once, like he can't quite help himself.

"Of course I meant it," I say and curl my fingers through his belt loops. "I can't believe you need to ask that."

He exhales, long and slow, and pulls his hand from the back of my shirt. I shiver at the loss of his warm skin against mine and gaze up at him, my chin on his chest. I want to remember this moment forever, my snow globe moment. Luka with desire on his face plain to see, a wayward lock of hair just starting to curl behind his ear, cheeks flushed with cold and with wanting.

Magic.

"Let's go inside."

He says it like a promise, his hands urging me up over the top lip of the porch, too impatient for me to take the action myself. I let him guide me back into the cottage, the door shutting firmly behind us, the snick of the bolt locking into place. Half of me expects to be pressed against it, lifted until our hips can match just right, but Luka just toes out of the boots he never bothered to lace, smiles, and makes a sweet sound when I kick mine off in the same general direction. He bends and straightens them into a neat line, the back of his hand skimming my calf, my knee, my thigh as he straightens. There's still Christmas music playing in the kitchen, softer now, a quiet croon from Ella Fitzgerald about a merry little Christmas. I watch his silhouette in the darkness of the hall, the strong line of his jaw, the curve of his shoulder.

"Listen, Stella. I'm going to be honest here." He drags his fingers through his hair, caramel brown strands a chaotic mess. "I'm having trouble holding myself back right now." I swallow and step closer, wanting to watch all that careful composure slip out of him. I want messy Luka, panting breaths and half-bitten curses.

"Are you feeling what I'm feeling?" he asks on a whisper, and I nod, stepping into him, my hand around the back of his neck as I tug him down to me. For all the energy lighting me up like a—well, like a Christmas tree—it's a gentle kiss. A sweet caress of his lips against mine. Then I tangle my hand in his hair and pull, and it's not so sweet.

Luka groans out a rough rumble of a noise and bends at the knees, palms smoothing from my waist down over my ass to the backs of my thighs. He grabs and lifts, earning a squeak from me that he smiles into, the curve of his lips delicious on mine.

"That's an interesting sound," he notes, wandering through my living room and bumping into every single piece of furniture I own. He grunts when his shins hit the coffee table.

"Shut up." I laugh into the skin of his neck, peppering small pecking kisses down the line of his throat. I undo the first button of his flannel shirt as he tries to navigate my cottage like he's never been here before in his life, and I press a deep sucking kiss to the edge of his collarbone, the hollow of his throat. He makes his own set of interesting sounds and drops me abruptly onto the arm of the couch, hands underneath my sweater and on the clasp of my bra before I even realize we've stopped moving.

"Fuck, Stella," he whispers, filling his hands with the swell of me. His thumbs brush over my nipples, and I wobble on the edge of the couch, curling my legs around his hips to hold myself steady. If kissing him in the snow was magic, then this is—this is sugarplum fairies and toffee brittle crunch on top of dark chocolate cupcakes. I fumble with the buttons on his shirt, abandoning the top to start from the bottom instead when he noses my head to the side and starts sucking at my neck. His thumbs caress, swirl, and tug, and I am mindless.

I lose all patience and pull at his shirt, trying to rip the thing in two. "Off," I say, wanting his skin against mine more than anything.

"But I'm busy," he says, trying to stretch the collar of my sweater wide enough for him to get his mouth where his hands are. He bites at my shoulder in frustration.

"Luka." I laugh and slip another teeny tiny button free on his shirt. When did flannel get so complicated? "C'mon."

"Ask nicely," he retorts into my skin with a smile, and I laugh again, wiggling my butt on the arm of the couch and pushing him back with my palms flat against his chest. He gives me a pout when his hands slip out from underneath my sweater, his fingers lingering over the top of my knees instead, his thumbs gliding back and forth at the line of my inseam. I pull my sweater over my head, and the pout disappears, a hunger settling instead, tongue at the corner of his mouth.

I reach up to the strap of my bra, ready to twist out of it and throw it in the general direction of my bedroom, but he shakes his head, steps forward into the cradle of my legs and slips his forefinger underneath the delicate strap. It's a plain, soft cotton, the same as the one I was wearing that night on the couch, but he looks at me like I'm in Italian lace. He drags his finger up and down the strap, toying with it, his knuckles glancing along my skin.

"Do you remember that music festival we went to in Philadelphia? The one with the Roots?"

"Um, I guess," I say, distracted. It's hard for me to think when his hands are on me. He switches his attention to the other strap, plucking at it with his fingers. He pulls it over my shoulder and back, my chest rising and falling with every careful touch.

"You were wearing this pale pink dress with the thinnest straps I've ever seen," he tells me. I remember that dress. It had been so hot, and I liked the way it flared out around my legs when I spun around.

He swallows hard, Adam's apple bobbing in the column of his throat. I'm stuck there, watching how his body moves when he's painted with desire. His thumb slips down to the cup of my bra and he traces the skin just above it, mesmerized. "You were dancing in front of me, and they kept falling down." He looks back up to me and presses his palms against my collarbones, fingers fanned out, pinkies tucked under each strap. He pushes his hands down slowly, taking the material with him until the straps are stuck at my elbows, the cups of my bra just barely covering me. He exhales a shaky breath, a half smile curling his lips. "I wanted to kiss you so bad."

I shiver. "Is that all you wanted to do?"

His smile eases into a grin, a wicked gleam in those brown eyes. "No."

He dips two fingers into the center of my bra and pulls the fabric away, leaving me topless on the arm of the couch. I resist the urge to cover myself, the lights from the tree painting my skin in tiny half moons.

"Wanted to do this," he says, settling closer, hands cupping my bare breasts. His mouth finds my collarbone and sucks—long, wet pulls against my skin. "I thought about slipping my hands in the top of your dress." His mouth brushes over my nipple. "I thought about putting my mouth on you."

"Please," I beg. I had meant for it to be teasing, silly, but I hear the need in my voice. Luka does too, if the way he starts fumbling at his shirt is any indication. It's a bit of a rush after that, both of us frantically discarding the rest of our clothes, trying to get as close as possible. I watch as his golden skin is revealed inch by inch, my eyes eagerly following the dark smattering of hair on his chest as it narrows into a thin line that disappears beneath his belt buckle. I busy my hands with that while he tries to pull down my jeans, practically pulling me off the couch with the force of his grip.

I laugh and hop on one foot, holding on to his shoulders while he pulls them down with a grumble, bringing his face back to mine for a kiss. He moans into it when I wrap myself around him, warm skin against warm skin. Finally.

Little hiccups of reminders keep hitting me as we stumble our way down the hall to my bedroom, stopping every few steps to touch and tease. I slip my hand into his boxers, stroking hard and tight, and have to remind myself that this is Luka gasping into my shoulder, my very best friend. It's Luka curling his hands into fists against the small of my back, chasing my touch with a roll of his hips, a grunt low in his throat. Luka grasping my wrist and tugging my hand away, marching us to the bedroom and tossing me onto the bed.

Pillows topple, and I swat them away as Luka crawls on top of me, his hands bracing over my shoulders. I'm eager to see him like this, his bare skin and flexing arms, the freckles on his skin muted in the moonlight.

"Hold on," he says, and he tucks his arm under me, guiding me up until my head is on the pillows and my knees are tipped open, my chest rising and falling with every shuddering breath. I can't seem to catch it, a frantic need burning through me. My lips feel swollen from his kisses, my skin tingling from the rough brush of his stubble against my skin.

"There," he says, and then he drops his body into the cradle of mine, skin scorching, the heavy thickness of him pressing against the wet softness of me. He rolls his hips down once and everything in me pulls tight. I gasp into a pale pink pillow in the shape of a crescent moon and wonder how it's possible I'm having the most intense sexual experience of my life with my underwear still on.

Luka slows the movement of his hips until he's still above me, his fingers catching in my hair and sifting through the dark strands. He arranges it carefully until it's not trapped by my shoulders, an artful halo of tangled dark curls. His gaze trips over my face, lingering I think on the curve of my lips. He sighs out, a little wistful, and I smile at the sweetness of it.

"What?" I ask. He's looking at me with a careful consideration that's beautiful in its honesty. He's saying a million things with that look. I just can't hear what they are.

"Nothing," he says, and his eyes trail down to the heavy swell of my breasts, the soft skin beneath. The flare of my hips and the dip of my belly button. I feel it like a fingertip at my sternum. He leans up on his knees between my spread thighs and tucks his thumbs into the material at my hips, dragging my underwear down an inch and then all the way when I move my legs to help. He gusts out a deep breath when I'm bare before him, his hands skimming over my knees.

"Thought about this too," he says. "When that pretty pink skirt brushed up against your thighs."

He finds the place where I'm almost embarrassingly wet, and I give in to the pleasure of his touch, my head tilting back into the pillows as everything within me rattles and groans. *Same*, I want to say, a little hysterical. *I've imagined this a hundred ways, a million different possibilities.*

"Fuck," he says, and I slit my eyes open to watch him touch me, one hand moving between my legs, the other sliding over my stomach to trace the bottom curve of my breast. He pulls at my nipple and I moan, thick and throaty. I have never once been touched like this.

"Fuck," he repeats, darker this time. His eyes blink up from between my legs to my face. He changes the angle of his hand between my legs, palm grinding down. I make another whimpering sound. "I could come just like this, Stella. Just by watching you. Hearing you."

My whole body tightens. But it's not what I want, to finish like this. Maybe later we can explore that particular idea, but right now I want to feel him pinning me down into the mattress, my arms around his neck and his mouth on mine. I want him desperate and panting into my skin, the both of us moving together.

I tell him this in a garbled breath, his laugh a little breathless as he pulls back from me.

"You don't need to worry about that," he mumbles, hands pulling down the waist of his boxers. "M'plenty desperate."

I reach for the drawer of my nightstand where I threw the box of condoms Layla delivered last week. She dropped them off at my doorstep with an obnoxious bow and a bottle of wine. I'm grateful none of the farmhands wandered by my cottage to spot the Costco-sized box of Trojans on my welcome mat. I pull out a whole strip and toss them at Luka, distracted by the sight of him in the moonlight filtering in through my window.

Long legs, solid chest, the dip and cut of his hip sharp in the muted light. His biceps flex as he tears a condom off the strip and rolls it on, the rest placed safely on the blanket chest at the foot of my bed.

"For later," he says with a wink, and I laugh, pulling him up and over me.

I sift my fingers through his hair. "That's presumptuous," I tease, like the thought of more doesn't send a thrill through me. I'm greedy for him and his touches, his sighs whispered into my skin.

He huffs a laugh and settles above me, a kiss dropped between my breasts, his mouth distracted by the swell of soft skin. He trails a meandering path over my chest until I'm gasping and arching beneath him, my hands in his hair guiding him harder against me. He's dragging just right between my legs, pressure everywhere I need it. I could come like this, and I tell him so, his answering groan rough and broken.

"It's been almost ten years of foreplay." Luka rises on his palms above me, arms flexing. "I don't think once is gonna cut it."

I'm the one who is impatient now, my hips dancing beneath his, my mouth tasting any skin I can reach. I bite at his ear, the curve of his jaw. I hungrily kiss his bottom lip and the tip of his nose. My hands grab at his shoulders, his forearms. It's like every moment of banked desire is spilling out of me in a cascading rush. I can't get enough of him, can't move fast enough for everything I want. Every suppressed thought, every hesitant touch, every half truth and daydream buzzes under my skin, making me antsy and frantic.

"It's okay," he soothes and cups the back of my head with his hand, tilting my chin up until he can kiss me slow and sweet, easing the tempo of my heart with long languid kisses. "Slow down a sec."

"I want—"

"I know. I want it too."

He calms me with gentle hands, guiding my legs wide and dragging his palms up and down until I relax back into the mattress. He smiles at me, eyes crinkling at the corners, and then steals the breath right out of my chest with a slow press of thick heat between my legs. I don't know if it's because it's been a while or just because this is— this is Luka, but my whole body comes alive with the pressure, the delicious fullness. He settles inside me, and I hiccup a moan, high and tight in the back of my throat. I feel like I can't catch my breath, the air stolen from my lungs by Luka. My blood thrums hot, a delicious shiver working its way from the place where Luka is clutching at my thighs with bruising fingertips to the slant of my shoulder blades against the mattress. I curl my hands around his biceps and squeeze, whisper out a breath when his hips shift against mine.

He drops his forehead to my collarbone and rocks his head back and forth once. "Stella," he says, no beginning or end to the thought, just the pleasure of saying my name into my skin.

I smooth my hands across his back and lift my hips, a shallow movement that doesn't do anything but frustrate me. "Luka."

He brushes a chaste kiss to my temple, hums low in his throat, and then he begins to move.

He starts slowly, picking me apart piece by piece. He's watchful, learning, every hitch in my breath cataloged, put to use. He squeezes my thighs and I sigh. He bites at my neck and I arch my back. He changes the angle of his hips until my left leg twitches in his grip, my foot kicking out against his shin. The laughter in his eyes becomes a low burn of determination, his eyebrows furrowing, tongue between his teeth. He shakes his head once and repeats the same motion, a slow drag and circle of his hips that I squeeze my eyes against.

"Don't do that," he rasps, hand cupping my neck gently, thumb stroking once over the hummingbird flutter of my pulse before settling in the hollow of my throat. "Don't hide from me."

"Feels so good," I mumble, wishing I could be more eloquent. Wishing I had the words to tell him how it feels like I'm breaking apart into tiny bits of stardust. I feel incandescent, iridescent, every fucking light on the Christmas tree blown out. But his hips are moving faster now, and he's angled himself slightly up on his knees, the hand not on my neck reaching between us to touch just above where we're joined. It only takes a few rough strokes of his thumb, his hips losing their finesse in favor of a desperate grinding movement that has me shifting up the bed, my hands braced above me on the headboard as more pillows tumble around us.

"Luka," I gasp as the sharp frustration of not enough turns into the perfect pull of exactly right, a rough shove off the edge into my release. It starts low in my belly and spreads down my thighs, settles in the backs of my knees and the press of my arms above my head. It steals the breath from my lungs as I chase it with rocking hips, stretching me out like taffy. Luka's hand on my neck twitches and then slides above me to tangle with mine, his one hand pressing both of my wrists into the mattress. I manage to open my eyes just as he tips over the edge too, his teeth biting down into his full bottom lip. He's beautiful like this. Another secret discovered.

Luka collapses on top of me, hair damp with sweat, nose nudging at my cheek. I welcome his weight and curl myself around him, ankles hooked over his. He squeezes at my hands and sighs, content. Like a jungle cat. Or a sleepy sexed-up boy.

"We should have been doing that for years," he murmurs, voice drowsy. He adjusts his position and groans. "Or maybe not. I'm not sure I would have survived it. I think you killed me. I'm dead."

"You'll be my favorite ghost of Christmas past, then."

I try to stretch beneath him, a warm and heavy blanket of Luka covering me from head to toe. I wiggle my toes and feel a brush of cotton, a sleepy, amused hum tucked into his collarbone.

"You're still wearing your socks," I point out. All I get in response is a snore, Luka curled possessively around me. I give in to the weightless pull of sleep, holding him just as tight, and let my dreams take me.

For once, I think reality might be better.

21

I WAKE UP to the smell of bacon, a rumpled Luka yawning at the edge of my bed with a mug of steaming coffee in each hand. He's not wearing a shirt, his sweatpants are on backward, and there's a distracting line of hickeys that starts just below his collarbone and drifts down the center of his chest. I shift onto my back and stretch my arms above my head with a pleased little smile.

"Yeah, yeah," Luka mutters, sliding a mug of coffee onto my nightstand and curling his hand around my ankle. He squeezes up my leg in a new twist on his familiar one-two-three, thumb just below the crease of my thigh. He strokes there once, and my whole body shivers, brown-gold eyes smiling down at me. "Awfully proud of yourself."

"You didn't sound like you were complaining last night," I say, remembering the way he had pressed his head back into his pillows with my mouth on his skin, my hands at his hips holding him steady. How he grit out my name in three separate syllables when I sucked the hot skin just below his belly button. *Stel-la-la*.

"Smug doesn't suit you," he tells me archly, mug at his lips.

I snicker and pat my hand around on the nightstand for my coffee. I slept with my best friend last night. I slept with him two . . . three times last night. After we had collapsed in a boneless heap the first time, I woke up sometime around two in the morning, stomach rumbling. I snuck into the kitchen for a bite of pie out of the tin, only for Luka to shuffle in the kitchen after me, sleepily steal a bite from my fork, and then prop me up on the kitchen counter.

"Want this," he had mumbled as he ducked down, teeth grazing my thigh, his mouth hot and wet on the inside of my knee. He had put his head between my thighs until I slammed my head back into the cabinets and then gently urged me down, turned me with my hips tucked tight to the counter, and fucked into me until I fell apart. I'm surprised he hadn't needed to scrape me off the kitchen floor after that one.

As it is, my body is sore in the very best of ways, and I indulge in another groaning stretch. Luka watches the bare skin at my chest with avid interest as the sheet slips down another inch.

"Hand me a shirt?" I don't like the idea of coffee burns on my boobs.

He grumbles but does as I ask, and I slip the warm faded material over my head. It's the same band shirt he was wearing under his jacket the other day, and it still smells like him. He is never getting it back.

I watch him sitting on the edge of my bed as we sip our coffee and wonder when this is supposed to feel weird. I thought maybe after Luka and I slept together, I would feel a combination of panic and regret, but instead, I just feel . . . settled. It's a relief and gives me hope that at the end of this week when the ambiguity around our relationship disappears, when the consequence-free mindset we've both adopted vanishes, I'll be able to fit myself back together just fine.

"I was thinking—" Luka kicks back on my bed, resting on one elbow over my hips. I'm distracted by the stretch of skin across his torso, the way his freckles dust down to the hem of his sweatpants. "I've got to move my stuff from New York next week. Maybe you could come with me if I go on Tuesday. It'll be slow, yeah?"

That should be fine. Beckett and Layla can handle a nonrush day. I'll have to check our reservations just to be sure, but I don't see why I can't. "Wait. Move your stuff?"

He curls his hand over my knee, the thin sheet muting the feel of his skin on mine. My seven hundred pillows are scattered around the room like they've survived a bomb blast. There's one balanced precariously on the lamp in the corner. "I told you about the job in Delaware."

"You told me you were thinking about it, not that you've made a decision." A giddy feeling sweeps through me. "You're doing it? You're moving to Delaware?"

He nods, his face lighting up when he sees my excitement. "Yeah, sorry. I thought I had told you, but I guess I didn't want to distract you with Evelyn here. Found a place and everything. It's a little house just off the beach. You can hear the waves when you open all the windows."

"That's—" I'm smiling so hard it feels like my face is going to split right open. Luka, a twenty-minute drive away. I can drive to his house for a cup of flour if I want. I can drive over in the morning, come back to my house, and then see him again in the evening. The possibilities are endless. "Luka, I'm so happy."

"Yeah?" He looks relieved. "Good. Me too."

"Tell me there's a taco stand close by."

He takes a long sip of his coffee, holding me in suspense. "There is a taco stand close by."

Luka within driving distance and tacos on the way. Life truly doesn't get any better.

"We can drive up on Tuesday to New York, pack up my stuff, and drive back the same day. I don't have too much, and I was planning on donating most of the furniture." He drops his mug on the nightstand and gathers mine too, placing it next to the open box of condoms. I blush. I really should put those away.

Luka crawls on top of my body and cages me with his arms, a gentle kiss on my nose. Gentle is the exact opposite of the ideas being laser-beamed at me from hooded, chocolate brown eyes. He drops another kiss to my jaw. "You could stay with me at the Delaware house." He scrapes his teeth over my neck. "We could find a creative way to break in the swing on the back porch."

It takes a second for my brain to catch up. I only had two sips of coffee before Luka took my mug, and his tongue is doing something interesting under my ear. But when it clicks, when I realize what he's just said, I go rigid underneath him.

Oh, hello panic. There you are.

"Wait. What?"

Luka presses up on the palms of his hands, wincing. Pink lights up the tips of his ears. "Sorry, I was joking about the swing. Sort of. Too much?"

I shake my head, change my mind, and then nod. I chew on my bottom lip and then shake my head again. Luka pushes back until he's sitting on the edge of my bed, his palm next to my knee. He scratches at the back of his head, confused.

"But Tuesday—" I try to collect the thoughts zigzagging through my brain. "Tuesday is next week."

He nods, eyebrows slanted low. "Yeah, it is next week."

"Our agreement was for this week."

"Our agreement?"

"Our trial run. You said we'd use this week as a trial run."

"Oh." His shoulders relax, the confusion melting from his features. I'm glad he understands. We can't keep . . . doing this past this week. We tried it; it was amazing; it's done and over. Out of our systems. We can go back to the way things were, and I don't have to ever risk losing him. He tries a smile. "I think it's safe to say the trial period was a success."

"Right. But it's called a trial because a trial comes to an end. We're not— Luka, we're not—" The words wither on my tongue. I can't say it. What does he think? That I'd be willing to continue a friends-with-benefits type of relationship with him? I look down at the twisted bedsheets, the box of condoms mocking me from the corner of my eye. I guess my actions didn't exactly dissuade him.

My cheeks burn hot, humiliated.

"I don't want that kind of relationship with you," I say quietly. "Last night was really fun, but I care about you too much for . . . for that."

Luka is basically a statue at the edge of my bed. "What is that supposed to mean?"

I refuse to look up from my bedsheets. "I don't want to be friends with benefits."

"Great. Neither do I."

I look up so fast, my neck cracks. "But you just said—"

"I phrased it wrong. I'm sorry, I just—your hair is all mussed from my hands and your bottom lip is swollen, and I guess I'm having trouble getting my mind straight." He grins at me, gathering my hands in his and tangling our fingers together. "I want you to see the house in Delaware, okay? We'll get tacos on the way. Custard too. If you want."

"Okay." I drag the word out until it's fifteen syllables long. "That means no sex, right?" I feel like I have to be crystal clear on this.

Luka is back to confused. His mouth opens and closes several times, his hands squeezing mine. "Well, I mean. At some point, yes, I would like to have sex with you again. But it doesn't have to be Tuesday if you don't want to."

"I thought you just said you don't want to be friends with benefits."

"I don't. Stella." He laughs, probably amused that we're going around this conversational circle again. I'm glad one of us is having a good time. "I want to be your boyfriend."

"Oh. Um." Not a single coherent thought enters my brain. "You do?"

He frowns. "Yeah, I do."

"No, I mean—" I shake my hand free of his and sit up on the bed. "You mean you want to finish out this week as my fake boyfriend, right? That's what you're saying."

"That's not what I'm saying," he says slowly, patiently. "I mean like actually be together, you and me, for real." The frown on his face spreads to that little line between his eyes, the one that appears when he's reading print too small or getting upset. "I thought we were on the same page."

When I shake my head that, no, we are not on the same page, Luka rubs at that little line with his thumb. Clearly we aren't even reading the same book.

"So, what—" His eyes dart above my head to my window, my nightstand, the floor. He's looking for answers in my white, flowy curtains and coming up blank. "What was last night, then?"

"I thought we had an agreement to do what feels right this week. See where it takes us."

"And you thought sex was a part of that deal? You thought— what—that I'd fuck you, and we'd go back to watching movies on the couch next week like nothing is different?"

"I had—um, I had kind of hoped so."

It's exactly what I wanted, actually. To have this week with him and then for everything to go back exactly as it was before. That's how everything stays safe. That's how I get to keep him.

He scoffs, a little bit angry now. "Stella, I wouldn't—" He rubs the bridge of his nose. "You're my best friend. You're not a one-night stand."

I drag my thumb over the quilt of my bed, wrapping more sheets around myself. It feels wrong that I'm not wearing underwear for this conversation. "You've had one-night stands before."

"But not with you," he says, and he's definitely angry now, the strong line of his shoulders tense. "Why do you keep bringing that up? I haven't had casual sex with someone in a long time. You keep acting like I'm—like I'm bouncing about town, fucking anyone I see."

"I don't know, Luka. This isn't—"

"I think I need to be more clear." He steamrolls right over whatever I was going to say, and I'm glad for it. This morning has gone to complete and total shit. Who knows what nonsense would have spilled out of my mouth next? Luka nudges my chin up with his knuckle and tilts my face until I'm looking right into his eyes, the burst of freckles across his nose.

"I'm in love with you," he says, frustrated and shirtless in my bed. He yells it at me, really, his dark eyebrows angry slashes over his eyes. "I'm in love with you and I want to be with you."

My stomach drops. I shut my eyes tight and dig my fingers into my sheets.

"Do you think—" I swallow. "Do you think you're just confused because of our arrangement?"

"Why do you think I agreed to this arrangement?"

"Luka." I'm getting frustrated now. He's pushing too hard. I'm cracking beneath the pressure.

"I wanted you to give me a chance. I wanted to know if you could see me like that."

I shake my head. "Don't you see how that could be misleading?" I try. "Maybe we're just really good pretenders. Maybe your heart is confused."

"Stop telling me how I feel, Stella."

"You can love me but not be *in love* with me. It's just—" I grasp for something to explain what's happening in my head and my heart. "It's just the—it's all of this tension. The sex, maybe. I don't know."

"Is that what it feels like for you?" He swallows. "Just tension? Just the sex?"

I open my eyes to see Luka gazing at me with such a devastated look on his face, it steals my breath. The best thing I can do in this situation is keep my mouth shut, certain that anything I say will just make it worse. Of course it doesn't feel like that to me. I've loved Luka for so long it feels like it's a part of me, but I'm also used to hiding it—suppressing it—and that feels like a part of me too. So I say nothing as I blink away and stare at the floorboards instead, one of his socks half hidden below my bed. Christmas lights twisted up and tangled together.

"Shit," he whispers. He huffs a dark little laugh, and I watch as his hand lifts from the bed, fixated on the imprint he leaves behind. Will I have marks like that on my thighs, my wrists, the swell of my hips? How long will I get to keep them before they disappear too?

"I feel like an idiot," he says, standing from my bed and picking up his sock. He starts looking around the room for the rest of his clothes, and I sink farther beneath my sheets.

Luka finds one of his old sweatshirts half hanging out of my dresser and pulls it over his head. I stole that three years ago and hadn't intended to give it back. He turns toward me but doesn't look up, standing on one foot and trying to slip on his sock. "I'm sorry I made you uncomfortable," he mumbles.

"Luka." *You didn't make me uncomfortable*, I want to say. *You've just scared the shit out of me.* "Stay, please. We can— I'll make us waffles. We can clear this up."

The sound he makes almost breaks my heart clean in two. "I don't see anything that needs to be cleared up. I'm just—" He hooks his thumb over his shoulder in the general direction of the rest of the house. I watch as he searches for an excuse and comes up empty. "I'm gonna go."

"Will you be back?" I hate how thin my voice sounds.

He nods, still looking at the floor. "Yeah, I'll meet you later. We're supposed to cut down a tree with Evelyn, right?"

I don't care what we have to do with Evelyn. Right now I only care about Luka and that faraway look on his face, how it feels like he's already a thousand miles away and he's standing right in front of me.

"Yeah, but—"

"I'll see you then."

And then he's gone, the door clicking shut quietly behind him.

❧ · ❧

I PUT ON some underwear. Wander into my kitchen. See the plate of bacon and waffles and Christmas cookies on the counter and almost start crying. I pick up a sugar cookie and nibble on it as I wander in circles. I've officially channeled every sad person in every sad movie I've ever watched. I'm listless, hollow.

There are signs of Luka everywhere. His gloves on the table by the door. Loose change from his pocket in the ceramic blue bowl I use for keys. The mug he was using for coffee this morning rinsed and drying upside down by the sink. That's the one that hurts me the most, I think. That even though he's upset and disappointed, he's still managed to take care of me.

Luka and I have had fights before. We once had a bickering fight in the drugstore below his apartment, the both of us getting so heated, the owner had to ask us to leave before I got the empanada I wanted. But we've always ended them with a hug or a peck on the cheek, his arms banded tight across my back.

This one feels different. I know it is.

I can't stop thinking about the look on his face, the way his eyes shuttered and fell when I let the silence build between us. I had been a coward, stupid to think this week could happen without one of us getting hurt. I thought it would be me. I would be able to handle it if it were me. But knowing that Luka is hurting too, that he felt like he needed to get away from me, I'm—I'm having trouble with that.

I go through the motions of getting ready for the day and pointedly ignore looking at the tender skin between my breasts, the place where his scruff left marks on my pale skin. I loop a scarf around my neck and then pull on a hat. Maybe if I put on enough layers, I'll be able to cover up this awful feeling in my chest.

I head out into the fields, aimless. The idea of sitting in my office right now with my bottom drawer full of tiny cardboard pine trees fills me with enough existential dread to send me stumbling over the cobblestone walkway. I'm not supposed to meet Evelyn for a couple of hours yet, and a walk through the cold fields feels appropriate. Maybe the fresh air will do me some good, but mainly I want to wallow.

So I wander.

I start in the west pasture and putter my way through the trees. The snow from last night is already gone, the trees as bright and vibrant as ever, untouched by the season's first burst of winter.

I am merciless as I recount our argument. Last night was amazing, but I think—I think he's been homesick up in New York. The new job, the move. He's looking for things that are comfortable. That feel good. I know Luka loves me, but he's not—he isn't in love with me. And I don't want to give in, give him all the pieces of myself that I've been holding close and have him figure out the difference a month from now. Six months from now. I don't think I'll be able to come back from that. Better to be a little bit broken by this than irreparable later.

Because I love Luka. I've been falling in love with him for close to nine years. Every day a little bit deeper. And if I give in to him now only for it to break apart later, I won't have anything left.

I start to get annoyed by pristine tree after pristine tree, so I turn on my heel and change directions. The dirt becomes rockier under my boots, the fields opening up as the trees become less dense. I see the first stump of twisted bark and peer over my shoulder. I've somehow managed to wander to the south pasture with the dead trees. I look at the one closest to me and thumb at a brittle branch, a large piece of black snapping off between my thumb and forefinger. Maybe I should cut one down and put it up in my house. It suits my mood.

I hear the sound of boots behind me and I turn quickly, hoping for Luka. I want to apologize, beg him to forget this morning ever happened. I just want us to go back to the way it was.

But it's not Luka. It's Evelyn staring at our twisted trees with a single arched brow. Another pang of regret hits me for a different sort of lie.

"Is this where dreams come to die?"

Mine do, apparently.

How do I even begin to explain Mr. Hewett and the soil moisture system and his quest for an alpaca farm? I decide it's not worth the effort.

"These trees got sick during the fall. A root rot, we think." I think I have a case of root rot. One that starts in my heart and burrows outward. By next week I'll probably look like one of these trees, hunched over and brittle at my office desk.

Evelyn narrows her eyes at me, zeroing in on my hat. I think it might be on backward. "You okay?"

No. I just made my best friend think I don't love him after he confessed his love for me over coffee. Oh, and we had an incredible night of passionate, all-consuming sex. He made waffles, and then I kicked him out of my house. I am unwell.

"Yeah," I say and try to fix the approximation of a smile on my face. Judging by Evelyn's wince, I'm not exactly successful. "Am I late for our tree adventure?"

She shakes her head and takes a step closer, her hands curled in her pockets. "No, you're not late. I was out here looking for you."

"Oh?"

"Yeah, I wanted to show you the first round of footage for the farm."

I get that feeling again, the low sinking in my gut. I hate that I've lied to her, made her think that this farm and my relationship with Luka is something it's not. It's not fair to her, and it's not fair to all of the other people competing in this contest. The ones who have told the truth from the beginning and need the money just as much as I do.

I sigh and make a decision.

"Before you do that, I should tell you something."

I don't know what to think about the way she rolls her lips and rocks back on her heels. "What's up?"

There's no easy way to say I faked a relationship to make my farm seem more romantic, so I decide to just launch into it. "I lied to you. About me and Luka."

Strangely enough, her mouth splits into a wide smile. She nods once and takes her hands out of her pockets, slapping her phone into her palm. "I am so glad you said that. I know."

"We aren't actually— Wait—" I blink a couple of times, look down at my boots and then up again. "You know?"

"Yes, I know." She nods and tucks a loose strand of dark hair behind her ear. "I was hoping you would tell me yourself."

"How do you know?"

"A big part of my job is listening to the things people aren't saying. And Stella, that's not hard to do here. The people of Inglewild talk . . . a lot. I was in town for maybe half an hour when I heard about the betting pool in the coffee shop."

Luka was right. This town is made up of a bunch of busybodies.

"I thought it was weird that you just recently got together with the long-term partner you supposedly own the farm with." She gives me a gentle smile. "Everyone really loves you guys together, for what it's worth."

That is . . . beside the point. "You knew I was lying? From the first day you were here? Why didn't you say anything?" I didn't think it was possible to feel any worse, but wonders never cease. I am mortified.

"I was going to ask you about it that first day, but, well, I got distracted." I remember her face when Beckett walked into the bakehouse. Fair enough. "And then I met Luka and saw you guys together and thought maybe I just misunderstood the town gossip. So I asked Gus when he drove me home last night."

"What did he say?" I'm not even upset. Just exhausted. All this trouble, and for what? To lose my best friend and humiliate myself in the process.

"He told me how glad he was to see you two together, that he won the town betting pool. I asked what the betting pool was for and put it together from there. I should tell you now, officially, that I have to disqualify you from the contest." She says it as gently as she can, but I still feel the twist in my stomach, the scratchy discomfort of embarrassment. "You checked off a box that said all the information in your application was correct, and if any proved to be false, your application would be voided."

I nod. I had figured as much. "I'm really sorry I lied. I knew it was a mistake from the start."

I just wanted to have my cake and eat it too, I guess.

She narrows her eyes at me, a secret smile playing on her lips. She taps her phone against her palm again. "But did you? Think it was a mistake?"

The lying? Yes, without a doubt. Every night I went to bed with a weight against my chest, thinking about that one line of copy in the application, my biggest lie. But the time with Luka? That part I'm less sure about.

"I don't understand." How many times can one person think and say the same sentence in one morning? Write this on my tombstone.

"It didn't take long for me to figure it out. I only had to see you two together. Do you even realize the way you look at each other?" When I just blink at her, she waves her hand. "Forget about it, never mind. Here's the deal. You're disqualified from the contest and the prize money, but I still see a story here. A good one. The kind of story I haven't told in a while."

"You do?"

"Yeah. This place is gorgeous. Stella, please understand that even if you were single and living in a tiny cave at the mouth of the foothills eating dog food out of a can, I would think this place is amazing. It's like the North Pole had a love child with Narnia. I want to live here forever."

I open my mouth, but she waves her hand again, cutting me off.

"So I'm going to feature you guys on my account. And I'd like to show you the video I made."

She closes the distance between us and hands me her phone, a video already pulled up on the screen. I stare at my tiny face in the thumbnail, standing in front of my office with a nervous smile and a peppermint hot chocolate. Her first day on the farm.

"Just watch. It'll make sense."

I glance at Evelyn and then back at the phone. I tap play with a shaking finger.

It opens on a quick clip of me standing on the porch of the office, gingerbread decorations bright and colorful against warm brown wood. "Luka put them up," I hear my tinny voice say, laughing. "I think I made him redo the licorice four times. He barely tolerates me."

It switches to another clip, Luka shouldering into my office with take-out coffee in both hands, me behind my desk. I hadn't even realized Evelyn had her phone out when this happened. He drops the take-out cup on the edge and then reaches for me, gloved hand curling around my elbow, pulling me close. It's hard to see the kiss, but I remember how I felt. The low swoop in my stomach. He pulls away and the small version of myself on-screen ducks her head. But Luka doesn't. It's just a fraction of a moment, but I see the look on his face. The way his eyes practically glow as he looks down at me. The slow smile that kicks up the side of his mouth. The surprise when he turns slightly and catches Evelyn in the corner. He hadn't even realized she was there.

The ice-skating rink is next. Luka shooing Jeremy away and wrapping himself around me. I watch as I tilt my head back into his chest and look up, his body moving back slightly to welcome the shift. We look . . . happy together, comfortable, my small body tucked into the security of his, his chin resting on my head as we watch the kids circle the rink.

Its clip after clip, faster now. Luka and me walking in front of Evelyn through the fields, our hands reaching for each other at the same time. Luka in the bakehouse with a grin and a blush, a candy cane half hanging out of his mouth as he says, "She's amazing and she doesn't even know it. She'd give you the sweater off her back." The two of us in my kitchen just last night, our backs to the camera as Luka smooths a hand down my arm. In all of these clips, he does not look like a man who is barely tolerating me. He looks like—

The last clip is an extended shot of me attempting to rehang a string of garland outside the Santa barn, balancing on a stool and rising on my toes. The camera drifts to the left, away from me, and I see Luka leaning against a fence post. He has that damned candy cane again, tongue twisting it back and forth in his mouth. But it's the look on his face that has me leaning forward until my nose is practically pressed up against the phone. Soft eyes lit up in the warm sun, a laugh caught on the tip of his tongue as his gaze lingers. Love and gentle adoration in the curve of his lips, the slant of his brows.

Luka hasn't been faking for a second.

"It's actually the second video," Evelyn announces, and I practically jump out of my skin. As it is, I drop her phone to the ground. God, I hope she has that video saved. "The first video is me explaining that I'm at Lovelight Farms where two idiots think they're pretending to be in love." She grins at me, proud of herself. "Do you understand now?"

She scoops her phone off the ground. "You think you've been lying to me, but you've just been lying to yourself this whole time."

22

LUKA LOVES ME.

Luka is in love with me.

I repeat it to myself on a loop. That look on his face in the video, I've seen it before. Of course I've seen it before. I've caught him looking at me like that in the early morning when I'm standing at the coffee machine whispering hello and begging for caffeine. When we've gone out on the bay on those little paddleboats shaped like dragons, a bag of crumbs in my pocket for the seagulls. He's had that look on his face pretty much every time I've ever seen him. The pieces slot together. Luka has been falling in love with me this whole time, and I've been too caught up in keeping myself safe to notice.

The bell above the door to the bakehouse jingles when I step inside, the tables empty, chairs still stacked in the corner. Layla doesn't open for another hour yet, but I know she's here somewhere, probably getting ready in the back. I spot Beckett sitting at the counter, a plate of donuts in front of him and an icing bag in his left hand. He likes to come here when he's stressed, eat his feelings, and pretend he's helping Layla out while he does it. Layla emerges from the supply closet, an apron around her waist and a streak of flour in her hair.

She stops short at the sight of me, Beckett turning with a glance over his shoulder.

"I fucked up," I tell them quietly.

Neither of them says anything, completely frozen at the counter. They look like one of those living art exhibits.

"Please say it's about Luka," Layla breathes.

Beckett rolls his eyes and goes back to filling his donuts. "Of course it's about Luka. She has a hickey on her neck and her hat is on backward." He places one perfect donut on the platter Layla has set out for him and drops a tiny icing mistletoe on top. "Plus, Luka has been hiding out at my house since this morning."

I'm relieved that Luka is still here on the farm. Despite his promise that he'd come back, a big part of me was worried he'd disappear back to New York, refuse the job in Delaware, and never return.

Layla waves me forward and clears space for me at the counter. She holds a donut up in front of my face. "Eat this and tell me what happened."

Beckett tries to grab the donut out of my hand, but I twist away from him. I need it more than he does.

"You're a mess." He grabs his own donut, biting the tiny mistletoe fondant on top clean in half. Layla frowns at both of us and moves the platter to the back shelf, out of our greedy reach.

"I'm going to have nothing left if you two keep trying to help me."

I swallow warm flaky pastry and buttercream filling and muster my courage. "Luka is in love with me."

Beckett and Layla stare at me. When I say nothing, Layla raises both eyebrows. "And?"

I drop my forehead to the counter with a groan. "Did everyone know but me?"

"Yup," Beckett answers. I hear the smack of a hand against bare skin and peek up just as Beckett rubs at his forehead, a glare aimed at Layla. "What? You know it's true. There was a townwide betting pool about it."

Layla ignores him. "Did he tell you?"

I nod and give them the abbreviated version of events. That he told me he loved me, and we argued. My conversation with Evelyn in the fields and the video she showed me.

"It shouldn't have taken a video for you to realize," Beckett says, squeezing out a bit of the donut filling onto his finger. Layla snatches that away from him too. "He's been showing you for years."

I look down at the countertop. "I didn't see it."

"You did," Layla disagrees gently and shoots a warning look at Beck when he opens his mouth. "You saw it, honey. You were just too afraid to do anything about it. You're comfortable in the friend zone, so you decided to keep yourself there."

I shrug, hapless. "How do I fix it?"

"I guess that depends." Layla turns and plucks a donut from the tray, splits it in half, and offers it to me. Beckett makes a pained noise under his breath. "Are you willing to be honest?"

❧ ❦

I HEAD BACK to my cottage after needling Layla into giving me another donut. I make the last turn around the big oak and stumble when I see a figure on my front steps. Luka is sitting on the stoop that leads to my porch, his legs apart, hands clasped loosely between them. He's staring down at the ground but looks up when my boots send a shower of gravel across my front yard, a donut still clutched in my hand.

"Hey," he says, hesitation making the word sound short.

After watching the video and examining every detail of every interaction we've had over the last month and a half, it's almost startling to see him sitting in front of me. I hadn't expected to see him again today. I had constructed a loose outline of a plan on my walk back home:

Find a bottle of wine.

Continue to overthink Luka.

Consume said bottle of wine and the rest of the pumpkin pie.

Apologize to Luka.

Beg for forgiveness.

Tell Luka I love him.

Eat some more pie.

The whole thing is a work in progress.

"Hi," I say back.

My heart lodges in my throat and makes it difficult for me to swallow. We watch each other, hesitant, and then Luka stands, unfolding his tall body from the bottom step to lean against the railing. I fumble around in my pockets for my keys, one of Luka's pine trees brushing at my knuckles. I never took it out after he kissed me in the barn. That feels like ages ago now.

Layla's words ring in my head. *Are you willing to be honest?*

I'm not sure I'm that brave.

"You have a key," I tell him, ignoring the pine tree and urging my feet forward. It's cold out this afternoon, a snap in the air that has my fingers numb to my knuckles. I wonder how long I was out in the fields, how long Luka has been on my front porch. I look at the ruddy color on his cheeks, the way his shoulders shrug up by his ears. He's not even wearing a scarf.

"Didn't feel right to use it," he says, gaze still locked on me despite the anxious line of his body. He's holding himself still, tight, away from me, and that more than anything makes me sad. I slip past him up the stairs, aware of the space between us. I want to throw his arm over my shoulder, curl into his side, and have him tease me about not being able to fit the key in the lock.

"You can always use it," I mutter, pushing open the door for us. My gaze catches on the Christmas tree in the window as I'm toeing off my boots, my bra hanging from one of the top branches. Luka follows my eyes and snorts when he sees it, a brush of color at the base of his neck where he isn't already painted pink by the cold.

"Ah." He scratches at the back of his head and arranges my boots into a neat line, almost like he can't help himself. That little gesture gives me hope that things aren't completely ruined between us. He shakes his head and diverts his attention from my new creative ornament. I should take that down before Dane comes over with the paperwork for Hewett. Luka rocks back on his heels. "I'm here for the thing with Evelyn."

"Oh." My little spark of hope snuffs out. "We decided not to do that this afternoon." There's no point since we've been disqualified from the contest. I suppose I should probably tell him.

"There's, uh, we don't have to pretend to be together anymore." I swallow and glance fleetingly at his face before losing courage and looking down at our socks instead. "I told Evelyn the truth. Turns out she already knew."

"She knew we weren't together?"

I nod. "Busybodies," I say. That's about all I can offer as an explanation right now. I nod my head toward the coffee machine in the kitchen. "Want to stick around, or—"

I don't want him to feel like he has to stay here with me, especially since it's clear he only came here to fulfill whatever responsibility he felt he had. He's free to go now, free to be clear of me completely if he wants. That sends a sour feeling rolling through my stomach. He must see it on my face because he reaches a hand out, taps once at my elbow. It's a valiant attempt at our previous physical affection, and I'm left wishing he curled his fingers around me instead, pulled me into his chest and rested his chin on my head.

"I'll stick around," he says, looking only mildly morose at the idea of it. His eyes bounce from the window to the curve of my chin, to my shoulder, and then back again. I hate how awkward this is. Even the first time we ever had lunch together, we didn't lack for things to say. I had been sad, withdrawn, a little bit lost, but Luka had filled the space between us with easy chatter—data patterns and his mom's cooking and the little pupusa stand in the city he liked to go to on Saturday mornings.

I start up the coffeepot in silence, the steady *drip*, *drip*, *drip* like a metronome. *Are you willing to be honest?* Luka sets himself at one of the kitchen chairs, eyes fixed out the window. I maintain composure through two series of drips before I can't take it anymore, my heart hammering in my chest.

I'm going to do it. I'm going to tell him the truth.

"Luka, I—"

"I want to—"

I huff out a laugh that is more nerves than amusement and nod for him to continue. If anyone deserves to have their say first, it's Luka. I'll follow his lead. I'll do whatever he wants.

He rests his hands on the table. "I want to apologize for this morning." My stomach sinks to my toes, and my face must show it because he rushes to correct himself. "Not—not for what I said, but for how I left. That wasn't right."

"I hurt you," I offer and pour two steaming mugs of coffee with shaking hands. If Luka had reacted the way I had this morning, I'd be on the first train out of town. I'd be out in the fields, digging a hole to bury myself in. I'm not sure I'd ever show my face in Inglewild again.

"You did," he agrees, and that sour feeling twists and pulls tight, making me frown into my mug. I take the seat across from him and fight to keep my gaze on his. "But I still shouldn't have left like that. I know—I know that's a big deal for you, the idea of people leaving. I think that's why you kept Beckett and Layla out of the loop on farm business. Because you were afraid they'd leave if they found out you were having some trouble." His voice is gentle, but his words hit their mark, landing like little hailstones against my heart. Each one leaves a little dent. "And when I told you I lo—" He clears his throat, avoids saying the words, and that hurts too. That I've given a sliver of my fear to him. "When I said what I said, and your reaction wasn't what I wanted, I did exactly what you were afraid of. I left. I'm sorry for that."

I can't stand to hear him apologize. Not after the way I acted this morning. Not after the way I've been acting since we started this whole thing. "Luka——"

"You know I buy those pine trees in bulk? Those little cardboard ones," he explains like I don't know what he's talking about. Like I don't have every one he's ever given me saved in the drawer of my desk, the overflow in a box in my closet. It smells like pine every time I open the door to get a sweater out, a little stale now, but I refuse to get rid of them. "The first one I got on a whim at the gas station down the street, but your face lit up when I gave it to you. I think it was probably then that I realized."

I hold my breath, captivated. "Realized what?"

He's shy, reserved, staring at his hands curled around his mug before he slides his eyes back to mine. His mouth hitches up at the corner, but he ignores my question. "I got greedy for that look. I didn't want anyone else to have it. I still don't want anyone else to have it."

You can have it, I want to say. *You can have all my smiles and looks and hugs and touches. My heart too. If you still want it.*

"Anyway, I guess what I'm trying to say is I still have about two hundred of those cardboard pine trees. And I have a recurring order. I'm—I'm not gonna leave, La La. I've still got plenty of trees to give you. As long as you want me around, I'll be here."

He digs his hand into his back pocket, hips lifting to pull something out. He places a small cardboard pine tree on the table and slides it over to me with his finger.

I stare at that tree for a long time, eyes hot, throat tight.

It's hard to love someone without restraint. To give yourself over to the swell and pull of it without fear of what might happen. I think it's only natural to hold a part of yourself back and protect what you can. My mom loved me fiercely, but she also never opened her heart to anyone else. Not after what my dad did. So I think I've—I think that's how I learned not to wish for too much. To play it safe and easy.

But it's hard to keep yourself from giving in too. Layla is right. These past nine years I've buried every glimpse of strong feeling with denial, yearning, and a sprinkle of deliberate misunderstanding. Every time I've even glanced at Luka, I've felt it. A hollow ring. A sharp tug. A persistent and uncomfortable ache.

I stand from the table abruptly, my chair rocketing backward across the hardwood floor with an angry screech. Luka stands too, eyes faintly panicked. I turn and head down the hallway, my whole body thrumming.

"Stella?" Luka stumbles behind me, hitting his knee on the edge of a vintage umbrella stand that I use for wrapping-paper tubes. He curses under his breath and hobbles after me. "Stella, wait a second. I didn't—"

I tear open the door to my closet, a cascade of sweaters and scarves and all of the other random things I shoved in here tumbling out. A garden gnome lands on my toe. Two boxes of extra string lights make a leap for freedom. I toss an old version of Candy Land over my shoulder. Luka skids to a halt inside my room.

"What are you— Oh my god." He cuts off abruptly. He sucks in a sharp breath, probably horrified at my messiness unleashed. Maybe I should have shown him this before he confessed his love. "Is that a fern?"

It's a fake monstera that one of Beckett's sisters bought him and he promptly deposited at my front door. I lower myself to my knees to drag it out of the way and reach behind it for the old KitchenAid mixer box. I don't even think I even own a KitchenAid.

"You don't own a KitchenAid," Luka says, folding up some sweaters behind me. "Can I help you with something, or—"

There's frustration there, a hint of sadness too. He just spilled his heart out and I'm rummaging through my closet.

"Here it is." I flip open the lid of the box and turn it over, hundreds of tiny cardboard paper trees falling to the floor between us. They slip over one another in a tiny waterfall of stale pine and curled green edges, the strings tangled. Luka abandons his folding and picks one up, eyebrows knit in confusion.

"I've got some data points for you," I tell him, voice wobbling at the edges. "After that day you took me to get a grilled cheese, I thought about your smile every time I walked past the hardware store. I still think about your smile every time I walk past the hardware store. I get heavy whipping cream when I go to the grocery store because you told me once homemade whipped cream is better than the canned stuff. Do you know how many cartons of cream I've wasted? I sometimes pretend I haven't seen a movie just so you can point out the best parts." I suck in a deep shaking breath. "That concert when I wore that pink dress? I wanted to kiss you too. When we took that first camping trip to the beach and I woke up with you wrapped around me, I could feel your heartbeat against my back. It was the first time in years I didn't wake up lonely and sad."

It's a relief to release every secret thought, every hidden feeling. I wipe my fingertips under my eyes and try to get control of my breathing. It's quiet between us, and I look down at the trees scattered across my floor.

Luka clears his throat, hands reaching for me. At some point, he decided to sit on the floor next to me. "I think data analysts—" His voice breaks off and he stops, collects himself, and tries again. "I think data analysts refer to that as a long-term trend."

"I want all your trees," I tell him. "You know I wrote *boyfriend* on that application on purpose?" I mirror his honesty from the kitchen with some of my own. "I had just gotten off the phone with you. You were laughing about some commercial you just saw, and you had those lines by your eyes—" I reach up and caress the faint smile lines by his left eye. "These. Right after we hung up, I filled out the application for the contest, and I wrote *boyfriend*. I was only thinking of you. I wanted an excuse, to have to pretend. I thought I could have you for a week, and it would be enough to make my feelings go away." I look down at my hands and start pushing the trees into a pile. "But all this week did was make it easier for me to love you. I'm sorry I wasn't honest. I'm sorry for the way I reacted, and I'm sorry I hurt you. I haven't handled anything right. I don't know, all of my excuses sound stupid now."

I remember what I told Layla. That if something were supposed to happen, it would have happened. I'm such an idiot. Things have been happening for years, I've just been clinging to this idea that if everything stayed exactly the same, I'd never have to be hurt again.

Luka pushes onto his knees in front of me, brushing the trees out of his way. He curls his hands over my thighs, ducks his head down until he can look at me. "How do you feel now?"

Are you willing to be honest?

I suck in a deep breath. "I'm still afraid," I tell him. I hold his eyes, hoping he sees how serious and terrified and stupidly in love with him I am. "I'm really afraid. You're my best friend. I need to know if we do this that I still get to keep you if it doesn't work."

"You will," he says, palms moving up and down, shifting closer. "You won't be able to get rid of me, I promise."

"Even if it goes bad."

"It's not gonna go bad."

"Luka."

He grins at me. "It's not gonna go bad," he says again, voice softer.

"I want it notarized." I sniff and run a shaking hand under my nose.

"We can get it notarized. Alex does that, right?"

"Yeah." I nod. "Okay."

"Okay." He nods, a smile starting in the corner of his mouth. The sun slanting in through my windows lights his eyes in shades of gold, the freckles on his nose a starburst. "See, was that so hard?"

I laugh. It's only been the hardest thing of my life.

"I'm really glad I asked you to be my fake boyfriend," I confess.

"I'm really glad I agreed to be your fake boyfriend."

"I love you." I sigh, and the change on his face is instant. His smile softens and spreads until his whole face glows with it, the hands on my thighs sliding up to my hips. He drops his forehead to mine until he's only colors. Gold, chestnut brown, pale pink. I sigh and close my eyes. "I love you so much."

I can feel his smile against mine, bright and beautiful. His hands squeeze my hips, my ribs, and then rise to cup my cheeks. His thumbs smooth under my eyes. "Fucking finally."

When he kisses me, it tastes like hazelnut lattes, the edge of a mini pine tree digging into my knee.

Finally.

23

LUKA

IT TOOK ALMOST a decade, but I finally got my shit together.

To be fair, Stella did her fair share of feet-dragging too. I think it makes us a good pair, unnecessary heartache aside. I tell her this while we're lying on the floor of her bedroom, my skin still sticky with sweat and my fingertips tracing between her shoulder blades, her pale skin glowing in the afternoon sun. I'm pretty sure there's a shoe digging into my back, but Stella keeps snuggling closer, her hair tickling my chin, and I wouldn't move if Beckett and all his kittens kicked in the door. Stella tilts her head up to glare at me after my comment of "Finally," but I see her hiding a smile too. My favorite Stella smile, dimples winking in her cheeks.

I should probably tell her she needs to get her bra out of the tree.

She sighs into my bicep, and part of me shifts, rolls, and settles. I've had my doubts that we'd get to this point. Before this social media thing, my plan for telling Stella how I felt about her was just a . . . general wear down, I guess. Keep coming around, keep feeding her Bolognese, maybe try and hold her hand. I told Beckett it was the long game. He called me a moron. When I explained the plan to Charlie, he just slapped me once upside the head and stole the rest of my beer.

I don't think she realizes it, but we've kind of been dating for the past nine years. Even when she's been with someone, I've been the guy she calls when she locks her keys in her car at the gas station. I'm the guy she calls when she accidentally puts dry ice down the sink and is afraid she's going to explode her plumbing. I'm really glad I'm the guy she calls when she needs a fake boyfriend.

The farm is going to be fine. With the monthly installments Dane has Hewett paying for all of the damage he's done, Stella won't even need the money from the contest. And she doesn't know it yet, but Charlie texted me earlier while Stella was wandering through the fields.

Elle has decided she's leaving Brian. Apparently, there was an incident with his secretary and seven other women at the firm. Not sure you can call it an incident when the number is over two, but I wasn't asking questions. As a parting gift, Charlie has decided to buy every dead and distorted tree from the south pasture and drop it on the front lawn of his father's house. I think it's a fine way to celebrate the occasion. I'm sure Stella will agree.

Stella presses a kiss to my chin, and I smooth my palm down her spine.

Here's the truth of it. Back when Stella asked me for my exit strategy for this fake boyfriend thing, I didn't have one. Frankly, I was too occupied with the idea of getting to touch her, hold her, be with her the way I've always wanted. But as soon as she asked, I knew what my answer was. I told her we'd continue and I meant it.

I have this memory of my dad that comes to me in bits and pieces. Vanilla ice cream. Sticky summer heat. Humidity that made my clothes feel like they weighed ten thousand pounds. And my dad's socks, one higher than the other, caught in the leg of his pants. Tiny bottles of ketchup on them, a gift from my mom.

I had just punched Jimmy Tomilson in the face on the playground at school, and my dad had picked me up early. He had been silent in the car and silent when we pulled up in front of the ice-cream shop. Silent in the line until he ordered us two cones to go. He walked us down the street to a little garden tucked away, surrounded by rosebushes with an empty fountain in the middle. I had been terrified of what he might say, the threat of his disappointment hanging over me like a thick cloud.

"Why'd you do it?" he had asked.

I told him that Jimmy was picking on Sarah Simmons, tossing mulch chips at her and tripping her every time she tried to hop on the slide. I told him to stop, and when he didn't listen, I punched him in the face. My dad didn't say anything at that, just took another slow bite of his ice-cream cone. He always did that. Bit his ice cream instead of licking it. My mom called it barbaric.

"You're not always going to know what the right thing is," he said. "When that happens, you continue."

I had blinked at him, ice cream melting down the side of my cone and over my knuckles. "Continue what?"

"You'll figure it out." Another bite of ice cream. "Continue. Listen. You'll find your way."

I've tried to figure that advice out as I've grown up. It's always been there in the back of my mind every time I've been confused or frustrated or impatient. Continue. Listen. But now, for the first time, I think I get it.

I'm going to keep stuffing Stella's pantry with whole-grain bread and protein bars and actual real-life fruit, because Cup O' Noodles and Oreos aren't a reasonable diet. I'm going to dance with her in the kitchen, her bare feet stepping on my toes every other step. Cook her ravioli and manicotti and garlic bread with extra cheese, because her face lights up when she sees me at her stove, chin on my shoulder as she tries to reach over me for a taste. I'm going to hold her hand when she needs it, tuck her close when she needs that too.

I'm going to love her in all the quiet ways, the slow ways, the loud and obnoxious ways. My heart has been moving steadily in that direction since she fell down the steps of the hardware store, right into my arms.

"Why're you smiling like that?" she mumbles into my chest, one eye squinted shut, her finger poking at the line in my cheek. I swat her hand away and tangle our fingers together. "S'weird."

"Mmm, you've got a way with words. Anyone ever told you that?"

She presses up on one elbow, her dark hair cascading over her shoulder in a riot of curls. She is stunning like this, all bare skin and rosy cheeks, tangled hair and a hickey at the curve of her shoulder. I push all that hair away from her face and trace the line of her jaw, the little divot in her chin, her full and tempting bottom lip. I don't know how I kept my hands to myself for so long. She presses a kiss into my palm and everything in me settles. I swear I didn't know how much I was rattling around in there until Stella curled her hand around my heart and tugged.

"Seriously though, what's with the look?"

"Just thinking," I tell her. I drop my head back to the floor. "Just happy."

She hums at that, a little shimmy of her body against mine. The silence is a warm comfort between us, her ankle hooked over mine. The wind whistles at the windows; the old clock in her hallway ticks an uneven beat. It's slow one second, too quick the next. I eyeball the mirror in the corner of her room and get some ideas.

She walks her fingers up my chest and then slides her palm down. "What's the plan now?" she asks, a little bit drowsy.

Move to the bed, I think. *See how many times I can make your breath catch.*

"Hm, I think that's obvious," I say. I tilt my head to look down at her. She props herself up, her chin in the palm of one hand, the other flat against my ribs. I don't think she realizes it, but she's tripping her fingers over each of my freckles, painting pictures into my skin. I grin.

She huffs and collapses back against me, her face in my chest. "Don't you say it."

I wrap both arms around her and hold on tight. I grin at the ceiling.

"We're gonna continue," I tell her.

EPILOGUE

STELLA

Two Years Later

I SNEAK A peek at Luka over the edge of my book.

It's a normal evening for us, squished together on the couch. I dropped my feet into his lap as soon as I shuffled over here, his hand immediately finding the curve of my knee, fingers spread wide. He's got a crossword propped on his thigh and an abandoned mug of tea at his elbow. Normal, all of it. I sit with my book, and I watch him, and I can't point to a single thing out of the ordinary.

But something feels off. Something just beyond my grasp.

He rearranged our tea collection four times this morning. He disappeared into his office for two hours and did god knows what with a series of spreadsheets.

Everything is exactly as it always is, and yet—

"You're being weird."

"You're being weird," he fires back right away, pen caught between his teeth. He always uses a pen, even though he gets seventy-five percent of the answers wrong. He slips the pen from his mouth, scribbles something down, and then glances over at me. "You're the one that's been staring at me for the last fifteen minutes like a little creeper."

"Because you're being weird." I nudge him with my foot and close my book. I set it to the side, right on top of the three other books I've started and abandoned this week.

Luka's mouth hitches to the side. A half grin. His hair is still stuck up on the left side, like it never quite figured out how to approach the day. "I'm going to need you to elaborate."

Maybe it was all that time back in his office. He doesn't usually do that on the weekend. Or maybe it was the whispering phone conversation he pretended he didn't have in our tiny hallway.

I don't know. Something is off.

I fix him with a look. "I've known you a long time, Luka."

The half grin spreads into a full one. He tosses his folded-up paper on top of my book and turns to face me, flopping his arm across the back of the couch. His eyes glow amber in the light of the fireplace, the sun just beginning to set outside the wide bay windows. From here, I can see pink and lilac cascading over the tips of the trees lining the fields. Winter finally beginning its slow crawl across the farm.

My favorite time of year.

"You have known me a long time," he agrees, voice low. "You know me better than anyone. Which is why you should know, beyond a shadow of a doubt, that I am not being weird."

I reach for my book again, eyes narrowed. I don't believe him, but that's fine. I'll let him work whatever this is out of his system and maybe rearrange the spice cabinet by country of origin. That always seems to put him in a better mood.

"All right."

His smile hitches higher. I want to bite the creases it leaves in his cheeks. "Okay."

"Okay," I respond.

A chuckle rumbles out of him. "All right."

I go back to reading my book. Luka goes back to tracing his fingertips up and down my leg. I glance up and catch him looking at me, eyes soft. He's wearing my favorite hunter green cable-knit sweater today. Socks with small embroidered silver bells.

I tuck my book against my chest. "What is it?"

He blinks twice and then swallows hard. It takes him a minute, face so serious I start to get worried. He clears his throat and sits up. "You want to go out and get a tree?"

I glance out the window. At the sun slowly sinking toward the horizon. "Now?"

He nods.

"It'll be dark before we get out to the fields." I wiggle farther down into the couch. "We can go in the morning if you still want to."

"Now is good too."

My suspicion grows. It's still two weeks until Thanksgiving, and usually I'm the one dragging him out for our tree. If we get one this early, it'll likely be a dried husk by the time the actual holiday rolls around. Not that it matters to me. I'd keep it up year round if Luka didn't get tired of sweeping up all of the pine needles.

I chew on my bottom lip and consider him. "Why?"

He fidgets, picking at a piece of imaginary lint on his knee. "Why what?"

"Why do you want to go get a tree right now?"

"Why do you have so many questions today?" he mutters, more to himself than me. He rolls his head to the side and meets my gaze, fond exasperation on every line of his handsome face. "I would like a tree right now, at this exact moment. And I'd like it very much if you came with me. Do I need a reason beyond that?"

I stare at him. Stare and stare and stare. "If you're going to break up with me, I'd like it if you did it inside where it's warm."

I'm only a little bit serious. Luka and I have been together long enough now that the fear of losing everything we've built is typically contained to the darkest moments of night—when sleep feels far away and my fears lurk with the shadows in the corners of our room. When my hands can't find him in the space next to me quick enough. When it takes him longer than usual to roll into me and press his face into my hair, arms tight around my waist.

He gives me a look that is entirely unamused. "And who will fold the laundry properly if I'm not here?" I note the clench in his jaw. "I'm not breaking up with you."

"Okay."

"All right."

"Fine."

He heaves a sigh from the very depths of his soul. He's going to need to rearrange the spice cabinet *and* the little drawer where we keep all of the hand towels. I worry for my haphazard shoe collection stuffed under the bed. The last time we disagreed about something, our house looked like an IKEA showroom.

He leverages himself off the couch and stares down at me with his hands on his hips. It is . . . distracting . . . when he gets bossy. "Go put your jacket on."

I have to adjust the collar of my flannel. "Okay."

Luka disappears while I'm looking for my boots. I've only managed to find one when he's suddenly there, holding the other in his hand. Prince Charming in winter gear. He's completely bundled head to toe, a thick scarf tucked neatly under his chin. He hands me a paper cup of something steaming and bends onto his knee to help me wedge my other foot into my boot.

It's something about the position, I think. Luka down on one knee. All of his weird behavior. The whispering and the insistence to get a tree now, when it's dark and—

"Oh my god," I whisper. "Are you proposing?"

Luka doesn't look up at me, still fighting with my foot and the boot. I'm wearing my thick inside socks today, the ones with the little grips on the bottom. I guess they make it difficult for sliding on boots. The only indication that he's heard me at all is the subtle tightening of his shoulders and the rosy blush that lights up the back of his neck like a Christmas tree.

My heart drums out something that sounds like *The Nutcracker* in my chest. My palms start to sweat through my mittens. It's a miracle I don't drop this cup of tea all over Luka's perpetual bedhead.

"Luka."

"Please," he sighs. "Please stop talking."

There's no heat in his words. Just a bemused sort of acknowledgment that this situation is not proceeding as planned. It's the same way he sounds when I don't bother separating out the laundry or when I only eat peppermint bark for breakfast. I roll my lips against a smile. "Can I—"

"You can't." He finally manages to get my foot in the boot. He pulls the strings too tight in the thrill of victory, and I go wobbling to the side. He steadies me with his other palm at my hip. When he stands up again, his cheeks are a bright flaming red, and he's looking at me like I've eaten the very last slice of pie. Like I've snatched away his favorite toy.

"Did I ruin it?" I whisper.

He rolls his eyes to the ceiling. "I did say you know me better than anyone else, didn't I?"

"You did."

"All right, well—" He shrugs, helpless. He turns me toward the door. "Let's go."

"Wait, wait, wait." I turn back toward him. He mumbles something under his breath. "I have something I want to ask you."

His lips flatten into a line, but I can see amusement dancing in his coffee-brown eyes. Amusement and adoration and years and years of friendship and love twisting and twining together. Everything we've ever been to each other. Everything we ever will be. "You're not allowed to ask me anything for the next twenty minutes."

"It will be my last question, I promise."

"And then we can go outside?"

"Yes. Then we can go outside. Find a tree, or . . . whatever."

"Whatever," he says with a laugh, quiet and low. He grabs the paper cup out of my hands and takes a fortifying sip. I guess he put something else in there besides tea. "Let's hear it."

"Okay." I slip both of my hands up his chest, rest one right against his heart. "Luka, will you marry—"

"Absolutely not." He cuts me off before I can finish my question, dropping the tea on the end table we always put our keys on. He bends at the waist and tosses me over his shoulder before I can so much as squeak. His boots stomp down the porch steps like a man possessed, making his way toward the northern fields, where our oldest trees grow.

With me thrown over his shoulder like a sack of potatoes.

I wheeze, scrambling to hold on to something so I don't slip down his back and fall flat on my face. I grab two fistfuls of his puffy jacket. The one I bought for him as a joke, but he ended up loving it without an ounce of irony or sarcasm. He says it keeps him cozy. He sifted through my email and found the receipt so he could get Beckett a matching one. Sometimes I sit on my porch and watch them wandering the fields together, two green-and-blue specks.

I clear my throat. As much as I can do so while upside down anyway. "Just so we're clear, were you saying no to marrying me, or—"

"Stop. Talking."

We walk in silence through the clusters of trees, branches catching on the arms of my jacket. He makes a *swoosh* sound every time he moves, and I try to match my breathing to it. I can't see anything but his incredible ass, and while the view isn't bad, I'm starting to get dizzy.

"Luka."

He finally slows to a stop, and I catch the dim glow of lights over the edge of trees. He tilts me forward and drops me neatly on my feet, hands on my shoulders until he's sure I won't tip head over ass into a Douglas fir. He holds me there and gives me his Luka look. The one that makes me feel like I'm floating and falling at exactly the same time.

"This isn't what I had planned," he says.

"You didn't plan on hoisting me into a fireman's carry for an evening walk?"

"Shockingly, no."

I toy with the zipper of his coat. "I bet you had diagrams, didn't you?"

Those lines by his eyes deepen. "I can neither confirm nor deny the presence of diagrams."

"Spreadsheets, at the very least."

"Oh, certainly." He glances over his shoulder, then back to me. It's hard to tell through his amusement, but I can see it. I can always see it, every shade of him.

Luka is nervous.

And in response, something in my chest settles. Eases.

I reach up and curl my hands around his wrists. I squeeze once.

"What was the plan?"

He lets out another deep, rattling sigh. His breath mists between us in a cloud of white, and his hands slip down my shoulders until they're holding me just above my elbows. Down farther to my wrists. A nice and slow version of his usual one-two-three.

"That's the thing. I couldn't really decide."

"Your plan?"

"Yeah." He nods and takes one step backward, closer to that ethereal glow rising just above the trees. "At first, I wanted to go to the hardware store on a quiet afternoon. Make you go inside while I waited on the front step for you to come back out."

The same way we met. "I probably would have gotten distracted by something. You might have been waiting for me for hours."

"I'm no stranger to waiting, La La." A grin curls his lips. "But you're right. The entire town would have been involved too. The phone tree is pretty quick these days."

"That's true." They've had a lot of practice in the busybody department over the last couple of years. I hum and follow him as he takes another step backward. "What else were you thinking?"

"Well, I thought maybe a romantic dinner would be nice. Something at home, just the two of us. Or maybe somewhere fancy. A place that needs reservations."

"Are there any places like that in Inglewild?"

"There are not. As you can see, we are currently standing in a field of trees."

"Ah."

"And so I thought maybe this might work." He releases one of my hands to scrub his through his hair, coming to an abrupt, adorable stop right in front of a massive pine. "I don't know. It's a miracle I managed to plan at all. I've been—" He cuts off with a sigh. "Do you know how long I've been carrying this ring around with me?"

My heart *ka-thumps* all the way up to my throat. Tears unexpectedly press at the back of my eyes. "So, there is a ring."

He ignores me completely. "I asked my mom for this ring two years ago. The same day you told me you loved me. I've been keeping it with the casserole dishes because I know you don't even bother with those. Sometimes I carry it around with me in my pocket when we go out, just in case it feels right. But here's the thing, Stella." He blows out a deep breath. "It's always felt right."

"What about now?" My voice warbles at the edges, and Luka tugs me into him until my chin is on his chest and my head is tilted back to meet his steady gaze. Stars like a halo above his head. His gloved hands smooth back my hair. "Does now feel right?"

He moves us forward until we're finally in the space all that light is coming from. "Now feels extra right."

A cluster of trees all twisted with red ribbon and vintage bulb lights. The ones I keep in a box in the back closet because they were my mom's favorite and she liked the way they made everything glow. A table I recognize from Layla's, set in the middle. A checkered red blanket used as a tablecloth. The one we use for picnics down by the pond when the weather is warm, Luka's head in my lap and a book open on his chest.

A plate stacked with what I'm guessing is grilled cheese wrapped neatly in foil against the cold night air.

"When did you do all this?"

He squints at something unknown in the distance. "I shimmied out the office window," he says faintly. "Made the grilled cheese at Beckett's place,"

I rub my fingertips against my lips. "Oh."

"Yep." He comes up behind me and wraps both of his arms around me, one across my collarbone and the other around my waist. He tugs me back into him until his lips are pressed in my hair, and I can feel every one of his inhales and exhales. "What do you say, La La? Want to marry me and keep ruining my best laid plans for the rest of our lives?"

I feel like one of the snow globes I keep on the very edge of my desk. Like he's just shaken me all up, and I'm twisting head over heels, glitter and snowflakes rushing around me.

The rest of our lives. That sounds pretty damn good.

His nose nuzzles my hair and he drops his voice to a whisper. "I want to wake up next to you every morning. I want to trip over boxes on my way out of the bedroom. I want to dance with you in the kitchen, and I want—I want to keep holding your hand. Every day. I want to be your husband. Do you want to be my wife?"

The word sends a thrill through me. *Wife.*

But there's another title that's still my favorite. "Best friend, too?"

I feel him swallow behind me. His arms squeeze me even tighter. I cling back just as hard. His voice is rough when he says, "Always that."

"I'll want grilled cheese every day," I manage. I spin in his arms until I can wrap myself around him. He drops his forehead down to mine, gloved hand at my cheek. "I'll probably want Christmas music in July, and I don't—I'd like to promise I won't be disorganized, but I think I'll always be a little bit messy."

His smile makes my heart beat double time. "That's how I like you best," he tells me.

I press up on my toes so I can nudge my nose to his. I don't know if he's realized it, but he's slowly started leading us into a dance. A gentle sway back and forth. I don't know if he hears a song in his head or if he's just turning us to the sound of the wind through the trees, but it's—it's perfect. The very best moment. He couldn't have planned it better.

I breathe him in with the nighttime air. I close my eyes and beg myself to remember this moment. The pounding of his heart against me and the shaky way he exhales. The glow of the Christmas lights and a red checkered blanket with a tear at the corner.

Luka and me right in the middle of it all. Together, like we're supposed to be.

"Yes," I say. "I want to be your wife."

He rocks us back and forth. His voice is rough and low. "Best friend, too?"

I hiccup a laugh into his neck.

"Always that."

❧ BONUS CHAPTER ❦

THIS BONUS CHAPTER is Luka's perspective of this scene in chapter twenty-one:

> *I slept with my best friend last night. I slept with him two . . . three times last night. After we had collapsed in a boneless heap the first time, I woke up sometime around two in the morning, stomach rumbling. I snuck in the kitchen for a bite of pie out of the tin, only for Luka to shuffle in the kitchen after me, sleepily steal a bite from my fork, and then prop me up on the kitchen counter.*
>
> *"Want this," he had mumbled as he ducked down, teeth grazing my thigh, his mouth hot and wet on the inside of my knee.*

LUKA

"LUKA."

I grunt and burrow my face deeper in the pillow I'm curled around, desperate to hold on to my dream. Stella with her knees on either side of my hips. My hands working down the line of tiny buttons on her oversized flannel. Her bottom lip caught between her teeth and all those curls a curtain around us both.

I bet I could slip right back into it if I tried. See what sort of lacy thing dream Stella is wearing. My brain certainly has enough practice coming up with explicit fantasies involving her.

My pillow moves. A fingertip presses between my eyes. "Luka."

I groan, edging further into consciousness and away from the bleary edges of sleep.

The huff turns into a laugh. Fingers drag through my hair. I peek open one eye, and it's Stella smiling in the moonlight, her lips kiss-bitten and hair a wild, tangled mess. It's so like my dream I have to blink four times and scrub a fist against my eye to make sure I'm not imagining it.

Everything comes back to me in flashes.

Stella in the front yard, snowflakes in her hair. Kissing her, the both of us tripping up the stairs to her house, unwilling to let go of each other. Peeling off her sweater until she was just bare skin in the glow of the lights from the tree. The freckle on the inside of her left knee. Both of her hands clenched tight in my hair. Her body, naked and wrapped around mine.

Everything she said when she stood in the kitchen, eyes right on me.

I stumbled off that step and he caught me, made sure I had my footing. He's sort of been holding me steady ever since.

I turn onto my side and brush a lazy kiss against Stella's shoulder. A small sigh slips from her lips, and I think I like that sound better than any of the ones she made last night. Better than the husk of her laugh in the dark or the bite of her moan pressed against the hollow of my throat.

I like the sound of her settling against me. I like hearing her happy. I've always liked that.

Her nails scratch through my hair again, and I wiggle my way closer through three down comforters and a novelty pillow shaped like an evergreen tree. I sling my arm around her waist and tug her toward me.

"Why are you awake?" I mumble. "And why are you poking my forehead?"

I can barely make out the lines of her face in the dark. I look for the little clock she keeps on the edge of her dresser. It blinks 2:23 a.m. back at me.

"I had a dream about pie," she whispers. Her voice is low and rough around the edges. There's a scratch to it that I like. Stella's sleepy voice.

I shuffle down farther in the bed until I can trap one of Stella's legs with both of mine. I nuzzle into her mess of chestnut hair. She smells like shortbread, whiskey, and wood smoke. I never want to move from this spot.

"Want me to get you some?"

"No, that's all right. I'll go see what we have."

I peer open one eye. "I can make you a grilled cheese, if you want."

I can feel her smile like a palm pressed to my cheek. "No," she says. "Though I'm tempted. You don't have to wake up. I just didn't—" She sighs and her mouth drops briefly against my forehead, bottom lip dragging. "I didn't want you to wake up and find me gone."

I smooth my fingers over the swell of her hip. That thing in my chest that's always belonged a little bit to Stella shifts, rearranges. Pounds harder. "Thank you," I manage.

"Sleep." I can feel her hesitate above me for one second, two, before she leans forward and brushes another kiss against my forehead. These new versions of ourselves together, trying to figure out how much we can get away with. "I'll be back in a second."

She slips out from beneath the blankets despite my groping hands, and I watch as she bands one arm over her bare breasts as she rummages around on the floor for a shirt. Her skin glows in the moonlight, and my greedy eyes trace her silhouette in the quiet of her bedroom. It feels like I'm still caught in the edges of my dream, getting to watch her like this. The gentle swell between her waist and hip. The tangle of hair that cascades over her shoulders. The thin white scar at the base of her spine I know she got from trying to jump into the pond six years ago. The full, lush curve of her breasts as she finds a flannel she clearly stole from me and slips it over her shoulders.

It takes her a minute to get the buttons right, and when she finally does manage it, they're haphazard and crooked. The one right between her breasts is left open, and I'm tempted to catch the end of that shirt in my fist and tug. Stella presses her chin to her shoulder and looks at me, blue eyes a deep sapphire. Her lips twist up at the corner.

"I'll be right back."

"Promise?"

The twist of her lips turns into a pleased grin that she does her best to fight. But it tumbles out of her just the same, like the starlight spilling in through her windows.

"Yeah, I promise."

She pads out of the room and I flip onto my back. I scrub my hands through my hair and yawn so wide my jaw cracks. Stella drops something in the kitchen, and I hear a muffled curse, socked feet against the kitchen floor.

"Okay?" I call, trying to urge myself awake. Stella's likely to lose a finger or set something on fire getting a slice of pie out of the fridge in the dark. I lift up on my elbows and try to see around the door. "Turn on the light, La La."

A light blinks to life in the kitchen and Stella grumbles some more. "M'fine!"

I snicker and collapse back to the bed. The sheets smell like Stella. Like Stella and me and sex and cinnamon, and my dream clings to me, the glimpse of Stella's skin as she slipped from the bed tightening the edge of my desire. My hands itch to touch every freckle I missed when we first fell into bed last night. I want to know every secret her body holds. Everything I've been thinking of for the past . . . decade.

God, ten years. It feels like a week turned into a year turned into a decade. I don't know how it's been so long. I know Stella's been afraid and I've been—I don't know. I guess I've been content to go at whatever pace she needs. Happy enough with her trust and the pieces of her heart I've slowly marked as mine over the years. It's hard to be greedy when I'm already the first person she calls when she wakes up, half mumbling something about a dream she had involving nutmeg and dancing chestnuts. When I get her weird snort laugh instead of the charming, polite thing she manages in front of everyone else. When half of her closet is filled with my shirts she thinks she's sneaky about stealing. I've always had Stella in the ways she's allowed.

But now I get her like this too.

Naked in her bed. Clinging to the damn evergreen pillow I drunkenly bought her two summers ago when I was alone in my apartment—a little bit tipsy and wondering what she was up to so damn far away from me.

I've spent so long thinking about this, hoping for it.

And I'm lying in her bed alone while she's in the other room half naked and eating pie.

I'm an idiot.

I slip from the bed just as she drops something else, finding my boxers hanging from one of the bedposts. I slip them on and follow the sounds of her muffled cursing until I find her at the kitchen counter, tinfoil rolled back over a half-eaten pumpkin pie, fork in hand. She doesn't bother glancing at me as I pad across the hardwood, scooping another bite of pie on her fork instead.

"Told you I'd *oomph*" Her sentence is cut off when I wrap myself around her, chin at her shoulder, arms banded low around her hips. She's soft and warm and smells like cinnamon, the curve of her ass pressed tight against where I'm aching for her. Again. Always probably. I don't know if I'll ever get enough of her like this.

"Did you want pie?" she asks, voice low. Her hips tilt back, and her eyelashes flutter against the curve of her cheeks. I nod and she lifts her abandoned fork, a bit of pie clinging to the edge. I curl my fingers around her wrist and guide it to my mouth, pumpkin and cinnamon exploding on my tongue.

"It's good," I say around a mouthful of flaky pie crust. She blinks at me, fork still hovering between us. All I can see of her like this is the blush creeping up her neck, the tempting rise and fall of her chest beneath her stolen flannel. I take the fork out of her hand until it's back on the counter and set my hands on her hips.

I turn her until every bit of her is pressed up against every bit of me, and she's looking at me with those dark, sleepy, wanting eyes. I've seen it in flashes over the years—the wanting. Shared glances in crowded bars. Lingering touches when we've both had a little bit too much to drink, and the leash I keep on myself slips just a bit. But I've never seen it like this. Up close. Constant.

Demanding.

I trace her cheek with my thumb to the little dip in her chin and try to memorize this moment. The hum of the refrigerator and wind creaking at the windows. Stilted breaths and anticipation pricking at my skin. Stella propped up against the counter with her eyes trailing down the length of me, smiling faintly at the cluster of freckles beneath my collarbone.

Her lips parted, candy apple red.

I drop my hands to her hips and urge her up. Her hip hits the pie tin and sends it skittering across the countertop. The fork goes . . . somewhere. Stella watches me with careful eyes, the insides of her knees pressing at my hips.

"What are you doing?"

I'm trying to go slow. I'm trying to hold myself together. I'm trying to look at Stella sitting in front of me in a shirt she stole from my closet and not tell her every word that's pounding a drumbeat right in the center of my chest. I let out a shuddering exhale.

"Want this," is all I can manage in response. Of all my fantasies of Stella, this has always been my favorite. The one I turn to when the wanting and the needing gets to be too much, and I have to fist my hand around myself. I close my eyes and picture her just like this, in front of me with her legs spread wide. Wild hair and kiss-bitten lips.

"You want some more pie?" she asks, voice shaky.

A sound rumbles low in my chest. A laugh, I think, if I could manage such a thing right now. "No, La La. I want more of you."

The floor is cold beneath my knees when I drop down in front of her, but Stella is warm everywhere else. Her thigh twitches when I brush my lips against the inside of her knee, and she smacks her head against the cabinet when I move three inches higher and nudge at the edge of the shirt barely covering her. I glance up at her from between her spread legs, and that seems to do something to her too. Me, like this, on my knees before her. Her breath comes faster, and I can feel my heart in my chest pounding to match.

"Okay?" I ask, and I know she knows I'm asking about more than her head.

"Yeah, um." She nods, eyes glazed. Her fingers clench the counter so tight her knuckles turn white. "Yes. This is good."

I huff a laugh against the inside of her thigh and her knees tip open just a bit wider. Lust roars through me. "Hopefully it's better than good."

She laughs back. "I guess we'll see."

I tease her with gentle swiping kisses against the inside of her legs—higher and higher, just below where she wants me most. Her skin is so soft here, so impossibly sweet. I drop a light kiss against the crease of her thigh, and I have to squeeze my eyes shut tight when I feel how wet she is. How warm.

"Luka," she says. The heel of her foot drums between my shoulder blades from where I draped her thigh over my shoulder. "Luka, please."

"All right. Okay, I'm—" I'm falling apart is what I am. I relent and curl my hands around her thighs as I press my mouth to the heart of her—a long, languid lick that has us both groaning.

"Luka," she says again. "*God*. Luka."

Her voice, like that, saying my name—it splinters my restraint. I yank her to the very edge of the countertop and drop my mouth to her. Again and again and again until she's gasping, yanking, tugging at me. I lick and suck and bite with both of her hands clenched tight in my hair, guiding me into the rhythm she likes best. Rough, fast, messy. I slip one hand into the waistband of my boxers and curl my palm around myself just as I thrust two fingers into her. She makes a sound that I'll hear in my dreams for the rest of my life. A whimper that blurs at the edges, mussed by desire.

It's perfect. She's perfect. She's everything I've ever wanted. Hoped for. Dreamed of. Her taste beneath my tongue is sweeter than that damned pumpkin pie left abandoned on the counter. The feel of her hot and wet and wanting is a goddamn revelation. I don't want to do anything else, ever.

"I'm—I'm so close," she says, voice two octaves higher than it usually is. I suck her clit into my mouth and she makes a whimpering sound that echoes in my bones. I do it again and her whole body trembles. I'm greedy for it. "Make me come. Please."

I pull away and rest my forehead against her leg, watching the way my fingers move against her. Her hips move with me, and it's a wonder I'm capable of any rational thought. I feel like I could come just from this. Watching her chase her pleasure.

I drag my gaze up until our eyes catch and hold. "What do you need?"

I drag a sucking kiss against her thigh. Her whole body shivers.

"Could you—" She drops her head back against the cabinets, watching me from beneath her lashes. "Could you put your mouth on me again?"

"Yeah." I nudge her with my nose and press a kiss right below her belly button. I tap my thumb over her once, and then again when a sound catches in the back of her throat. I've dreamed of exactly this so many times, Stella flushed and panting and asking for me. I try to gather the threads of my control. "I can do that."

I can do anything you want, is what I want to say. *Anything you've ever thought of.* I bite back the words and set my mouth to her instead. Firm, unrelenting pressure and quick strokes of my tongue. Her thighs tighten around my ears, her moans muffled. I close my eyes and feel the way she unravels against me, her whole body giving in to her release.

I stay with her through it, gentle kisses and careful touches until she calms, legs spread haphazard and limbs loose. She watches me with dark, interested eyes as I drag the back of my hand against my wet mouth.

"That was—" She blinks twice, the blue in her eyes luminescent. "It was good. If you were—if you were wondering."

"I gathered that."

"Oh? What gave it away?"

I grin at her and stand. I thumb at the blush on her cheeks, the strand of hair sticking to her neck. "The look on your face." I gather all of her hair into a fist and then release it with a wistful sigh. Her head lolls into my touch. "The way you shrieked my name."

One imperious eyebrow rises on her forehead as she flicks me in the center of my chest. I catch her fingers with my hand and hold. "I did not shriek."

"You shrieked."

She curls her hand around my jaw and tugs me closer until she can angle her mouth to mine. She licks into my mouth with a sigh, and goose bumps light up my arms.

"I didn't shriek," she whispers against my lips.

The bottom half of my body feels like it's a hairpin away from something devastating and embarrassing. Probably equal parts both. I wonder how Stella would feel if I yanked my boxers down and touched myself to the sight of her, messy and spent. God knows it wouldn't take long.

Her mouth moves to my neck and I'm tired of teasing. "Okay, okay. You didn't shriek." She did though. "Can I—" I fumble with the mismatched button over her breasts that I've been fixating on. I want to see her skin. I want to watch the way she moves when she takes me inside her. "Can I have you again?"

She nods, pink on her cheeks. A little bit bashful. Entirely adorable. Completely mine.

"How do you want me?"

Every way, my mind supplies. *Here, in your house. In this kitchen and in your bed and up against the door to your horribly unorganized closet. With me always.*

Her eyes flash a shade darker, like she knows exactly what I'm thinking. After ten years, she probably does. I urge her from the counter with gentle hands and spin her in my arms until she's bent at the waist. I tug the shirt off her until it's a crumpled heap on the floor. She's nothing but smooth curves in the low light, elbows resting on the countertop and ass in the air. Another fantasy.

"Is this okay?"

She nods, frantic. "Very okay." Her hands are busy fighting with the hem of my boxers as she tries to urge them down with her body twisted away. "Come here, please."

It's the *please* this time that sends me over the edge. I grab one of the condoms Stella helpfully left by the pie tin and roll it over myself, one palm on the small of her back. I press into her slow, slow, slow until I'm buried in her. Until I can lean forward and tuck a deep sound of appreciation against her neck.

I hold myself there, overwhelmed by the feeling. I nose through her hair and catch the edge of her ear with my teeth.

"Did you plan this?" My voice sounds like it's coming from some-place very far away. I roll my hips and heat rolls up my spine. Back down again. Everything pulls tight.

"What? The pie?" Her breath is almost as fast as mine, her hips rocking back like she's too impatient to wait. Like she'll take me how-ever she can get me. It's driving me wild. "Of course I planned the pie. I'm always planning for pie."

"Not the pie." I smooth my hand down the length of her spine. I pull out slowly and then thrust back in with all of my pent-up . . . everything . . . I've been feeling since I woke up with Stella naked next to me. She makes me feel like I'm out of control. Like I can't have everything I want fast enough, hard enough. Like I need to bend her over her kitchen counter just so she can understand how badly I *want* all the damn time.

I thrust into her again, and the mugs we left on the counter earlier rattle. We both make strangled sounds of pleasure. Matched as al-ways, even in this. "You wanted me to fuck you, didn't you?"

"There you go with that word again."

"I knew you liked it best."

"I don't know, I'm—" Her breath hitches when I angle my hips and hit that spot. That spot I found last night, when I pressed her flat to the bed and curled my hands around her hips, chasing our pleasure until she was shaking beneath me. "I'm pretty partial to *bumping uglies*."

I'd laugh if I wasn't so focused on the way she's still reaching for me, her nails biting into the skin of my hip. The way her breasts bounce every time I move against her. *Christ.* This is better than any dream, anything I could have ever thought up.

"Noted," I grit out, and then I lose myself to her. To the wet heat between her thighs and the flush of her skin. The way she pushes back into me harder when I try to slow down, try to make it last. I tilt my head back and catch a glimpse of us in the tiny window above her kitchen sink. Stella and all those alabaster curves glowing like stardust. Me right behind her, making her shiver.

"Fuck." The sight of us together tosses me right over the edge. I drop my chin to my chest and grind my hips against Stella, deep and slow and messy and perfect. I come the moment just before she does, her hands scrambling against the counter, knocking over an old coffee canister. It rattles across the floor as I collapse in a boneless heap against her back, my ear pressed to her shoulder. The steady thump of her heart lulls me into some sort of hypnotic trance. I could fall asleep right here. Just like this.

"Do you remember that time you took me to that food court in Annapolis?" I mumble against the curve of her back. She's still plastered against the kitchen counter, but she doesn't seem to be complaining. She tilts her face to the side until she can glance at me out of the corner of her eye. The pads of her fingers sooth over the marks she left on my skin.

"The one with all the different pizza places?"

One food court. Fourteen different pizza options. Deep dish. Stuffed crust. Flatbread. "That's the one."

Her eyes crinkle at the corners. "You told me it was the best day of your life."

I blow out a deep breath and leverage myself off her. My legs feel like Jell-O. Like someone just shot me with a tranquilizer gun. I haul Stella up after me and tuck her neatly against my chest. I collar my hand around her throat and trace her fluttering pulse, a zigzag line all the way to where her heart is thumping a steady beat. I press my palm there and close my eyes.

I hope she can feel it. Everything I haven't said yet. Everything I want to.

"New best day," I mutter.

She tangles her fingers with mine and raps our hands against her heart. Like maybe she wants to tell me some things too.

She tilts her head and presses a smacking kiss to my jaw. "Back to bed?"

Soon. I'll work up the courage to tell her everything else soon enough.

I smooth my hand down her hip and smack her ass. "Anywhere with you."

⚘ ACKNOWLEDGMENTS ⚘

My first thank-you goes to you, reader. I can't believe this book is out in the world being read by people—real-life people! Thank you for giving this little book some of your time. Writing this has been a dream come true, and I couldn't have done it without the support of two very important people.

Did you know this is the first thing my husband has ever read by me? Thank you, E, for your support as I tip-tapped away on the patio, the couch, the floor, and everywhere in between. You have always believed in me, and I love you so much. I promise to listen to you talk about fantasy football now.

Annie, my gateway drug into romance novels. You've been cheerleading me for close to a decade. This book one hundred percent would not be what it is if it were not for you. Thank you for editing, but more importantly, thank you for holding my hand.

Keep reading for an excerpt from the next novel in the
Lovelight series

IN THE WEEDS

BECKETT

March

"DO YOU PLAN *on coming back to bed?"*

Her voice is raspy with sleep, and she has a hickey at the base of her throat, a deep purple bruise that I can't stop staring at. She stretches her arms above her head, and the sheet slips half an inch, the swell of her breasts rising from beneath. I want to catch that sheet in my teeth and drag it down until she's bare beneath me. I want a hundred other things too.

I shake my head from where I'm perched on the desk in the corner of the room, taking another sip of coffee instead.

Restraint, I tell myself. Have some goddamn restraint.

She smirks at me.

"Oh, I get it." She drops her hands back down, one twisting through her hair, the other slipping beneath the sheets. One eyebrow arches high in invitation. "You like to watch."

I'm pretty sure I'd like just about anything with Evie. I want all that black silky hair wrapped around my fist, that smiling mouth at my neck. Last night she spent twenty-two minutes tracing the tattoo across my bicep with her mouth, and I want that too. I want to return the favor with the freckles on the inside of her wrist and the marks at her hips.

I push off the desk and set my cup to the side. I step toward the bed and watch the movement of her hand. She swipes it low across her stom-

ach, a wicked smile on her pretty face. I plant my knee on the bed and find her ankle, her bare foot dangling off the edge.

"I love to watch," I tell her as I grip her thigh and make room for my body between her long legs. I drop a kiss to the inside of her knee, and her whole body shivers. I drop another kiss just above it. "But I like to touch more."

A finger digs into my ribcage as I'm violently yanked from my favorite daydream.

"Are you paying attention?"

My knee jolts and my boot catches on the chair in front of me, sending Becky Gardener rocking precariously to the side. She curls her hands around the edges with a white-knuckled grip and shoots me a look over her shoulder. I fix my attention on my boots and mumble an apology.

"I'm paying attention," I tell Stella, and swat her hand away.

Kind of. Not really. There are too many people in this room. All of the business owners in town are sandwiched together in the conference space at the rec hall, an old room that I'm pretty sure is used to store Easter decorations if the slightly terrifying six-foot bunny in the back corner is any indication. The air smells like stale coffee and hairspray, and the ladies from the salon haven't stopped cackling since they stepped through the door. It's like sitting cross-legged in the middle of a parade while the drumline marches around me. All of the sound pulls my shoulders tight, an itch of discomfort pricking at my neck.

And I keep making eye contact with that bunny.

I don't usually come to these types of things, but Stella had insisted. *You wanted to be a partner*, she said. *This is what partners do.*

I thought being a partner meant I could buy the fancy fertilizer without checking in with anyone, not attending meetings that serve absolutely no purpose. There's a reason I chose a job where I spend seventy-five percent of my day outside.

Alone. In the quiet.

I struggle with talking to people. Struggle with coming up with the right words in the right sequence at the right time. Every single time I come into town, I feel like everyone is looking right at me. Some of that is in my head, I know, but some of it is—

Some of it is Cindy Croswell pretending to fall in the aisle at the pharmacy just so I have to help her up again. Or Becky Gardener from the school asking me if I can host a field trip while eyeing me up like I'm a rare steak with a side of potatoes. I've got no idea what goes on half the time I come into town, but I feel like people lose their damn minds.

"You're not paying attention," Layla chimes in from my right, legs crossed and hand rummaging around in the giant bowl of popcorn she brought with her. Layla runs the bakery at the farm, while Stella holds down the tourism and marketing side of things. Since Inglewild is the size of a postage stamp and Stella has a bone-deep urge to make Lovelight Farms a "cornerstone of the community," we seem to be expected to be involved in a lot of town business.

I don't even know what this meeting is about.

"Where did the popcorn come from?" I ask.

I glance at the gargantuan bag stuffed under her chair. I know for a fact there's some brownies and half a box of crackers in there. She says the Inglewild bimonthly small business owner's meeting is a drag without a snack, and I'm inclined to agree. Not that she's offered to share.

Layla circles one finger right in front of my face and ignores my question. "You have that moony look on your face. You're thinking about Evelyn."

"Was not." I sigh and roll my shoulders, desperate to relieve the tension that sits between them. "I was thinking about the pepper crop," I lie.

I'm distracted. I've been that way since two hazy nights in August. Sweat-slicked skin. Hair like midnight. Evie St. James had smelled like sea salt and tasted like citrus.

I haven't had my head on straight since.

Layla rolls her eyes and crams another handful of popcorn into her mouth. "Okay, sure. Whatever you say."

Stella reaches across me and snatches the bowl out of Layla's hands. "They're getting ready to start. If we could pretend to be professional, that would be great."

I raise both eyebrows. "For the town meeting?"

"Yes, for the town meeting. The one in which we are currently in attendance."

"Ah, yes. Always very professional."

At the last town meeting, Pete Crawford tried to filibuster Georgie Simmons during a vote on new parking restrictions in front of the co-op. He had reenacted *Speed*, complete with props and voices.

Stella levels me with a look and turns back to the front of the room with the bowl in the crook of her arm. Layla shimmies closer and rests her chin at my elbow. I sigh and look up at the heavy wooden beams that cut across the ceiling and pray for patience. There's a deflated balloon stuck up there, probably left over from the Valentine's Day event they had last month. A speed dating thing, I think. My sisters had tried to make me go, and I locked myself in my house and turned off my phone. I stare at the balloon and frown. A faded red heart, deflated and stuck, string wrapped around and around.

"Have you talked to her since she left?"

A couple of times. A bland text sent in the middle of the night after one too many beers. A generic response. A picture from her of an open field, somewhere out there in the world, a line of text that said, Not as nice as your farm but still pretty nice. I had fumbled my phone into the dirt when that message came through, my thumb tracing back and forth over her words like I had my hands on her skin instead.

A social media influencer. An important one, apparently. I'm still trying to wrap my head around that. Millions of followers. I looked her up one night when the silence of my house felt suffocating, my thumb tapping at the screen of my phone. I checked her account and couldn't stop staring at that little number at the top.

I never checked her account again.

I've had one-night stands before. Plenty of them. But I can't get Evie out of my head. Thinking about her is like a hunger in the hollow of my stomach, a buzzing just under my skin. We spent two nights together in Bar Harbor. I shouldn't— I don't know why I still see her when I close my eyes.

Twisted up in bedsheets. Hair in my face. That half smile that made my heart hit double-time.

"I was thinking about peppers," I say again, determined to hold on to this lie. It's best not to give Layla an inch. She'll take a mile and the shirt off your back for the trouble of it. I grew up with three sisters. I can sense the inquisition like a wind change.

"Your face does not say you're thinking about bell peppers," Layla snaps. "It says you're thinking about Evelyn."

"Stop looking at my face."

"Stop making the face you're making, and I'll stop looking at it." I sigh.

"I just think it's a shame, is all." Layla reaches across me and grabs another handful of popcorn, and a kernel lands in my lap. I flick it off and hit Becky Gardener right in the back of the head. *Christ.* I wince and sink farther in my chair. "You two seemed to hit it off."

What we seemed to do is circle each other like two skittish kittens. After I went to visit her at the bed-and-breakfast, I promised I'd give her a wide berth to do her job. It had been harder than I expected, keeping that promise. Seeing her standing among the rows and rows of trees on the farm, a smile on her face, her hands passing over the branches—well, it was like taking a baseball bat to the face. Repeatedly. But the contest meant everything to Stella, and I wasn't about to ruin our chances with a . . . with a . . .

A crush? A flirtation?

I don't even know what.

All I know is that it was a challenge for me to be around her. I couldn't stop thinking about my body curled around hers. The way the skin just below her ear tasted. How it felt to have all that hair brush against my jaw, my shoulders, the tops of my thighs. I found myself wanting to make her laugh, wanting to talk to her.

I can count on one hand the number of people I *want* to talk to.

But we figured it out, settled into a routine while she was here. Cordial conversation and polite nods. A single slice of shared zucchini bread on a quiet afternoon—plenty of space between us. That same electric current that tugged us together at a dive bar in Maine knit slowly back together in a thin thread of connection.

And then she left. Again.

And unfortunately for me, I still haven't figured out how to stop thinking about her.

"What kind of peppers?"

I shake my head once, trying to pry loose an image of Evelyn standing in between two towering oak trees on the edge of the property, her face in profile and tilted toward the sky. The sun had painted her in shimmering golds, leaves fluttering lightly around her. I clear my throat and adjust my position in the folding chair, my knee knocking sideways into Layla's. I'm way too big for these chairs, and there are too many damn people in this room. "What?"

"What type of peppers are you planting?" Layla asks, enunciating each word. "I haven't seen any markers for peppers out in the field."

The back of my neck goes hot. "You never go out in the fields."

"I'm in the fields every day."

Layla walks through the fields, sure, on the way to the bakehouse, situated smack-dab in the middle of them. But she never finds herself in the produce crop. Not unless she needs something. I scratch at my jaw, frustrated. I'd bet my savings she finds something she needs out there tomorrow morning.

"Bell," I manage between clenched teeth.

Shit, now I need to go out and plant bell peppers.

Layla hums, eyes alight with mischief. "What color?"

"What?"

"What color *bell pepper*"—she puts an annoying emphasis on the words—"have you planted?"

"He planted red bell peppers in the southeast fields in two rows next to the zucchini. Which you will get absolutely none of if you do not pay attention," Stella snaps.

Layla and I both glance at her in shock. It's not like Stella to get aggravated. Not to mention that is . . . not a true statement. And we both know it.

Some of the steel melts out of her shoulders, and she slumps, handing Layla back her popcorn bowl.

"Sorry. I'm stressed."

"Clearly," Layla says in a laugh, hand back to rummaging around in her snacks. Her eyes find mine and hold, narrowing until all I can see is a glimpse of hazel. She still has some jelly in her hair from baking earlier today. Strawberry, by the looks of it. She points her finger right between my eyebrows and taps me there once. "Don't think I'm going to forget about this."

I swat her hand away. She could persist on this topic for the next six months for all I care. It'll just sound like background noise.

I turn my attention to Stella and wedge my boot against hers. She stops the nervous tapping of her foot and grimaces. "Sorry."

"Nothing to apologize for." I shrug and scan the edges of the room. "Luka not coming?"

If Luka were here, he'd smooth his hand between her shoulder blades, and she'd melt like butter. They were like that before they got together, and it took them a stupidly long time to see what was right in front of them. I didn't win the townwide betting pool, but it was close. Gus over at the fire station hasn't shut up about it, going as far as making a plaque to hang above the ambulance bay at the firehouse. It says, INGLEWILD'S TOP MATCHMAKER, like he had anything to do with Luka and Stella orbiting each other for close to a decade. I slip down farther in my seat and try to rearrange my legs so I actually fit in this damn chair.

"He's on his way," she says, eyes darting to the door and holding like she can make him appear by sheer force of will. Her hand pushes tangled chestnut curls off her face. "But he's running late."

"He'll be here," I assure her. Pretty sure Luka wouldn't miss this for anything. Even if his tiny Italian mother and all her ferocious sisters were blocking the door. If he said he'd come, he'll be here.

"Hey." I lower my voice and lean closer, conscious of Layla still snacking away on my right. She's started tossing pieces up in the air and catching them in her mouth. Accurate every time. "I didn't plant any bell peppers."

That seems to relax Stella a bit, a coy smile turning the corners of her lips. "I know that."

"Why'd you lie, then?"

"Because you looked like you needed an out. And I know a thing or two about having to sort through feelings before you can share them with everyone else." The door to the rec hall creaks open, and Luka steps inside, eyes searching. His hair is sticking in every direction, the edge of his shirt half tucked into his jeans. He looks like he ran straight here from the Delaware border. Stella breathes out a sigh and a grin pulls her mouth wide. An answering smile blooms on Luka's face the second he finds her in the crowd. Watching them together is like shoving a cupcake directly into my face.

"Plus—" Stella's eyes don't blink away from Luka as he tries to climb his way through rows of people to get to the empty seat next to her. He knocks over a folding chair and almost sends Cindy Croswell to the ground with it. "I've been wanting bell peppers on the farm for ages."

"Ah, okay. There it is."

"Luka makes really good stuffed peppers." She chuckles as Luka slips into the space next to her. His hand immediately sneaks under her hair, and her shoulders do a little shimmy as she leans farther into him. I avert my eyes to the front of the room, where Sheriff Jones is getting ready at the wooden podium, but I don't miss the low murmuring between them, the way Stella folds her body into his. How Luka's foot hooks in the bottom of her chair to pull her a little bit closer.

Not for the first time, I'm jealous. I've never had that with another person. Never been able to slide into someone's space and press my fingertips to their skin, watch them lean farther into me.

I think of my thumb against a full bottom lip, red as a cherry, and shift in my seat. The metal squeaks ominously beneath me.

I'd really love to stop thinking about Evelyn.

Layla leans around me, her bowl digging into my ribcage. "The maintenance closet is available if you two want to get a room."

I snort a laugh. Stella groans.

Luka bends forward and scoops his hand in the popcorn bowl. "Does it have a lock?"

Layla cackles loud enough to attract attention from the front of the room. Some of the salon ladies stop their conversation to give us a look, and Alex from the bookstore raises his coffee in greeting. I notice Deputy Caleb Alvarez standing just behind the sheriff, a smile twitching on his lips, his gaze fixed on Layla.

I catch Stella's eye and she grins.

"All right, let's get this show on the road." Sheriff Dane Jones clears his throat and then clears it again, the chatter in the room quieting as everyone settles in for the meeting. "First order of business. Ms. Beatrice, the police department would appreciate it if you stopped trying to tow the cars in front of the café on your own. You don't have the equipment for it, and using your vehicle as a battering ram has resulted in a few complaints."

"She tried to kill me," Sam Montez shouts from the back of the room, his hat falling off sideways as he jumps from his chair. "I was out of my car for a minute—two tops—and she tried to kill me!"

I hide my smile behind my fist. Sam has a bad habit of double-parking. Not usually a problem on our small town roads, but annoying all the same. I can just barely make out the top of Ms. Beatrice's head sitting at the end of the front row, her gray hair pulled into a messy bun. She mutters something that I don't quite catch. Dane frowns, and Caleb practically swallows his tongue.

"Well, there's no need for that kind of language. If someone is blocking the loading dock, you can give me or Caleb a ring."

She mumbles something else and Shirley from the salon gasps. Dane pinches the bridge of his nose between thumb and forefinger. "Bea, what have I told you about making threats of physical violence in front of a police officer. Sam, sit down."

Sam drops down in his seat and scoops up his hat. Luka reaches across me for another handful of popcorn from Layla's bowl.

"You undersold this meeting, La La."

"They're not usually this colorful," Stella tells him, accepting a piece of offered popcorn.

"Yes, they are," Layla and I reply in unison.

"Next up—" Dane glances down at the stack of papers on the podium and lets out a muffled groan. He glances at Caleb with a pleading expression. Caleb shrugs and Dane turns back to the room. "Ms. Beatrice, if you could kindly remove the WANTED posters from the window of the shop, that would be great."

This time I'm not the only one who has to stifle a laugh. The room breaks out into a low murmur, and Caleb has to completely turn around to hide his grin, his back facing the audience and his shoulders shaking. Ms. Beatrice has been putting up WANTED signs in her windows for months now, ever since she caught two tourists in the back bathroom using the sink in new and creative ways.

Dane tilts his head to listen to whatever Ms. Beatrice has to say on the matter. "I agree public indecency is a crime, but again, just give me or Caleb a call." He holds up his hand to cut off her response and glances down at the podium, eager to move the conversation along.

But whatever he sees has him folding up the whole stack of paperwork with a grunt. "All right, Beatrice, clearly you and I need to have a side conversation. We'll table the"—he flips over the paper and glances at it again—"other seven things for another time."

"Do you think someone complained about how she refuses to buy almond milk?" Layla whispers out of the corner of her mouth. She did buy it, actually. She just put it in a canister that says HIPSTER JUICE on the side.

"Probably something about Karen and the latte incident," I reply. I rarely come into town during the afternoons, but I happened to be walking by the day Ms. Beatrice refused to serve Karen Wilkes on account of her being rude to the waitstaff. A latte somehow found its way all over Karen's faux fur bomber jacket. Can't say I blame her for that one.

"All right," Dane's voice booms over the room and everyone settles again. "Next up. The pizza shop is, uh . . ." He hesitates, rubbing his fingertips over his mustache and down his chin. He taps there once and glances around the room. "Matty would like you all to know there's a special this month. Half the profits on Wednesdays go to the elementary school to fund their science trips."

Stella's hand shoots into the air. Dane looks like he wants to walk out the door and keep walking. "Yes, Stella?"

"Is this an appropriate time to share that I think you two are the cutest couple I've ever seen in my life and express my congratulations that you've finally moved in together?"

"I like the wreath you put on your door," Mabel Brewster adds from somewhere in the middle of the room. "And the birdbath in the front yard. Didn't know you had such an eye for gardening, Sheriff."

The rest of the room bursts into a series of comments and questions about the sheriff's love life.

"Did you see them at the farmers market? I swear I've never seen Dane Jones smile so much."

"Do you mean he smiled once? Because I think that's the standing record."

"They were holding *hands*. He bought Matty *flowers*."

"Where is Matty? You can't keep him locked up just because you two are an item now."

I sink farther in my chair, the hum of sound rising up and over me. It's like a buzz in the back of my head, a ringing in my ears. I press my thumb deep into my palm and try to focus there instead.

Dane looks about ready to burst at the front of the room, his cheeks a flaming red above his beard, hands fussing with the hat tucked under his arm.

I nudge Stella with my elbow. "You're not worried this is going to turn on you?"

"What do you mean?"

I gesture between her and Luka. "When are you two moving in together?"

"Oh"—she waves her hand, unconcerned—"as soon as we can figure out how to add more space. I don't think Luka is ready for me in my full messy glory quite yet."

Stella lives in a cottage on the opposite side of the farm from my cabin, a tiny house filled to the brim with old magazines and half-empty coffee mugs. It looks like an eighty-year-old woman with a hoarding problem lives there, Luka's interference be damned. I once heard them arguing about kitchen towels with gnomes on them. Stella didn't want to throw them away because, apparently, they're a conversation piece.

"We'll move in together when we can add a bedroom or two so he has someplace to cry when I don't fold his T-shirts exactly right." She shrugs, jostling Luka's arm around her shoulders. He pinches her lightly without even looking, and her smile spreads into a grin. "I'm happy to share that with anyone who asks. All of this—Dane needs to know we love him. We love *them*. He told me once he didn't think he was enough for Matty. He was afraid to take the chance." She leans into Luka, her temple against his chin. "He deserves to know he's got the town rooting for him. That we're glad he's happy."

That's all well and good, but Dane looks like he's about to melt into the floor.

"Even if it derails the rest of this meeting?" I say.

She grins. Luka shouts something about matching china patterns. There's an answering cheer throughout the small room, and Dane presses his fist to his forehead. "Especially then."

I lean back in my seat with a chuckle and cross my arms over my chest, pull my baseball cap low over my eyes, and stretch my legs out as much as I'm able. Best just to wait these things out, in my experience.

I close my eyes, breathe in deep, and think about peppers.

Photo by Marlayna Demond

B.K. BORISON lives in Baltimore with her sweet husband, vivacious toddler, and giant dog. She started writing in the margins of books when she was in middle school and hasn't stopped. *Lovelight Farms* is her debut novel.

CONNECT ONLINE

BKBorison.com

AuthorBKBorison

AuthorBKBorison

Ready to find
your next great read?

Let us help.

Visit prh.com/nextread

Penguin
Random
House